M000310660

JATOUCHE

Pyreans Book 3

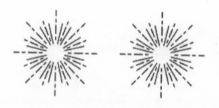

S. H. JUCHA

This book is a work of fiction. Names, characters, places, and incidents either are products of the author's imagination or are used fictitiously. Any resemblance to actual events or locales or persons, living or dead, is entirely coincidental.

Copyright © 2018 by S. H. Jucha.

All rights reserved, including the right to reproduce this book or portions thereof in any form whatsoever. Please do not participate in or encourage piracy of copyrighted materials in violation of the author's rights. Purchase only authorized editions.

Published by Hannon Books, Inc.
www.scottjucha.com

ISBN: 978-0-9994928-4-0 (e-book)
ISBN: 978-0-9994928-5-7 (softcover)

First Edition: September 2018

Cover Design: Damon Za

Acknowledgments

Jatouche is the third book in the Pyreans series. I wish to extend a special thanks to my independent editor, Joni Wilson, whose efforts enabled the finished product. To my proofreaders, Abiola Streete, Dr. Jan Hamilton, David Melvin, Ron Critchfield, Pat Bailey, and Mykola Dolgalov, I offer my sincere thanks for their support.

I wish to thank several sources for information incorporated into the book's science. The bone replacement copy (BRC, pronounced brick) originated from the website of EpiBone and commentary by CEO Nina Tandon.

The El car diamond-thread cable concept was borrowed from Penn State Professor John Badding and Dow Chemical Company senior R&D analytical chemist Tom Fitzgibbons, who isolated liquid-state benzene molecules into a zigzagging arrangement of rings of carbon atoms in the shape of a triangular pyramid — a formation similar to that of diamonds.

I'm a fan of James White and his Sector General series of twelve, science fiction novels, which were set aboard the Sector 12 General Hospital, a huge hospital space station. The facilities were designed to treat a wide variety of life forms, with a broad range of ailments and life-support requirements. I'm pleased and proud to pay homage to Mr. White's legacy by borrowing his concept for Rissness Station.

My thanks to Michael Fossel, MD, PhD, with whom I've had formative discussions about telomere lengthening, which I mention in this story. I highly recommend reading his book, *The Telomerase Revolution*.

Despite the assistance I've received from others, all errors are mine.

Glossary

A glossary is located at the end of the book. Some alien names are used frequently. For pronunciation of many of them, refer to the glossary. For instance, Jatouche is pronounced as jaw-toosh, with a hard "j," as are all the Jatouche names beginning with "j."

CONTENTS

Acknowledgments

-1-
Arrival

Jatouche Q-gate number two's flash of blue light merged briefly with the overhead dome. A small coalition of humans and aliens appeared on the gate's platform, having journeyed from the faraway system of Pyre.

"Come," Her Highness Tacticnok said, directing the three humans to follow her, as she and her Jatouche stepped off the Q-gate, which had transported the individuals from Triton, a Pyrean moon.

Tacticnok expected the three Pyrean engineers to follow her. They'd heard her command in their ear wigs, which were a gift from her species to humans. The tiny devices managed translations between the Pyreans and the Jatouche. The humans had Tacticnok's sympathy. They were the first of their species to travel via a quantum-coupled gate.

Instead of obeying Tacticnok, the humans were transfixed by the parade of aliens coming and going from the dome's other platforms. The Jatouche were the first and only aliens who Pyreans had previously met. The discovery that there were other sentient races had come as a shock to humans.

One of the engineers, Pete Jennings, reached a hand to his crotch and felt around. When Pete caught Olivia Harden's quizzical glance, he muttered, "Just checking to make sure everything came through okay."

Despite the warning from Captain Harbour, a notable Pyrean captain, who informed the engineers that they should expect to see other sentient races on their arrival, the engineers stood frozen on the platform, mesmerized by the cavalcade passing by.

Jaktook, the Jatouche dome administrator, who had become Tacticnok's close advisor, regarded the stunned humans. "Perhaps we should have prepared them better," he whispered to Tacticnok.

"How does one prepare a young race for this scene?" Tacticnok asked, sweeping an arm at the dome's activity.

As experienced engineers, Olivia Harden, Bryan Forshaw, and Pete Jennings, despite their incredulity, were registering an assortment of minutiae, such as the Jatouche dome had six platforms versus the single platform found at their moon. The center console had six stations, but only five platforms were active. A sixth platform was enclosed in a three-meter high wall, with equipment poised on top of the wall, which pointed inward and downward.

However, the majority of the Pyreans' attention focused on the indescribable parade of unusual individuals, arriving and departing via the other platforms. Olivia, Pete, and Bryan gawked at the diverse species walking, crawling, and slithering past them. In reverse, the engineers were the first humans to be observed by these other members of the alien alliance. As such, stares were exchanged in both directions.

"We probably look as odd to them, as they do to us," Olivia shared with her companions.

"You sure about that?" Bryan asked. His remark accompanied the passage of a creature obviously capable of flight, even though it was walking.

The avian's membrane-covered wings were tightly folded, but the one facing Pete appeared to be damaged. Pete leaned forward to examine the injury, and in response, the alien paused, craned its long neck, and extended a sharp beak toward Pete. Human eyes and alien orbs regarded each other silently before the avian walked on.

"This is going to take some time to get used to," Pete muttered.

The humans stepped toward the platform's edge, but Tacticnok signaled them to stop. They heard, "Wait," in their ear wigs.

Four Jatouche in uniforms escorted a tank of semiclear, light-blue liquid past the humans. The tank was as tall as a human and measured about two meters wide by three meters long.

Two small aliens led the way, clearing a path. Another Jatouche wore a headset and transmitted commands to the tank's carrier, which floated about fifteen centimeters off the deck, and directed the tank's movement.

A fourth individual followed the tank and acted as a buffer from those behind her.

As the tank silently passed the engineers' platform, the humans saw waving tentacles appear and disappear, as the appendages neared the tank's clear walls. Several tentacles evidenced burn, and Olivia flinched in sympathy.

The entity within the tank pressed close to the wall to view the oddly formed creatures staring at it. Four alien orbs regarded three pairs of human eyes, as the sentients observed one another.

"We're definitely not on Pyre anymore," Pete commented.

"Technically, we never were," Bryan replied. He was referring to the fact that two of them were spacers and the other served on the YIPS, the Yellen-Inglehart Processing Station. None of them lived downside in one of Pyre's domes.

"Did you see that alien's mouth parts?" Pete asked.

"It's probably saying to itself, 'I wonder what happened to their mouth parts. Maybe they're here to have them reattached,'" Olivia replied.

That's what had brought the three engineers to Jatouche, technically to Rissness, the Jatouche moon, where the dome had been built by the alien race known as the Messinants. They had what Her Highness Tacticnok had euphemistically referred to as decorations, severe injuries each had suffered.

"Come," Tacticnok repeated, when the medical unit escorting the tank cleared their platform.

The engineers stepped off the gate and joined Tacticnok and her team. The Jatouche led the Pyreans across the dome, toward the exit, which was a wedge that slid aside to allow egress and ingress to the Q-gates via a ramp.

Despite the number of aliens, cargo, and other sundry items in transport, all appeared to be orderly and fairly quiet, until a console operator announced in a strong voice, "Crocian is arriving."

"Come quickly," Tacticnok said sharply to the engineers.

The Pyreans didn't need their ear wig translations to understand Tacticnok's urgency. Her gestures and fearful expression were enough to galvanize them.

However, before the small contingent could reach the ramp and descend below the dome's deck, a platform's blue light flashed, merging with the shield above, and an alien appeared, who was more imposing than the humans could have imagined. Across the deck, Jatouche and other aliens scuttled aside, leaving an open pathway for the Crocian.

The engineers felt tugs on their arms, intended to pull them free of the Crocian's path. Unfortunately, the Jatouche failed to comprehend the kind of lives the engineers had endured. The harsh conditions of space had mentally toughened them, and their minds were populated with the memories of horrendous calamities. In simple terms, they weren't easily intimidated.

"Ugly as this one is, it's got to be a sentient, right?" Bryan whispered to Olivia and Pete.

"That's my thinking," Olivia whispered in reply.

The Crocian waddled on a pair of thick, squat, hind legs toward the ramp. His muscular tail, which trailed a half meter on the deck, balanced his heavy body. His hands and feet were uncovered and ended in blunt, black claws. He wore a simple sheath and was a head taller than the humans, who blocked his path.

The audience on the deck resembled a tableau, as they watched and waited for the inevitable confrontation to unfold.

"What're you supposed to be?" Olivia challenged the alien, her arms defiantly folded across her chest, not caring whether the scaled entity understood her or not.

"I'm Mangoth of the Logar," the alien announced.

The Pyreans glanced at one another, surprised to hear their ear wigs managing translations for the Crocian.

"Nice name," Pete shot back. "Why are you frightening our friends?"

"I'm Crocian. Many cower before our magnificence," Mangoth replied. To emphasize the point, the alien's maw opened, displaying long rows of blunt, conical teeth.

"Well, Mangoth, despite your glorious presence, it looks like others are more magnificent than you," Bryan replied, indicating the extensive scars on the Crocian. Deep grooves along Mangoth's jaw appeared to be made by claws. Punctures in the muscled shoulder indicated teeth or a weapon had delivered the injuries, and a digit on the formidable right claw was missing.

"Who are you to ask?" Mangoth demanded.

"If you don't like our questions, waddle your bulk around us," Pete replied hotly.

"Crocians step aside for no race, especially upstarts who haven't joined the alliance," Mangoth retorted.

"And there you have it," Olivia replied, laughing. "We aren't members of the alliance, which means we don't know the rules."

"You're impertinent creatures," Mangoth said, his tongue lapping the top of his open mouth.

"I don't much like that word creature," Bryan said, glancing toward his friends, who concurred by shaking their heads.

"Now," the Crocian demanded.

"Now what?" Olivia asked.

"Are you moving?" Mangoth demanded.

"Why should we?" Bryan retorted. "There's room for you to go around."

Mangoth loosed a low and rumbling roar. The sonic waves vibrated through the engineers' chests. "I like your impudence. You're audacious," he boomed. "How do you call yourselves?"

"We're humans. We come from Pyre," Olivia volunteered.

"What happened to you?" Pete asked, pointing toward Mangoth's deep wounds. "Did you say something wrong to your mate?" he joked.

Mangoth's long jaw snapped shut. His yellow eyes regarded the three humans. Then his head drooped.

"I have no mate," Mangoth admitted. "These marks were received in a mating bid."

"Ouch," Bryan remarked, "I take it that you didn't win."

"The fighting was fierce, but I acquiesced to my opponent's greater strength," Mangoth said. "I'm here to remove these shameful scars. It will improve my opportunity when next I compete."

"Good luck with that," Olivia said.

"My thanks for your comment, human," Mangoth said. "I see you're in need of repair yourselves, but how is it that you've been brought here?"

"We're here at Her Highness Tacticnok's invitation," Olivia replied, indicating the Jatouche, who stood quietly aside, with her team.

Mangoth eyed Tacticnok. "Commendable," he said, tipping his head minutely at the diminutive royal member. Turning to the engineers, he added, "I look forward to the filing of your race's application to join the alliance, if it is ever submitted. Now, how will we accommodate our predicament?"

"As a courtesy to an individual, who might someday be a fellow alliance member," Olivia said congenially. "We will step aside today. One day, it will be your turn."

The Crocian bellowed his laughter, as the engineers made way for him.

"Be polite to our friends," Bryan whispered to Mangoth's scaly back. The only response he received was a subtle lift of the alien's heavy tail.

The Jatouche watched the Crocian waddle down the ramp. They stared open-mouthed at the Pyreans. Tacticnok's team members were anxious to speak, but she silenced them with a motion of her hand.

"Let us proceed," Tacticnok said, leading the party down the ramp. "I regret, Olivia, Pete, and Bryan, that you must remain at the dome until I secure permission from my father to proceed."

"And if he doesn't give his approval?" Pete asked.

"Then we'll immediately return you to Triton," Tacticnok replied.

A host of questions stirred in the engineers' minds, but suddenly the Jatouche seemed reluctant to speak. A partial answer was provided in the corridor beneath the dome. Despite the greater width of the passage than the one at Triton, it was crowded with pedestrians, tanks escorted by uniformed Jatouche, and cargo haulers.

As Tacticnok indicated, the party didn't reach the corridor's end, which would have led to the dome's exit. Instead, Jaktook, who fronted the group, stopped and touched a glowing glyph on the wall. A door recessed and slid aside. The lit glyphs covered every surface of the dome. In this case, the activation of the door uncovered a ramp, and this one led to another lower level.

The engineers saw only Jatouche in the new level, where the group descended. It appeared to them that the levels below the primary sublevel were only accessible by the host race. It made the engineers wonder if they would have access to the lower levels at Triton. Humans had learned that they were the second race to occupy Pyre. According to Tacticnok and Jaktook, the original race was the Gasnarians, who were destroyed in a long-running war after they attacked the Jatouche.

Partway along the third level's corridor, Jaktook touched a second glyph and walked through the doorway.

"Oh, superior accommodations," Olivia remarked, relishing the room's gracious appointments.

"I must leave you," Tacticnok said, her expression portraying her apology. "You will receive word of my father's pronouncement in a matter of cycles. Jaktook will keep you informed."

Tacticnok's gaze lingered on Jaktook. He flashed his teeth at her, attempting to buoy her spirits, and she tipped her slender muzzle in appreciation before she turned and left.

Jaktook led the Pyreans around the room, demonstrating the facilities. The engineers, who hadn't visited the accommodations on Triton, were fascinated by the glyph-activated beds that slid from the wall, the self-warming pallets, and the food dispensers.

For modesty's sake, Kractik, the female console operator, showed Olivia the operation of the personal facilities. Afterwards, Jaktook trained the men on the hose receptacle and the controls for the mister.

With the beds extended and the Jatouche lying on their sides and humans sitting upright, there was finally an opportunity to talk.

"Will Tacticnok's father approve access for us to your planet's medical services?" Bryan asked.

"This is unknown," Jaktook replied. "There will be those speaking for you and others speaking against your presence."

"Your sixth Q-gate is enclosed. Why is that?" Olivia asked.

"Actually, that is gate number five," Kractik corrected. "It leads to the Colony."

"The colony of what?" Pete asked.

"That's the name of the group of species that were elevated by the Messinants," Jakkock, the linguist, explained. "They are a composition of aggressive species that act in support of one another. Their actions have made it impossible to establish diplomatic relationships. Without knowing their true name, they've been called the Colony."

"Why has diplomacy failed?" Pete persisted.

"They bite first and ask no questions," Kractik remarked, evincing a sour expression.

"The mandibles of the species strike deep and inject venom into the body," Jaktook explained. "Within moments, a bitten individual is catatonic and dies soon afterwards. Their poisonous bite kills anyone whose skin they are able to penetrate."

"The Jatouche first visited the Colony's Q-gate dome centuries of annuals ago," Jakkock continued. "At that time, there was no species in the dome. Over the annuals, we visited many more times, watching the planet's development. We were aware when the sentients achieved spaceflight and knew they would soon decrypt the console's information."

"They came to Rissness late one evening," Kractik said, picking up the story. "Gate number five activated, and the console operator called the dome's commander. Individuals of the Colony arrived before the soldiers could reach the deck. The dome's records detailed the event. Every trainee console operator is required to view the attack. It's chilling to watch."

"In the moments it took the soldiers to gain the deck, the Colony members attacked every sentient in sight, biting and clawing them," Jaktook said. "The presence of two Crocians was invaluable. The pincers of the Colony members were unable to penetrate the Crocians' scaled hides, and the alliance members' massive jaws rendered the centipede-like and millipede-like sentients in two."

"Three gate activations delivered more than thirty of the aggressive entities," Jakkock added. "By the time the attackers were stopped, only the

Crocians and half the soldiers survived. Every other visitor caught on the deck eventually died from the bites."

"The Messinants informed us via the console that obstructing the platform with an object would prevent the arrival of anyone or anything through the gate," Kractik said. "Immediately after the attack, soldiers heaped parts of the Colony members on gate five's platform. But we hadn't comprehended the Colony's cleverness. They found a way to call to our platform, activate it, and send our obstruction to their dome. Once our platform was clear, they swarmed in again."

Jakkock spread his hands in exasperation, as he said, "The soldiers grew tired of replacing the platform's obstacles. That's when our scientists and engineers created the wall and the weapons emplacement. The Colony members are free to visit and be eliminated on arrival."

"A Q-gate's weaponization is a contentious subject, as far as the alliance is concerned," Jaktook said. "The taking of sentients' lives can result in the species' expulsion from the alliance. That the Colony killed thirty-four individuals from various other races, in addition to our soldiers, has had a great deal to do with moderating alliance reactions."

"Have you sent anyone to the Colony's dome?" Pete asked.

"When?" Jaktook replied, confused by the question.

"After the Colony began attacking you," Pete clarified.

Jaktook and Kractik regarded Jakkock briefly. It was their thought that the translation application had failed.

To dispel the confusion, Jakkock said, "You've heard of the dangerousness of the Colony, and yet you ask if we've sent our soldiers or citizens to the Colony's dome after they began attacking us?"

"That's correct," Pete replied pleasantly.

The Jatouche stared at the Pyreans in amazement.

It occurred to Jaktook that the humans had met a Crocian for the first time and braced the individual. They wouldn't have known that Mangoth, a Crocian, was a combative male. And here they were asking if the Jatouche had investigated the Colony's dome, knowing that death waited there for whoever journeyed through the gate. A formative thought to aid the Jatouche occurred to him, which he kept to himself.

Each race spent time discovering the more mundane things about each other. The discussions ranged across subjects of food, sleep habits, work schedules, and personal preferences. The time passed enjoyably for the group. Meals were eaten, and soon it was time to sleep.

The Jatouche cringed, as Bryan uncoupled small sensor relays that connected his prosthetics to the nerve endings in the stumps of his upper arm and upper thigh.

When the propulsion engineer pulled off his artificial limbs, Olivia quipped, "Yeah, I'd love to remove mine too, if only for the night." Her ruined face was the result of an explosion, while working aboard the YIPS. The deadly gas fire took the life of her husband, who'd been walking next to her.

"Our medical personnel will permanently remove it for you, Olivia," Kractik said, with great sincerity.

Jakkock chittered at Kractik to chide her.

"What?" asked Olivia, her eyes boring into Jakkock. She wasn't in the mood for secrets. There was already too much the engineers didn't know about the Jatouche, their world, and the alliance.

Jakkock chastised himself. It was a mistake to think of the Pyreans as an undeveloped species by viewing them through the lens of technological development. In social matters, he was dealing with individuals who could read him as well as he could read them.

"It's not known if our present medical techniques are compatible with your physiology. It's logical to assume that they aren't. Time and funds will need to be spent to generate the science that will enable our medical teams to repair your decorations," Jakkock explained, attempting a touch of humor by borrowing Tacticnok's term for their infirmities.

"Are we talking about a short period of time or a lengthy one?" Bryan asked.

"First, Tacticnok must obtain permission from His Excellency Rictook," Jaktook finished for the linguist. "After that, it will be a matter of weeks in Pyrean time to adapt our technology."

"Then how long will it take to fix us?" Pete asked.

"Patience, my friends, you're asking the wrong individual. These types of questions must be reserved for the medical director," Jaktook replied, which ended the discussion.

Rumors

In the nearly three hundred years that humans occupied the orbital stations and domes of Pyre, there hadn't been any greater shocks experienced by humans than those that had recently been delivered. An alien dome had been discovered on a distant moon and accidentally activated. Then, if that hadn't caused enough consternation, aliens arrived, and Pyreans learned that the dome housed a gate that connected to a distant world.

The astonishment receded when the aliens, the Jatouche, gifted the Pyreans a massive device, an intravertor. The device was constructed at the YIPS and deployed by humans, implanting it on the planet's surface. The intravertor filtered the heavily laden atmosphere of dust and noxious gases. In addition, humans discovered that the alien's device produced excess energy, which was transmitted to the YIPS to help power one of the smelting lines.

Naturally, enthusiasm about every aspect of these events was spotty. This was because of the pronounced schisms in Pyrean society. Privileged downsiders occupied the planet's domes. Their primary contribution to the populace was food. The topsiders occupied two stations, the YIPS and the Jenkels Orbital Station or JOS. The YIPS produced metals, gases, mechanical parts, and circuitry, and the JOS was the population center for topsiders.

Then there were the spacers, who supplied the YIPS with ores and slush, frozen gases, for processing. A particular group of spacers, who worked for Captain Jessie Cinders, had formed an unlikely bond with Pyre's empaths. It was an involved story as to how the independent-minded spacers had taken a young empath, Aurelia, under their protection.

And their actions had earned them the respect and support of Captain Harbour, the leader of the empaths.

An indication of the current state of thinking of spacers, active and retired, could be heard at the Miner's Pit, a cantina owned by Jessie Cinders.

"Would you go with the Jatouche, Maggie?" a retired spacer asked the manager and hostess of the Miner's Pit.

Maggie paused in the midst of passing the table of spacers. "Do you mean would I go to Na-Tikkook to get rid of this lovely thing?" she said, hoisting her prosthetic arm. Then she added, with gusto, "Just let me know which ship I catch for Triton, when the shuttle's departing, and how much coin I have to pay."

Benny turned to his fellow retirees, who filled out the table. They were finishing their food and drink and had been discussing whether they would take the opportunity to get their injuries repaired, if offered the chance. Between them, they had three prosthetic limbs, two missing fingers, a lost eye, and a considerable amount of scar tissue. For most spacers, it was a matter of luck if they made it to retirement with some coin and no injuries. Usually, it was the ships' officers who were the fortunate ones but not always.

"If the engineers come back looking whole, I'm asking to be put on the list just as soon as I can figure out who's keeping one," Benny remarked.

"What if they look whole, but there's something alien in them?" a spacer asked the table.

That comment shut down the conversation, and soon thereafter, Maggie directed them to the bar to finish their drinks to make room for more diners.

The Starlight cantina, with its expensive clientele, was experiencing different conversations. The individuals were often company or ship owners or people who had inherited coin from family members. As such, the topics weren't about the prospects of repairing damaged bodies. They concerned the burgeoning opportunities presented by the Jatouche intravertor.

Around a small table sat four investors, who met regularly.

"What's the latest from the YIPS?" Trent Pederson asked.

"Same thing," Hans Riesling replied. "The intravertor is performing within Jatouche specifications. It's spitting out globules of fused atmospheric dust and gases and delivering power to the station."

"The same amount of power?" Dottie Franks asked. "Isn't it supposed to be clearing the air, which would mean the energy waves would be more likely to pass, wouldn't they?"

Dottie was new to the group. She'd been left a substantial amount of coin when her husband was killed while mining. She'd decided to adopt the three savvy investors as mentors, joining their weekly evening meeting. An attractive widow, the elderly patrons were happy to have her company.

"The intravertor doesn't clear out a space around it, Dottie," Hans explained sympathetically. "Atmospheric conditions constantly mix the air."

"According to engineers, it will take thirty or forty intravertors working for years, if not decades, to make a considerable difference in the atmosphere," Oster Simian added.

"And we only have the one," Dottie replied in a desultory fashion.

"For now," Hans said. He had a twinkle in his eye that attracted the stares of his friends.

"What?" Trent asked.

Hans said genially to the others. "I find it interesting that the three of you think of the Jatouche primarily as aliens. Yes, yes, they are," he added quickly, waving away the comments before they could be made. "Let's not forget that it was probably the Jatouche engineer who was the target of the plumerase gas attack on the YIPS. And what did the Jatouche do in retaliation? They did nothing. They completed the intravertor, packed up their gear, and disappeared back through the gate. In addition, they took with them the three engineers, who helped them the most, to repair their bodies. Now, if they were humans from another world, what would you think about them?"

While the men contemplated answers, Dottie piped up. "I'd think they were extremely generous and tolerant."

Her comment had Trent and Oster nodding in agreement.

"You're thinking that the Jatouche aren't done with us," Trent proposed.

"I think they're just getting started with us," Hans replied, with a self-satisfied smile.

Downside in a dome, the three heads of the nascent domes' council, Dorelyn Gaylan, Idrian Tuttle, and Rufus Stewart, met to discuss the ramifications of the Jatouche intravertor. The council had usurped the power of the domes' governor, Lise Panoy, but had left her nominally in place. They'd taken the precaution of removing her powerful and dangerous security chief, Jordie MacKiernan. His body, like those of many other downsiders, was buried beneath Pyre's ash-covered surface.

"What timeline do the engineers give us?" Rufus asked, worry evident on his face.

"Are you concerned about your bodies already?" Idrian riposted.

"This aspect of our discussion is premature," Dorelyn scolded. She was the head of the Gaylan clan, which in economic terms was one of the domes' most influential families. "There are more immediate concerns. Captains Jessie Cinders and Harbour grow more prominent in Pyrean eyes with every step they take. Right now, the conversation on everyone's lips is whether the Jatouche can rehabilitate the engineers and what will happen next with the aliens."

"It's ironic," Idrian said, sitting back in his chair and frowning. "Not long ago, the domes were the center of Pyrean power and attention. Now, it's a moon with an alien gate."

"And let's not forget that the families don't own a single ship that can reach Triton," Dorelyn remarked. "We're at the mercy of spacer captains if we want a seat at the table."

"Are you referring to negotiations with the Jatouche?" Idrian asked.

"What else?" Dorelyn replied. "I've no idea what form the discussions will take, but as sure as I'm sitting here, I know they'll happen. The Jatouche will be a part of Pyrean life for generations to come, if not forever, and we must ensure that the council is not left out."

"Why are you so positive?" Rufus asked. He didn't like the idea of aliens being involved in human society, especially if they might upset the balance of power.

"Harbour," Dorelyn replied simply.

Dorelyn hadn't counted on the empath leader becoming a political force, but the previous governor's foolishness had ignited a tumultuous cascade of events. Years before, Markos Andropov had kidnapped a young empath and fathered two children by her. It was the escape of the elder daughter, Aurelia, who was taken in by spacers, which had led to the liaison of Captain Cinders and Captain Harbour. Suddenly, two fringe groups of Pyrean society, the spacers and the empaths, had banded together to form a strategic entity that was in the right place at the right time to welcome the Jatouche.

"Worse, the captains are getting wealthy hauling slush in that ancient colony ship," Rufus added with envy.

"You can stop referring to Captain Harbour's ship in that manner, Rufus," Idrian commented. "Everyone calls the ship the *Honora Belle* or simply the *Belle*. The captain has put her coin to good use. She's hired crew, engineers, and techs, who've brought their families aboard the ship, and she's spent much of her surplus on upgrade equipment."

"It would take a good-sized crew a few years to turn that aging vessel into a rehabilitated and robust ship," Rufus retorted.

"Rufus, you really must keep abreast of information on subjects that can affect our business, even if you don't care much for them," Dorelyn remonstrated. She watched a red flush of embarrassment creep up the sides of Rufus' neck. Her eyes held Rufus, waiting for him to object. When he didn't, she continued. "One of the clever things that Harbour did with her slush coin was buildout a large cantina onboard the *Belle*. It's reported that the spacers in Cinders' company love to rotate aboard the colony ship, while they're at Emperion harvesting slush. They have access to comfortable cabins, a cantina, and the company of empaths."

Rufus shuddered at the prospect of passing empaths in the ship's corridors at every turn. He'd always abhorred the prospect of someone entering his head and manipulating his emotions.

Dorelyn and Idrian politely chuckled at Rufus' reaction.

"Well, Rufus, Cinders' crews don't see it quite the same way you do," Idrian said. "The rumors are that the spacers spend their downtime working on the ship's needs, celebrating in the cantina at night, and enjoying the attention of grateful empaths."

"Enough enjoying yourselves at my expense," Rufus growled. "Dorelyn, what is it that you wanted to speak to us about?"

Dorelyn grew serious, and her sharp gaze demanded the men's attention. "What I need the two of you to do is help me sell a project to the council. The families need to invest in a ship."

"You want us to become miners?" Rufus moaned.

This time it was Idrian who threw a disappointing glance at his friend. "What type of ship, Dorelyn?" he asked.

"We must have the first passenger ship that will be capable of transport between the YIPS and Triton. It must be capable of landing on the moon and docking with JOS terminals arms," Dorelyn replied.

Rufus' mouth clicked shut. Dorelyn was thinking far in advance of him. He realized he'd spent the majority of the conversation's time displaying his weaknesses, and he was determined to change that. "How far have you gotten toward locating a ship architect, estimating a budget, and determining a delivery date?" he asked.

Rufus was pleased when Dorelyn gave him an appraising glance, and he promised to spend more time accumulating knowledge on the spacers and empaths, especially those working for Cinders and Harbour.

At the same moment, Harbour was sitting at the salon table in her captain's quarters, sharing greens with fellow empaths.

"I think I'd like an emotional tasting of our engineers when they return," Sasha Garmenti, Aurelia's younger sister said. "Can you imagine the emanations of three people who've had their bodies made whole again?" She wore a dreamy expression, envisioning the sensations she might enjoy.

The empaths around the table laughed at Sasha's remarks. There was little doubt that Sasha would be able to pick up more from the engineers than most empaths. Although only a teenager, she was already one of the most powerful empaths and was growing stronger day by day. However, her capabilities were ruled by a blunt and determined personality.

"I think the most important point is that the engineers do return fully repaired," Yasmin, Harbour's close friend, commented.

"I have no doubt they will," Harbour added. "Although, Jessie said that the Jatouche might need to augment their skills to deal with humans."

Small smiles danced across the faces around the table. In this intimate group, Harbour had given up referring to Captain Cinders in a formal manner. At certain times, when Harbour's guard was down, the empaths sensed her emotional reactions at the mention of Jessie's name.

"Then what comes next?" Lindsey Jabrook asked. She was a miracle to the empaths and a sign of the evolution of their powers. Age had been a detriment to empaths, weakening their ability to keep the emotions of others from assaulting their minds.

Sasha had played a game of protection with her mother, Helena Garmenti, defending her against her stronger sister, Aurelia. In repeating the game with Lindsey, they discovered Lindsey's mental guards were gradually repaired. Thereafter, Sasha had gone from one isolated empath elder to another, helping to restore their balance.

"I think the next move must come from the Jatouche," Harbour replied quietly.

"What do you think that will be?" Aurelia asked. She was only a year past her teenage years and had been shuttered in the downside governor's house for most of her life. However, her tutelage under Captain Cinders and senior spacers showed her accelerated maturation.

"I've an inkling of what might come from Tacticnok, but it's a matter of what her father says," Harbour replied. "I would hear your thoughts first, Aurelia."

"I don't know what the Jatouche might offer, but I've an idea of what it will entail," Aurelia replied. Greens paused on their way to lips, as the empaths waited to hear her thoughts. The young empath smiled at the attention she'd suddenly received. "It's nothing momentous," Aurelia said quickly. "It's more about the mechanics of our response."

"Do tell," Harbour enticed.

"Well, whatever the Jatouche request, it'll probably entail a journey through the gate to speak with them, their ruler, I mean," Aurelia explained. "From my experience, I can tell you that the downsiders won't want to be left out."

"I don't think any faction will want to be left out," Nadine commented.

"I have visions of a great line of Pyreans waiting at the dome's platform to be whisked away by the blue light," Sasha said, reaching for the pitcher of greens.

Lindsey slid the pitcher away from Sasha. She was gentle in her reprimand. "Three greens are giving you more than enough visions for now."

Sasha's scowl fell impotently on Lindsey's implacable face, and the teenager acquiesced. Lindsey was one of the few individuals who could direct the headstrong girl.

"As I was saying," Aurelia continued, "to reach the dome we'll be riding aboard spacers' shuttles."

"Aha," Harbour exclaimed, and Aurelia grinned in reply.

"And this means what?" Yasmin asked.

"You have to be vac suit qualified to ride aboard spacers' shuttles, no exceptions," Aurelia replied, a mischievous smile twisting her lips.

"This piece of information should be kept quiet until the right moment," Nadine cautioned Harbour. Everyone, except Sasha, was nodding in agreement.

"Harbour, what was your thought about what the Jatouche might say or request?" Yasmin asked.

"Tacticnok spoke to me about a Pyrean envoy journeying to the Jatouche home world as a preliminary step toward membership in their alien alliance," Harbour replied.

Mouths fell open. Harbour was speaking about a future that staggered the imagination.

"I've a question," Sasha piped up. "Who gets to be the envoy?" She looked around the table, but no one was returning her gaze. Instead, the others were staring at Harbour.

"Afraid so," Harbour admitted. She was inundated by warm waves of affection sent her way. Harbour kept her gates partially closed to manage the emotions sent by Sasha. The teenager still tended to have two levels of power, on and off.

-3-
Rictook

His Excellency Rictook, the ruler of the Jatouche system, chose to hold his meeting in the formal court due to the number of attendees and the disparate groups represented.

The aging ruler was the last to enter the grand court after he'd been informed that everyone was present. Immediately, he noted the absence of the usual seating arrangements. The senior advisors weren't grouped together. Instead, they sat apart, surrounded by their supporters. Even his daughter, who normally sat alone, was accompanied by another.

So, it will be one of those meetings, Rictook thought, with resignation, as he settled on the centuries-old throne, with its rearward slot for his tail.

The audience patiently waited for Rictook's signal to begin their presentations. However, he seemed intent on examining the faces of those assembled. The confidence and brightness in the eyes of Rictook's daughter told him that she believed her arguments would win the day. For that reason, Rictook recognized Roknick, the master strategist, first.

"Your Excellency," Roknick said, rising, as was required in the formal court setting. "It is with regret that I report the abysmal failure of our team's interactions with the humans."

The soft hissing from many of the attendees told Rictook that Roknick was speaking for the minority. Rictook raised a hand ever so slightly off his thigh, and the audience quieted.

"Gitnock, what did you encounter that resulted in your failure to deploy the intravertor?" Rictook asked.

Tacticnok kept her muzzle tight. Otherwise, she would have flashed her teeth in amusement. Her father's health might be failing, but his mind was as sharp as ever.

The elderly scientist, Gitnock, rose and replied, "Deployment was successful, Your Excellency. The device is performing as expected and even supplying the Pyreans' fabrication station with limited power."

Rictook nodded and returned his eyes to Roknick, expecting a response.

"I beg your pardon, Your Excellency, I didn't mean to mischaracterize our engineers' efforts," Roknick explained. "It was in regard to security and any future interactions with the humans that I deem our experience wholly unsatisfactory. The humans attacked Drigtik and their own citizens with a hallucinogenic gas."

"This is distressing to hear," Rictook commented. "And how are you feeling now, Drigtik?" the ruler asked.

"Wonderful, Your Excellency," Drigtik replied, nearly bouncing out of his chair to answer.

"I can see that," Rictook said, the slightest hint of teeth showing before he eased the curl in his lips. "Have you been seen by our medical services?"

"It was absolutely unnecessary, Your Excellency. The empaths cured me," Drigtik enthused. "They possess a fascinating capability."

"And this is the danger I speak of, Your Excellency," Roknick insisted. "The human empaths have the ability to control Jatouche minds with their emanations. They can't be allowed to visit this world."

"Who, of our citizens, was hurt by these empaths?" Rictook asked. His eyes roamed over the audience. When no one spoke, he continued, "I see. This is a potential threat that you speak of, Master Roknick, which despite the length of time in the empaths' presence didn't materialize."

Roknick drew breath to speak, but a subtle motion from Rictook's hand bade him take a seat.

"Master Tiknock," Rictook said, recognizing the elderly scientist, who sat next to the engineers, Gatnack and Drigtik.

"Yes, Your Excellency, the intravertor was successfully deployed, as Gatnack reported," Tiknock said. "I'd like to report some encouraging news about the Pyreans' technological capabilities, but I can't. They're woefully behind even the poorest of alliance races."

"Master Pickcit," Rictook said, inviting the senior economist.

"With regret, Your Excellency, after interviewing the team's members, I can perceive of no trade advantage in a liaison with the Pyreans," Pickcit replied and then reclaimed his seat.

Rictook's gaze swung to his daughter, but Tacticnok cut her eyes to the right to indicate Jaktook, who Tacticnok had requested catch a transport from the dome to attend the meeting.

"Dome Administrator Jaktook," Rictook said.

Had this been Jaktook's first meeting with royal family members, his tongue might have failed to work. Instead, his time in Tacticnok's presence had created a familiarity with royalty that allowed him to speak his mind.

"Your Excellency," Jaktook began, after rising and tipping his head courteously. "I can't disagree with Masters Tiknock or Pickcit, but I wonder if trade and technology are the only means by which we can measure the value of an alliance with humans."

Jaktook turned to the economist and asked, "Master Pickcit, when you interviewed the team members, how did they seem to you?"

The slightest hint of teeth accompanied the master advisor's nod, as he rose to reply. "While I'm not truly qualified to summarize a citizen's mental and emotional health, I was struck by the overwhelmingly positive attitudes displayed by each individual. Of course, that excludes Jittak, who appeared quite despondent."

"And how do you account for Jittak's reaction, Pickcit?" Rictook asked.

"Again, I'm not a medical expert, Your Excellency, but I would hazard to say that our medical teams wouldn't be able to explain it either," Pickcit replied, spreading his hands in apology. "I can only rely on the reports of certain individuals who have confided in me their experiences with the female empaths."

"Continue, Jaktook," Rictook requested.

"I'll speak of Jittak's exception to the team's general mood later, Your Excellency," Jaktook said. "We were asked to offer reasons to start negotiations with the Pyreans that would benefit the Jatouche. We're known throughout the alliance for our medical services, although we're not necessarily highly prized as a member. What I envision is an adoption of human empaths by our medical services. We repair bodies, but they repair minds. I ask you to consider how the Jatouche might be elevated within the alliance if we were able to offer this unique service. And while you dwell on that thought, I would point out something that occurred at the dome, which every citizen is aware of, and yet Master Roknick failed to mention in his opening remarks."

Jaktook felt the brief touch of Tacticnok's hand on his forearm, and he temporized, "I think my second point might be better expressed by Her Highness," he said, taking his seat.

"The point that Jaktook was about to make concerns the encounter of our three human guests with a Crocian for the first time," Tacticnok began.

"I've heard this story," Rictook noted. "Its nature has grown with every telling."

"One had to be standing there, Your Excellency, as I was, to know that no retelling could capture the incredulity of the moment," Tacticnok said. "As expected, every sentient on the deck gave way to Mangoth of the Logar but the three humans. These four individuals engaged in the oddest of conversations, while they wrangled over who would give way to whom. By the end of the exchange, the Crocian was laughing and telling the humans that he looked forward to viewing their application to join the alliance, if and when it was put forward by us. After that, the engineers politely made way for him, but not without informing Mangoth that he was to stop frightening their friends ... by which the humans meant us."

Roknick motioned to be heard, and Rictook accepted his request.

"I think this underscores my argument, Your Excellency," Roknick said. "This proves that humans are an aggressive race, if they could encounter a Crocian for the first time and confront him so casually."

"I can agree with you, Master Roknick," Rictook replied, which did much to buoy the advisor's confidence that his argument would prevail. "Their actions do demonstrate contentious tendencies, although I note that it was offered in defense of individuals who they perceive as friends."

Roknick deflated and reclaimed his seat.

Tacticnok stood without being recognized. Despite being the ruler's daughter, it was still an inexcusable breach in protocol. However,

Tacticnok did wait for a motion from her father's hand. When she received it, she said, "At issue is the question as to the degree of human combativeness. Did the engineers confront the Crocian? Yes, they did. And what weapons did they wield? The answer is none. And I would point out that the only time a truly aggressive nature was demonstrated at Pyre, besides the gas attack, was when Jittak ordered his soldiers to deploy their weapons against the Pyrean leaders."

"I deemed it necessary, Your Excellency," Jittak said vigorously, jumping out of his chair.

The audience was aghast at the odious breach. Rictook said nothing, while Roknick whispered fervently to Jittak. Evidencing chagrin, Jittak sat down.

Rictook was surprised by the news, but he reserved his comments for a private meeting with his daughter. He motioned to Tacticnok to continue.

"I've nothing more to say about the incident with Jittak," Tacticnok said tersely, "except to state that the captains didn't ascribe any blame to our team. They viewed it as the foolishness of a single individual, which it was. Suffice it to say, aggressive actions can be evidenced in both our societies. We must ask ourselves which of these incidents are to be embraced and which are to be shunned."

Roknick indicated he wished to be heard, and Rictook knew the advisor wanted to repudiate Tacticnok's comments, but he refused to recognize the master.

Jaktook signaled politely that he would like to be heard, and Rictook beckoned with a single digit.

"Your Excellency, I enjoyed an evening's conversation with the human engineers the first night they arrived. I would welcome the opportunity to share our discussion with you in private, at some future time. Her Highness is aware of the details."

Jaktook sat down before his knees gave out. He'd just requested an audience with his world's ruler. A glance toward Master Tiknock, with whom he'd developed a friendship, revealed the elder's eyes dancing with mirth.

"Perhaps, daughter, you'd like to accompany your ... advisor. We'll speak immediately after this meeting," Rictook said, and Tacticnok tipped her head in acknowledgment of the request.

Rictook gazed across the attendees and opened the subject, which was to be the heart of the meeting. "We've three guests. I would hear more about why they're here."

Tiknock surreptitiously pointed at Drigtik, and Rictook took the hint and requested the engineer speak.

Drigtik rose and said, "Your Excellency, these three humans have been excellent companions in work and at play."

On hearing the word play, Rictook minutely cocked his head. It was an unusual term to hear from the mouth of a Jatouche concerning members of another race.

"They've suffered for years with their injuries, and it seemed a fitting gesture to return the favors they granted our team," Drigtik continued. "For those kindnesses alone, I would have requested Her Highness to extend the invitations. However, in my case, I can never repay the immediate and unstinting loyalty paid to me. When I inhaled the powerful hallucinogenic, the two station crew members who approached us turned into nightmarish monsters. I was frozen in place and felt sure that I would die on the spot. Instead, I was whisked away by one of the engineers, Pete Jennings. He cradled me as we ran in absolute fear, and he never let go of me."

"Remarkable," Rictook whispered. The thought that an alien, who had so briefly encountered his race, should treat one of his citizens as if they were one of their own deeply moved him.

When Drigtik took a seat, Tiknock gestured toward Gatnack, and Rictook invited him to speak.

The aging metallurgist stood and said, "Your Excellency, I've met many races in the course of my life. I've found many of them interesting and some of them technologically inventive, but I've never found one as intriguing as the humans. I don't care if they aren't advanced or if they don't offer valuable trades. Before I pass, I would like to visit with them again and take some of my family with me. I echo Drigtik's sentiments. These three engineers deserve whatever medical services we can offer."

Rictook needed no more time to deliberate. There were too many factors that recommended the Jatouche investigate the Pyreans further.

"Tacticnok, you have my approval to allow our guests to receive the attentions of our medical services," Rictook pronounced. With that announcement, the ruler sealed the wedge that Roknick and Jittak had been hoping to drive between the Jatouche and the Pyreans.

"Attend me, daughter, and bring your advisor," Rictook said, rising slowly from his throne. He was headed for his private lift, which would return him to the uppermost apartment, where he resided.

The audience quietly departed after Rictook left the throne room. Gatnack and Drigtik briefly gripped forearms, celebrating the ruler's decision.

The open doors of the lift beckoned Tacticnok and Jaktook, and they hurried to catch up and prevent Rictook from waiting. At the ruler's advanced age, standing for any length of time was a challenge.

The lift's ride to the top floor was swift and silent. The technology wasn't Jatouche. Like many things in the alliance, it had been borrowed from another race.

Attendants in the royal chamber were quick to make Rictook comfortable, and he reclined on a pallet set atop a centuries-old, ornate pedestal.

Tacticnok and Jaktook were offered pallets, and the attendants hurried to provide refreshments.

When Rictook had an opportunity to partake of some small repast, he said, "Master Roknick put forth the idea that the human engineers could be empaths in disguise."

"An interesting theory, Your Excellency," Jaktook said hesitantly, "although, I can't give it much credit. We worked closely with these three individuals on a daily basis for a long period of time. If they had these mental abilities, we'd have known it."

Tacticnok added, "It should be noted, Your Excellency, the empaths are quick to declare themselves so that other humans know who they are.

Additionally, it appears that only females are empaths. The more dangerous sex doesn't possess these powers."

Rictook's teeth flashed briefly at his daughter's jab at the male sex. He couldn't disagree with her. It had been borne out too frequently among the races. Yet, there were exceptions. Some races were ruled by their females, and there were other societies that multiplied without two sexes or by complex biological processes.

"Enough of Roknick's unreasoning fears," Rictook said. "I would hear what you would have to say, Jaktook."

"Our guests are excellent engineers," Jaktook began. "As such, they note details quickly. During our conversation, they asked about Q-gate five."

"How detailed were these conversations?" Rictook asked.

"The humans learned the history of gate five, as we know it, Your Excellency," Jaktook replied. "They know of the Colony's attacks, of their aggressiveness, the alliance sentients killed, and the venom they inject."

"It's a wonder that you didn't frighten our guests so badly that they insisted on returning to their home world without partaking of our medical services," Rictook said.

"That was my fear, Your Excellency, but we both would have been wrong," Jaktook pronounced without thinking. When he realized his gaffe, he quickly began to stammer an apology, but Rictook waved it away.

"Continue your story, Jaktook," Rictook requested.

"Yes, Your Excellency," Jaktook replied, dipping his head courteously. "Instead of displaying horror or revulsion, they continued asking questions about the Colony. They wanted to know if we'd visited the Colony's dome after the attacks."

"After the Colony's invasion?" Rictook clarified.

"Yes, Your Excellency, afterwards," Jaktook confirmed. "They asked many other questions that indicated they were ignoring our comments about the Colony's deadly attributes."

"You don't think this was a question of them not understanding the nature of the Colony or a problem with translation?" Rictook asked.

"No, Father," Tacticnok interjected.

That his daughter addressed him in an informal manner in front of the dome administrator indicated a personal relationship between Tacticnok and Jaktook that Rictook had suspected was growing. Tacticnok's remark was an indication of how far it had developed.

"The translation application was perfected long before we returned," Tacticnok continued. "And although the humans aren't technologically advanced, their society's complications have acquainted the empaths and their comrades with the perfidiousness of their own citizens."

"A complex race," Rictook mused. "It's hard to reconcile the events you've shared: the gas attack, the rescue of Drigtik, the lack of offense at Jittak's behavior, the engineers bracing the Crocian, the claim of our citizens as friends, and the inquiries about the Colony dome, as if it would be a day trip into the forest. It makes it difficult to discern their natures and our next steps."

"I've already taken it, Father," Tacticnok replied. "I've spoken to Captain Harbour about becoming the Pyrean envoy to the Jatouche." She waited for a response from Rictook, but he merely regarded her quietly. Then Tacticnok added deferentially, "I told her a formal invitation must be approved by you."

"Considerate of you, daughter," Rictook admonished.

Tacticnok could tell by her father's tone that he was amused by the exchange.

"I'll consider what has been shared here," Rictook said. "You must be aware, Tacticnok, that any challenges resulting from steps taken with the Pyreans will fall on your shoulders. The process will take time, and I won't be around to guide you."

Rictook could see the pain in Tacticnok's eyes in reaction to his words. He considered his daughter too young to rule and too headstrong to search out an older mate to help her. For a brief moment, he regarded Jaktook and wondered what strength of fiber was woven throughout his being.

-4-
Rissness Station

Jaktook exited a transport at Rissness and made his way from the shuttle through the moon's tunnels toward the dome. The question of who would visit the dome and take the engineers to the medical station had resulted in Jaktook and Tacticnok's first contentious exchange. Tacticnok had insisted that it should be her responsibility. Jaktook had countered that her presence would create unrealistic expectations on the part of the engineers.

"Tacticnok, I've already communicated with the station's research director, Zystal," Jaktook had said. "The Mistrallian confirms that they will need to develop new tissue replication processes for humans."

Jaktook had studied Tacticnok's eyes. He could sense the arguments sifting through her mind, while she stared hotly at him.

"Tacticnok, if you think I'm usurping your duties or claiming credit for your rightful accomplishments, I'm not," Jaktook stated. He was torn between speaking his thoughts and staying silent to preserve his relationship with the ruler's daughter.

"I don't think any of those things," Tacticnok replied, the anger in her eyes slowly fading.

"What you've started, Tacticnok," Jaktook said, reassuringly touching Tacticnok's forearm, "is quickly evolving and taking on a dimension that I think neither of us envisioned. Now, we must act strategically. We must think far into the future."

In a bold move for the Jatouche royal daughter, Tacticnok placed a hand over Jaktook's. Rather than look him in the eye, which would initiate something that neither of them could afford now, she stared quietly at their hands. Finally, she gently patted her friend's hand, and Jaktook withdrew his.

"How far into the future are you looking?" Tacticnok asked.

"I don't know the length of time, but I see a point when you're ruler and the Pyreans are part of the alliance," Jaktook replied.

Tacticnok's mouth dropped open, and then she chittered. "Do you realize how many obstacles lie between here and then?" she exclaimed.

"Do you realize how insurmountable those obstacles will be if we don't consider them and prepare to surmount them?" Jaktook riposted.

"You're telling me that my obligations are here and yours are with the engineers," Tacticnok replied, deflating.

"For now, yes," Jaktook replied. "You must speak to your father and the advisors, even Roknick, and inform them of the steps you imagine and the path you think the Jatouche should follow."

"What if I don't know the path?" Tacticnok objected.

"I don't see how you could," Jaktook replied. "But I do know that discussing these thoughts with our learned individuals will clarify the possibilities for you. In the end, you must listen to their advice but choose your own path."

"And why should that be the process?" Tacticnok asked.

"Someday, your father and his master advisors will not be around to advise you. When that time comes, the fate of the Jatouche will lie in your hands. I hope that you'd be content with the direction you've chosen to take us, regardless of our circumstances in that future time."

Where the tunnels ended, Jaktook waited with others to pass through the air containment system that protected the dome. When a group exited, he stepped into the space with others. On the other side, while other journeyers headed for the upper deck and the platforms, Jaktook accessed the door that led to the lower level. When he entered the room that held the engineers, he was taken aback by the greeting.

"Go away," Pete growled, "we're busy."

The engineers were lounging on their beds, and Jakkock and Pickcit were tittering at Pete's remark.

"It's a human mannerism," Jakkock explained. "We've been learning a great many methods by which Pyreans speak. Depending on the circumstances, humans express themselves in a variety of ways that are contrary to what one might expect."

"And in this particular case?" Jaktook asked Jakkock.

"Pete is bored by the cycles that he's spent in this room," Jakkock explained. "He's pleased to see you, but expresses his frustration by telling you falsely that he's busy and you're to leave." Jakkock flashed his teeth, pleased with his ability to translate the spacer's idiomatic expression. He extended his hand across the space to Pete, who tickled the back of their fingers together.

"I see I've missed much," Jaktook said.

"Don't mind Pete," Olivia said. "What news do you have for us?"

"Well, I'm not sure that you'll like what I have to say. It's probably best that I leave and return in a few more cycles," Jaktook announced, turning for the door.

"Wait," Pete cried out. When Jaktook turned around and flashed his teeth at him, Pete knew that Jaktook had gotten the better of him.

Everyone, Pyrean and Jatouche, applauded Jaktook's performance.

"Enough teasing, you two," Olivia remonstrated. "I'm ready to hear the news."

"His Excellency Rictook has approved your admittance to the Rissness Medical Station," Jaktook announced happily.

The Jatouche looked with delight at the three engineers, who remained quiet, sitting on their beds.

"This isn't good news?" Kractik asked.

Olivia regarded her companions, and they returned her solemn gaze.

"I suppose it is," Olivia replied. "There was a good chance that we wouldn't get the green light, and maybe a part of each of us was hoping for that. We've learned to live with these injuries over the course of many years. It's a little frightening to think of returning to the world of normal."

Kractik reached out a small, dark-furred hand to Olivia, who took it. The little Jatouche female said, "I, for one, would enjoy seeing you return to the world of normal. That way, you would stop sharing your food with me."

Olivia laughed and held a small cloth to her mouth that she kept handy. At moments like this, she used it to prevent spraying saliva from the ruined side of her face.

"Do you wish time to consider?" Jakkock asked gently.

Olivia looked at Pete and then Bryan. Both men were shaking their heads. "No," Olivia replied. "When do we leave?"

"Whenever you're ready," Jaktook said. He was surprised when Bryan hurriedly reattached his prosthetic limbs, while Olivia and Pete leapt off their beds and ran for their lockers to retrieve their vac suits.

"Wait," Jaktook called out. "I don't wish to sound authoritative, but much of what will take place will seem strange, perhaps odd, to you. You must let us guide you."

The engineers halted and waited expectantly for Jaktook to continue. He said, "Your personal equipment, vac suits, and the items that you carried will be collected by medical access teams. They will be transported for you and kept until your recovery."

"Where are we headed that we don't need a vac suit?" Pete asked.

"It will be aboard a transport, Pete, but you can be assured that the risk of failure has been reduced to near zero," Jaktook replied.

"There hasn't been an accident in centuries, Pete," Jakkock added.

"So we go as we are?" Olivia asked, holding out her arms to indicate her coveralls, skins, and deck shoes.

"Yes, please follow me," Jaktook said, heading toward the door.

When Olivia realized that Kractik and Jakkock weren't accompanying them, she hurried to the Jatouche female, knelt down, and opened her arms. The two females briefly embraced, and Olivia whispered her thanks.

"Is it permissible for me to receive one of those?" Jakkock asked. When Olivia nodded, he enjoyed a hug too.

Turning to Pete, Jakkock held out his arms.

Pete growled and said, "That's a female thing."

Jakkock chittered and replied, "We continue to learn."

Olivia slapped her male companions on the backs, as she hurried to join Jaktook, who waited in the corridor.

When the group reached the second deck and joined the throng, reality intruded quite quickly on the humans. Once again, they were the intriguing species not seen before by the alliance members, although, in fairness, the engineers were ogling them too.

After passing through what the engineers accepted as the dome's exit airlock, they entered a spacious rotunda. Multiple tunnels led off around its circumference, and Jaktook joined the wheel of movement to work his way through the crowd of individuals and transport tanks toward a far tunnel.

As opposed to the dome's levels, which were covered in glowing, blue runes, the rotunda and the tunnels were brightly lit, without being glaring.

The foursome joined a short line, which was moving quickly, and the engineers, with their height advantage, had a clear view of the tunnel's transport mechanism. It looked like a collection of open cars, with front canopies. The cars were arriving, emptying their passengers, and waiting for the next group to load. When it was their turn, Jaktook ushered the engineers inside, pulled down seats for them, closed the small half door, and tapped a panel at the front of the car.

The little vehicle accelerated smoothly, and the engineers realized the reason for the protective, clear canopy at the front. The transport achieved a tremendous speed. However, soon it was decelerating, and the group was exiting their vehicle and walking down a ramp. At the end of the ramp was a pair of heavy blast doors. The engineers noted the heat-darkened metal on the exterior sides.

"For this transport, Jatouche crew will manage each one of you," Jaktook instructed. "Please follow their instructions implicitly." When he received nods, he proceeded through the hatch.

"It's a shuttle," Bryan whispered.

"And we don't have vac suits," Pete replied, which sent chills down the engineers' spines.

The Jatouche transport's interior was entirely unexpected. It wasn't open seating. Jaktook was welcomed by a crew member and then ushered into a small structure. It was bright metal on the exterior and plush inside. The crew member extended a seat for Jaktook and strapped him into it.

The top half of Jaktook's structure was opaque and projected various scenes of Na-Tikkook. The bottom half was solid and heavily padded. Suddenly, Jaktook's structure was whisked away and another took its place. The structures appeared to be cages on a carousel system.

Olivia looked at the men, who appeared fixed in place. "Cowards," she whispered and stepped forward.

The crew member signaled her cage, and it expanded slightly in height. He seated her, strapped her in, and she too was quickly moved away.

The humans discovered that their transport was prepared to gimbal their cages during the flight. The crew waited until the shuttle filled. During liftoff, the engineers experienced the usual g-force encountered on smaller moons, but not that of Triton.

Their cages gently rotated during the flight. It wasn't long before the shuttle decelerated, and they were waiting to unload. One by one, it became their turn, and a medical technician gathered them to the side, after they exited the shuttle, to wait for Jaktook.

Much of the shuttle's disembarkation traffic flowed down a brightly lit corridor, seemingly sure of their destination. In contrast, the medical tech led them down a side corridor to a transport mechanism. They climbed aboard a small car with the tech. Several times, the transport entered a carousel, and the tech guided it onto another track.

"How big is this station?" Bryan asked, before he realized that Jatouche units of measurements might have no meaningful translation.

Jaktook thought for a moment and replied, "Rissness Medical Station is a set of stacked cylinders, which have been added over time, and it's more than three times the length of your *Belle* and encompassing much more volume."

Bryan let out a soft whistle.

"Is that an indication that you're impressed?" Jaktook teased. He found he enjoyed the emotional natures of humans. They expressed their feelings and thoughts in vibrant manners.

Bryan grinned in reply and said, "A little."

When they finished their routing, much of it ascending vertically and some of it while under minimal gravity, the tech led them down another corridor to a gleamingly austere, circular room. A low platform sat in the center, and a broad wall of glass ringed half the room. Liquid filled the space beyond the glass wall.

"Zystal, the Pyreans are here," the tech announced and exited the room, the door sliding closed behind him.

"Welcome," the foursome heard in their ear wigs. "Is this translation tone pleasing or would you prefer another version?" Zystal repeated his greeting multiple times using different voices.

"I like the second one," Olivia said. When the others agreed, that one became the voice they heard.

"I'm Zystal, a male Mistrallian, and the head of genetics research for Rissness Station," Zystal said. "It will be my duty to analyze your genetic structures and prepare the cellular growth mechanisms that will be employed to repair you. However, my first step is to discern the extent of your injuries. You'll forgive my awkward questions. You are the first of your species that I've seen, and I'm pleased to have the privilege to work with you."

There was a pause, as if Zystal was mentally preparing to proceed. "Dome Administrator Jaktook, will you stay?" Zystal asked.

"Her Highness Tacticnok expresses her gratitude and confidence in the medical services of Rissness Station. However, as Pyreans are new to our society, she wishes me to remain close to them and guide them."

It was easy for Zystal to parse what Jaktook was saying. It wouldn't change his procedures, but he'd been made aware that the Pyreans were important to Her Highness. He quickly made note of the fact for the others who would work with the humans.

"Would you like to proceed separately or as a group?" Zystal asked. "I'm not aware of your preferences for privacy."

The men eyed Olivia. As far as they were concerned, it was her choice.

"Together," Olivia said.

"If one of you would remove your coverings and step on the platform," Zystal requested.

Olivia took a step forward but was stopped by Pete's hand on her arm.

"You climbed aboard the shuttle first. This one is my turn," Pete said. He shucked his coveralls, skins, and deck shoes in quick order. Then he stepped on the platform. Tiny beams were emitted by an overhead ring and from the base of the platform, and they scanned Pete's body.

"Please announce your name and sex, if it is appropriate," Zystal requested. When Pete complied, Zystal said, "Now state exactly what we're to repair."

Pete hung his head. The majority of his body had been flashburned. JOS medical teams had a problem separating Pete's clothing from his skin, which left the surface wrinkled in some areas and patterned in others.

"My skin is scarred. It's the result of burns," Pete stated firmly. He worked to control his temper, which was driven by the embarrassment of exposing his infirmity.

"Apologies for my misunderstanding," Zystal said calmly. "Where on your body is there a significant area of original covering?"

Pete thought for a moment and lifted his arms overhead.

"Excellent," Zystal replied, and the beams scanned again. "To what extent do you wish the texture repeated over your body?"

"Texture?" Pete queried, dropping his arms.

"Yes, at the apex of your limb and central mass you have a texture of fine filaments. Should your body's covering have this in full or in a pattern?"

"Oh, for the love of Pyre," Pete moaned. He was at a loss as to how to explain a human male's physiological appearance to the alien.

Quickly, Bryan stripped off his clothing and stood next to the platform. "Step off, brother," Bryan ordered gently. He took Pete's place on the platform and announced, "I'm Bryan Forshaw, a human male."

Bryan let the beams scan his body. Then he raised his arms, and said, "My friend's skin should appear smooth like mine but with his coloring. The hair you see on my body is the natural distribution for a human male. Pete's hair should mimic the hair's color on his head."

"Most instructive, Bryan Forshaw; your participation is appreciated," Zystal replied. "Pete Jennings, please regain the platform."

After Pete replaced Bryan, Zystal held a discussion about details of the final appearance, including requesting if there were any marks gained over his lifetime that he'd like replaced.

"What kind of marks?" Pete had asked.

"Some of our clients request the restoration of marks of honor gained through ritual combat," Zystal explained.

"Humans don't engage in those types of things," Pete had replied.

"Commendable," Zystal commented.

When Pete was finished, Zystal proceeded with Bryan. This engineer's case was easily resolved. The primary question Zystal asked was whether symmetry was to be observed or whether there were specialized limbs that were missing.

Bryan turned his head and grinned at his comrades. "Do you think I should get something unique ... maybe an extra powerful arm?"

"Behave," Olivia scolded. She sounded fierce, but she was smiling and shaking her head in disbelief at Bryan's humor. Even Jaktook was chittering at the display.

"Symmetry would be appreciated, Zystal," Bryan finally acknowledged.

"Please, step down," Zystal instructed. "And now our final client, if you would."

Olivia stripped off her clothing and gained the platform. In contrast to the men, Olivia wasn't as uncomfortable displaying her body as much as she was her face. She said, for Zystal's benefit, "Olivia Harden, female."

"Is there a difficulty in turning your head forward, Olivia Harden?" Zystal asked.

"No," Olivia replied, straightening her neck. She thought it was odd that she was embarrassed to show her ruined face to an alien, who would have no idea of what was normal for a human woman.

"I assume you're in search of symmetry, Olivia Harden?" Zystal requested, when the beams had scanned her.

"Yes," Olivia politely replied.

"Does this include your ocular elements?" Zystal inquired.

"To a degree," Olivia said. Before she could expound on her answer, Zystal responded.

"Yes, I see the subtle differences in the males who accompany you. Do you have imagery for me to emulate?" Zystal asked.

On a dark day after Olivia's recovery, she'd deleted all the photos and vids of her before the accident. She hadn't wanted to be reminded of how she had once appeared.

"No, I don't, Zystal, I'll depend on your creative efforts," Olivia replied.

"I'm humbled by your offer, Olivia Harden. It's my hope that you'll be pleased by my efforts," Zystal said. The genetics director had a few more questions for Olivia before he excused her.

Olivia dressed and joined the men.

"Excuse me," Zystal said, "I'll resume our conversation shortly."

Jaktook explained, "The beams have penetration capability. Zystal is examining the data to see the extent of injuries beneath the surface."

As time continued to pass, Jaktook realized he was frowning and smoothed his face before the Pyreans noticed it. Unfortunately, he wasn't quick enough. Olivia had caught him, but she didn't say anything.

"Thank you for your patience," Zystal finally said. "As non-alliance members, I've observed that your medical services haven't maintained your bodies in optimal conditions."

The engineers burst into laughter, and Jaktook hurriedly offered an explanation to prevent Zystal taking umbrage. "The Pyreans are evincing responses that are meant to be taken as agreeing to your words," he said. "They feel that you've severely understated the situation."

"Thank you for the clarification, Dome Administrator Jaktook," Zystal said. "Clients, deep analysis of your bodies indicates significant wear. Many aspects of your bodies indicate a younger age than the appearance of joints and bones. These elements are easily repaired while you're under our care. Do you wish them restored at the same time?"

"Is he kidding?" Pete asked Jaktook.

"Zystal takes his position as genetics director quite seriously," Jaktook explained. "Our medical services are much more extensive than you might imagine. If Zystal is offering these services, you can be assured that the Rissness medical teams can deliver them."

The three engineers turned toward one another. Their mouths were open in mock surprise, and then they yelled, "Yes," in unison.

"We'll be pleased to honor your requests. My duties with you are complete. A technician will show you to another office where samples will need to be collected from you. Are there any questions for me?" Zystal asked.

"Could we see you?" Olivia asked.

"I'm extremely foreign to you in appearance," Zystal said. "Are you certain that you wish this?"

"Yes," Olivia replied, although the men, especially Pete, weren't sure they agreed.

Digits, which ended in broad suckers appeared out of the murky, gray green liquid and stuck to the glass. Thin limbs pulled a pod-like body covered in smooth skin and decorated in red, orange, and brown tones. A bulbous head, with little definitive shape and containing two extremely large eyes, swam close to the glass.

"As you see, I've a unique shape among alliance members," Zystal said. A thin band encircled his throat and picked up his voice.

"At least, among your race, you're normal," Olivia retorted. "Among my people, this," she said, circling a finger around her face, "has frightened many of my species."

"We will repair that, Olivia Harden. You have the bond of Zystal of Mistral."

"Aren't you rather confined if you have to live in there?" Olivia asked, approaching the glass.

"I'm honored that you would be concerned for my mental well-being, Olivia Harden," Zystal replied. "The genetic director's position is rotational. A Mistrallian fulfills it for one annual, and then another of my race assumes the position for the next cycle. We're well compensated for our duty here, and it provides security for our futures. Mistrallians compete fiercely for an opportunity to serve a rotation."

When Zystal finished, he faded into his watery domain, and on cue, a Jatouche technician entered the room and beckoned them to follow her.

The engineers had another ride to reach a narrower corridor, where the gravity was close to that of their stations. It was a familiar comfort.

During a brief stop in a clinically furnished room, samples were collected from nearly every aspect of the engineers' bodies. To their amazement, the harvesting of cells was so minimal, as to be unnoticeable, even when the Jatouche med techs sought deep samples.

Afterwards, Jaktook led the Pyreans to a dorm-style room. He stood in the doorway and said, "I've taken the liberty of requesting a room where the four of us can remain together, unless you'd like to make other arrangements."

"You're welcome to stay with us, Jaktook, if you can put up with Pete's snoring," Bryan teased.

"As long as Pete doesn't mind mine," Jaktook riposted, which had Olivia and Bryan laughing and Pete protesting that he didn't snore.

Restorations

The wait for the final phase of the engineers' restoration to begin might have been punctuated by days of tedium, except Jaktook was determined to prevent that from happening. Tacticnok and he had a plan, and Jaktook attempted to execute it to the best of his ability.

The dome administrator led the Pyreans on daily excursions around the station until he wore them out. The engineers met as many different alliance members as Jaktook could manage introductions. But it wasn't simple greetings that Jaktook sought, it was conversations. To his surprise, it was easier than he thought. Once the parties crossed paths and Jaktook ensured the translation app was functioning, inevitably, one of the Pyreans propagated the exchange.

Jaktook discovered the engineers' curiosity was unrestricted. They were a gregarious lot, willing to speak with every entity. To his delight, the Pyreans often challenged an alliance member who was curt or gruff with them. He found it interesting that a member, who had been braced, often became a willing participant in a conversation. It made him wonder if the timidness of his species hadn't been at fault for the Jatouche failing to achieve a more respected position within the alliance.

The common subjects in the meetings' discourses were the injuries that had been suffered, but that soon led to questions about how the damage had occurred, which slowly morphed into comparisons of cultures. Time and again, the alliance members expressed interest in reviewing the Pyreans' application when it was put forth by the Jatouche.

"I should have taken my comm unit out of my carryall," Pete groused after another full day of touring the station. "I could have gotten some great images. Most of what we've seen is going to be difficult, if not impossible, to describe."

"Your devices haven't been returned for a reason, Pete," Jaktook explained. "The alliance members, who are here at Rissness Station, expect privacy. The publication of their injuries can lead to the loss of important positions or opportunities within their societies.

Late one evening, Jaktook received word that the restoration teams were ready. He shared the message with the engineers, pleased that their tour day had been especially rigorous. Soon the Pyreans were fast asleep, and it was Jaktook who lay awake for a lengthy spell. He knew he shouldn't be worried about the expertise of the Rissness staff. Over the annuals, new races were continually introduced to them. But Tacticnok and he thought this species was unique and that they could make a critical difference in the lives of every Jatouche.

The following morning, Jaktook woke the Pyreans early. "Relieve yourselves, but don't bother to wash. The medical teams will manage that."

"Can we eat?" Pete asked.

"Regrettably not," Jaktook replied.

"You could have told us this last night," Pete complained.

"Which is why I didn't," Jaktook riposted.

"How long do you expect these operations to take?" Bryan asked.

"I've no idea, Bryan," Jaktook replied. "Your injuries are significant, which means you'll be under for at least twenty cycles."

"By then, I'll really be really hungry," Pete declared, delivering a grin at Jaktook. "I'm first," he said, as he hurried toward the facilities.

When the Pyreans were ready, Jaktook met a medical technician in the corridor. The tech took the ensemble via a transport car toward the station's center.

"Are we headed toward zero-g?" Olivia asked the tech.

"Close to it, Olivia Harden. It aids the restoration processes and allows the clients to rest more comfortably," the tech replied.

"Twenty or more cycles on a bed or an operating table doesn't sound like it would be comfortable for any species," Bryan commented.

"Who would put you there?" the tech asked.

"Bryan, your restoration process will take place while you're suspended in a tank of specialized liquid," Jaktook explained.

"Oh," was all that Bryan could manage to reply.

The tech deposited each Pyrean at a different door. Jaktook escorted each engineer inside, telling him or her that he would be waiting when their restoration was complete.

Within each medical suite, the processes for the Pyreans were the same. Clothes and prosthetics were removed, and bodies stepped on platforms. In Bryan's case, a support was given him so that he could stand erect. Then beams scanned again to check for subtle changes in bodies. The introduction of embryos, while visiting Rissness Station, had been known to happen.

After the scans, a cleansing cycle preceded a final examination by a variety of thin, probing, metal arms. The robotic approach frightened the Pyreans, who thought that this might be the beginning of their restoration processes. But the engineers never witnessed the final preparation steps. An ultrathin needle injected a small amount of fluid into their necks, which put them to sleep.

The tables on which they rested were taken to the suites' next rooms. There the engineers were prepared for the long periods of restoration. A tank containing a liquid would support them. The fluid was supersaturated with oxygen and would fill their lungs. A slender web of electrical contacts would keep the engineers unconscious, and various tubes were connected to handle nutrient supply and excretion.

When the techs finished the bodies' preparations and suspended the engineers in their tanks, they exited the room, leaving the next steps to the senior medical personnel, who would run the restoration programs.

The engineers' long wait until this point was due to the time needed to generate the various body parts that were required to complete the transformations.

Pete received sheets of skin the Rissness laboratories had grown for him. Limb by limb, skin was excised by tiny surgical arms, and the rolls of new skin were wrapped, trimmed, connected to underlying tissue and the ends sealed. When the transformation was complete, it would require days for the skin grafts to take. Afterwards, there would be subtle operations to ensure the finished transformation was seamless, which meant more time in the tank.

Bryan's operations were more complex. His replicated arm and leg were ready, but the engineer's truncated limbs had to be opened. When those steps were complete, bone, muscle, nerves, and circulatory vessels were exposed. Working from the inside out, the surgical program started with bone connections. The entire attachment process was only the beginning for Bryan. The health of the new limbs was monitored, and the attachments proved successful, as expected.

The follow-up steps for Bryan were stimulations of the arm and leg muscles via the brain. This would accelerate the engineer's adoption of the new limbs. Later, the skin attachment would be finalized.

Olivia's repair represented the greatest challenge to the medical teams. Face reconstruction was recognized as the most difficult of operations. The majority of species identify their individuals by these critical visuals.

A debate about Olivia's symmetry had overtaken the medical teams. Symmetry was prized, but Olivia had no images of how she appeared before the accident. The argued question was whether to give her superlative symmetry or imbue a certain amount of asymmetry, which, of course, brought up the subject of to what degree.

The medical directors sought out Jaktook, which caused the Jatouche a great deal of consternation. Never in his life had he been asked to offer such an important opinion on which he had so little knowledge. He thought about the many Pyreans he'd met. Few humans exhibited a high degree of symmetry and balance, which the directors assured him they could provide. Regarding symmetrical features, only Envoy Harbour and Yasmin came to Jaktook's mind, but few others qualified.

In the end, Jaktook said, "Olivia Harden is a plain-speaking, well-intentioned individual, who is a talented human engineer. I don't think she would appreciate suddenly becoming a marvel of Rissness sculpting. On the other hand, we wish to send a message to the Pyreans as to the quality of our medical capabilities. Does that answer your question?"

Judging by the intense discussion that broke out among the directors, Jaktook didn't think it did.

Thereafter, Jaktook received updates on the restoration progress from the directors, but it was nothing more than *progress continues*. It wasn't much, but at least, it wasn't bad news. Every evening, Jaktook relayed the same terse message to Tacticnok.

Jaktook truly appreciated the nightly contact with the royal heir. Little did he know that Tacticnok shared his feelings. Each, in their own way, had plans for the future of the Jatouche, and they revolved around the Pyreans. Their common fear was that they lacked the power to make the crucial decisions and they lacked the experience to navigate the process of liaising with a new race.

"I think we're doing ourselves a disservice with these types of conversations," Tacticnok had said one evening.

"Are you implying that we should cease lamenting over our shortcomings?" Jaktook posited.

"Yes, they're making me despondent," Tacticnok replied. "The lack of action on my father's part is bad enough, but I'm concerned events might be transpiring on Pyre that will upset our plans."

"Understood," Jaktook replied. "I propose that we converse and strategize as if we had the power to command the next steps," Jaktook proposed.

"In that case," Tacticnok replied brightly. Then she launched into the edicts she'd enact if given the authority to liaise with the Pyreans. In the back of her mind, there was the niggling thought that she was acting out a fantasy.

* * * *

Rictook assembled the same individuals in the throne room — Tacticnok, senior advisors, and supporters — who had met with him soon after the human guests had arrived. The only individual missing was Jaktook, who kept vigil over the Pyreans' restoration.

Rictook eased into his throne, when everyone was present. The past cycles had been particularly hard on him. The medical services had urged him to make a personal exception to the life expediency regulation, which limited to one time the lengthening of an individual's lifespan by altering a portion of the genes' lengths within the body's cells. It wasn't Jatouche law. It was a requirement that any race had to adopt if they wished to join the alliance. But, Rictook wouldn't listen to their entreaties.

That wasn't the only medical service Rictook had chosen to deny his mate and him. The couple had elected to let chance rule the sex of their offspring. This was an unpopular decision, but Rictook wished to set an example that medical technology shouldn't rule their natural lives.

"I've reached a decision about the Pyreans, and it is this: I'm not the one to make it," Rictook announced. "It is foolish for the most senior of a race to make world-changing decisions about a future in which they won't abide. The generations to come must have a say in how their society develops, and we're selfish if we deny them their inherent rights. Therefore, I'm giving my eldest, Tacticnok, the right to choose how to proceed with the Pyreans. It is my hope that all of you will offer her your counsel and guide her in this endeavor that could well command the future of the Jatouche."

Rictook turned a hand palm up and indicated that Tacticnok should rise. By her delay to stand, he could see that she had been stunned by his decision. *Such is the heavy price of leadership, daughter,* Rictook thought.

Tacticnok furiously considered her options. She didn't want to uselessly expend this opportunity by making weak statements of thanks to her father and expressing intent to develop plans sometime in the future. The conversation with Jaktook came back to her, particularly his advice that she should listen to the advisors but choose for herself the path for the Jatouche. In her heart, she knew what she needed to do.

Finally, Tacticnok rose. Rather than speak from her position in the court, she ascended the shallow dais to stand beside her father's throne. Briefly and gently, she touched his shoulder before she addressed the assembly.

"Jaktook has spent a considerable amount of time with the Pyrean engineers, while they waited for their restoration, which they're now undergoing," Tacticnok announced. "During his time with them, he ensured that the humans met as many alliance members as possible. On that subject, I've received an excellent report. The members have expressed overwhelming interest in reviewing the Pyreans' application, if and when we submit it."

Tacticnok paused to order her thoughts, and then she continued. "Unfortunately, the alliance members know nothing about the conditions of Pyrean society. His Excellency, the master advisors, and I agree that under no foreseeable circumstances would the alliance approve the Pyreans' application. In fact, most likely, there would be condemnation for contacting a species that had yet to solve the Messinants console and gate transport."

Tiknock indicated he would like to be heard, and Tacticnok recognized the master scientist.

"Surely, Your Highness, the alliance would give credit to our efforts to save the Pyreans' planet, which had been devastated by our weapon," Tiknock said.

"That has been considered, Tiknock," Tacticnok replied, "and while our actions regarding contact and delivering the first intravertor might be forgiven, it would not favor an application for Pyrean admission to the alliance."

Tacticnok caught the brief flash of Roknick's teeth. *You think you've won,* she thought of Roknick's display just before she said, "However, I refuse to let the opportunity to explore this new race slip through our hands. As such, I'll be requesting an envoy from the Pyreans."

Tacticnok's comment elicited some hisses, but the majority of the audience flashed their teeth in approval.

"Understand me," Tacticnok said, raising a hand to quiet the room, "this isn't a prelude to submitting a Pyrean application to the alliance. That might not happen for many annuals or might never happen. The alliance places too much weight on a species' technological advancement. It follows the guidelines of the Messinants, which are contained in the consoles."

Pickcit, the master economist, signaled and stood when Tacticnok nodded to him. "I would be interested to hear what you believe you'll accomplish by taking this direction, Your Highness," he said.

Tacticnok stoically withheld her reaction to Pickcit's leading question. She knew that Tiknock and he were ardent supporters of hers, but she didn't want to broadcast it.

"It's no secret that the Jatouche, despite our mastery of medical services, are treated as junior members of our illustrious organization," Tacticnok replied. "I have this belief that a liaison with the humans can change that."

Roknick motioned, and Tacticnok reluctantly recognized him. Once again, Jaktook's words were in her ear, when he urged her to allow Roknick to voice his counsel.

"If the Pyreans can't qualify for membership and can't offer us anything in the way of trade or technological innovation, what good is a liaison with them?" Roknick asked. The audience could hear the advisor's tone, which bordered on insolence.

"I'm pleased you asked that question," Tacticnok replied congenially, at which point Rictook carefully touched his nostril to cover his muzzle and the subtly exposed teeth.

"I believe humans can offer us something unique," Tacticnok continued, "and if you're tempted to ask me what that might be, I can tell you that I don't know. This is why I will invite an envoy and explore the opportunities."

"I hear and accept Her Highness Tacticnok's pronouncement," Roknick replied, straining to regain lost ground, "but I would urge her to request an envoy who represents the majority of the Pyreans. I'm told by Jittak that this collection of humans live in domes on the planet. The offer should be made to them to choose a suitable envoy."

"I will take Roknick's advice into account before I make my final decision," Tacticnok said gracefully. "However, as someone who spent more time in the company of the humans than Jittak, I can tell you that the invitation of a Pyrean envoy will generate a greater conversation among the humans than you could imagine."

-6-
Welcome Home

JOS station security sergeant, Cecilia Lindstrom, was notified by a terminal arm manager of an accident, which occurred while stationers were boarding a ship. She relayed the location to the medical teams to attend the two injured stationers and filed a report with her superior, Lieutenant Devon Higgins.

The incident had Cecilia wondering to what extent the Jatouche would be able to help Pyre's engineers. If the aliens were successful, she considered the extensive number of injured stationers and spacers. More important, she wondered how Pyreans could induce the Jatouche to help them.

About the time the medical teams arrived on the JOS terminal arm to aid the stationers, a bridge tech aboard the colony ship, *Honora Belle*, uttered, "Uh-oh, they're back."

Beatrice "Birdie" Andrews turned her head around to regard the monitor the tech pointed out. It was a fixed transmission from the Triton dome. The light from the platform was fading, and three Jatouche stood on the platform.

"Dingles, Jatouche arriving," Birdie snapped out over her comm device.

"Understood, Birdie. I'll notify Captain Harbour and then alert Captain Cinders aboard the *Spryte*," Dingles, aka Mitch Bassiter, replied. He quickly relayed the message to Captain Harbour, who was near the bridge.

Kractik descended the dome's platform and hurried to the console. A few taps on a panel engaged a comm transmission protocol to the Pyrean colony ship, which she'd programmed after their first arrival.

"Hello, Kractik, welcome back," Birdie greeted the console operator, when her face appeared on a comm monitor.

"Thank you for your generous words, Birdie," Kractik replied. "Her Highness Tacticnok would speak to your Captain."

"She's on her way," Birdie replied.

"Birdie, connect Captain Cinders to this comm," Harbour sent, as she hurried to the bridge.

"Ituau reports that he's on the way to the *Spryte*'s bridge. Be there in three," Birdie replied.

"Thank you, Birdie," Harbour acknowledged.

When Harbour entered the colony ship's bridge, her face lit up, and Tacticnok's image on the monitor responded in kind.

"It's good to see you again, Your Highness," Harbour said.

"The feeling is reciprocated," Tacticnok replied.

"We have Captain Cinders," Birdie whispered.

Harbour hand signaled Birdie, who split the screen for Tacticnok's view.

"Your Highness," Jessie said, when his monitor reflected the *Belle*'s transmission.

"After such a period of time since we last met, Captain Cinders, I would have expected you to have adopted a greater vocabulary," Tacticnok riposted.

Jessie observed Harbour's laugh, Tacticnok's flash of teeth, and the smirks and chuckles of his bridge crew.

"I like to save them up so that I have plenty to throw at the people who annoy me," Jessie retorted in a growl, but he punctuated his statement with a grin.

"I'm pleased to see you both in good health," Tacticnok said.

"We're fine," Harbour replied. "What of our engineers?" she asked.

Tacticnok was delighted to hear Harbour's first question after pleasantries were exchanged. It did much to confirm that she'd made the right choice for envoy.

Jaktook tapped Kractik on the arm, and the tech initiated the Q-gate's transfer and shifted the console's view to encompass the dome's deck.

The bridge crews of the *Belle* and the *Spryte* saw the platform light, and three figures dressed in spacer skins and a stack of crates appeared.

The figures raced to the console, and Kractik shifted the view.

"Hello, Captains Harbour and Cinders," a woman, with an inviting face and broad smile, said.

"Olivia," Harbour exclaimed, recognizing the engineer's voice.

"Fantastic, isn't it?" Olivia enthused. "No more sharing my food with whoever is seated beside me." She laughed, and it was a rich, full-throated sound.

"Check this out, Captain," Bryan said. He held up his new arm and waggled his fingers at the console. Then he danced a few steps to demonstrate his new leg.

"I can't believe it," Harbour enthused, joyfully clapping her hands.

"I'd be happy to show you my repair," Pete declared, with a broad grin, and spread his arms wide.

"Don't listen to him, Captain," Olivia shouted, laughing. "He's been dying to say that to the first Pyrean woman he met after returning. We've had to put up with his endless parading around our room, while he showed off his new appearance."

The Jatouche watched the enormous delight the engineers got from displaying their repaired bodies. *And such a simple thing,* Tacticnok thought, incredulous that any sentient society didn't possess these medical capabilities.

"Your Highness, I can't thank you enough for what you've done for our people," Harbour said, tears forming in her eyes for the generous gift bestowed by the royal daughter.

"I think you can, Captain," Tacticnok replied.

Quickly, Jessie sat forward in his captain's chair, and Harbour's eyes dried.

"My father, His Excellency Rictook," Tacticnok continued, "has left it to me to choose whether to develop a relationship with Pyreans. And, I've decided to request the Pyreans send an envoy to Na-Tikkook, specifically you, Captain Harbour."

"There are others who are much more qualified than me, Tacticnok," Harbour replied, slipping into the familiar address, despite the audience who was witnessing the exchange.

Ituau noticed Jessie's frown and wondered what aspect of the conversation concerned him.

"I thought you might wish to offer others in your stead, Captain," Tacticnok replied. "It's one of the reasons that I've chosen you. To help you in your decision, Captain, I've two inducements."

"Uh-oh," Jessie muttered under his breath.

"Rissness Station will accept twenty Pyreans who are in need of medical services. This will continue in a cycle of every half-annual, while you're the envoy and our talks demonstrate progress."

"That isn't fair, Tacticnok," Harbour objected.

"What's the second inducement, Your Highness?" Jessie asked.

Logical and business-minded, Tacticnok thought of Jessie. "The crates on the platform are for Pyre. We're prepared to send your world the intravertor parts to build more devices at the rate of three each quarter annual."

"I take it the stipulation is that we get the parts as long as Captain Harbour accepts your proposal to become the envoy," Jessie clarified.

"You understand me correctly, Captain," Tacticnok replied.

"Captain," Bryan said, stepping close to the console, "there is an incredible world on the other end of this gate. Pyreans need to be part of it."

Harbour took in the expectant faces of the engineers.

"Captain," Jessie said, his heart heavy at what he was about to propose, "I think you might need to step up and shoulder the responsibility."

"I'm pleased to hear you say that, Captain Cinders," Tacticnok said. "I have one more condition, Captain Harbour. You'll need a master advisor, and I've selected Captain Cinders for you."

"Oh, for the love of Pyre," Ituau whispered.

Jessie shook his head at the masterful way that Tacticnok had played her hand. "One day, you'll be a clever ruler, Your Highness," he said.

"It's my hope, Captain Cinders," Tacticnok replied.

"Choosing me as an envoy is one thing," Harbour said, "but I'll be ineffective without the support of Pyre's leaders."

"This was expected, Captain," Tacticnok replied. "I offer the medical services for the twenty Pyreans and these parts to build the next intravertor in the hope of helping you resolve your internal politics successfully. Kractik will program the console so that your engineers can call us when your people are ready. Also, she will train them in initiating a call to you on the *Belle*. To your success, Captains."

Tacticnok and Jaktook mounted the platform, and Kractik sent them home. Then the call to the colony ship ended.

"Birdie, Captain Cinders on a private link to me," Harbour said, waving her device at the comms operator. She exited the bridge and headed for the captain's quarters. The link was established before she made her door, but she waited until she was inside to respond.

"I'm not sure what just happened, Jessie," Harbour said in a rush. She was pacing and holding a hand to her forehead.

"We were played by a young royal heir, who has learned a great deal from what I suspect is a wise, old father," Jessie replied, chuckling.

"Why are you laughing?" Harbour asked, with exasperation.

"Look at what Tacticnok did," Jessie replied. "It was masterful. She returns three of our people fully rehabilitated and looking years younger. On top of that, she entices you with the offer of sending twenty more Pyreans."

"Don't forget about the intravertor parts," Harbour reminded him.

"The parts aren't for you, or us, for that matter, Harbour," Jessie replied. He was taking the call from his quarters, sitting forward in his favorite chair, with his elbows on his knees. "Tacticnok was smart and adroit in her offers. The first one was extended to you, and she knew it would tempt you."

"The medical services," Harbour said, realizing what Jessie was saying.

"Yes," Jessie acknowledged. "The parts are bribes for the Pyrean leaders, who will object to the heir choosing you."

"I've got to think on this," Harbour said. She checked her unit's chronometer. "You haven't got much time, Jessie, you'd better hurry."

"What?" Jessie asked, failing to understand Harbour's segue.

"You need to get your butt over here for dinner and start advising me. That's your new job, isn't it?" Harbour asked pointedly.

"Be there soon," Jessie replied.

Harbour could hear Jessie's laughter, as he closed the connection.

"Ituau, ready a shuttle," Jessie called over his comm unit. "I'll be there in five."

"I've a shuttle standing by for transport to the *Belle*, Captain," Ituau replied. "And, Captain, there's time to clean up before you go."

Ituau heard Jessie's growl before he ended the call, and she smiled to herself.

There was a knock on Harbour's door. She was tempted to ignore it, but called out, "Enter."

Yasmin came through the door first, carrying a green. She was followed closely by Dingles, the colony ship's first mate and a true spacer.

"Thought you could use this," Yasmin said, handing the glass to Harbour. "Are we preparing dinner for two?" she asked, concerned for the paleness of Harbour's face.

"Absolutely," Harbour replied, gulping down half the glass.

"Birdie updated me, Captain," Dingles said. "How can I help?" He too was disturbed by the impact the offer was having on Harbour.

Harbour turned away, took a few steps, and swallowed the other half of the green. She employed one of the techniques of ordering her emotions, as if she was soon to meet with a client. When she was ready, she returned the empty glass to Yasmin, saying, "Thank you. Captain Cinders will soon be on approach."

Yasmin slipped out of the door, and Harbour focused on Dingles.

"I can't think about the broader view, right now, Dingles. The only thing I can focus on is the offer to rehabilitate twenty Pyreans. How would you go about choosing them?"

"Easy one, Captain," Dingles replied, "we call medical and ask how many they have in serious condition. If it's more than twenty, they choose them. If it's fewer, we call Maggie and she selects the rest of them."

"Make the call to JOS medical, Dingles, but ask the director to keep it quiet until we resolve this," Harbour ordered.

By the time Harbour had an opportunity to prepare for dinner, she'd received word from Dingles that Jessie's shuttle was landing. She pinned up her hair, zipped her skins, and stepped out of the facilities. Nadine and Yasmin were setting the table for two. There was none of the usual banter. The royal heir's request was weighing heavily on everyone's mind.

A firm rap at the door had Harbour responding, "Come in, Jessie," before she caught herself. She'd just made a personal error. Her empathetic gates were open, and she'd identified Jessie by reading his emotions.

Nadine and Yasmin ducked their heads in commiseration with the chagrin on Harbour's face.

Jessie entered the salon. His narrowed eyes expressed his displeasure at Harbour breaking the rules that governed their meetings. But the empaths' apologetic expressions gave him pause. It struck him that he was holding on to an image of what had been, instead of accepting that the situation was in flux. And rules would be bent if not broken to accommodate the future. He eased his frown and said, "No harm done. I imagine Tacticnok has created quite a stir over here. She certainly has among my spacers."

Jessie was rewarded with brief smiles from Nadine and Yasmin, who returned to completing preparations for dinner. However, he was observing Harbour and her expression hadn't changed. Something Ituau said to him a while back came to mind. She'd said, "There's nothing wrong with choosing to live alone, Captain. But, if you do find someone you like and you've not practiced sharing your life, you're going to find it tough to build a relationship. Personally, I never was good at the give-and-take thing, and I don't think you'll be any good at it either."

Fortunately for everyone, Dingles rapped on the open doorframe to get Harbour's attention.

"I've the response you requested from JOS medical," Dingles said.

Jessie swiveled from Harbour to Dingles. *You're lagging behind, Jessie. Time to burn some reaction mass and catch up,* he thought.

As Dingles stepped into the salon, Nadine and Yasmin slipped out, closing the door behind them.

"What did medical have to say?" Harbour asked.

"They have twenty-three critical, Captain. Five are too serious to make the trip to Triton," Dingles reported.

"Do you know the status of the eighteen?" Jessie asked.

"According to the medical director, they are stable enough to make the trip out, but it has to be taken soon," Dingles replied.

"And all our ships are here at Emperion," Harbour replied, referring to the moon where Jessie and she had been earning serious coin by slinging slush and filling the *Belle*'s enormous array of tanks.

"We have an option, Captain," Dingles said, addressing Harbour. "One of the injured in medical is the first mate of the *Splendid Metal*. The captain just brought him in, and the ship is still docked on a JOS terminal arm. I took the liberty of talking to Captain Tanner Flannigan under the cover of a spacer's word that the information wouldn't be shared. He's waiting on the comm to talk to you, Captain."

"Birdie, transfer Captain Flannigan to me," Harbour ordered. She switched her comm unit to speaker.

"Captain Flannigan, you have Captain Harbour, Captain Cinders, and First Mate Dingles," Harbour announced, when the link was completed.

"I've heard some amazing things from Dingles, Captain Harbour, and no disrespect to him, but I find them hard to believe," Tanner said.

"The Jatouche completely rehabilitated three of our people ... facial reconstruction, a new eye, new limbs, and enormous amounts of skin grafts. I'm not privy to the methods, but we've witnessed the results. The rehabilitated engineers are at the Triton dome," Harbour explained.

"So, this is for real," Tanner said, still a little incredulous.

"Captain Flannigan, I know your first mate," Jessie said. "Nelson Barber's a good man. I'm sorry to hear about his injury. Is he stable enough to travel?"

"Just barely, if I were to launch soon," Tanner replied.

"I'll cover your flight out and back, all costs," Harbour said.

"That's unnecessary, Captain," Tanner replied. "As soon as you make this public, which I'm assuming you will shortly, the commandant will receive my bill. After all, this is an emergency medical flight."

"Contact the medical director, Captain, get the eighteen transferred now," Harbour said. "I'll be adding two more passengers for your flight. Send me your ship's location, and I'll relay it to Maggie at the Miner's Pit. The engineers at the dome will contact your ship when you're close and give you instructions. No Pyrean medical personnel will be allowed to accompany the injured on the final leg of the trip through the Triton gate."

"Aye, aye, Captain," Tanner replied. Harbour's rapid-fire instructions and authoritative manner had made him feel like a first mate again being directed by the captain to hook on.

Jessie was as surprised as Captain Flannigan at the terse and commanding instructions. A glance toward Dingles caught the first mate's smirk.

"Well done, Dingles, thank you," Harbour said, dismissing the first mate, who touched two fingers to his brow. When the door closed behind Dingles, Harbour tapped on her comm unit again. "Birdie, connect me to Maggie at the Miner's Pit."

There was a momentary lapse, before Maggie answered. The sound of diners and drinkers could be heard. The Miner's Pit was busy.

"Captain Harbour, don't tell me you've run out of alcohol. You know I can't make deliveries this late at night," Maggie quipped, followed by a throaty chuckle.

"And here I was told by Jessie that you could do anything," Harbour replied, acting severely disappointed.

"Before you answer the Captain, Maggie, know that you have another listener," Jessie announced.

"You're a bad woman, Captain Harbour, trying to get me in trouble like that," Maggie chastised.

"All kidding aside, Maggie, you have a task to perform. It has to be done quietly and quickly," Harbour said.

"The place is jam-packed, Captain. Can it wait until tomorrow morning?" Maggie asked.

"Hook on, Maggie May," Jessie said sternly.

"Aye, Captain, latched on," Maggie replied reflexively.

"Maggie, I'm sending you the terminal and dock location of Captain Flannigan's ship, the *Splendid Metal*. You must choose two spacers who you believe are most worthy of complete rehabilitation."

"Captain Harbour, I'm latched on, but I don't understand where this is going," Maggie complained.

"The Jatouche have completely repaired three of our engineers and have offered to do the same for twenty more Pyreans," Jessie interjected. "This is to be kept quiet until we make our broadcast. Captain Flannigan's ship will get underway in a few hours with a group of seriously injured patients from medical. There are two slots left. We can use them or lose them."

"There are so many who are deserving," Maggie lamented. "This seems unfair to choose only two."

The captains waited while Maggie absorbed their request. Suddenly, she said, "I know just the two. What can I tell them?"

Jessie held up a finger to Harbour, requesting he supply the answer, but Harbour waved him off.

"Tell them that if they want complete rehabilitation, they will follow Captain Cinders' orders exactly as I'm relaying them to you. They speak to no one. They grab small packs and board the *Splendid Metal* within the hour. In a couple of months, they'll return from the Jatouche home world with new parts for whatever they're missing."

"I don't mind telling you, Captains, this seems unreal, but I'll get it done," Maggie said and closed the comm.

Harbour dropped into a chair, appearing exhausted by the emotions of the last hour. Jessie sat quietly next to her. As the owner-captain of a mining company, he was used to daily upheavals. Space mining was an unpredictable profession.

Maggie approached a brother and sister, who were eating at a small table.

"You two, drop your drinks and utensils and get your butts outside," Maggie ordered.

The siblings glanced at each other before they quickly struggled up from the table on their prosthetics. Gone was the affable tone of their hostess. In its place was a space officer's commanding voice, and they hustled to follow Maggie out into the corridor.

While in their early twenties, the brother and sister had been together on a work gang, chasing a vein of heavy metal. They were in a deep shaft on a massive asteroid when the mine's ceiling collapsed. The brother's legs were pinned. Rather than abandon him, the sister tried to free him, when there was a second cave-in. By the time the youths were rescued, four limbs between them were too badly shattered to restore without the use of BRCs. Unfortunately, they were two individuals whose bodies rejected the implants.

"I'm supposed to tell you that I've orders from Captain Cinders, and while he knows about them, they really come from Captain Harbour," Maggie said. Urgently, she whispered the details that she was to share, including the ship's location.

The brother, Dillon Shaver, was unconvinced, but the sister, Tracy, was ready to sprint as fast as she could to the *Splendid Metal.*

"This sounds awfully flimsy," the brother commented. "How much time do we have to think about this?"

"You don't have any," Maggie replied. "You go now or I walk in there," she said, pointing to the door of the Pit, "and I select others."

"If you walk in there, Maggie, you're selecting one more," Tracy said, with determination. "I'm packing my duffel and catching that ship. You coming?" she added, poking a finger in her brother's chest.

"I'm not letting you go alone. That's for sure," Dillon replied.

Tracy kissed Maggie on the cheek, whispered a thank you, and set off down the corridor on her prosthetic leg. Dillon hesitated for a moment, and Maggie shooed him off with a wave of her fingers. "Thank me when you return," she added.

Aboard the *Belle*, Nadine rapped softly on the door and entered to ask if dinner should be served. The captains sat in chairs, alone with their thoughts, and she quietly closed the door.

Harbour ceased her musings and stared across the table at Jessie. "Do you think Tacticnok was serious?" she asked.

"Deadly," Jessie replied perfunctorily.

"We have to present Her Highness' offer to Pyre, but not before we define a means of selecting an alternate envoy," Harbour said.

Jessie was trying to reconcile the two versions of Harbour he was witnessing. There was the one, who when presented with the opportunity to help twenty Pyreans, had fired off orders like some ancient general commanding her army. Then there was this one, who appeared to be in denial about accepting a strange and confounding responsibility that was being thrust upon her.

"Well, as your advisor," Jessie started, his lips twisting in an ironic smile, "I need to straighten out your thinking here. There will be no alternative envoy. In Tacticnok's mind, it's you or no one else."

"The Pyrean leaders aren't going to like that," Harbour pointed out.

"No, they won't," Jessie admitted, "which is why we've got to broadcast the entire conversation. They have to hear it from the royal heir herself. And it's going to stir up a huge commotion."

The Twenty

Events were moving swiftly, and Harbour and Jessie decided that they should broadcast Tacticnok's announcement immediately. When the pair gained the bridge, Dingles was standing by and said, "We're ready when you are, Captain."

"The entire broadcast?" Harbour asked.

"Didn't see any way to shorten it, Captain," Birdie replied. "It's one of those all-or-nothing things."

"Did I miss something?" Jessie asked Harbour. "When did you order the broadcast set up?"

"Captain Harbour didn't, Captain Cinders," Dingles replied authoritatively. "She doesn't have to. It's our jobs to anticipate her needs."

"I stand corrected," Jessie said.

"Any announcement of the broadcast?" Harbour asked.

Dingles grinned and ducked his head momentarily. "Couldn't figure out the timing on that one, Captain. Guess we haven't perfected our anticipation skills yet."

Jessie laughed and said, "Maybe not, but you're getting close."

"Let's start it, Birdie. I want Captain Cinders and me in the view," Harbour requested.

"Keep it simple, Harbour," Jessie whispered. "Let Tacticnok do the talking."

Harbour didn't agree with her new advisor, but Birdie cued her that the *Belle* was transmitting Pyre-wide.

"Captain Cinders and I have important information for Pyrean citizens," Harbour started. "Following our words, you'll witness a recording made after Her Highness Tacticnok's arrival at the Triton dome. She has made an announcement, and there are several elements to her statements. I urge you to carefully consider each of them. First and foremost, our three engineers have returned and look wonderful. Jatouche medical skills are astounding."

Jessie picked up the thread that Harbour focused on, recognizing that the rehabilitation was a neutral subject that every Pyrean could appreciate. "Her Highness Tacticnok has offered medical services to twenty more Pyreans. You'll hear why she's being generous when you listen to the broadcast. In response to the offer, Captain Harbour has requested that JOS medical services select the twenty Pyreans. They could only send eighteen, who could survive the trip to Triton, and two spacers have been selected to fulfill the count. The twenty will be sailing for Triton in a matter of hours."

Jessie deliberately didn't mention the ship's name. He wanted the *Splendid Metal* to undock and gain headway before the general public was aware of its mission.

"We'll be at Emperion for two more weeks," Harbour said, "and then we'll have a long trip to the YIPS. I would suggest that everyone watch the broadcast and think about what's being offered by Her Highness. The commandant's meeting this month would be a perfect time for leaders to share their views. The *Belle* out."

Harbour thanked Dingles and the bridge crew for their support, sending them a wave of appreciation. Jessie was a collateral recipient, and it clarified for him why Dingles and the others worked so hard to anticipate Harbour's and the other empaths' needs. There was a thank you, and then again, there was an empath thank you.

Jessie and Harbour retired to the captain's quarters, and they were served dinner.

* * * *

It was late evening aboard the JOS. Medical personnel were wheeling eighteen stretchers with attached support equipment and supplies. They were using a lower level corridor to reach the terminal arm before they surfaced and accessed the cargo level.

Behind the row of stretchers, spacers from the *Splendid Metal* shoved cargo sleds that carried the personal items of the medical personnel, who would accompany the injured Pyreans, and airtight transport tubes to safely move the injured from the shuttle to the dome. Only six medical techs would accompany the injured and make the trip to Triton and back.

At the appropriate point around the orbital station's circumference, Theo Formass, the JOS medical director, accessed a lift and directed the first load of stretchers into the car. "You're loading through the cargo level," Theo reminded the medical personnel. "It's gate six. More crew from the *Splendid Metal* will be standing by to assist you."

Theo sent the next to last group of stretchers up the cargo lift, when he caught sight of two young people coming around a corner, with duffels over their shoulders. His experienced eye immediately identified the various prosthetics they wore. At this time of night, he could think of only one reason that two young people, carrying kits and sporting prosthetics, were hurrying toward this particular terminal arm. He waved them over.

"Sir?" the brother, Dillon, asked.

"Are you nineteen and twenty?" Theo asked.

Dillon hesitated, but his sister, Tracy, piped up. "Yes, sir, boarding the *Splendid Metal* and bound for Triton."

"We're accessing the ship via the cargo level," Theo replied. "I suggest you join the crew members over there. You can add your duffels to the sled."

Dillon paused, a frown on his face.

"Having second thoughts?" Theo asked.

"I'm just wondering if this is for real," Dillon persisted.

"Who chose you two?" Theo asked.

"Maggie, hostess of the Miner's Pit," Tracy replied.

"And who does Maggie work for?" Theo continued.

"Captain Cinders," Dillon supplied.

"Well, the offer to ship my patients to Triton to make the journey through the gate came from Dingles, the first mate of the *Belle*. So, you have Captain Cinders and Captain Harbour directing this project. Which one of them, or is it both of them that you don't believe?"

Theo wasn't entirely convinced of the saneness of this adventure, but he acknowledged that much of his angst stemmed from his tendency to be overprotective about his patients. Exposing them to the trip's lengthy journey was bad enough, but turning their medical care over to aliens really bothered him. However, he intended to project a brave face and convince his patients and the medical personnel that this was a superb opportunity.

The frown on Dillon's face remained, and Theo took sympathy on the youths and decided to offer a bit of advice. "I can see that the two of you have not been treated fairly by life. You're young, and you're already wearing multiple prosthetics. But my warning to you is this: Don't let your accidents turn you into cynics. Always keep your eyes and ears open for new opportunities. Sometimes they can come at you in odd ways like this one. Now, join the crew."

Tracy punched Dillon in the arm and jerked her head toward the crew, standing next to the sleds. On the way over, she said, "You ask anyone else about the legitimacy of this opportunity and I will personally throw your butt off the ship. And I don't care if it's underway. I'm tired of wearing these hunks of metal in place of my arm and leg. I want the chance to get rid of them."

Dillon started to object, and Tracy stuck a finger in his nose. "Don't!" she said, in a tone that Dillon recognized was his sister's final word on the subject.

* * * *

Knowing that they wouldn't be picked up by a ship for two to three weeks, at the earliest, the engineers descended to the dome's secondary level to pick out accommodations. By now, using spacer parlance, they were achieving what they considered level-one dome qualification.

When Pete headed for the traditional glyph that marked the room with the most cursory appointments, Bryan halted him.

"Anybody else interested in exploring?" Bryan asked.

"I am," Olivia replied. "If the domes are similar in layout, except for maybe the number of platforms and levels, there should be an access door to the third level down there," she added, pointing the way. "I'm curious to see if this dome's subtler attributes will respond only to the long-gone Gasnarians or they'll be available to humans too."

"Do you remember the glyph?" Pete asked.

"I remember the one Jaktook touched," Olivia replied. "I'm hoping it will be the same."

Near the end of the corridor, Olivia began searching for the glyph among the multitude of etched, glowing symbols that festooned every Messinants surface, including the decks. After a while, Olivia dropped her hands to her side, admitting her idea was probably wrong.

"I thought Jaktook walked in farther than this after we passed through the airlock," Bryan supplied, eyeing the distance to the Messinants exit hatch.

"And I think you're looking too high, Olivia," Pete commented. "Jaktook reached to just above his head."

"I was considering that this place was built for the Gasnarians, who were similar in height to us," Olivia replied.

"I stand corrected," Pete said. "You're right in your thinking. Bryan, how far down the corridor do you think we should look?"

Bryan measured the distance and stepped about fifteen paces toward the dome's platform ramp. He faced the wall, held his arms out, and said, "We search this area. If we don't find it, I'm at a loss for any other ideas."

Minutes later, Olivia loosed a shout of glee and touched a glyph. A hidden door recessed and slid aside.

"Well done, Olivia," Bryan congratulated, and the two men studied and memorized the glyph.

The engineers descended to the third level. This time, the three of them recognized the glyph that would open the room similar to the one that they stayed in at the Rissness dome.

"Hard to believe," Olivia remarked, when she walked through the door and threw her duffel down. "This room probably hasn't been accessed for centuries, but it looks and smells clean."

Pete touched a glyph to extend a bed from the wall. He dropped his duffel, plopped down on the pallet, and declared, "Home sweet home!"

Bryan accessed the food dispensers. He didn't ask if anyone else was hungry. Following their rehabilitations, all the engineers were experiencing increased demands for calories. Olivia and Pete hurried to a table, while Bryan served them paste and water.

"Hope our pickup doesn't take too long," Pete said, around a mouthful of paste. "I'm getting tired of this stuff."

"I was wondering if we should contact Captain Harbour now," Bryan mused, as he took a seat at the table.

"I think we should wait," Olivia offered. "Captains Cinders and Harbour have to be stunned by Tacticnok's offer."

"I agree with Olivia," Pete said. "I had no idea that Her Highness was going to propose what she did, and it nearly pried my deck shoes free."

"None of us knew the specifics, but I can't say that I was surprised that Tacticnok made the offer," Olivia replied.

"Why's that?" Bryan asked. He paused for a moment to look at his new hand, as if it was a stranger that had dropped by to visit him.

"Ask yourself why the Jatouche, specifically Tacticnok, are being so amazingly generous," Olivia replied. "First, she gives us free medical treatment. Then she offers medical services to twenty more of our people and intravertor parts if Captain Harbour takes the envoy job."

"So why do you think she's doing this?" Pete asked.

"I don't have an answer, but we need to put our heads together and think on it," Olivia declared. She was tempted to divert her head. In this intense mood, she was likely to lose control of her saliva, and people had often been sprayed. However, Pete and Bryan had taken to sitting on either side of her. It was their means of training her that she no longer needed to do that.

"We've been to Rissness," Olivia persisted. "We've met alliance members. There are things we've seen and done that have made impressions on the Jatouche, and Captain Harbour needs to be given a heads-up about what the Jatouche might want from Pyreans and her."

"So, we enjoy our paste, and then we do some thinking. We can talk to the captains in the morning," Bryan concluded.

The engineers talked late into the night, scouring their memories for every incident witnessed on the Jatouche moon and station. They picked apart the conversations they'd had and what they observed. It was fascinating to them that comparisons of visual details revealed a great deal of commonality, but memories of conversation were often quite disparate.

When they were mentally exhausted, they slept and slept hard. Many hours later, Olivia woke, glanced at her comm device, and jerked upright.

"Time's a wasting, boys," she shouted. "Facilities, paste, and top deck, in that order," she called, as she raced to be first in the facilities.

In short order, the engineers were standing in front of the dome's console. Pete and Olivia were relying on Bryan. As a propulsion engineer, Bryan constantly monitored readouts and ran diagnostic applications via panels and submenus. His experience most closely related to the console's operation.

"Let's see if I understood this correctly," Bryan said, which didn't engender any confidence from his companions.

Bryan touched a panel and selected the third item down. A menu popped into the air. From the menu, he selected the fourth item from the top. He hoped he'd selected the comms connections submenu, because the glyphs remained indecipherable. The panel projected various icons overlaying the Gasnarian system. Each icon was representative of a ship. The colony ship's icon was the one that Kractik had taught them, and it was stationed at Emperion. Bryan smiled as he selected it.

"Well done," Olivia said, clamping a hand on Bryan's shoulder.

"This is the *Belle*. Are you aliens or humans, because I don't recognize you?" Birdie quipped. She had the engineers' faces on her monitor.

"Handsome Pete is back, I'm happy to say," Pete crowed.

"Of all the people, Drigtik and Gatnack had to invite to Rissness," Birdie lamented, shaking her head. Then she snapped upright, and asked, "Say, you don't think the Jatouche could make people look younger?"

"Good question, Birdie," Olivia replied. "You'll have to ask Tacticnok, when she comes back."

"I think I might be afraid to know the answer," Birdie said, wincing. "Do you three want one or two captains?"

"Captain Harbour, private conversation, Birdie," Olivia replied.

"Understood," Birdie replied and connected the comm call to Harbour, as requested.

"Captain, we need a few minutes of your time," Olivia requested.

"One moment," Harbour replied. She put off her next meeting, entered her study, and hooked up her comm unit to a monitor for a better view of the engineers. She marveled again at the sharp image the dome's console transmitted.

"I still can't get over how well the three of you look," Harbour marveled. "How do you feel?"

"Ten years younger," Bryan replied. "Zystal, the Mistrallian, asked us if we'd like our structural deficiencies repaired. He was referring to our bones, muscles, and joints."

That the engineers so glibly talked about alien species and their members, as casually as you'd mention crew members, gave Harbour an inkling how immersed these three were in Jatouche culture.

"And to what do I owe the pleasure of this call?" Harbour asked.

"Do you have an idea why Her Highness wants you so badly, Captain?" Olivia asked.

"Or maybe it's Pyreans in general," Bryan quickly added.

"I think it's both," Harbour replied.

"Why do you think that is, Captain?" Pete asked.

"I've bits and pieces but no sure conclusion. Why?" Harbour asked.

"Could you share with us your thoughts? It might be important," Olivia requested.

Harbour spoke for a while about the conversations she'd had with Tacticnok and Jaktook, and the impressions she gathered from their inadvertent comments. When she was done, the engineers engaged in an internal dialog. It lasted long enough that Harbour cleared her throat to gain their attention.

"Sorry, Captain, it would take us days to recount some of the incidents that we experienced on the other side of the gate," Olivia apologized. "But our overriding impression of the Jatouche that we gathered from our visit is that they are greatly respected for their medical services but not much more."

"Be more specific, please," Harbour requested.

"That's just it, Captain, we can't be more specific," Bryan protested. "There might exist a wonderful alliance, encompassing sentient races, but it's not like all members enjoy equality. Our impression is that the Jatouche are lesser members, and they think, in some way, Pyreans and you can help them with that."

"Are you going to accept the envoy position, Captain?" Pete asked.

Olivia smacked his shoulder for his impertinence.

Rather than be upset, Harbour laughed. "It's good to see the Jatouche didn't change anything about your personality, Pete. I would have missed that part of you."

Pete grinned, as if he had been vindicated.

"If you go, Captain, pay particular attention to Rissness Q-gate five. It has a defensive placement around it," Olivia said. "I think you should talk to Tacticnok and her father about the Colony." She saw Harbour check her comm device and figured they might have used up their time. "We can tell you more later, Captain, if you have to go."

"My time is short, but there are some things I have to relay to you," Harbour replied. "The *Splendid Metal* is headed your way with twenty individuals aboard for transport through the gate. I'm accepting that portion of Tacticnok's offer. I need the three of you to do several things."

"We're ready, Captain," Pete announced.

"Can you communicate with Captain Flannigan when he achieves orbit position?" Harbour asked.

"Bryan can," Olivia volunteered.

"I'm fairly certain I can, Captain," Bryan qualified, frowning at Olivia.

"You'll need to train them on where to land the shuttle, how to approach —" Harbour began explaining.

"Captain," Olivia interrupted. "You're talking to three experienced, detail-minded engineers. We'll take care of the landing party and educate them about the dome."

"Of course you will," Harbour apologized. "Most important, eighteen of these individuals are critically injured. They came straight from medical."

Harbour heard Olivia's sharp intake of breath. "Exactly," Harbour continued. "Transport to the dome will be difficult, and you need to have Jatouche medical personnel come to our side of the gate to administer to them."

"Will JOS medical personnel travel with the injured through the gate?" Bryan asked.

Harbour quietly observed the engineers, wondering how to phrase her next request.

"You want us to go with them, Captain, don't you?" Olivia guessed.

"Yes, I do," Harbour admitted.

"And here I was getting excited about showing off handsome Pete to the women who missed me," Pete exclaimed.

"Just think, Pete," Bryan interjected, "if you go back, you can ask Zystal to fix the injuries to your personality."

"Behave, you two, Captain Harbour feels bad enough about asking us to go," Olivia said. "Truth is, Captain, we'd be happy to go. There's more to learn over there that can help Pyreans, and it's a pretty exciting place."

The fact that Bryan and Pete were nodding in agreement made Harbour feel a great deal better.

"What about the intravertor parts, Captain?" Pete asked.

"Stage them at the exit lock," Harbour requested. "Captain Cinders spoke to Captain Flannigan. He'll transport those to the YIPS. The injured are your priority. Once the Jatouche prepare them for transport through the gate, I'd like you to accompany them and stay with them until they're returned."

"Anything else, Captain?" Bryan asked.

"Only that the *Splendid Metal* launched late last evening from the JOS, and Captain Flannigan is burning reaction mass to get to Triton in the shortest possible time. One of the severely injured is his first mate," Harbour replied.

"We'll take care of them," Olivia promised.

"Thank you," Harbour said, wishing she could send the engineers some of the affection she felt for their sacrifice.

"No need to thank us, Captain," Pete replied. "Look at us. We're looking fine, thanks to your efforts with the Jatouche. The women will have to wait a little bit longer for their handsome Pete."

"I don't know about that, Pete," Bryan shot back, "There was that blue-skinned female with the complicated ocular structure. I think she had most of her eyes on you."

While the men bantered back and forth, Olivia said, "Triton dome out," and closed the connection by touching the *Belle*'s icon.

-8-
Commotion

Jessie Cinders was right about one thing. Their broadcast of Tacticnok's announcement did cause a tremendous commotion Pyre-wide. Much of the populace had gotten over the shock that aliens existed and that they were able to move through gates created by mysterious entities called the Messinants.

As long as the aliens stayed on their side of the gate, there was a certain amount of comfort among Pyrean citizens. Now, new concerns arose. Pyreans had journeyed to the alien home world and returned appearing renewed, and more humans were being sent there.

The fearful wondered if the newly rejuvenated were entirely human anymore. Thankfully, for Pyreans, this was the minority view. There were a good number of spacers and stationers who had suffered irreparable injuries and wondered if they could journey to the Jatouche home world and receive the same treatment. Of course, the questions that followed those thoughts were: how to gain transport to Triton, the price of the medical services, and how to pay an alien race for them.

Then again, there were other citizens who were thinking in much more strategic terms. Another load of intravertor parts and the offer of many more meant that someday the entire surface of Pyre would be habitable. There was a significant problem with the path to that kind of future. Her Highness Tacticnok wanted Harbour as the envoy, and she'd been abundantly clear about that.

For wealthy downsiders, such as the council's triumvirate, that was unacceptable, and they schemed how to minimize that condition of Tacticnok's offer.

"Most important," Dorelyn Gaylan said to her audience, "Harbour has to be assured that we support her accepting the envoy position. That's critical. Without her, there are no more intravertor parts."

"What about the bodies?" Rufus asked.

"If you hadn't buried so many out there, you wouldn't have so much to worry about, Rufus," Lise shot back.

"Let me ease your mind, Rufus," Idrian interjected. "I had some tests done. The gases that have permeated this planet's surface layers are incredibly corrosive to flesh and bone. So, if you stop burying bodies, all evidence will be gone in about three to four more years."

"Enough," Dorelyn scolded. "We need to focus on the bigger picture."

"Why are you meeting here in my office?" Lise demanded.

The council had effectively reduced Lise's governorship to that of a figurehead. The domes' families had decided they couldn't accept the economic instability of a competition for the governor's position or, worse, the return of another dynasty, such as the recently ended Andropov family.

"You're required to verify our transition announcement, Lise," Dorelyn stated coldly. "It's time the council emerged from the background. Afterwards, you can enjoy your family's wealth in peace and quiet." Dorelyn accented the last word in a warning to Lise. In essence, be quiet or be prepared to join the bodies of the criminals and competitors that the families' security chiefs had buried just beyond the domes.

In eleven more days, the commandant's monthly meeting would be held, and Dorelyn planned on using that occasion to accomplish several things: announce the council, support Harbour for envoy, and limit the captain's power in that position.

In the same time frame, other strategic discussions were underway among Pyre's societal sectors. In the Starlight, the usual foursome was enjoying evening drinks in the posh cantina.

"You were right," Oster Simian said, raising his glass in a toast to Hans Riesling. "I have to admit that I thought you were far off the mark in your opinion that the Jatouche would return."

"And they brought presents," Dottie noted.

"Presents with strings attached," Trent Pederson added. "Why would the little alien want Harbour?"

Dottie chuckled at Trent's remarks. She leaned forward and said quietly, "Let me correct your viewpoint there, Trent, because just about every Pyrean man secretly wants Harbour."

"Point taken," Trent admitted, "but I was speaking about the alien."

"And while we're correcting one another," Hans interjected, "all of us had better learn to say Captain Harbour or Envoy Harbour and Her Highness Tacticnok. To say otherwise and be overheard is to earn the ire of their supporters, and that would be a mistake."

"Well, Hans, you were the one who had the vision. Now, what are you thinking?" Oster asked.

"I find it fascinating that Her Highness knows Captain Harbour so well," Hans replied.

"What do you mean?" Dottie asked. The three men were considerably older than her and had accumulated enormous amounts of coin over a long period of time. In contrast, she was newly widowed, and the sale of her husband's ship and mining rights had recently elevated her into the rarified strata of the station's wealthy.

"Her Highness offered two gifts to Captain Harbour," Hans said. "Which of those would have tempted us?"

"The intravertors," Oster and Trent chimed together.

Hans directed his attention toward Dottie, who said, "The intravertor was for the likes of us. The offer to rehabilitate twenty Pyreans was for the captain."

Hans nodded his agreement and paused to sip on his drink. "So, the little alien, as you call this very savvy member of a royal family, crafted an offer to simultaneously appeal to the captain and the rest of Pyre."

"And Her Highness was probably testing her knowledge," Dottie mused. When the men regarded her, she said, "She couldn't know how her offer would be received by Captain Harbour. Yes, she crafted the terms and had to hope she'd calculated properly. I wonder what she'll think when she gets the call that there are twenty Pyreans at the Triton gate, who are ready for Jatouche medical care."

"That is capital thinking, Dottie," Hans said, raising his glass to her.

"Let's get back on point," Oster requested. "What's next? I mean, we've gotten just the one load of intravertor parts, which have to be assembled with our shells and which we have to pay for, I might add."

"My goal is the same," Hans replied. "I want a future for my grandchildren on Pyre. We need more intravertors, which means we must convince Captain Harbour to accept the offer of envoy."

"The families aren't going to like that," Trent warned.

Oster and Trent were looking at Hans for a reply, but it was Dottie, who said, "I think they will, at least, in a convoluted way."

Hans struggled forward in his chair. He was on his third drink. "Go on, Dottie," he said encouragingly.

"Well, um ... the downsiders saw the same broadcast we did, and no one doubts that the envoy must be the captain or it's no deal," Dottie explained. "And, I'm thinking the downsiders, by that I mean the families, want the intravertors as bad as we do. Everyone wants the surface of Pyre reclaimed someday, sooner than later."

"So they'll support Captain Harbour for envoy even though they don't like it," Oster concluded.

The men sipped on their drinks, seeing Dottie Franks in a new light. Originally, they thought of her as an attractive widow, years younger than them, and they were flattered by the attention. The more discussions she participated in, the more they realized there were brains behind the beauty. Her insights tonight told them that Dottie had become an asset to their group.

"There's the commandant's meeting coming in a week," Hans said quietly. "You can be assured the governor will have something to say about Captain Harbour's acceptance of Her Highness' offer."

"That's the part I don't get," Trent complained. "If the families encourage the captain to accept the envoy position, how will they maintain control of her negotiations? Intravertor parts are one thing, but Captain Harbour could be making all kinds of deals with the Jatouche that none of us will like."

"The families will proceed in the same manner we will," Hans replied. "We must have a seat at the negotiations table or whatever the Jatouche use."

"You mean go through the gate with the captain?" Oster asked.

"How else?" Hans inquired of the group

"But who would we send?" Dottie inquired. Her heart fluttered, when the three men quietly appraised her.

Two days before the investors met in the Starlight, Commandant Emerson Strattleford spoke with Major Liam Finian, who was his second in command. The commandant had broad sway over the JOS and was responsible for the station's capital expenditures, maintenance, medical support, and security. The one thing that he didn't control and wished he did was the justice system. That purview belonged to the Review Board, which was led by Captain Henry Stamerson.

"This can't happen," Emerson ranted. "Harbour can't be allowed to attain this much power over our people."

"What does the governor say?" Liam asked quietly.

Emerson froze in the middle of his tirade and glared at Liam. Ever since the arrest and conviction of the last governor, Markos Andropov, Emerson had felt a powerful undercurrent of distrust from his subordinates toward him. He was uncertain as to why, but he feared his people knew he was in league with the governor.

"You'd do well to listen to what I'm saying, Major. Your position might depend on it," Emerson fired back. "Now, the general mood of the stationers is that they're supportive of Harbour, and there's nothing we can do about that. But what we can do is assign security to protect the envoy!"

"You want to send one of our security personnel through the gate to keep a grip on Harbour's communications with the Jatouche?" Liam asked incredulously. He had to admit he never saw this coming, and he racked his brain to figure a way to convince the commandant it was a bad idea.

Emerson took a moment to gloat. He saw the hesitation on Liam's face and knew that he'd caught the major off guard.

"And while you're thinking on that," Emerson crowed, "Let me tell you that the security person will either be you or Lieutenant Higgins. You two can fight it out. Dismissed."

The only groups who weren't concerned about being well represented to the Jatouche by Harbour were the spacers, the empaths, and the *Belle*'s residents.

* * * *

The commandant was forced to hold the monthly meeting in a JOS auditorium due to the number of attendees who clamored to be present. A nascent media group was given permission to cover the meeting and broadcast the proceedings Pyre-wide.

Two individuals wouldn't be present for this historical meeting — Captains Harbour and Jessie Cinders. Their ships were headed for the YIPS and the JOS from Emperion. The *Belle* and the *Unruly Pearl* were loaded were slush, and the captains anticipated another superlative payout of coin.

Jessie Cinders spent hours calculating the best investment for his company's growing surplus of coin. With the earnings expected from the upcoming YIPS delivery, Jessie had enough to order another ship. If he chose to take that route, the question he faced was what kind of ship he should add. The arrival of the Jatouche and Tacticnok's proposal had complicated his decision.

Harbour and Jessie decided to join the commandant's meeting from her quarters. Engineers had set up a high-resolution pickup at the end of the salon table, and the captains chose to sit side by side, within a single frame.

On Dingles' request, Birdie had contacted JOS security, specifically Major Finian, to plan how to maintain a presence in the commandant's meeting.

"Are you interested in a two-way audio patch?" Liam had asked Birdie.

"Only if you think the meeting will host significant discussions," Birdie had replied sarcastically.

"Point taken," Liam replied. "I'll hand you off to Sergeant Cecilia Lindstrom."

Cecilia understood Birdie's request, and she quickly arranged the kind of technical presence that made the *Belle* comm specialist smile.

When the conference attendees filed into the auditorium, the principals, except for the commandant, were shocked to find that they didn't have a central forum from which to lead the discussions. They were relegated to the front rows of general seating.

Lise Panoy smiled to herself at the commandant's maneuvering to hold hostage the meeting's central role. She surmised that it was the novel media coverage that had prompted Emerson's decision.

After the attendee's filled the auditorium and station security closed the doors, turning away stationers and spacers, Emerson strode onto the stage. His confident step faltered, when he spotted the huge screen that occupied a space beside the podium. He frowned at Major Finian, who waited in the wings, but Liam merely stared passively back at him.

"The meeting will come to order," Emerson announced officially from the podium. He enjoyed the way his voice was projected throughout the auditorium. "Two important participants aren't present, but that can't be helped," he said.

"Now," Liam whispered over his comm unit, and Cecilia transferred the *Belle*'s link from security operations to the monitor on the auditorium link. Simultaneously, she cued Birdie, who relayed the signal to Harbour.

The audience watched the monitor next to Emerson spring to life, displaying Captains Cinders and Harbour sitting side by side in a spacious, well-appointed salon.

"We're pleased to be able to join this important meeting today," Harbour said. Specifically, she didn't address Emerson. Unknown to the auditorium's attendees, the captains had two monitors stationed beside their pickup. One unit displayed an image of the commandant, and the other showed a wide view of the audience.

Emerson swiveled his head around, looking for the culprit he suspected had engineered this undercutting of his moment. Unfortunately for Emerson, Liam, who the commandant wished to blame, was no longer standing in the wings. The major, wearing a satisfied smile, was descending the backstage steps to access the front of the house.

In the front row, Lise raised her hand. *Time to get this ignominious moment over with,* she thought.

Emerson recognized the governor, appreciating that the meeting would begin on a familiar note.

Lise chose to stand to make her announcement. A media pickup hovered near her. "There has been a significant change in the manner in which the domes will be governed," Lise said, which elicited a round of noise from the attendees.

Emerson called for quiet and requested Lise continue.

"The domes will no longer be overseen by a governor," Lise continued. "Effective immediately, the power of my office is passed to a council made up of the families and directed by three individuals who have been chosen by the council. I'd like to introduce them."

One by one, Lise asked Dorelyn, Idrian, and Rufus to stand and greet the audience. Then Lise sat down, as did Idrian and Rufus.

"I'll be the primary participant, representing the domes, for the important subjects to be discussed today," Dorelyn said. She wasn't looking at Emerson. She was staring straight and hard into the monitor on the stage.

Jessie signed to Harbour in plain view of the audience, and Dorelyn frowned. She was unable to understand the waggling digits. But what irked Dorelyn was Harbour's sly smile. It was obvious to her that the captains had a means of communicating without speaking.

Across Cinders' ships and the *Belle,* spacers, empaths, and residents were laughing out loud. Jessie was using sign language, which he'd learned from Kasey, a tech aboard the *Spryte.* After Jessie used the technique to free his crew, when they were trapped in the dome, sign language had been adopted by nearly everyone aboard the captains' ships. It had become a game to demonstrate the greater proficiency. However, underpinning the spacers' efforts was the thought that one day it might be a tool that saved their lives.

Emerson called for attention, annoyed that the audience was focusing on the monitor. He was tempted to push the unit and its stand offstage but thought that would make him appear petty.

Dorelyn had remained standing, and Emerson said, "Dorelyn Gaylan, you have the floor."

"The domes' council wishes to go on record that we support Captain Harbour taking the position of envoy to the Jatouche," Dorelyn stated formally, which elicited a buzz from the audience.

Jessie signed to Harbour, "Watch out. A second deck shoe will drop."

True to Jessie's warning, Dorelyn proceeded to say, "However, careful attention needs to be paid to those who will accompany Captain Harbour. Specifically, these should be individuals who reflect the population's balance."

A loud grumbling erupted from the audience. They knew where Dorelyn was headed.

When Emerson quieted the crowd, Dorelyn continued. "We don't want to overwhelm the Jatouche with an extensive envoy party. Therefore, it seems prudent to work in close approximation to the ratios of our diverse society. The domes will contribute four representatives, stationers two, and spacers one. Captain Harbour represents spacers and empaths, which means that a position has been taken. All that remains is for the JOS to choose its two representatives."

The audience erupted into angry shouts that drowned out Emerson's protestations. It was apparent that not only was Dorelyn's suggestion not appreciated, but that many stationers had intentions of accompanying Harbour.

A burly mining captain stood and bellowed for quiet. He got everyone's attention, and Emerson was able to restore order.

Jessie glanced at Harbour and signed. She replied in kind. Those aboard the captains' ships read Jessie as saying, "This is a problem." Harbour had replied, "Be patient."

A prominent stationer stood without being recognized. He directed his comments at Dorelyn. "With all due respect to the downsiders, their lives have been good. It's those of us up here who've had to struggle. That's something the families and their kind would know little about. If anyone is going to accompany Captain Harbour, it should be stationers, and we'll keep you apprised of our negotiations."

The stationer's comments elicited thunderous cheers and applause.

When the opportunity presented itself, Dorelyn answered. "The council is adamant on this subject. We've a right to be fairly represented by our numbers and our wealth. You want to be careful that your protestations don't create a rift that can't be repaired."

The outrage over the threat teetered on the brink of disrupting the meeting. Once again, it was a captain who got everyone's attention. She loosed a warning via a portable horn. The terrific noise cut through the shouting and silenced the crowd.

"I have enough loads in this horn to sound it twenty or more times," the captain said. "If you like your hearing, I advise you to communicate in a calm, peaceful manner. I, for one, wish to witness a conclusion to this discussion."

Emerson had his opportunity, and he was intent on making his own point. "The domes' council leader has neglected to mention another sector of the populace. Security is responsible for every function of Pyre. As far as I'm concerned, that includes this potential envoy party. I insist an officer of my staff accompany Captain Harbour for her protection and to represent the functions of Pyre security.

Hans Riesling raised his hand. He stood and said, "There are many of us who invested heavily in the first intravertor. We intend to continue to do so for as much coin as we can afford. For that reason alone, I believe we have a right to have a say, and I don't mean after negotiations are all said and done."

Originally, Harbour had sincerely wished that she was present at the meeting to sense the emotions. Recognizing the level of chaos, she now appreciated the fact that she was comfortably sitting beside Jessie in her salon.

Harbour raised her hand, which Emerson didn't see. However, many people pointed at the monitor.

"Captain Harbour," Emerson said, turning to face the monitor, "much of this discussion is predicated on your acceptance of the Jatouche offer. All this is moot, if you intend to refuse it. And, Captain Cinders, will you accompany her if she does go?"

Jessie replied first, "If Captain Harbour decides to go, then I'll follow, as her advisor." He felt a subtle wave of support flood through his mind.

"I'll tell this audience under what conditions I'll accept participants," Harbour said, in a clear, strong voice.

"With respect, Captain Harbour," Dorelyn said, cutting the captain off, "this discussion is bigger than you. This group must decide what's best for Pyre."

Dorelyn wore a self-satisfied expression, and Lise Panoy thought, *Bad move, fool.*

"I've an idea for you, Dorelyn," Harbour replied. "Why don't you charter a mining ship, travel out to Triton, set the Messinants console for a journey to Rissness, and ask Her Highness if you can dictate to me the formation of the envoy party?"

The audience erupted in laughter, and anger burned in Dorelyn's eyes, bright enough so that Harbour had no need to be present to sense the downsider's wrath.

"In a roundabout way, Captain Harbour brings up an important point," Jessie interjected. "Whoever goes must be vac suit qualified to reach the dome."

"I'm sure accommodations can be made to circumvent the usual requirements," Emerson said. He saw his sponsorship shifting from the governor to the council, and he was attempting to placate Dorelyn.

"I would like to know how you intend to accomplish that," Captain Henry Stamerson asked. "Captain Cinders is quoting the Captain's Articles. Every captain is a signatory of that agreement, and they jeopardize their right to sail a vessel if they violate any portion of the Articles."

Emerson was stumped. He gazed across a row of captains, hoping for an alternative suggestion. Unfortunately, his glance met with hard-eyed stares that said there would be no breaking of the Articles.

"What this implies," Harbour said, "is that anyone who is selected to go with me must be willing to undergo vac suit training and be rated by a ship's officer. No exceptions."

"That will include you, Captain Harbour," Dorelyn stated evenly. She thought she'd discovered the point of leverage she needed.

"No, it won't, Dorelyn," Jessie replied. "Captain Harbour is already rated, as attested by First Mate Mitch Bassiter."

Dorelyn didn't recognize the name, but she wasn't familiar with many more than a handful of captains' names, much less ships' officers. Out of the corner of her eyeline, she saw captains nodding their acceptance of the first mate's name. Having misstepped twice, Dorelyn chose to remain silent.

Harbour used the opportunity presented by the sudden quiet. She said, "To reply to the commandant's query and in light of the evident desire of the attendees to engage the Jatouche, I'm officially announcing that I will accept Her Highness' proposal. I'll become the Pyrean envoy to the Jatouche. That said, I'll tell you the conditions under which I'll accept participation in any negotiations with the Jatouche. I recognize the need to have a representative from every group who should have a role. Captain Cinders, who has graciously granted to support me, and I will represent the voices of the spacers and the empaths."

When Jessie heard Harbour speak about him, he felt the kind of mental lift that Aurelia shared with him, when they explored Triton and the drudgery of the days in evac suits took their toll on him.

Mental lines blurred for Jessie. He'd considered Harbour and Aurelia as occupying two separate categories — two individuals, with nothing in common other than their unusual capabilities. He saw that as a mistake. First and foremost, the women were empaths. It was the fundamental nature of their personalities, and, through no fault of their own, they were forced to constantly guard their powers in the company of normals, individuals like him. He saw his irritation at Harbour's occasional emanations, which might encompass him, as his weakness not theirs.

"Despite my status as a spacer and empath," Harbour continued, "I can tell you that I'll be more concerned with ensuring that all Pyreans benefit from our liaison with the Jatouche. As to other groups who wish to participate, downsiders, stationers, investors, and security, they may each choose one person to ensure their voices are heard."

Harbour waited for the audience's raucous reaction to die down. It took the female captain raising her air horn in warning to hush the crowd.

"You have two weeks to choose your representatives," Harbour said. "By that time, Captain Cinder's ships and the *Belle* will be docked at one or the other of the stations. Soon afterwards, we'll be launching for Triton.

-9-

Rescue

The engineers at the Triton dome discussed Harbour's notice of the *Splendid Metals* flight to Triton.

"When should we let the Jatouche know about the mining ship and the injured aboard?" Pete asked. He eyed the small stack of cubes that Drigtik had left with them. It irked him that their instructions weren't written, but that was the problem with two species with no common alphabet. They were reduced to recording the steps as Kractik spoke and capturing images on their comm units.

"I'm in favor of sooner rather than later," Bryan replied. "We're unqualified to do much more than direct shuttles onto the plains and the crew to the dome."

"I agree," Olivia said. "The Jatouche are the medical experts, and we don't know how long it will take them to mobilize their services."

"They could choose to wait until our injured appeared on their platform," Pete mused. When he received annoyed looks from his companions, he added, "But probably not."

"No time like the present," Bryan announced, deciding for the group.

Paste and water were consumed, containers and cups were recycled, and a cube snatched, and then the engineers headed up two levels to the dome's deck.

Bryan paused in front of the console, opened his comm unit, and rolled through the recording. Pete was about to volunteer what he viewed on his device, but Olivia laid a hand on his forearm to stop him.

"Okay, we need the comm submenu, again," Bryan mumbled out loud, tapping the panel, and selecting the correct items. "Then we need the cube comm subsection, which is the seventh item, and then we install the cube on the adjacent panel."

Olivia dutifully placed the cube where Bryan pointed. Immediately, the panel lit, and the cube glowed.

"Contact," Pete rejoiced. He tapped Bryan's shoulder, saying, "Step aside." Then he gestured to Olivia to face the console's center. "You're better at this communication thing than either of us," he said.

"Okay, give me a second," Olivia replied. She closed her eyes and organized her thoughts. When she was ready, she nodded to Bryan and cleared her throat.

Bryan tapped the panel's icon, and Olivia said, "This message is for Her Highness Tacticnok, Jaktook, or Kractik. Captain Harbour has accepted Her Highness' offer of twenty Pyreans for rehabilitation at Rissness Station. A mining ship is inbound for Triton carrying eighteen medically critical humans. Two others are in need of repair but aren't critical. You are aware of the length of our cycles, and we estimate time of arrival in twelve to fourteen days. Please advise us how best to accommodate the transfer of the injured to Rissness."

Bryan touched the glowing icon on his panel, and the cube went dark.

"Ready?" Pete asked. When Bryan nodded, he snatched it off the console, hurried over to the platform, and placed it in the center.

Bryan took a deep breath and blew it out slowly.

Olivia laid a hand on his shoulder. "You're doing great, Bryan," she said.

Bryan glanced briefly at Olivia, who resisted the habit to turn her face away. He whispered, "I've got this stupid feeling that because I've got new limbs that I should be smarter, more capable somehow."

Olivia smiled sadly and replied, "I catch myself looking at my new face in the reflective metal of the facilities door, and I think, for a moment, that my future will be entirely different, new and exciting. Then I realize that inside ... it's the same old me."

Bryan and Olivia heard Pete clear his throat. For the first time since they had come out of the tanks at Rissness Station, Pete wasn't displaying his upbeat, handsome Pete smile.

"Sorry to eavesdrop," Pete said. "You two aren't the only ones feeling unsure about yourselves. I hated my scars for years, but over time I realized that my relationships with people had become more real. Now, I don't want to go back to being the man I was."

"Then stop parading around our dorm room in the nude," Bryan objected, laughing, and the other two joined in.

"Okay, let's see if I can send this little thing," Bryan said, turning back to the console. He accessed a different panel, located the item he needed, and selected it. The attached icon glowed, indicating the platform at the other end of the gate was clear, and Bryan touched it. The platform's blue light merged with the dome, and the cube disappeared.

"Oh, for the love of Pyre," Bryan said, exhaling in a rush. "I just sent a cube across the galaxy."

"Probably the first human to ever do that," Pete added, grinning.

"Come here, you two," Olivia said, holding out her arms. She folded the men into a warm embrace. When she let go, she had tears in her eyes. "We have to recognize that the Jatouche only repaired our bodies. Yes, that's been a shock to each of us. Now, we have to ask ourselves: What are we going to do with these gifts?"

"I think Captain Harbour is ahead of us," Bryan replied. "Think about these twenty who are coming. Do they know what's about to happen to them? And what about the critical ones? I mean, are they conscious? What happens when they wake up on Rissness Station, and they're surrounded by alien faces?"

"Yeah, some really odd faces," Pete added.

"It looks like we're going to be their guides during the treatments," Olivia said, "which reminds me. We need to instruct the twenty to hand over their comm units."

"What are you thinking?" Pete asked.

"Zystal and the other medical directors might need images of the patients if they have facial damage," Olivia replied.

The engineers continued their discussion for a while longer, leaning against the console. They talked about how to help the new patients, what they might need, and what fears they might face.

Bryan noticed a transfer panel light up. "Uh-oh," he said, and the others followed his gaze, which was directed toward the platform. It lit, and two figures resolved, as the light faded.

"Kractik," Olivia declared, clapping her hands in delight.

"I'm pleased to see you, again, Olivia, and you, Bryan," the small alien replied, as she hopped down from the platform.

"How about me?" Pete asked plaintively.

"And, of course, you, handsome Pete," Kractik replied, chittering.

"Okay, who told her?" Pete challenged, eyeing his companions.

Kractik interrupted the engineers' exchange. "This is Ristick, the dome's emergency medical director. He wishes to communicate with individuals who are knowledgeable about the injuries of the prospective clients."

After introductions were complete, Olivia said, "The *Splendid Metal* is on approach, Kractik, we can contact them and translate between Ristick and the medical teams."

Immediately, Kractik stepped to the console and her small digits flew over the panels.

"She makes it look easy," Bryan commented.

In moments, they heard over the console, "This is the *Splendid Metal*, Captain Flannigan speaking. Identify yourself."

"This is the Triton dome, Olivia Harden, Captain."

"Good to hear from you, Olivia. We're still a long way out from Triton," Tanner replied.

"Understood, Captain. We have a Jatouche medical director here who wants to ask questions about the status of the injured. We can provide the translations," Olivia said.

"Wait one," Tanner replied.

After a few minutes, the Triton group heard, "This is Med Tech Jameson."

Once Olivia explained the circumstances, Ristick held up his tablet, tapped a few times on it, and asked his first questions. She was relieved that his initial queries were general in nature. Ristick requested a name, the nature of the injuries, and the medical status of the first patient.

However, Ristick soon transitioned to more technical questions. Olivia had to ask for clarification of the medical terminology, and she ended up going back and forth between the two males just to establish an understanding of the question.

Aboard the *Splendid Metal*, Tracy made her way around the ship's gravity wheel. She'd been in the ship's meal room, when she heard from a crew member that the captain was talking to the dome. Tracy tapped politely at the hatch to the bridge, and the captain stepped away from the conversation.

"Yes, what is it?" Tanner inquired brusquely.

"This might help," Tracy said, holding out a tiny ear wig.

"What is it?" Tanner asked.

"It's a translation device. Maggie May gave it to me. She said she received it from Major Finian," Tracy explained.

Tanner took the ear wig and examined it. "It's a Jatouche device?" he asked.

"I don't know anything about it, Captain," Tracy replied. "When Maggie gave it to me, she said, 'Use this when you want to understand the Jatouche.'"

"Thank you," Tanner said, smiling. He interrupted the bridge conversation and handed the ear wig to Jameson, who was eager to test the device.

On the other end, Ristick repeated his last question. The bridge crew heard the same chittering nature of the Jatouche language, but this time, Jameson broke out in a smile and quickly answered.

Unfortunately, not all proceeded smoothly. It became evident that Ristick wanted medical information that Jameson couldn't provide. It was simply a matter of the different levels of technology that the two species possessed. The medical director and the tech plowed on, sharing as much information about the injured Pyreans as they could, until they exhausted the subject.

Hours later, when the conversation ended, Kractik set the console and told the engineers that they would return before the *Splendid Metal* arrived.

Ristick and she hopped up on the platform and left in the usual flash of light.

Aboard the mining ship, Jameson removed the ear wig and stared at it. "That's ingenious," he remarked breathlessly. "Ristick sounded like a human in this thing."

Jameson attempted to hand the ear wig to the captain, but Tanner pointed at Tracy, who lounged at the hatch. "It's hers," he said.

"Not right now," Tracy replied. "I'll take it back before I go through the gate."

* * * *

Daily, the engineers watched the progress of the *Splendid Metal* through the awe-inspiring capabilities of the Messinants console. Bryan would access a panel, run down submenus, and project the nearby system's bodies and the ships. By trial and error, he learned how to touch two items at once — the mining ship and Triton. In response, the panel projected a series of glyphs.

"I wish we could read those," Pete griped once again.

Olivia and Bryan had heard the complaint so many times, they'd tuned it out. Bryan decided to occupy his companions' attention by forcing them to run many of the subroutines he'd memorized. One of the more enjoyable exercises was to call the *Belle* and chat with the bridge crew.

One day, Harbour, walking past the bridge hatch, discovered a large group crowded onto the bridge. Crew, residents, and empaths filled every meter of the deck, and a few children were hoisted on adult shoulders. The engineers could be seen on the monitor, and they were regaling their audience with tales about their initial medical examinations. She heard Bryan exclaim, "That's when Zystal asked if I wanted symmetry."

Harbour heard Bryan's audience roar with laughter. As she walked on, she heard Bryan say, "I had to give that one some thought." Another round of laughter faded, as she turned a corner. Harbour smiled. In the engineers' inimitable way, they were teaching her people that there was no need to be frightened of the aliens.

One morning, it was Olivia's turn to run through the basic subroutines. She wasn't as quick as Kractik, but she was becoming quite skilled.

"The *Splendid Metal* has to be close," Pete said, examining the distance between the ship's icon and that of Triton.

"Time to call the ship," Bryan said, looking at Pete.

Olivia stepped aside, and Pete sucked on a lower lip before he reset the panel to the primary menu and dove down the submenus to the comm section. When the ships were displayed, he touched the ship's icon, which was next to their moon.

"Captain, it's that same odd ID," the second mate of the mining ship said, when he saw his comm panel light.

"Put it on speakers, and call Jameson, in case we need that ear wig," Tanner replied. When the second mate cued him, Tanner said, "Captain Flannigan here."

"This is the Triton dome, Captain. Pete Jennings here. We're checking in with you. The console's display shows you're close, but we can't read the glyphs that it displays."

"We'll begin deceleration in fourteen hours," Tanner replied. "We expect rendezvous over the Triton dome in less than two days."

"How are the patients doing?" Olivia asked.

"They're stable. Thank you for asking," Tanner replied. "The med techs had to jumpstart three of them, one twice. They say the deceleration and the transfer are going to put them in jeopardy."

"Do they know where they're going?" Bryan asked.

"Most do. It doesn't seem to matter. They know there isn't much choice," Tanner said. "One thing has helped. We played the *Belle*'s broadcast of your arrival. Many of them remembered Pete and Bryan. The new images have given them strength to hold on."

"How's your first mate, Barber?" Bryan asked.

"He's the individual the med techs had to start twice. He's the most seriously injured," Tanner replied. His voice dropped in strength, when he spoke. There was a pause in the conversation until Tanner resumed. "Are the Jatouche standing by?"

"Negative, Captain," Olivia replied. "They haven't returned yet."

"Wait one," Tanner ordered. Turning to his second mate, he ordered some select individuals to the bridge. When they were assembled, Tanner resumed the call. "I have the key people with me who will be responsible for the landing and the transfer. Talk us through what to expect."

The engineers discussed the landing point on the plains, the type of ground rubble that would be encountered, and the dome's entrance tunnel.

"How do we get in?" Tanner asked.

"Don't worry, Captain," Bryan replied. "We'll meet you outside the tunnel. But, we'll be teaching you how to enter the dome, access the rooms, and feed yourselves."

"Is that necessary?" Tanner asked.

"Captain Harbour's orders, sir," Pete replied.

"Jameson here," the med tech said. "Once we reach the dome's deck, what's the plan?"

"Captain Harbour has requested we accompany the injured through the gate, and we're happy to do that," Olivia replied.

"What about my med team?" Jameson asked.

"Not this time," Olivia said. "Only the twenty the *Splendid Metal* is carrying and the three of us go on this trip."

"Understood," Jameson replied.

The engineers could hear the relief in the med tech's voice. If required, he'd stay with his patients, but he wasn't anxious to travel through a Q-gate to an alien world.

When questions were exhausted, Tanner ended the comm call.

The engineers regarded one another. It was Pete who expressed their common thought. "I expected the Jatouche would be here by now."

"Remember, it's Kractik who knows these consoles intimately," Olivia volunteered. "Maybe she could determine the arrival date of the ship." Unfortunately, Olivia's tone lacked assurance.

That evening the engineers unpacked their gear, laying out their vac suits.

"Oh, for the love of Pyre," Pete moaned. "We have no way to charge our tanks."

Bryan looked at his tanks, lying at his feet, "And when was the last time we charged them?" he asked.

Olivia knelt next to hers and checked the readout. "Mine indicate full," she said.

When Pete replied that his were full too, Olivia glared at him.

"Yeah, I know," Pete said, raising his hands in protest. "Check them out first before I panic everybody."

The engineers slept, rose, used the facilities, ate, and climbed to the deck. They walked into a hive of activity. Jatouche medical services teams were arriving in groups. A mechanical bot was picking up tanks and depositing them on the deck, and then a tech would control the tank's carrier and direct it out of the way.

Kractik hurried over to them. "Olivia, Pete, and Bryan, we're here," she said exuberantly.

"I can see that," Olivia replied. "Are you planning to perform the medical services here?"

Kractik frowned until she figured out what might have initiated Olivia's question. "Oh, no, we're following the precautions laid out by Zystal. These are transfer tanks for severely injured individuals. After the initial investigation, each of the eighteen clients will be transferred to these."

Ristick hurried over to the group. He asked anxiously, "Have you spoken to the ship recently?"

"Yes," Bryan replied. "The eighteen injured are stable, but they've had problems with three. They had to jumpstart them."

Ristick ducked his head and touched his ear wig. Then he looked at Kractik for help, and she shook her head. "Please clarify, Bryan. What was done to them?"

"When their heart stopped, an electrical charge was applied across the chest to restart it," Olivia explained.

The engineers watched Ristick's eyes widen in shock.

"I think Jaktook did explain to Zystal that our medical technology isn't comparable to yours," Pete said defensively.

Kractik nudged the medical director, who quickly closed his mouth and apologized for his response. He looked toward the console, and Kractik caught the hint. She hurried over to it and checked the disposition of the Pyrean ship.

"It's making orbit," Kractik announced.

"Good timing," Ristick said approvingly. He began shouting commands to his teams, who collected their gear and tanks, moving them toward the ramp.

"How can we help?" Bryan asked.

"We will stage our stabilization tanks on the second level near the exit door," Ristick explained. "If the three of you could facilitate the transfer from the surface through the doors, it would save my team having to deal with suits."

"We can do that," Olivia acknowledged.

For the next several hours, equipment was staged, and Ristick reviewed his expectations with the medical services teams. The engineers were surprised to note the extent of the Jatouche party that arrived. It constituted eighteen tanks, seven transfer bots, a medical director, and sixty medical techs.

In a private moment, Pete whispered to his companions, "Do you get the feeling that Her Highness wants the captain really badly?"

"Um, yeah," Bryan whispered, "as in no request by the captain is too small or too big."

Kractik opened a comm connection to the *Splendid Metal* and left it open. Anyone within earshot of the console could hear the bridge call.

Hours passed, as the engineers lounged on the deck. They heard Tanner's voice announcing, "The shuttle is departing."

"Acknowledged, Captain," Pete replied, having been the first to reach the console.

Drigtik kept her muzzle closed. Without training, humans were unaware that they could speak from anywhere on the deck and the console would transfer their voice clearly.

"Are all twenty aboard?" Olivia asked.

"Affirmative," Tanner replied. "Eighteen are in transfer tubes, and the other two are mobile, wearing vac suits. There was only room for one rover."

There was some swearing in the background, which the engineers couldn't discern.

Tanner came back on the comm and said, "I intended to drop the second shuttle with more crew and another rover, but I'm told there's a reaction mass flow warning. My engineers will need several hours to troubleshoot the problem."

"How many crew aboard the shuttle?" Pete asked.

"Only six med techs, a rover driver, two crew members, and two mobile spacers with prosthetics," Tanner replied. "The pilot has to remain with the shuttle, as you know. Each transfer tube with equipment and injured takes four individuals to load and unload.

Bryan did some quick calculations. Looking at his companions, he said, "If Pete and I assist at this end with the rover, Captain, you can leave eight individuals at the shuttle."

"That would help," Tanner replied. "Are the Jatouche ready?"

"They're here in numbers," Olivia replied, her voice reflecting her confidence.

"Well, my crew and the med techs will do their best. After that, it's all in your hands," Tanner said. "Will I get an update?" he added.

"Doubtful, Captain, but we'll try," Olivia said.

The engineers hurried below to the third level and donned their vac suits. When they returned to the second level, the med techs were standing beside their tanks, which lined the corridor from the inner airlock door to the ramp. Several Jatouche stood at the exit door to assist the transfers.

Olivia explained that her companions would support the unloading of the transfer tubes from the rover and through the airlock.

"How many can the rover transfer?" Ristick asked.

"I'm not sure," Pete replied. "I would guess four tubes at most." His fellow engineers nodded their agreement.

"Olivia, I task you with a critical portion of this operation," Ristick said. "I must have an accurate transfer of the name, injuries, and status of each client. This information must correlate between our tanks and my log." He waved his tablet to illustrate where his data was kept.

"Understood," Olivia replied, although she wasn't sure how she was going to accommodate the process.

Kractik communicated updates to the Jatouche and the Pyreans. She told them when the shuttle touched down, when the rover began its trek across the surface, and when it neared the dome.

It was bright outside, when Pete and Bryan cycled through the airlock. They'd expected to have to direct the rover to the entrance, but the driver was unerringly following the tracks of the many rover trips made by other parties.

With no fanfare or time wasted in greeting, the two engineers helped two med techs unload a tube and place it on the deck of the airlock. The woman was conscious and staring up at them through the clear material. Pete gave her a little wave, and she smiled weakly. After three more transfers, the rover driver set off at top speed for another load.

Pete cycled the airlock, and Olivia was faced with her first problem. Luckily, Bryan thrust a comm unit in her hand. It was locked open.

"This is Jameson's," Bryan said. "It has the medical files in it. They're coded to the transport tubes."

Olivia breathed a sigh of relief. She tapped the comm unit to the metal tag on the top of the tube, and a patient's information came up. "Ready," she said to Ristick, who nodded to the first medical services team.

Pete taught the Jatouche how to shut off the tube's air supply, release its seals, and crack it open. There was a great deal of chittering, as the first team relayed the instructions to the other groups. Olivia stood next to Ristick and read off the medical information he required.

When Olivia finished, Ristick ordered various services, and the med team delivered them. Soon, the woman, the first patient, was asleep and transferred to a tank. Supports were attached to arms and legs to keep her position steady. Then the Jatouche medical team directed the tank toward the ramp, where the transfer bot would manage the load up the incline.

In quick order, the next two injured were processed. For the fourth individual, Ristick paused when he heard the medical information. Olivia noted that the injured spacer was Nelson Barber, the *Splendid Metal*'s first mate. Ristick personally examined the spacer and attached a device to the bare skin over the man's heart. Then the next med team transferred the sleeping spacer.

Olivia was conflicted, wondering if she should have accompanied the first group of injured, who were already on deck and might have already been sent to Rissness. However, she couldn't abandon her present duties. So, she quickly dismissed the notion.

It took four more trips of the rover to complete the transfer of the eighteen injured, and Dillon and Tracy rode alongside the last two tubes.

Bryan spoke to the rover driver, Jameson, and a second med tech over his comm and requested that they accompany Pete and him inside. They paused at the entrance and showed everyone how to navigate the dome's airlock.

Jameson and the Pyrean med tech watched in awe as their last two patients were sedated and immersed into tanks of liquid without oxygen masks.

"You'd have to see this to believe it," Jameson whispered.

Olivia regarded the two spacers with prosthetics and introduced herself. Then she said to Bryan and Pete, "I'm taking these two to the platform deck. You need to introduce these three to the glyph system and the accommodations on the third level."

Olivia steadily regarded each of the three men from the mining ship and said, "Use your comm units to take images of the glyphs and make notations about what they do. As you can see," she added, gesturing around her, "there's no shortage of them."

By the time Olivia reached the platform deck, the director, the medical teams, and the tanks, with patients, were gone. The transfer bots were standing idly to the side. She breathed a sigh of relief when she saw Kractik waiting for her.

Dillon and Tracy dropped their duffels, and Olivia introduced them to the console tech.

"I'm pleased to greet you," Kractik replied pleasantly.

Dillon frowned at the odd chittering noises, but Tracy said, "And I'm pleased to meet you. Thank you for what you're doing for us."

Kractik flashed her teeth in surprise, and Olivia leaned to the side to spot the ear wig Tracy wore, which she'd retrieved from Jameson.

Soon the group from below deck trooped up the ramp, and Bryan walked them through the process of connecting to the *Splendid Metal.* The three men from the mining ship wore glazed expressions, as if they had seen more than they could process.

"Overwhelming, isn't it?" Olivia asked sympathetically.

Pete didn't give the men a chance to reply. "Test time," he announced. Then he asked each of them to show him on their comm units the glyph to access the third level and the glyph to access the room. They passed Pete's test.

"My turn," Bryan announced. He had reset the panel to the main menu, while the men weren't looking. "Now, call your captain."

Immediately, the med techs looked at the rover driver, who grumbled, "Great." He eyed the panel and then accessed his comm unit. He'd taken several still images, as Bryan had worked through the menus. Eventually, he touched the icon for his ship, and a smile spread across his face when Captain Flannigan answered the comm call.

"We're happy to report, Captain, that all eighteen severely injured were successfully transferred to the Jatouche. They've already departed," Jameson said.

"Excellent news," Tanner replied. "What's next?"

"This is Olivia, Captain. The last of us will be leaving, momentarily. We've shown your people the basics of the dome so that they or other crew members can maintain themselves here if it's required."

"Olivia, please convey my respects to Her Highness Tacticnok. Whether the Jatouche are able to save all our people or not, I want her to know that I deeply appreciate her efforts."

"I'll convey your sentiments, Captain, when I'm able," Olivia replied. She ended the call.

Pete slapped the rover driver on the shoulder and said, "So, are you going to stay a while and enjoy the comforts of the dome?"

The rover driver looked stricken. "Are you kidding?" he asked. "We're leaving now."

There was a bit of a race between Jameson, the rover driver, and the second med tech, as to who could get down the ramp quickest.

"There's no accounting for taste," Pete quipped.

"Ready?" Kractik asked. It wasn't an offhand question. She was looking at Tracy.

"We are," Tracy replied resolutely.

"This way," Bryan said, walking toward the gate.

Kractik waited until the group had ascended the platform, and then she tapped the icon for the transfer and hurried to join them for the journey to Rissness.

-10-
Envoy

Harbour was notified by Dingles when the Jatouche medical teams arrived in the Triton dome, and she'd watched the transfer of the Pyrean injured through the gate. She kept an eye on the proceedings via her comm unit, while she went about the ship's business.

As ordered by Harbour, Birdie sent a Pyre-wide notice to citizens to check the JOS channel that carried the dome console's deck view.

Seeing twenty Pyreans delivered to the Jatouche for medical care convinced Harbour that accepting the envoy position was a worthy course.

Pausing to watch Kractik join the final group of individuals on the platform and the gate to send them to Rissness, Harbour whispered to herself, "Now, I have to find something of worth to the Jatouche to ensure these services continue for our people."

It also occurred to Harbour that the number of Pyreans who could benefit from rehabilitation was a significant portion of the topsider population. At a pace of twenty citizens per half annual, it would take decades to service them all.

At the moment, the YIPS was pumping dry the slush-containing tanks of the *Belle* and the *Pearl*. Jessie had the *Spryte* and the *Marianne,* aka the *Annie,* dock at the YIPS too, rather than proceed to the JOS for downtime, which set the crews abuzz with rumors.

Aurelia tapped lightly on the captain's door, which was open, and Harbour motioned her inside.

"Take a seat," Harbour said, walking around her and closing the door. "Do you remember when I told you that your education, while you were trapped in Andropov's home, was severely limited, and you needed to find opportunities to broaden your horizon?"

"Yes," Aurelia replied. She was sitting comfortably in the plush salon chair, no longer a nervous teenager, but a confident young woman.

"Are you ready for an adventure?" Harbour asked. She opened her gates wide to read Aurelia's emotions. In the silence, while Aurelia considered the question, Harbour sensed touches of anxiety and sadness, but they were overshadowed by excitement.

"Does this have something to do with you accepting Tacticnok's offer?" Aurelia asked.

"It might," Harbour hinted, "but I want to know how you feel about a change."

"I'd miss the crew of the *Annie*," Aurelia admitted, "but lately I've been considering my future."

"And," Harbour prompted.

"The spacers were my first place of refuge," Aurelia said. "For that, I can't ever thank them enough. But I've been wondering if I want to remain a spacer, attend officer training programs, and work toward a captaincy. The answer I came up with was no."

"So, what do you want?" Harbour asked.

"The Jatouche have changed everything," Aurelia replied. "I want to be part of opening Pyre to these new worlds. I was disappointed when I heard the debate about who would accompany you. There's no room on your team for a lowly spacer and a downside escapee, at that."

Harbour felt Aurelia's turmoil. The two women were communicating empath to empath, and Aurelia wasn't withholding her emotions.

"There might be a need for a vac suit qualified individual," Harbour said quietly, and Aurelia's head snapped up. "I expect four individuals to join us from the station and the domes," Harbour continued. "You can bet that two of the four, if not more, will not be vac suit qualified."

"But I can't qualify them," Aurelia objected.

"I know that," Harbour pointed out sternly.

Aurelia belatedly realized her error. Harbour's time as captain had greatly increased her knowledge of spacer routines.

"My point, Aurelia, is that if I'm performing my duties as envoy, I don't have time to keep an eye on a downsider or some stationers who haven't a clue when to latch on."

"And Captain Cinders can't watch them because you'll need him with you," Aurelia surmised.

"Now, you're catching on," Harbour said. "It would look bad for me, as envoy, to report to Pyre that we'd lost one of the team and needed a replacement."

"Or worse, that we needed two or three," Aurelia added, smirking, before her demeanor sobered. "Will you be able to get the Pyrean leaders to agree?"

"I don't intend to ask them, Aurelia. I'll be telling them," Harbour replied. "Now, I have an assignment for you. I want you to think about what you heard in the commandant's meeting and what that means concerning Pyrean attitudes about a liaison with the Jatouche."

Aurelia frowned at Harbour.

"You don't think the primary reason that you're being invited to go with me is to babysit some vac suit newbies, do you?" Harbour asked, releasing a strong wave of emotional support.

Dingles passed Aurelia after she left Harbour's quarters. The young woman's contented smile was abundantly evident.

"You wanted to see me, Captain?" Dingles asked, after rapping on the doorframe.

Harbour invited him into the salon, and Dingles noted that the chair he chose was still warm from Aurelia. By Aurelia's expression, it appeared that she'd received good news. He was fairly certain that he knew his wouldn't be.

Dingles watched Harbour pour a glass of green, and he judged that her day had been filled with a good many emotional exchanges. It made his decision easy for him, which was to make things easy for her.

"Captain, I want you to know that I'll give my best to whomever you select to be the *Belle*'s captain," Dingles said.

Harbour watched her first mate and trusted friend wring his ever-present cap in his hands. She was reminded of the first time she met

Dingles in security administration. He'd told her that his space dementia was closing the walls of his detention cell in on him, and he didn't expect to survive the ever-pressing, gnawing fear.

The empaths had cured Dingles' space dementia, and the spacer had returned the favor a hundred times over through his diligent attention to the *Belle*'s needs.

"I appreciate you saying that, Dingles, and I've made my choice," Harbour said. "I've selected an extremely competent individual, who I believe the people of this ship can support."

Dingles nodded his head in agreement with Harbour's remarks. He was still nodding, when he heard her say, "I've chosen Mitch Bassiter."

"That's fine —" Dingles said stoically, and then froze.

When Harbour saw tears form in the old spacer eyes, she deluged Dingles with the strength of her affection for him. Dingles closed his eyes and leaned his head back, as if the warm wind of emotion that blew through his mind had physical strength.

Harbour eased her gates closed, and Dingles opened his eyes.

"You sure, Captain?" Dingles asked.

"I've never been surer of anything in my life," Harbour replied, with a generous smile.

Dingles stood up. He stared at the cap he'd twisted in his hands. Straightening it, he sat it atop his head, squared it, and saluted Harbour with a couple of fingers to the brim.

"Captain Dingles," the old spacer said softly. "It has a nice ring to it."

"Yes, it does," Harbour replied.

* * * *

Hours later, Jessie took his captains and his first mate, Ituau Tulafono, to a dinner with Harbour in the captain's quarters of the colony ship. While most were enjoying a drink before dinner, Jessie met with Ituau in Harbour's office.

"I'm not sure how long Captain Harbour and I will be gone," Jessie said.

"Not to worry, Captain, I'll take good care of your ship until you return," Ituau replied.

"That's just it, Captain Tulafono. The *Spryte*'s no longer my ship. It's yours."

In Ituau's momentary speechlessness, Jessie smiled and said, "That's a new state of affairs for you, Captain, isn't it? To be at a loss for words, I mean."

"I'm elated and worried, at the same time, Captain," Ituau replied, deciding to be forthright with Jessie.

"With your promotion, Ituau, which you've earned, goes a captain's share of the profits," Jessie added. "Hiring and promotions are your duties, effective immediately. However, we must discuss one aspect of your new role."

"Would that be my behavior in downtime?" Ituau asked.

"Yes. I know you've curtailed the more ... strenuous elements during your downtime over the past few years, and I appreciate that," Jessie said.

"Say no more, Captain," Ituau replied quickly, waving a hand to end the discussion. "I'll keep a respectful distance from any of our crews, including that of the *Belle*, and I'll be discreet aboard the stations."

"As a captain should be," Jessie noted.

"Anything else?" Ituau asked.

"What remains to be discussed will be shared with the other captains," Jessie replied.

"Well, I know you frown on this, and I can't promise this will be the last one," Ituau said, as she stepped quickly forward and grasped Jessie in an embrace.

A whoosh of air escaped Jessie, as Ituau's heavy arms encircled him. She was right. He wasn't a man who hugged or liked to be hugged. But, in this instance, he patted Ituau's wide back several times before she released him.

"Let's join the others before I regret my decision," Jessie said, scowling, and Ituau laughed at the pretense.

When Jessie entered the salon, Harbour gazed at him, and he nodded in return. The two of them had planned the means by which their responsibilities would be handed off and how they would keep the coin flowing in their absence.

Harbour handed a pair of crystal glasses to Jessie and Ituau. They were filled with some select choices from the captain's stock.

"A toast," Jessie announced, raising his glass. "To Captain Ituau Tulafono."

There was the slightest hesitation, and then the present company cheered loudly. Harbour bathed in the heartfelt emotions that the senior captains shared with Ituau and her with them.

Harbour signaled the empaths, who were ready to serve dinner. As they swept into the salon, with food dishes and drink carafes, they could sense the powerful emanations from everyone but Harbour. For the empaths, it was another major step in a direction they coveted. Where once they'd been considered the outcasts of society, they'd been fully adopted by one of the most independent-minded sectors of the Pyrean populace — the spacers.

Harbour and Jessie let the captains consume a major portion of their meals before they began updating them.

"Captain Harbour —" Jessie began.

But Harbour interrupted Jessie. "Everyone is a captain at this table. I suggest we dispense with formality."

"Agreed," Jessie replied. "Harbour and I see no reason to change what's been working. After the *Pearl*'s tanks are emptied, Leonard, you'll sail your ship for Emperion with Yohlin and the *Annie*. The *Belle* will need more time to be emptied, and we can use this period to send the shuttle to the JOS to pick up any additional family members, new crew, and supplies. Ituau, I presume the crews' usual attitude exists in that they don't wish downtime on the JOS."

Ituau tipped her head in agreement.

"Do you anticipate any negotiations with Evan Pendleton?" Leonard Hastings, captain of the *Pearl*, asked.

"Difficult to say," Jessie replied. "If so, be prepared to take a hard line with the YIPS manager. There might be an attempt in my absence to see if the YIPS can negotiate a better deal for our slush."

"Understood," Leonard replied.

"Now, let's talk about my arrangements," Harbour said. "Yohlin, I'll be relieving you of one of your spacers."

"Rules," Yohlin Erring, captain of the *Annie*, replied, referring to Aurelia by the name the empaths gave the spacer, when she was in hiding.

"Yes," Harbour said simply. "As far as anyone is concerned, it's to babysit the vac suit newbies. Any rumors to the contrary are to be ignored."

"And what is the truth?" Yohlin asked. Harbour stared evenly at her, and Yohlin acquiesced. "Understood, Envoy Harbour."

Yohlin's address of Harbour was a statement to the others that more than one individual's status had changed.

"Ituau," Harbour said, "we'll be collecting the delegates from the JOS, after they're selected, and then making for Triton. Afterwards, you'll proceed to Emperion. The slush cycle will continue until we return."

"What about the vac suit newbies?" Ituau asked.

"Excellent point," Harbour replied. "I've no idea what we'll get in that regard. We might have to be outfitting them at the Latched On, if no one has done that for them."

"We have the trip to Triton to train them," Jessie interjected. "Harbour and I think the best way to do this is to let Belinda Kilmer train and qualify them, and Rules to assist in every step."

"Smart," Ituau allowed. "Rules can't be in charge of training them, but by participating, she can qualify as a team safety member."

"That's the plan," Harbour said, "and I want that qualification in the logs."

"Aye, aye, Envoy," Ituau replied, with a grin.

Harbour's mouth twisted in a sour manner, and she asked, "Why does that sound unsettling, if not ominous?"

"Pyre's future is now in your hands, Envoy," Leonard added, spreading his arms wide.

"Okay, stop people. You're scaring me," Harbour quipped. The polite chuckles she received settled her. Years ago, a warning from Pyre's most powerful empath that she was scared would have sent Pyreans running for safety. Now, this intimate group felt comfortable teasing her and not worrying about her reaction.

"What about Belinda's position as second mate on the *Annie*, if she's making the trip to Triton on the *Spryte*?" Yohlin asked.

"Why are you looking at me?" Jessie riposted.

"Um ... apologies, Captain Tulafono," Yohlin said, turning toward Ituau. "At your earliest convenience, I'd like to discuss Belinda's transfer and your thoughts on your ship's officer positions."

Ituau graciously nodded to Yohlin's offer and her adroit recovery from the gaffe.

"Kindly include me in that discussion," Leonard added.

Harbour sensed Jessie's contentment with the promotion of his new captain. Now, it was her turn to see how the table reacted to her choice.

"I'd like to announce one more promotion," Harbour said. The emotional temperature of Jessie's captains changed radically. The Emperion venture's success had poured coin into everyone's pockets. A poor choice for the *Belle*'s captain could upset the familiar and profitable routine.

Harbour picked up her comm unit and signaled.

The table's attention turned to the salon door. When it slid open, Dingles stepped through. He wore a crisp pair of captain's coveralls with shoulder bars. Atop his head was his ubiquitous, frayed cap.

"Yes," Ituau exclaimed, bolting out of her chair. "She rushed to give the *Belle*'s former first mate a bone-crushing hug.

"Easy there, girl," Dingles replied. "These bones aren't as firm as they used to be."

"Won't you join us, Captain?" Harbour asked, walking around the table and handing Dingles a glass. She turned to the table and said, "To the *Belle*'s new captain, Mitch Bassiter."

There was a round of cheering, and Harbour carefully sampled each captain's emotions. Only when she was satisfied that her choice of captain had been unconditionally accepted did she smile and relax.

Jessie had carefully observed Harbour, even as he participated in the festive congratulations of Dingles. For the second time in a period of weeks, he made a significant readjustment in his thoughts about Harbour and her powers. Her ability to perceive the emotions of others would be a major asset to an envoy, and as the envoy's advisor, he had to be a willing participant in her use of those powers if they were to ensure that the negotiation tables wouldn't be turned against them.

-11-
Selections

The *Pearl* and the *Annie* sailed for Emperion, and the deadline for delegate selection was fast approaching. In truth, finding individuals who could make the momentous decision to journey to a distant world for an unknown amount of time was difficult.

"Why me?" Lieutenant Devon Higgins said to his superior, Major Finian.

"It's either you or me," Liam replied.

"Why don't we tell Emerson that neither of us will do it?" Devon protested.

"We can, Devon, and then we can both start looking for new jobs," Liam replied.

When Devon stared at him in consternation, Liam added, "The commandant's exact words, I'm afraid."

"So if I refuse, I'm fired, and you have to go or get fired too," Devon said.

"That's about the size of it," Liam replied.

"I knew I shouldn't have let my vac suit qualification lapse," Devon grumbled. An idea occurred to him and he pointed a finger at Liam, saying, "You get me alien hazard pay while I'm gone, and don't let that tightwad skimp on the coin either."

"That I can do," Liam said, laughing. He was greatly relieved that Devon agreed to go. It wasn't that he feared joining the envoy party. It was that there were too many unresolved issues with the commandant. He had to stay to keep an eye on the man.

Downside, the discussion was direct and terse.

"It's you, Idrian," Dorelyn said.

"How do you figure?" Idrian asked, with trepidation.

"It has to be a member of the council," Dorelyn replied. "Rufus can't go. You know he's a xenophobe. And if I go, can you keep the family heads in line?"

Idrian had to admit that Dorelyn's logic was unassailable. He did make one last, albeit weak, argument. "You know I'm not vac suit qualified."

"Oh, for the love of Pyre, Idrian, none of the family heads are," Dorelyn replied in exasperation.

Aboard the JOS, a discussion was floated among the station's investors who had taken part in ensuring the deployment of the first intravertor. They were, in large part, male and aging. At a private meeting, it was discovered that only three individuals were young enough to participate in the envoy party and had no family members. Dottie Franks was one of them.

The two younger male investors, who did qualify, were adamant about not going. That left Dottie standing alone, but her time with Hans, Trent, and Oster had taught her a thing or two about negotiations.

Dottie stood in front of the group and said, "I'm willing to represent you in negotiations with the Jatouche. However, I see my absence from Pyre as a loss of opportunity to further my investments." This wasn't entirely true, because her three friends had promised to invest a portion of her coin in their enterprises.

Dottie negotiated a tidy agreement for the length of her absence from Pyre. Rather than this upsetting the investors, they were pleased to discover that their representative was a savvy businesswoman.

The sum of these discussions meant there was only one slot left to fill on the envoy mission. The station would select one of their own who wasn't an investor. This was the only post that would be filled by a broad topsider referendum.

"This is ridiculous," Captain Stamerson said to Sergeant Cecilia Lindstrom and Lieutenant Devon Higgins.

The security personnel were helping Henry research the backgrounds on some of the many individuals who had placed their names on the ballot. Name after name was found to be a less-than-respectable individual.

"Too many unknowns, Captain," Cecilia commented.

"If you could be a little more precise, Sergeant," Henry requested.

"The working stationers can't afford to take the trip ... loss of coin or job. And there are too many unknowns about this trip for those who can afford to go. So, it's the less reputable, who have nothing to lose, that are signing up," Cecilia explained.

"There are a good many ex-spacers, who wanted to put their names on the ballot, but they were told by the commandant that they didn't qualify," Devon added. "There were some good candidates among them."

"There is only a day and a half to go before the ballot closes," Henry complained.

"Wait. Another name has just been added," Cecilia announced. She searched for the individual in security's database. "This one is a clear winner. Two tours in security confinement, both times for brawling and putting his opponents in medical."

Devon and Cecilia regarded Henry's crestfallen face. Cecilia glanced toward Devon, widened her eyes, and nodded toward Henry. Devon, who was seated on a desk slightly behind Henry, grimaced and held up a hand in protest, which caused Cecilia to repeat her motions in an exaggerated manner.

Devon took a breath and said, "Well, Captain Stamerson, I could use the company."

Henry turned partially around and studied the lieutenant's face. He'd thought to outright object to the suggestion, but the more that he mulled it over in his mind, the more he wasn't so sure the idea didn't have merit. Henry turned back to regard Cecilia, who was smiling and nodding her head in agreement.

"Envoy Harbour and Captain Cinders would welcome someone of your stature and experience on the team," Cecilia suggested.

Henry was about to tell the sergeant that flattery wouldn't work on him, when Devon interrupted. "Captain, think about the others who are going. We have an investor. From what we can determine, Dottie Franks is a good woman, but she represents the wealthy. I'm going for security's sake, but I doubt I'll take part in the negotiations. Then you have Idrian Tuttle, who we've just learned is a member of the domes' council, which is an organization that we've never heard of before. Who's going to speak for the stationers ... one of these malcontents or felons?"

Henry had always considered himself a deliberate man. He was a person who weighed the pros and cons, judged the risks, before making an important decision. In a departure from that lifelong history, he said to Cecilia, "Add my name."

"Yes, good company," Devon said excitedly, slapping his hands together.

"A final adventure, if I'm selected," Henry commented, with a wry smile.

Captain Stamerson needn't have wondered about the outcome. Except for a few friends, family members, and drinking partners who voted for each of the other thirty-four names on the ballot, the stationers overwhelmingly selected Henry as their representative.

* * * *

"Welcome aboard, Envoy," Claudia, the copilot of the *Belle*'s premier shuttle, said.

Harbour smiled genially, as she climbed the ramp into the shuttle. It felt as if she had only recently become accustomed to being called captain when her title had changed again.

Danny Thompson remained in the pilot's seat. It eliminated his need to stump down the aisle on his prosthetic legs. In Harbour's mind, Danny would be one of the next twenty individuals to visit Jatouche medical services, if she could convince him to go. Then again, it occurred to her that the best way to convince Danny was through his copilot and new love, Claudia.

Harbour strolled to the pilot's cabin, while other passengers found seats. The shuttle's interior looked as good as it had when first delivered. The exterior had taken a beating when it entered Pyre's harsh environment to drop the Jatouche intravertor, and a substantial amount of coin was spent to resurface the hull and return it to a pristine state.

Harbour's visit with Danny was cursory. She said hello, shared her appreciation emotionally with him, and left to find her own seat.

The shuttle flight was from the YIPS to the JOS, and it was full. Notably, Dingles, Belinda, and Aurelia accompanied Harbour. Dingles wore his best skins and new coveralls with captain's patches on the shoulders.

After docking at the terminal arm, the passengers disembarked. Those who were intent on shopping were allowed to go ahead. Then the remaining passengers followed Harbour along the arm toward the transition ring.

Groups of spacers caught caps, transferring through the station's ring, until only four people remained on the arm. Harbour, Dingles, Belinda, and Aurelia loaded into a cap, rode the ring, and exited into the station.

Harbour's entourage waited for her. The first few times Harbour had received this type of treatment, it had embarrassed her. She no longer felt that way. The spacers formed a column, which occupied half the width of the station's promenade corridor.

Dingles walked proudly beside Harbour at the front of the column. Stationers opened comm units as they passed. Many wanted to be the first to share the news about the arrival of the envoy and the *Belle*'s new captain.

But the critical messages that were hurriedly shared by the stationers concerned Aurelia Garmenti, who walked beside the envoy. In the minds of Pyreans, Aurelia was the young woman who toppled the Andropov dynasty, and she had finally set foot again aboard the JOS.

It remained to be seen whether the commandant would confront Aurelia. Harbour had held a captain's court, presented evidence, and declared Aurelia innocent of murder by reason of self-defense. However, the young empath had never faced the JOS Review Board, much less returned downside to face the families' justice, as they had demanded.

The spacer phalanx reached the Latched On. The store's owner, Gabriel, was waiting for Harbour, and he welcomed her inside. For a moment, he was taken aback by the numbers who accompanied her, but only two women followed Harbour inside.

Harbour's entourage lined the store's face, staring impassively at the pedestrians who passed by. Dingles' position was nearest the door. The spacers had no intention of denying access to the store, but their mere presence deterred customers from entering, choosing to put off their business until later.

"The four delegates are waiting, as you requested, Envoy," Gabriel said. "Belinda, good to see you appearing so well, and, Aurelia Garmenti, I don't believe I've had the pleasure. Welcome to the Latched On." Then he led Harbour and her companions to where the delegates waited.

"Thank you for meeting us," Harbour said graciously to Henry, Dottie, Devon, and Idrian. "Our purpose today is to check on your vac suit qualification and see you properly outfitted, if necessary. Let me introduce your primary trainer and qualifier, Belinda Kilmer, second mate on the *Annie*. The assistant trainer will be Aurelia Garmenti, known as Rules by spacers."

Harbour gazed briefly at Dottie before her eyes settled on Idrian. "Does anyone have any issues with my choices for your trainers?"

Idrian was quick to shake his head. Harbour had opened her senses to taste the emotions of the foursome. She was sure that Aurelia had done the same thing. More than anything, Harbour felt combinations of excitement and anxiety, which she attributed to nervousness about the vac suit training, the flight to Triton, and the journey to Rissness.

"We're taking the *Spryte* to Triton. It's a mining ship, which I'm sure most of you know," Harbour stated. "The question is who, besides Captain Stamerson, has been aboard one?"

When the other three delegates shook their heads, Harbour briefly eyed Belinda, who signed her acknowledgment. There would be a necessity for more than vac suit training.

"Next question is the status of vac suit training," Harbour requested. "Let's go left to right. Captain, if you'll start."

"My qualification expired, Envoy, and I wouldn't trust my old suit," Henry replied.

"I've never even been on a terminal arm," Dottie said. Her embarrassment was evident.

"We'll take care of you, Dottie," Harbour said. She sent the woman some emotional support, knowing that due to Henry and Devon's proximity to Dottie they would feel some of her power. Harbour meant it as a reminder to the three of them that the title of envoy was in addition to her capability as an empath.

Dottie smiled briefly at the unusual sensations that flowed through her mind. She remembered telling her associates that she'd never had contact with an empath. The thought crossed her mind that she now had two obligations as a delegate. She must look after the interests of her fellow investors, and she must be careful to maintain a cordial relationship with the envoy.

Harbour moved on to Devon, who replied, "Vac suit qualification was seven years ago. It's expired, and my gear is old."

When Harbour regarded Idrian, he said, "Apologies, Envoy, my circumstances are much the same as those of Dottie."

Harbour had been prepared to dislike the domes' delegate, but Idrian didn't seem to be formed from the same mold as the likes of Markos, Lise, or Dorelyn. But that didn't mean she intended to forget or forgive the fact that Idrian Tuttle was the head of a dome family.

"I'm not aware of which of you has the coin to pay for a quality vac suit or who will be reimbursed for your purchases," Harbour announced. "Therefore, I'm purchasing your equipment today, and I'll appreciate you taking Belinda's advice in all things. Captain Stamerson, for the sake of expediency, I request your cooperation in this regard."

"I never argue with someone who is choosing to spend their coin on the purchase of quality equipment for me," Henry replied. His smile was warm, and Harbour sensed the retired mining captain's genuine affection for her.

"You speak as if we're departing soon," Dottie said. "I thought we would need weeks to become vac suit qualified."

"You'll be trained on the way to Triton," Harbour replied. "It will keep you occupied."

Henry hid his smile. A mining ship's journey to its destination could be tedious, the height of boredom. It was the reason that captains kept their spacers busy and carefully monitored the camaraderie of the crew. A slovenly crew and an unharmonious ship meant accidents waiting to happen.

"And regarding our departure date, Dottie, we'll be sailing as soon as everyone can be ready," Harbour said. "Captain?" she added.

"Tomorrow morning," Henry said, sending Dottie an apologetic expression.

"Lieutenant?"

"The same," Devon replied.

"Idrian?"

"I see no reason why I can't keep the same schedule," Idrian replied.

When Harbour turned her attention on Dottie, the woman said, "Well, I don't want to be the one holding up the works, but someone is going to have to collect me from the station's side."

"We'll send you a message as to which terminal arm our shuttle is docked, Dottie, and we'll meet you and the others on station," Belinda assured the woman.

Harbour turned around and found Gabriel watching. She twitched her head in the delegates' directions. In turn, Gabriel signaled several clerks, and then he hurried forward. The clerks followed, towing sleds.

"Gabriel, I've requested Belinda and Aurelia select captain's quality gear for the delegates," Harbour said. To the foursome, she said, "I'll leave you in these spacers' capable hands." To the store owner, she said, "Gabriel, I need a rush order."

"Certainly, Envoy. How soon do you need it?"

"Tomorrow morning," Harbour replied.

There was a moment while the two individuals eyed each other. Gabriel was trying to figure out what it would cost to put fabrication teams on the order around the clock to meet the schedule. Harbour was telling Gabriel through her focused stare that she wanted it done.

"The rush charge will be exorbitant, Envoy," Gabriel cautioned.

"As long as you can meet the goal," Harbour replied. She sent him a wave of appreciation, spun, and walked out of the Latched On.

Previously, Harbour had been extremely reserved about dispensing her powers among stationers. Since the start of her liaison with Jessie and his spacers, she found she was less concerned about keeping her abilities under wraps. She wondered how stationers would react to the change in her habit. Then again, she quickly realized the effect would be minimal. She was leaving for the Jatouche home world tomorrow.

In the station's broad corridor, a small group of spacers fell in behind Harbour. Dingles and the majority of the crew continued to wait outside the store. Those observing from the restaurant windows across the corridor considered the spacers weren't securing the delegates, more likely, they were protecting Aurelia.

-12-
The Crossing

The following morning, the *Belle*'s shuttle docked at JOS terminal arm three. Dingles and Belinda led a group of spacers onto the arm. They transferred through the caps to the station and met the delegates in the arm's access corridor. Gabriel was standing behind them with clerks and sleds of equipment.

Dingles immediately noted something was wrong. Henry and Devon stood to one side of the corridor with duffels at their feet. Idrian and Dottie stood on the other side with an assortment of sleds near them, and they weren't happy.

"Uh-oh," Belinda mouthed to Dingles.

It was Dingles' time under Harbour's tutelage that allowed the old spacer to approach the problem diplomatically instead of barking questions.

"I'd say good morning, but that doesn't seem to be the case for everyone," Dingles said. Turning toward Idrian and Dottie, he said, "How can I help?"

"According to the captain," Dottie said, pointing at Henry, "you won't allow us to take this meager amount of luggage."

Dingles, whose entire possessions had fit in two duffels, eyed the loaded sleds. With no stretch of his imagination could he have applied the term meager to the four mounded sleds. Dingles looked at Henry for clarification.

"More accurately, Captain, I was trying to educate my fellow delegates about the challenges of space travel," Henry replied.

"I must admit that more closely resembles what Captain Stamerson said," Idrian added, which earned him Dottie's displeasure.

"The ship is full of spacers," Dottie objected. "Why can't we borrow a few of them to manage our things until we get to the Jatouche home world?"

"First, you'll be on a mining ship," Dingles explained. "It's not a passenger ship, and it'll be carrying more people than it's built to accommodate. Can your gear be stowed in an unpressurized bay?"

"Certainly not," Dottie said defiantly.

"More important," Dingles continued, "only the envoy and her party will be traveling through the gate. You'll arrive at a dome on a moon far from this world. We have no idea how you'll be transported to the Jatouche home world or another station. Every time you transfer from dome to ship to station and back, you'll be responsible for managing your gear."

Dottie forlornly regarded her sleds. "Captain Stamerson, I apologize for my remarks," she said. She regarded Idrian, and the two individuals seemed at a loss as to what to do next.

"Gabriel, I need four duffels, if you please," Dingles requested.

Gabriel glanced at the nearest clerk and tipped his head toward the Latched On, which set the clerk running toward the store.

"Lieutenant Higgins, I'll need someone to secure the delegates' extraneous gear in whatever manner they request," Dingles said.

Devon stepped away, pulled his comm unit, and spoke into it quietly.

"Now," Dingles said, approaching Idrian and Dottie. "I think it best that you separate your possessions into what will fill two duffels, such as those you see at Captain Stamerson's feet."

Gabriel signaled the clerks, who hurried forward to help pull bags off the sleds and open them for the delegates. The corridor became a display of personnel wardrobe and comfort items. At one point, Devon regarded Henry and quirked his eyebrows, forcing the captain to cover his grin.

Belinda knelt next to Dottie to advise her, and Dingles did the same with Idrian.

When the Latched On clerk arrived, carrying four duffels, they were filled to overflowing. That necessitated some more fretting and reordering by the delegates to consider what was necessary. When the final decisions had been made, the clerks helped the delegates repack the bags that would be left behind and return them to the sleds.

By this time, Sergeants Lindstrom and Rodriguez were standing by.

"I'd like my things returned to my cabin," Dottie said.

"I'll secure them for you," Cecilia assured the woman.

"I've nowhere on station that's private," Idrian said.

"Sergeant Rodriguez, please store Delegate Tuttle's gear in security's lockup," Devon ordered. He had kept his eyes on Idrian and received a nod from the downsider, indicating that it was a satisfactory arrangement.

"Then I believe we're ready," Dingles said. "Gabriel, if your people would assist," he requested, nodding toward the duffels.

The clerks scooped up the eight duffels and added them to the sleds carrying the vac suits. Then Gabriel and his people made for a lift to drop to the arm's cargo level, while Dingles, Belinda, and the delegates turned to catch a cap and transition to the arm's passenger level.

As the cap doors closed, Devon saw his sergeants give him small waves, and he lifted his hand in recognition of their farewell.

When the cap doors opened on the terminal arm, Belinda asked Dottie to wait, while the others exited the cap. Then she unbuckled and released her shoulder restraint. Standing in front of Dottie, she cautioned, "Always one foot on the deck, and when we're in zero-g, you will always hold the hand of an experienced spacer. I don't care who that person might be."

Dottie had thought to object to Belinda's tone. Then she recalled Harbour's instructions. This officer would be her trainer, and she had to vac suit qualify to be allowed to journey through the gate. She visualized the embarrassment of standing before the investors and admitting that she'd been dismissed from the envoy's party at Triton.

"Understood, Belinda," Dottie replied. Then, she quickly forgot her instructions.

Belinda unbuckled the delegate, and Dottie shoved up on her restraint. Her feet hit the cap's floor, and she instinctively flexed her legs to take her weight. In the next moment, she would have smacked the cap's overhead, except that Belinda had grabbed her.

"Oops," Dottie muttered, annoyed with her actions.

"In space, mistakes will get you killed, Dottie," Belinda cautioned. "You have to listen to what we teach you and incorporate those lessons into your thoughts. Think about them over and over ... in your cabin, in the facilities, in the galley ... everywhere."

Dottie nodded. She reached out a hand, which Belinda took. Then Dottie stretched out both legs and connected to the deck. "One foot on the deck at all times," she repeated to herself. The women's exit from the cap was slow and careful, as Dottie practiced what she'd just learned.

Idrian, who had ridden the El hundreds of times, was familiar with the transitions from Pyre's gravity to an arm's zero-g. Despite that experience, he noted that he was bracketed by both captains, who walked shoulder to shoulder with him.

Dottie, who was proud of her shoulder-length hair, was suddenly disconcerted by it floating around her face and obscuring her vision. She felt a tug on her hand and halted her step. Belinda gathered Dottie's hair, pulled on the back of her skins, and tucked it inside.

"Thank you," Dottie muttered. From the corridor, where she'd packed her duffels, to where she now stood, she'd already had several eye-opening, if not terrifying, lessons. The future looked extremely daunting to her, and it had nothing to do with being a delegate.

Once the group boarded the *Belle's* shuttle, Dottie and Idrian felt a bit of confidence return. The shuttle's quality elicited oohs and aahs from Dottie and several polite comments from Idrian.

Listening to the other delegates, Henry and Devon regarded each other. They knew the *Spryte* would be several orders of lesser comfort compared to the colony ship's new shuttle. Dottie and Idrian were about to receive some rude awakenings.

* * * *

Harbour and Jessie waited aboard the *Spryte* for Belinda and the delegates. Their goodbyes to those on the *Belle* had been said.

Danny dropped Belinda and the delegates at the *Spryte* and then returned to the *Belle*. Soon after, Dingles gained the bridge and ordered the colony ship underway. The course was set for Triton. This was a common routine for Dingles, but, this time, he stood straighter, with his hands clasped behind his back, proudly accepting his new responsibility.

Aboard the *Spryte*, Idrian and Dottie were disoriented by the mining ship's boarding routine. Belinda led them down a long corridor, which was the ship's axis. She turned and navigated a tunnel that was festooned with handles. She called it a spoke. Finally, she entered a huge curved structure she announced was the ship's gravity wheel.

"Which we get when?" Dottie asked.

"After the ship is underway," Belinda explained.

A shifting of cabin assignments was necessary to accommodate the delegates. Jessie had given up his captain's quarters to Ituau, telling her that it was necessary to underline her new status. In turn, Ituau gave up the cabin to Harbour. She said it was necessary for the delegates' impression of the envoy, which made Jessie smile.

Idrian was bunked with Henry. Dottie shared a cabin with Belinda. Ituau confiscated Nate's cabin, and the second mate moved into a spare cabin with Devon.

As soon as Ituau could manage it, she got the ship underway. If nothing else, Ituau hoped to help Dottie, who evinced a slightly green complexion from the effects of zero-g.

Despite Dottie and Idrian's initial impressions about the lives of spacers, they weren't given time to dwell on their thoughts. Instead, the delegates and Harbour joined the crew in drills for fires, emergency decompressions, vac suit failures, and every other form of danger the spacers faced.

In addition to the shipwide drills, Belinda and Aurelia put the delegates through their vac suit training.

Aurelia ran Henry and Devon through the newest operational requirements. Also, the equipment had technological updates that the men hadn't seen. All in all, the men enjoyed their leisurely training exercises. Not to mention, they had good-natured Aurelia as their training instructor.

Idrian and Dottie struggled to adopt their lessons. Belinda was patient, but she was a stern taskmaster. Often, Aurelia used her power to moderate reactions, while physically stepping in to assist one or the other of the delegates.

After the first week, a transition took place. Devon and Henry were rated by Belinda. Then rather than sit out the training, they joined Dottie and Idrian. Now, there were multiple individuals assisting the two delegates who needed the most help.

During a morning meal in the galley, Dottie quipped to Belinda, "I always wanted to lose a few kilos and tone up. Who knew I only had to take a jaunt as a spacer?"

Belinda didn't have the heart to tell Dottie that traveling aboard a mining ship was the easiest part of a spacer's life. It was making a living by digging out ore and slush from the surface of asteroids and moons that crippled and killed most spacers.

Idrian was eventually rated. And only three days out from Triton, Dottie passed her exam, much to the relief of Belinda, Harbour, and the other delegates.

Harbour took the opportunity to announce to the delegates the final member of the envoy party. She met with them and Jessie in the captain's quarters.

"Let me start by saying congratulations to every one of you on your ratings achievement," Harbour said, addressing the delegates. "I think your participation in the drills and the training helps you comprehend the dangerousness of space travel. Among you, only Captain Stamerson knows what it's like to transfer from a ship to a shuttle, land on an airless body, and walk its surface. This is exactly what we'll be doing on Triton, going to and from the dome."

"Envoy Harbour," Henry interrupted. "Before you continue, might I suggest we dispense with titles? I think this group will have many intimate discussions, and we can probably save a great deal of time."

Harbour glanced at Jessie, who nodded, and she replied, "Consider it done."

"While we're laying down some basic rules," Devon said, "I'd like this group to know that I see my primary role as addressing the team's safety concerns."

"Negative," Harbour said firmly. "We'll be entering locations populated by aliens, exercising customs of which we have no knowledge. We'll rely on the Jatouche for direction and security. You'll play the same role as the other delegates."

"By representing security's concerns?" Devon asked in confusion.

"Do you think I'm representing the Review Board?" Henry asked Devon.

"The stationers elected you," Devon objected.

"Because I was the only decent choice," Henry replied, his lips twisting wryly.

"Devon, you might speak to Captain Ituau," Jessie volunteered. Devon frowned at the suggestion, and Jessie explained, "Her circumstances are similar to yours ... a trained officer who has been elevated and must deal with a greater level of responsibility."

"I want it understood that, as far as I'm concerned, each of you is a Pyrean delegate," Harbour said. "In private conversations, you may discuss the concerns of those you represent, but when we communicate with the Jatouche or any other alien race, we will speak as one. Is that understood?"

"That wasn't why we were selected," Idrian objected.

"I'm not concerned with why your peers selected you, Idrian," Harbour replied. "You'll follow my rules or find yourself sent home."

"You might consider the fact, Idrian," Henry interjected, "that being sent home means you'll journey from the Jatouche dome to Triton. Then you'll wait there, hoping a captain will take pity on you and divert his or her ship for you."

Idrian looked around at the other delegates for backing, but none of them offered him any semblance of moral support.

Jessie regarded Harbour. His eyes shone in appreciation for her adoption of her new role. It occurred to him that she'd done the same thing when she'd been elected the *Belle*'s captain. At first, Harbour had resisted the residents' desire to have her lead, but once she chose to accept the situation, she'd dived wholeheartedly into learning what she needed to know to be effective.

"At this time, I want to inform you that we'll be adding another member to our team. Aurelia Garmenti," Harbour announced.

This time, Idrian bristled. "In the space of a few minutes, you've chosen to change the team's dynamics twice," he declared hotly. "These are issues that should have been shared with our leaders before the delegates were chosen."

"Let me ask you, Idrian," said Jessie, his voice hard. "What would Dorelyn have done if Harbour had announced that Aurelia would accompany us?"

"That's unknown," Idrian replied quickly, "but she should have been given the opportunity to respond."

Jessie smiled, his eyes narrowing, and Idrian realized that he'd openly admitted that Dorelyn was responsible for choosing him as the delegate.

"I can tell you what would have happened, Idrian," Jessie volunteered. "Dorelyn would have strenuously objected, and Harbour would have heard her out and then ignored her. What I think you're forgetting Idrian is that Harbour wasn't selected by Pyreans. This envoy team exists because Her Highness Tacticnok requested her. These two females spent months in close proximity and had hours of intimate discussions. It's their relationship that we're trading on. Anything you do that interferes in this tenuous twining runs the chance of disturbing, if not ending, negotiations."

"Idrian, Jessie has a valid point," Dottie said quietly. "I might represent investors, but first and foremost, we must secure a position of confidence with the Jatouche and discover our mutual benefits. The representation of our individual groups will come later when negotiations become more detailed."

Idrian didn't appear to be mollified, but he quieted.

"The primary reasons that Aurelia will be accompanying us are that she is qualified as a vac suit team safety member and she's an empath," Harbour said. "Think of it this way. If you have suit problems, an empath will sense your fear before you can comm or signal someone. Saving those precious seconds can mean saving your life."

"If you care to talk to this ship's crew," Jessie said, "you'll discover that, first and foremost, they think of Aurelia as a spacer and a good one. Yes, she's employed her power on them, including me. In every instance, it was to help a bunch of tired, worn-out spacers forget their aches and pains for a little while."

"We should have had an empath aboard every mining ship," Henry said. It might have sounded like a lament, but his eyes were hard, as he recalled the dangerous and exhausting toiling of his crew.

While Dottie looked at Henry, she imagined her husband. As usual, they'd said goodbye in their cabin before he sailed on the trip that led to his death. Both men looked older than their years. Her eyes blurred, and she blinked back the tears. She'd hoped that no one noticed, but she caught Harbour regarding her with sympathy.

"There is one more thing I might as well mention," Harbour said. "As an empath, I have abilities that are assets to me and this team, and I intend to use them. If you have personal objections to that, you have two choices ... curb your emotions in my presence or choose to remain aboard this ship."

"But isn't the *Spryte* sailing for Emperion after Triton?" Dottie asked.

"Yes," Jessie replied. "You'll be out there for about six months while the crews sling slush off the moon's surface. If nothing else, the *Belle*'s accommodations have become first rate."

"Do you intend to read us continuously?" Dottie asked.

"No," Harbour replied, laughing lightly. "That would exhaust me. But there will be times when I need to know what you're feeling."

"Why?" Idrian asked.

"To see if your words and your emotional context match," Jessie supplied.

"That's invasive," Idrian replied.

"You could consider it that way," Henry interjected. "Then again, if you're saying what you believe, what's the difference? Personally, I've no problem with being read. I intend to tell Envoy Harbour what I believe."

-13-
Journey

A crew member picked up Henry's duffels and headed around the gravity wheel toward the bay, and Henry took the opportunity to visit the bridge. It was near the end of first watch, and he expected to find Ituau on duty. He was right and tapped at the hatch to catch her attention.

"Captain Stamerson, nice of you to visit before you launch downside," Ituau said.

"I wanted to congratulate you again on your captaincy," Henry said. "I look forward to buying you a drink at the Miner's Pit when I return."

"I'd appreciate that," Ituau replied, with a smile. When Henry paused, she asked, "Is there something else?"

"No ... well, maybe," Henry said, his words tumbling out. "I believe I owe you an apology, Captain. Many years ago, I was present in a cantina when you had an altercation with two spacers ... big men, both of them. You wiped the deck with them, and I remember thinking that you would never rise in rank. At that time, you were a third mate. I'm pleased to see that I was wrong."

Ituau laughed deep and hearty. "At that time, Captain, you had a good chance of being right," she said. "I tried to mitigate my behavior, but I ran into trouble with a senior officer when I was a second mate. It was Captain Cinders who gave me another chance, and I've worked hard to repay him."

"It looks like you've done a fine job of it, Captain," Henry admitted.

"I can tell you something that makes your life easier," Ituau said quietly, as if she was sharing a secret. "Hang out with the empaths. They do a great job of mellowing you out."

Henry smiled, touched two fingers to his brow, and made his way around the gravity wheel to the vac suit room. *Yes, they do,* Henry thought.

Jessie had Ituau fill the shuttle with a rover and crew. The rover would transport the delegates. But Jessie's purpose in taking Nate Mikado, the newly promoted first mate, and other crew members was to instruct them in the dome's operation.

When Harbour and the delegates were suited up, Belinda and Aurelia led them through the axis and into the bay. The group settled into seats that were saved for them, and Belinda and Aurelia ensured everyone was properly secured. The shuttle launched, and a short flight later landed on Triton.

"Makes you appreciate the *Belle*'s shuttle," Idrian whispered on a private comm channel to Dottie. He didn't receive a reply, and he glanced at her. She had her eyes closed and was repeatedly swallowing.

"We're on the surface, Dottie," Aurelia said to Dottie and Belinda, to alert her fellow spacer. "The rough ride is over. I want you to breathe deeply."

Harbour sensed Dottie's overwrought emotional condition, but she waited. As she hoped, Aurelia came to Dottie's aid. Despite being seated across the shuttle from the delegate, Aurelia focused her power and inundated Dottie with sensations of calm.

Dottie felt her fear shoved aside by a sense of well-being. It gave her strength, and she held on to it. Slowly, her breathing returned to normal, and she opened her eyes. The wonderful wave continued to wash through her mind, as she stared across the shuttle at the young woman who stared intently at her.

When Dottie felt ready, she said, "Thank you, Aurelia."

"My pleasure, Dottie," Aurelia replied and smiled.

Seated on either side of Dottie, Idrian and Belinda felt some of the effects of Aurelia's power. Idrian was slightly annoyed, which mitigated the opportunity to enjoy it. On the other hand, Belinda relaxed into the sensation, savoring it.

On an open channel, Belinda said, "We load the delegates in the rover now."

It was an uncommon procedure, but Jessie and the crew accepted Belinda's pronouncement as an order. Jessie noted that the rover had been backed into the shuttle. Access to a shuttle, while housed inside a bay, was through a hatch amidships, which made loading through the rover's rear hatch easy.

Jessie signed to Nate, "Rover backed into shuttle."

"Captain's orders," Nate signed in return.

"Smart," Jessie signed.

"Crew thinks so," Nate signed back.

From Nate's simple remarks, Jessie learned that the crew had accepted, even welcomed, his choice for captain of the *Spryte* and a significant load was taken off his mind.

"If no one minds," Henry sent over the open channel, "I'd like to walk on the surface of Triton."

Jessie signed quickly to Harbour that he could accompany Henry, but Harbour signaled him to wait.

"Aurelia, you have the captain. I'll ride in the rover," Belinda replied. Her first thought had been for Dottie's emotional well-being. Then she realized that Harbour would be in the rover with her. More important, this was a perfect low-level test for Aurelia.

"Belinda, I'd like to go with Captain Stamerson," Devon requested.

"Aurelia?" Belinda queried.

"I have them," Aurelia replied confidently. "It's a nice night for a walk."

Nate swung open the rover's hatches, which bracketed an airlock large enough for one crew member. He slipped up to the front seat, Jessie took the navigator's position, and Harbour, Dottie, Idrian, and Belinda climbed aboard.

Aurelia, Henry, and Devon remained seated, while the pilot dropped the shuttle's wide rear ramp. Nate drove the rover off and waited until crew members surrounded the vehicle. Then he set off, following the tracks of previous visitors to the dome.

The last personnel off the shuttle were Aurelia, Henry, and Devon. When the threesome stepped off the ramp onto the loose aggregate of Triton, Aurelia turned to her charges, unclipped the safety lines on either side of her belt, extended them toward the men, and said, "Hook on, delegates. I'm not about to lose my first trainees."

Henry accepted a line, snapped it on his suit's ring, and replied, "Aye, latched on."

Devon took his line, clipped it to his suit, and said, "I'm good too."

Behind their visors, Aurelia and Henry smiled. There was no quicker means of identifying a stationer than failing to hear the iconic response to the request to hook on.

The rover was a hundred meters ahead, moving slowly. Its lights lit the moon's dark landscape, and Aurelia let the men set the pace. Their heads were on swivels, as they absorbed the unreal landscape. Aurelia gently steered the delegates around rocks and craters, while they focused on the stars overhead and the outlines of distant ridges.

"Unbelievable," Devon shared over the comm channel.

"My times in these environments have always been while working," Henry said, "and my mind was focused on the crew and the ore. It's a rare thing to enjoy this without the responsibilities. Thank you, Aurelia."

"It's a small thing to do for a lifelong spacer," Aurelia replied.

Aurelia's feeling of satisfaction leaked through her gates, and the men's heads swung toward her.

"Did I just feel your power, Aurelia?" Devon asked. "I mean, this is an airless environment."

"Empaths ... we're such mysterious women," Aurelia replied enigmatically. She realized Harbour was right about the opportunity to expand her horizons. *I just might enjoy this journey*, she thought.

At the dome's entrance, Jessie waited until Aurelia and her charges arrived. Once the rover was unloaded, he led a class on understanding the dome's glyphs and basic operations. At every step of the way, he instructed which glyphs should be recorded in comm units and what text should be annotated to the images. He was bombarded with questions, the majority of which he couldn't answer. It became a constant phrase of his: Ask the Messinants, when you see them.

Using the information supplied by the engineers, Jessie led the group to the third level and walked through the processes of food, water, sleep, and facilities.

"Didn't you say the engineers stayed here for weeks?" Idrian asked.

"That's correct," Jessie replied.

"How did they clean up the place, for instance, the pallets?" Idrian asked.

"You close them into the wall. When you open them hours later, they're clean," Jessie replied.

Afterwards, the Pyreans trooped to the deck level. Jessie walked through the basic comm operation of the console. Nate and a few others studiously captured images and recorded lengthy notes by voice to ensure they understood the routine.

While Jessie trained individuals, the rover returned to the shuttle and offloaded the duffels that would accompany the envoy team to Rissness. The gear was deposited in the third level's dorm room. When Jessie finished his lessons, Nate and Belinda wished the envoy party good luck and, in the company of the *Spryte*'s crew, departed.

Jessie, Aurelia, and the delegates were arrayed around Harbour on the dome's deck.

"Is it appropriate to ask, what now?" Dottie inquired.

"Now we say hello," Harbour replied. She held up a cube that she'd taken from the stack on the counter where the engineers had stayed. She opened her comm unit and played the sequence that the engineers had broadcasted to the *Belle* and Birdie had recorded for her.

Jessie assisted Harbour in the setup of the cube to prepare it for recording. When all was ready, Harbour asked Jessie to stand beside her, and the delegates and Aurelia to stand in a ring behind her. Jessie touched off the final submenu icon and stepped back. When the cube lit, Harbour recorded a brief message to Tacticnok, saying that she was formally announcing acceptance of the envoy position and that her team waited at the dome for transport.

Harbour handed the cube to Aurelia, who ran to place it in the center of the platform. Then, Jessie and Harbour worked through the instructions to send the recording. The delegates watched in awe as the platform's blue light speared the dome and the cube disappeared.

"It's one thing to watch that happen on a monitor," Devon said in awe, "but it's another to stand here and witness it."

"I wonder if they've ever had an accident," Dottie said softly. When she became the center of attention, she added, "With the sending of individuals back and forth, I mean."

"If you can get fresh paste out of a dome that was shut down for centuries and beds cleaned by sliding them into a wall, then the aliens can certainly handle something as simple as quantum-coupled gates," Devon said offhand, which elicited strained chuckles from most of the party.

"Now we wait," Harbour said, leading the party to the dorm room.

Dottie looked around at the gear piled in a corner and the duffels arranged in pairs. "We're all staying here? There aren't separate rooms or cabins?" she asked.

Dottie had been shocked by the sharing of a cabin aboard the *Spryte*, but she'd assumed that was a temporary inconvenience due to the constraints of a mining ship. Now, the accommodations seemed determined to get worse.

"I know the glyph sign for a dorm room on the second level," Jessie offered. "Its appointments are simple though."

"The offer is appreciated," Dottie replied pleasantly. "I suggest the women take this room, and the men take the alternate one."

Harbour smiled, but it didn't reach her eyes. "If you wish more privacy, Dottie, I'm willing to accommodate that request. We'll install you in the second level room with whoever wishes to accompany you. Meanwhile, I'll stay here and discuss with whoever remains some of the strategies that we can employ in our negotiations with the Jatouche."

Dottie looked around for support, focusing lastly at Idrian, who looked away from her, as had the others.

"Pick up your duffels, Dottie. Jessie will lead you to your private room," Harbour said. She was staring evenly at the woman, but inside, she was working hard to control her anger and keep her gates tightly shut.

"I rescind my suggestion," Dottie said, a bit miffed, but Harbour could sense the woman's rush of fear and guessed it emerged from the prospect of sleeping alone in a room built by aliens.

The Pyreans shucked their vac suits, displaying various qualities of skins, and Jessie showed them how to access the lockers to store their suits.

He couldn't resist a glance or two at Harbour in her exquisitely decorated skins.

Aurelia picked up on the subtle surge in Jessie's emotions, checked where he was looking, and hid her smile. When the suits were stored, Aurelia set about serving paste and water, while Harbour gathered the others at a table.

"I'm setting some more rules," Harbour said bluntly. "We must be compliant with whatever the Jatouche offer us, regarding accommodations or practices that are their social norms. Under no circumstances must we argue with them on these types of subjects. Understand that Tacticnok is a royal family member and, at some point, we'll be meeting His Excellency Rictook."

Harbour's point didn't seem to penetrate, and Jessie chose to elaborate. "There is no equivalent to a royal person in Pyrean society," he said. "And I get that to many of us it sounds like a nice title, like commandant or governor. But imagine an individual who can look at us and say, 'Leave,' and his security will whisk us aboard the next shuttle, ship us to their dome, and send us home without question."

"In other words, his power is absolute," Henry paraphrased, and Jessie nodded his agreement.

"The good news is that we'll be dealing with Tacticnok, the daughter, but she'll be listening to her father's advice," Harbour noted. "What I'm trying to stress is that we're guests, who are invited to communicate with representatives of an alien nation, which is incredibly more advanced than us."

"Then why the invitation?" Devon asked.

"Excellent question, Devon. I'm glad you're joining the delegate side of the party," Harbour quipped. "I've had various hints from Tacticnok, and most of them have to do with the Jatouche place in the alliance. Keep your ears tuned for comments, no matter how subtle, about the alliance. A final thought on this subject. When we arrive, and I understand the sight will be unnerving, scan for an odd platform with an emplacement around it."

"An emplacement?" Henry echoed.

"According to our engineers, on the other side of that gate is a dome, which is held by a vicious species of sentients, referred to as the Colony," Harbour explained. "That might be another subject to explore."

"Any other ground rules?" asked Idrian, his pique in evidence.

"Tacticnok requested that Jessie be my advisor," Harbour replied. "That's a royal daughter's way of politely expressing her demand. In Jessie's role, there might be times when he and I are meeting privately with Jatouche. In our absence, Devon will act as lead delegate. However, in any matter that pertains to your physical safety, during operating conditions, Devon will take Aurelia's advice."

"Acceptable," Henry said before anyone could object, which left Dottie and Idrian, one by one, acquiescing to the arrangement.

The small company chatted for a while longer, while they consumed their paste and water. Then beds were extended and facilities visited. When the team lay down, they either slept or used their comm units for entertainment.

Over the following days, Harbour was pleased to see the delegates fall into an easy arrangement. Even Dottie came to accept their circumstances, although she noted the men were careful to allow her a little more accommodation.

In contrast, Aurelia's experience as a mining ship's spacer was in evidence. She demonstrated an unflappable demeanor in the presence of mixed company and was equally comfortable conversing and teasing every team member.

Harbour sensed Devon's heightened reactions to Aurelia's interactions with him. She was certain that Aurelia had noticed too, but the young empath didn't appear to treat him any different than the other men. But Harbour carefully tucked away those observations.

* * * *

Tacticnok, Jaktook, and Kractik exited the shuttle from Na-Tikkook and made their way to the tunnel's conveyor system. Jaktook and Kractik exchanged glances, having noted Tacticnok's subtle indications of impatience.

"Your Highness, I believe the Pyreans won't leave before you arrive," Jaktook said.

Kractik held her breath. Jaktook's statement boarded on the edge of criticism.

Tacticnok eyed Jaktook. It was a mark of the development of their relationship that she took no umbrage from Jaktook's comment. "Anxiousness is a royal prerogative," Tacticnok riposted, flashing her teeth.

When Tacticnok caught Kractik's release of breath, she commented, "I allow Jaktook the occasional impertinent comment for his value, but he knows better than to take advantage of my patience."

Kractik glanced at Jaktook, whose expression indicated his amusement at Tacticnok's flippant bluff, and Kractik blinked twice. The shift in the manner in which a royal daughter was being treated was disconcerting.

Jaktook quietly bantered with Tacticnok until they reached the dome's platforms. It occurred to Kractik that Jaktook's irreverence was successful at distracting Tacticnok. It made her wonder if she had value in this manner, but years of training kept her quiet.

The bored Rissness console operator of gate two was alerted that Her Highness was on her way to his gate. When he abruptly straightened, the other console operators immediately assumed more officious stances, as their eyes furtively searched for the reason.

Tacticnok maintained a measured step, as she walked through the dome's lower corridor, climbed the ramp, crossed the deck, and mounted the platform. Jaktook and Kractik assumed positions slightly behind her. At a nod from Tacticnok, the console operator energized the platform and sent the threesome to Triton.

The operator remained much more erect, having had the honor of sending a royal member on a journey. It was a rare occasion, and one he would celebrate with his mate.

Tacticnok was ready to jubilantly greet Harbour on her arrival at Triton. Instead, the threesome was presented with an empty deck.

Belatedly, she realized that in her rush to get here, she'd forgotten to check the Pyrean's cycle.

"One moment, Your Highness," Kractik said, hopping down from the platform and rushing to the console. She accessed a panel and queried it for the locations of sentients within the dome. The console displayed a map of the accessible levels. On the platform deck, three icons were evident. In a room on the third level, there were seven more.

"The Pyreans are here, Your Highness," Kractik said triumphantly.

"Lead us, Kractik," Tacticnok instructed.

Kractik hesitated and said, "Your Highness, the icons are in parallel lines. I believe the Pyreans are asleep."

"It would be a most auspicious moment for Jatouche history," Jaktook said. "Our historians will relate the momentous event when Her Highness greeted the Pyrean envoy by disturbing her sleep."

"When I return to Na-Tikkook, I must find myself a suitable advisor," Tacticnok grumbled.

Jaktook had the good sense to maintain a neutral expression.

"We wait," Tacticnok said, acquiescing to circumstances.

The Jatouche sat or sprawled on the platform, watching the stars twinkling overhead. During a quiet moment, Tacticnok slid a hand over Jaktook's forearm, patting it twice before she retrieved her hand.

Down below, Harbour woke. She glanced at Aurelia, who had the pallet next to her. She was awake too. Harbour opened her mental gates wide and concentrated on the extremely weak sensation she was receiving. When she glanced at Aurelia, the young empath signed that she didn't know the source. For a brief moment, Harbour wondered if Dottie was a latent empath, but the direction was wrong.

Suddenly, Harbour sat upright, smiling. "Everyone up," she said loudly, clapping her hands repeatedly. To the confused faces, she announced, "We have visitors on the deck."

Aurelia broke into a smile. She had sensed the faint emanations, but lacked the experience to identify the direction of such a weak signal. She focused her power in the direction of the dome's deck, locking in the sensation.

"Do we have time to use the facilities?" Jessie asked. He wore a wry smile.

"Apologies, yes," Harbour replied. "We eat, prepare for the day, and then greet Her Highness."

"If Her Highness is among those who came," Idrian remarked.

"She's here," Harbour said definitively.

Kractik occasionally visited the console's display to check on the Pyreans' disposition. In time, she announced, "The Pyreans are moving around."

Jaktook checked his chronometer, which he'd set to the Pyrean cycle, using data from the console. "They've risen early," he commented.

Tacticnok eyed him for a moment, and then she touched her temple.

"You think the envoy sensed us?" Jaktook whispered. "They're on the third level."

"Perhaps, the envoy didn't sense all of us. I was the agitated one," Tacticnok admitted with chagrin.

"Unimaginable," Jaktook muttered quietly.

It wasn't long before Kractik said excitedly, "The Pyreans are ascending the levels."

Tacticnok placed herself well back from the ramp, and Jaktook and Kractik stood beside her.

"Greetings, Envoy Harbour," Tacticnok announced formally when Harbour gained the top of the ramp.

"I'm happy to see you, Your Highness," Harbour replied.

"I believe we'll do great things for our cultures, Envoy," Tacticnok said, clasping Harbour's hand.

"That's my hope too, Your Highness," Harbour replied.

"This will announce you as an alliance envoy," Tacticnok said, offering Harbour an ornate, crescent-shaped medallion on a delicate silvered chain. "May I?" she asked, holding it up, and Harbour bent on one knee to allow Tacticnok to place it over her head.

"It's beautiful work," Harbour said, admiring the craftsmanship.

"Jaktook will escort you to Rissness when your party is ready," Tacticnok said. "I look forward to working with all of you," she added, acknowledging the others. Then she quickly mounted the platform, and Kractik hurried to the console to send the royal daughter home.

14

Medallions

"Under the circumstances, I expected a little more pomp for the occasion," Idrian commented, when Tacticnok left. He adjusted his ear wig, and said, "I must have missed some of the dialog."

"Afraid not," Devon commented. "I found it a little disappointing too."

The envoy party looked at Jaktook, who seemed to be as confused as they were.

Indeed, Jaktook had been caught off guard. It was unlike Tacticnok not to personally escort someone as important as the envoy. However, Tacticnok and he had been in lockstep about their plans for their citizens' future. In that regard, Jaktook was confident that Tacticnok had her reason for what she did, even if he didn't know the specifics.

"Yes, well," Jaktook said temporizing, "Let's gather your personal belongings."

"None of you are wearing vac suits," Jessie noted.

"Completely unnecessary," Jaktook replied. "There's never been an accident while journeying through a dome."

"From your dome or from this one?" Henry asked.

"Via any Messinants dome," Jaktook replied, "unless you consider the firing of weapons within a dome an accident. You may wear your suits if your rules require it, although they do appear archaic. If, for some reason, you require suits during your stay in our system, we'll fit you with our equipment."

"An alien vac suit," Aurelia enthused, and a small amount of her power escaped.

Jaktook blinked and swayed.

"Apologies, Jaktook, that one got away from me," Aurelia said.

"A youth's enthusiasm is understood," Jaktook replied. "But you must be careful to control your abilities on the other side of this gate."

Aurelia felt truly admonished, and she hung her head in embarrassment.

"We'll leave our vac suits behind," Jessie said, and looked at Henry for agreement, which he received. "It's duffels and a crate topside," he ordered, and led the team down the ramp.

When the duffels were collected and deposited on the platform, Jessie tapped Devon's shoulder, and the two men retrieved Harbour's crate from below.

"What's in the crate?" Devon inquired.

"The makings of greens for Aurelia and me, and some gifts for the royal family," Harbour replied.

The envoy team and Jaktook took up positions on the platform. Kractik set the console for a delayed transport. Dottie slipped her hand into Aurelia's, and the young spacer gripped the delegate's hand firmly. Kractik hurried to join the group, and the Pyreans took their first journey between the stars.

Having experienced the engineers' reactions, Jaktook and Kractik were content to stand on the platform and wait for their guests to absorb the scene.

"This is beyond what I imagined," Devon whispered to Henry, who was unable to reply.

"Who would have guessed that aliens came in all these shapes?" Aurelia marveled.

"All sentient too," Jessie added.

Harbour's attention was quickly usurped by the passing of three aliens in front of their platform. They paused, turned toward her, and briefly bowed their blunt-horned heads before continuing on their way.

When the envoy's party appeared settled, Jaktook led them off the platform toward the ramp.

The Pyreans noted the similarity between the domes. Except for the number of platforms, they were identical. Eyes swung toward the enclosed gate. This was the subject the Pyrean engineers had hinted could be an opening in negotiations with the Jatouche.

Along the now familiar path across the deck toward the ramp, every alien, except those accompanied by Jatouche medical services, paused to pay homage to Harbour. She realized that the medallion, which she thought to be a static symbol, was broadcasting her status. As proof of her thought, individuals, whose backs were to her, stopped, turned, and paid their respects.

What gave Harbour pause was that while she was mesmerized by the incredible diversity of alien shapes, her appearance made no difference to them. She was an envoy, an individual with a lofty purpose within the alliance. Suddenly Harbour felt totally unprepared for the position. She clamped her gates shut, lest her fear leak out and broadcast to the host around her.

Jaktook led the party down the ramp. Tacticnok waited at the bottom. Harbour smiled at her and said, "You're a devious female, Your Highness."

Tacticnok flashed her teeth in reply. She said, "I wished you to experience the esteem in which envoys are held by alliance members."

Jessie glanced at the medallion. "It's broadcasting your status, isn't it?"

"Yes, Advisor," Tacticnok replied. "Come," she added. "We've an audience with His Excellency to attend."

* * * *

The envoy party followed the same route as the engineers, when they left the dome for Rissness Station.

Harbour took the opportunity to ask Tacticnok about the status of the twenty Pyreans in the hands of the Jatouche medical services.

"I receive daily communications, Envoy," Tacticnok said. "Every Pyrean was stabilized and safely transported to the station. Most are now undergoing repair. Each will require a different length of time to complete their needs. More than likely, we'll discover the value of our negotiations before every citizen is ready to return to Pyre."

On the one hand, the envoy party was delighted with the news about the injured. On the other hand, Tacticnok had reminded them that their mission to Jatouche was tenuous.

The group's trip down the last tunnel ended at the ramp to a shuttle. However, this ship wasn't built with the same features as the one that flew the engineers to Rissness Station. That one was prepared to accommodate species of all kinds.

Typically, only Jatouche boarded a shuttle flight to Na-Tikkook, and the Pyreans found themselves slightly uncomfortable in the undersized seats during takeoff. It was fortunate that Rissness' lighter mass made for a low-g launch compared to Triton.

"It appears that we hadn't considered all aspects of the envoy's visit," Jaktook whispered to Tacticnok.

"This is a detail too small to have been foreseen, under the time constraints," Tacticnok replied quietly. "However, I want new seats installed for the Pyreans for their return trip." Tacticnok glanced at Jessie, who was once again shifting in his seat in an attempt to ease his discomfort, and her embarrassment rose.

At Jaktook's request, the pilot ceased acceleration for short periods of time. It allowed the Pyreans to stand and enjoy the freedom of zero-g, except for Dottie, who preferred the safety of being strapped to a Jatouche-sized seat.

The Pyreans had anticipated a flight lasting weeks and were surprised that it was much shorter. In a matter of days, they felt the shuttle flip over and the deceleration burn commence. They endured the vibrations, as the shuttle fell through the planet's atmosphere and the press into their seats, as the ship landed tail down.

After touchdown, it was Aurelia who remarked, "Despite the child-like seats, the Jatouche shuttles are a good deal more comfortable and faster than ours and that includes the *Belle*'s new shuttle."

"Yes," Jessie murmured, who had been thinking the same thing. "It's technology we could use, especially when Pyre's surface opens up."

Jaktook ushered the Pyreans off the shuttle through an exit tunnel. In a brightly lit space, cars arrived and whisked passengers away. Four Jatouche royal security members stood next to a car, waiting for Tacticnok's party. Once passengers and gear were loaded, Tacticnok directed the car to take a circuitous route at a lesser velocity to the royal residence.

Deliberately, the Jatouche didn't initiate any conversation during the ride. The Pyreans were left in peace to be mesmerized by the view.

"So, this is what a planet can look like," Henry commented in awe.

"It makes you sad to think about what we have," Dottie added.

Harbour detected Tacticnok's mental flinch and made a note to chat with her team. They weren't to mention the subject of Pyre's disrupted surface in the presence of the Jatouche.

"Have you ever seen so much greenery?" Devon asked.

"I saw things like this from the upper floor window of the Andropov home, although I was never allowed outside," Aurelia said. "Every family head supposedly has an expanse of green like this.

Hard stares were directed toward Idrian, and Harbour could sense the anger from the other Pyreans. She was tempted to calm them, but the Jatouche sat too close. Instead, she changed the subject, and asked, "Is that snow on the peaks of those elevations?"

There was a momentary pause among the Jatouche, while the translation failure was checked.

"Ah, yes, a form of crystalline water ... snow," Jaktook acknowledged.

During the remaining part of the trip, following Aurelia's remarks, Idrian kept his mouth shut. The families' homes did have significant gardens, festooned with fruit trees and flowering shrubbery for birds, bees, and other pollinating species.

Arriving underground at the royal residence, the Pyreans were shown to their rooms. One room was allocated to each person, much to Dottie's delight.

"The royal servants will see to your every need," Tacticnok announced to the envoy party. "You need only ask. No request will be considered too much or too mundane. Please refresh yourselves. We'll collect you in two hours, as measured by your chronometers, for the audience."

"Your rooms are at the end of the hall, Envoy," Tacticnok said, leading Harbour and Jessie in that direction. "Should Advisor Cinders' personal baggage be placed in your room?" she asked.

Harbour regarded the royal daughter. The little Jatouche had asked a sincere question.

"Not at this time," Harbour replied.

"Hmm ..." Tacticnok hummed under her breath, "Strong females have the most difficulty finding mates."

Harbour recognized that the royal daughter was speaking for both of them. She laid a hand on Tacticnok's shoulder in sympathy, and said, "But it's important that we don't settle for anyone less than we deserve."

Tacticnok thought about that and then flashed her teeth in agreement. She directed the servants to deposit Jessie's bags in the room next door.

Harbour was left in the apartment's salon, with two Jatouche servants standing by for her requests. She stared at the expanse of space. Her eyes were directed toward the view on the other side of the room, and she crossed quickly to stare out the wall-to-wall, floor-to-ceiling window. The lush greenery and rolling elevations of Jatouche stretched out before her.

Tears formed in Harbour's eyes and soon rolled down her cheeks.

"Are you ill, Envoy Harbour?" the senior servant asked. "Should medical services be called?"

"No, I'm sorry to upset you," Harbour replied. "I've never seen the likes of this. Our planet is shrouded in deadly gases and dust. "I've lived my entire life aboard a station or a ship enclosed in cabins."

"We're aware of the circumstances of your planet," the younger servant said. "You have our condolences."

"Enough of this lament," the senior servant said with authority. "We must prepare you, Envoy, for your audience with His Excellency. Your mind should be at rest, and you should look your best."

The two servants hustled to unpack Harbour's duffels.

"I need the contents of this crate," Harbour directed, "and I require the presence of Aurelia Garmenti."

The senior servant directed the younger one to fetch the requested individual, while she requested additional staff to unpack the crate.

Harbour had considered using her comm unit to call Aurelia, but she was reticent to use her device for communication without first checking with the Jatouche.

By the time Aurelia arrived, two male staff members were laying out the contents of the crate. It had been Harbour's intention to prepare greens for both of them, but something else caught her attention.

"Can I offer you a green?" Harbour asked, smiling.

"Oh, for the love of Pyre, is that what you brought? I thought I would have to go the entire trip without one," Aurelia replied enthusiastically.

The older servant watched Harbour lay out the ingredients, and she made careful note of each item and its quantity.

"Now, all we need is a means of combining them." Harbour lamented, when she discovered a blender hadn't been packed.

"The royal daughter has instructed that no request is too great or too small," the elder servant commented. With a quick order, another staff member came running with a device. It had a slender body and was topped by a small hopper.

The senior servant directed Harbour to load the ingredients into the hopper. Afterwards, Harbour turned around to look at the servant for the manner of starting the blender. She caught Aurelia's smirk and looked at the device. The blended green had filled the bowl at the bottom without a sound.

"I want one of these," Harbour exclaimed.

"It's yours," the senior servant replied, dipping her head.

Aurelia signed, "Be careful how you speak. You're an exalted person."

"Please bring two glasses to the facilities," Harbour requested of the servant. "Come with me," she said to Aurelia. "You have to see this."

Harbour opened the door to a room and waited for Aurelia's reaction.

"I don't get it," Aurelia said. "Why would they leave their drinking water in the open like that?"

"That was my thought," Harbour said, laughing. "Then I was informed that it was for bathing."

Aurelia stared aghast at Harbour. "You immerse your entire body in there?" she asked. "How deep is it? Could you suffer from water inhalation?"

Harbour laughed again. "Remember, it's built for the Jatouche. It can't be that deep."

"Should we?" Aurelia asked.

Harbour could sense the young woman's excitement, and she was happy to share. She signed to Aurelia to calm herself, when she heard the servants coming.

"We'll enjoy the water, while we take our drinks," Harbour directed the servants. She expected the drinks to be left, and the servants to vacate the room. Instead, they stood waiting.

"We don't wish to surprise you with our appearances," Harbour protested.

"Envoy, I've served the royal family my entire life," the elder servant replied. "I've seen alien forms that stretch the imagination. Most important, you are an envoy, and all care should be taken to ensure that your needs are well attended."

Aurelia shrugged and immediately shucked her skins. After a moment of indecision, Harbour followed. The servants hurried to assist. The Pyrean women eased into the water, pleased to find a shelf to sit on, while their legs dangled in deeper water.

"It's warm," Aurelia said in surprise.

"Is the temperature comfortable?" the younger servant asked.

"Yes," Harbour replied.

Soon the water began circulating, and Aurelia softly moaned in delight, which made Harbour snicker.

The older servant offered a colorful display of products in delicate glass jars. "These are cleansers made from plants found on our planet. They have delicate scents."

The women slipped off the tops and sniffed each container. Together they chose one that smelled of flowers. The servants used long-handled brushes to dip into the container and meant to apply them to the women's skins.

"Please," Harbour said, holding up a hand. "This courtesy will not be necessary, and she reached for the brush."

The servants flashed their teeth, having realized that they had reached the limit of their ministrations. They sat the greens next to the women and exited the facilities.

"I don't know," Aurelia said, taking a deep swallow of her green. "I might have enjoyed being scrubbed from head to toe."

Harbour stared evenly at Aurelia until the young spacer added, "Okay, maybe not," which set the women to laughing.

15

Audience

The royal daughter was delighted to discover Harbour and Aurelia in relaxed moods when she came to collect them. In the elegantly decorated hallway outside the envoy's apartment, the rest of the party waited.

The captains wore clean and pressed coveralls with shoulder bars over their skins. Devon's skins were covered by his security uniform. Idrian and Dottie proudly displayed their expensive and colorful skins, and Harbour wore her silver filigreed skins that Makana made for her.

Dottie was a little miffed when she saw Harbour. She'd thought to outshine the others with her expensive taste, but she realized that it didn't matter what Harbour wore. The envoy would always attract the attention of every human.

It was Aurelia who was feeling a little embarrassed. Usually, she wore inexpensive spacer-black skins, but Harbour requested Makana make something special for her. The artist chose to embed what appeared to be metal that reflected colors in a gentle pattern. The design began on each shoulder and disappeared down the arms. It was the right touch of attention for a young person.

The young empath stood with her hands locked in front of her, knowing she was the center of attention and was unsure what to say.

"Quite appropriate," Jessie said, breaking the silence, and Aurelia broke out in a grin.

Tacticnok led the group upstairs to the royal court. The rest of the audience was waiting in attendance, and Tacticnok made introductions for Harbour to every individual. In turn, Harbour introduced each member of her party.

The attendees took their places, and soon afterwards, Rictook entered from the back of the hall and assumed his throne.

The empaths could feel the ruler's discomfort. When Aurelia eyed Harbour, the envoy signed, "Wait."

Tacticnok rose, signaled Harbour to do the same, and said, "Your Excellency, I've the honor of introducing Envoy Harbour of Pyre to you. We wish to receive your favor so that we might enter negotiations for the benefit of our races."

"Eldest daughter, your request is granted," Rictook replied. "Envoy Harbour, welcome to Na-Tikkook. I wish you success in your endeavors."

"I thank you for your generosity, Your Excellency, in providing this opportunity to my people," Harbour replied. She was unsure of what to do next until she saw Tacticnok's signal to be seated.

"I ask all of you to work together to find the means by which our cultures can prosper. I wait to hear what you devise," Rictook said. "At this time, I've only one request of the envoy."

Harbour immediately stood when Rictook mentioned her name.

"I would feel this power that you possess," Rictook said.

Roknick leapt out of his seat, calling out harshly, "This isn't wise, Your Excellency."

Rictook's aging eyes delivered a piercing gaze that stilled Roknick.

"Apologies, Your Excellency," Roknick said, dropping his head.

"I'm ready," Rictook declared to Harbour, bracing his hands on the throne's arms.

To Harbour, the ruler's preparatory actions might have appeared comical if the situation wasn't so fraught with complexity and tension.

"You appear to hesitate, Envoy. Why?" Rictook asked.

"There are opposing views about human empaths, Your Excellency. I don't want to inflame the polarization," Harbour replied.

"A considerate and wise opinion, Envoy. However, I'm requiring this to allow the negotiations to go forward," Rictook replied. Despite his age, there was force in his voice.

"As you request, Your Excellency," Harbour replied. She approached the throne to focus exclusively on him and heard sharp intakes of breaths from the Jatouche.

The fingers of Rictook's left hand rose slightly, and the sounds abated.

Harbour thought of the hopes she had for the success of their mission, opened her mental gates, and ever so slowly leaked her power out.

Rictook's jaw fell open, his eyes closed, and he slouched in his throne.

Harbour heard a cry from behind her. Then Tacticnok yelled, and Harbour slammed her gates closed.

Rictook returned to full consciousness. He surveyed the audience. Jatouche were staring hostilely at one another, and the Pyreans were anxiously wide-eyed.

"That was disconcerting," Rictook commented to Harbour.

"Apologies, Your Excellency. That wasn't what I wished you to experience. You're extremely susceptible, and your audience became alarmed at your reactions," Harbour explained.

"Only one of us couldn't control himself," Tacticnok accused. Her eyes were aflame and staring at Roknick.

"It's my duty," Roknick declared loudly, forgetting again where he stood.

"Enough. Leave me," Rictook requested.

"This way, Envoy Harbour," Roknick said, trying to take control of the situation.

"You misinterpret my request, Master Roknick," Rictook said firmly. "I wish to be alone with the Envoy and my daughter."

"Your Excellency —" Roknick started to object.

"It's good that you remember my title, Roknick," Rictook said, cutting the master advisor off. "For a moment, it sounded as if you ruled the Jatouche."

Royal servants ushered everyone in the audience out, save Harbour and Tacticnok. The Jatouche were left milling around in the antechamber, and the Pyreans were led to their rooms.

"Now, if we might begin again, Envoy," Rictook said, when the hall was cleared. "I'd like to experience this effect as intended."

"Your Excellency, I'll do as you request on the condition that we find a more comfortable place for you," Harbour replied.

"This is a fair request, Father," Tacticnok urged.

Rictook accepted, and the threesome exited the throne room via the back passageway and took a lift to the royal chambers. The ruler reclined on a soft pallet, and Tacticnok chose to sit on one near her father. She flashed her teeth at Harbour, admitting that she hoped to share in the sending.

"I believe we're both ready, Envoy," Rictook said, catching his daughter's expression.

Harbour had to calm herself and eliminate the fear that had arisen from Roknick's outburst. When she was ready, she started again with less power than she'd used the first time. As before, Rictook's jaw fell open, but instead of slumping, the ruler stretched out on his pallet and slowly closed his eyes.

Harbour carefully monitored Rictook's emotional return. Earlier, she'd felt his pain. Now, she adjusted her sending to encompass elements of calm and serenity. She sensed the ruler's emotional return. He was keenly sensitive to her power and relished the sending.

Harbour glanced at Tacticnok, who sat cross-legged on her pallet. The royal daughter was swaying gently in the throes of the sensations. Harbour waited until she felt she'd given Rictook a generous amount of relief, and then she eased off on her power, allowing Rictook to be weaned off her emanations.

When Harbour finished, she stood waiting. Rictook was slow to come around, but it wasn't due to any disorientation. Rather, he was basking in the relief from pain and noticing that it didn't immediately return.

"Impressive and delightful," Rictook finally said. "Will these feelings last for any length of time?"

"Periods of mental well-being can be elongated with continual support from an empath, Your Excellency," Harbour replied. "But physical pain can't be kept at bay for too long."

"That's regrettable," Rictook replied. "Ah, well, Envoy. Now I would experience a negative emotion, something dark."

"I'm sorry, Your Excellency. I won't do that," Harbour stated firmly.

"Even if your refusal endangers our negotiations?" Rictook asked.

"Sharing negative emotions is not something that empaths choose to do," Harbour explained.

"Has it ever been done?" Tacticnok asked.

"Mistakes have been made by the untrained," Harbour said. She was thinking of Aurelia's fight to protect herself, and her childhood manipulations of parents and friends.

"I'll allow you time to reconsider," Rictook said, sitting upright and feeling better than he had in a long while.

"My answer will remain the same, Your Excellency. It'll be no," Harbour stated emphatically.

"A diplomatically clever answer and one that might be thought to conceal the truth," Rictook challenged.

"As with most things, Your Excellency, the truths of an individual's words are borne out over time and shown in their efforts and accomplishments," Harbour replied. She waited. When Rictook failed to answer her, she asked, "Should I be requesting a shuttle to Rissness?"

"That won't be necessary, Envoy. However, I've a final question and a stricture," Rictook replied.

"Yes?" Harbour queried.

"What portion of your power did I receive?" the ruler asked.

Harbour considered a means of expressing the minor amount of sending that Rictook received. Then she said, "It was less than I shared with your daughter aboard my ship, and that was less than what is used with humans during their healing."

Rictook's eyes narrowed, having spotted the omission in the explanation. "And what portion of your power is given to humans?" he asked.

Harbour felt cornered. She'd tried to give Rictook an honest answer, even if it was incomplete. Forthrightness had served her well, and she chose to hold true to that habit. "Understand, Your Excellency, an empath's power hasn't ever been measured by human instrumentation," Harbour offered. She paused, and Rictook drew breath to speak, but Harbour raised her hand to still his question.

Tacticnok hid the flash of her teeth at Harbour's inconsiderate display. She noted with interest that her father took no umbrage with the gesture.

"Power varies from empath to empath, as does the skill," Harbour continued. "I'm considered to be the most powerful empath. I can tell you that, during my sessions with humans, I employ only a small amount of my abilities. Since I've attained adulthood, I've never used all of it, at any one time."

Harbour waited for Rictook's response, but the ruler sat quietly with his thoughts. She glanced at Tacticnok, who signaled patience and to be seated. She'd seen her father ruminate on questions or concerns for long periods of time, while his audiences were forced to wait quietly.

It was nearly a quarter hour by Pyrean time before Rictook spoke. He said, "My one stricture, Envoy, is that you never use your power on any Jatouche until your race is admitted to the alliance. At that point, we'll set the conditions for your empaths' use of their powers. Agreed?"

Harbour let out a sigh, resigned to failing as an emissary for her people, "No, Your Excellency," she replied quietly.

"No? You refuse my request?" Rictook demanded.

Tacticnok was fascinated by the interplay. She'd witnessed her father's bargaining processes many times. They were often used not to reach a desired conclusion but to test the nature of the individual in front of him.

"I must, Your Excellency," Harbour replied sadly. "It's not a choice I would make as envoy. It's one I would make as an empath, which is what I am. If I were to see one of your citizens in distress and know that I could help, I would do so. I won't let individuals suffer needlessly."

Rictook examined Harbour for a moment. Then he said, "That's an adequate explanation, Envoy. I rescind my stricture. However, I depend on your good sense to keep your sharing and that of your companion, Aurelia, sparse and only when absolutely necessary."

"You have my word, Your Excellency," Harbour replied, grateful for the reprieve.

"If you will excuse us, Envoy," Rictook said. "Please wait in the outer chamber. Tacticnok will join you shortly."

After Harbour was escorted from the royal chamber, Tacticnok waited for her father to speak. It was their custom. More important, her father approved of her demonstration of patience.

"I must admit that I had misgivings about this entire adventure, Tacticnok," Rictook said. "After the calamitous history with the Gasnarians, many of our senior citizenry thought it unwise to revisit their dome. Most of these individuals were appalled that I sent you."

"What tipped your decision?" Tacticnok asked.

"Two of my preferred advisors were in favor of the exploration and, thereafter, meeting with the humans," the ruler explained. "As to why I allowed you to go, it was your siblings. They have great confidence in you."

Tacticnok nodded gratefully and kept quiet. Her father would signal with a finger or two when he was done.

"I wait to see what develops with these humans," Rictook continued, "but let me say now that I'm extremely proud of you, my daughter. I'm intrigued by the possibilities of negotiations with these humans. And, despite the envoy's nearly hairless appearance, I find her absolutely delightful. Now, go. Rescue her from her worries."

Tacticnok leapt off her pallet, ran to her father, rubbed her cheek alongside his, and then hurried to join Harbour.

In the antechamber, Tacticnok found Harbour pacing and frowning. "Enough of that," the royal daughter admonished. "We've overcome the first obstacle. Now, let us attack the next."

-16-
Negotiations

The next obstacle, as Tacticnok referred to these events, was more contentious than the first. It involved a planning meeting between the master advisors, the envoy party, Tacticnok, and Jaktook.

"I would know why each delegate is here," Roknick demanded.

"Why are you asking?" Harbour replied.

"We've heard reports that there is great division among Pyreans," Roknick replied. "We're His Excellency's master advisors, and it's important for us to know and understand the motivations of the envoy's party members, with whom we must communicate."

"Ask," Harbour said, gesturing toward the delegates.

Immediately, Roknick focused on Aurelia. "Are you a delegate?" he asked.

"No. I'm here to watch over the safety of the delegates," Aurelia replied.

"Why?" Roknick inquired.

"The envoy was unaware of the circumstances under which the delegates would be traveling and thought it prudent to include me. I'm qualified as a vac suit safety team member," Aurelia replied.

"And you're like the envoy," Roknick persisted.

"If you're asking if I'm an empath, the answer is yes," Aurelia replied.

Harbour was proud of Aurelia's mature responses.

"How does your capability compare to the envoy's?" Roknick demanded.

"You asked to understand the motivations of each member of the envoy's party," Pickcit, the master economist, interrupted. "You have Aurelia's answer."

Roknick's eyes smoldered, but the stares of Tacticnok and the other masters were hard and resolute.

"And you, Advisor Cinders?" Roknick asked, moving on.

"I was invited to this meeting by the royal daughter. Can you say the same thing?" Jessie asked.

"This is my right as a master advisor," Roknick fired back.

"Understood, but were you invited?" Jessie said. He wasn't bothered by Roknick's angry stare. He'd encountered spacer captains who presented much greater challenges during business negotiations.

"You've not answered my question," Roknick persisted.

"That's true," Jessie replied easily. "And I don't intend to reply. I believe your line of questioning isn't pertinent to our negotiations."

Tacticnok could have nuzzled the captain's face in celebration, despite the fact that she found its pale hairlessness slightly repugnant.

"Envoy, I demand you order your advisor to respond," Roknick stated hotly.

"My advisor did reply, Master Roknick, and he, like all Pyreans, is free to speak his mind," Harbour replied. She was of a similar opinion as Tacticnok. She could have kissed Jessie, and unlike the royal daughter, she would have enjoyed it.

Roknick wasn't to be put off. He switched his attack to the delegates, but Jessie had set the model for truncating the master strategist's interrogations. In short order, Roknick received responses in the same vein as Jessie's.

"I'm completely dissatisfied with these answers, Your Highness," Roknick declared, jumping up from his seat. "I'm tempted to register a complaint with His Excellency."

"I invite you to do just that, Master Roknick," Tacticnok returned. She was working hard to control her temper. It was a test she knew she mustn't fail.

When Roknick hesitated, Tacticnok added, "You've asked questions and aren't satisfied with the delegates' and an associate's answers. You've every right to communicate your ire to His Excellency. I suggest you do that now."

Roknick's indecision was apparent. He'd hoped to sway Tacticnok to force the delegates to reveal the schisms among the Pyreans, which he could use to create dissension among them. But the envoy's members had closed ranks against him, and Tacticnok was now calling him on his threat.

"Now," Tacticnok repeated. "Consider this a royal request."

In a huff, Roknick exited the meeting room.

"Well, that was pleasant," Tiknock, the master scientist, said. "My congratulations on the patience that all of you exhibited. I believe Master Roknick was hoping to tempt you into displaying some kind of emotional outburst or perhaps provoking you, Envoy, to use your powers."

"He'd have to try harder than that, Master Tiknock," Harbour replied. "Apparently, he's never dealt with Pyrean spacers."

Harbour's comment elicited chuckles from Jessie and Aurelia.

The small company launched into discussions about technology, economics, financial systems, and a variety of other subjects. Jessie, Dottie, and Idrian fielded most of the questions and replied with their own. Unfortunately, before the morning passed, the conversations came to a close.

"This was as we feared," Pickcit said. "The early reports from Her Highness, Jaktook, Drigtik, and Gatnack indicated that there might not be an opportunity for trade between our species."

"I'm loath to end our conversation here," Tiknock said. "Might we have missed a subject that interests you, Envoy, which hasn't been explored?"

Harbour was reminded of the discussions she had with the engineers before they returned to Rissness with the injured. "Tell us about the protected gate?" Harbour requested.

The question caught most of the Jatouche off guard. It was the last subject they expected the envoy to bring up.

Jaktook wasn't put off by the question. Instead, he began detailing the contact history with the Colony.

The envoy party hadn't expected to hear Harbour delve into this subject so soon. As Jaktook talked, Jessie and Aurelia became extremely interested, as evidenced by their body postures, which showed them sitting forward on the chairs and leaning toward Jaktook.

"Have you ever investigated the Colony side of the gate?" Jessie asked at one point.

"Your engineers asked the same question," Jaktook replied. "How is it that Pyreans hear of the Colony's insidiousness and deadly capabilities and yet wonder if we've journeyed there?"

"You're speaking to spacers," Jessie replied. "Curiosity enables our success, despite the dangers."

Henry and Aurelia nodded their agreement to Jessie's point.

Harbour had heard enough about the Colony. Now, she wanted to explore a different subject but for the same purpose. She cleared her throat to call attention to her.

"From many sources, I've gathered that the Jatouche aren't comfortable with their position in the alliance," Harbour said.

"There is little that we can do about it," Tacticnok replied.

"I'd hear more details," Harbour pressed.

"There is a certain order within the alliance. It's not identified in the agreement, which must be ratified. Rather, it's a subtle condition based on the perceived contributions of the individual races," Tiknock explained.

When Harbour stared expectantly at him, Tiknock continued. "One of the greatest factors forming this perception is the number of species, which are introduced and accepted into the alliance, by a race."

"We came late to the alliance," Pickcit said. "Of our six gates, we found four were active with alliance members, and two led to species that hadn't progressed far enough. Of these last two, the Gasnarians learned the dome's functions first. While our liaison with them was growing, we encountered the Colony, much to our regret."

"Were the Gasnarians submitted to the alliance for membership?" Dottie asked.

Harbour regarded Dottie out of the corner of her eye. It was an astute question.

"No," Jaktook said. "Before they qualified, they attacked us, and we were locked in a war with them."

"How did the alliance perceive that situation?" Idrian asked.

It amazed Harbour that her two troublesome delegates were pursuing the subject she had broached.

"Alliance members hold the senior party responsible for failure to develop a young sentient species properly," Tiknock replied.

"Have other alliance members experienced the same situation as the Jatouche have with the Colony?" Devon asked.

"There are a number of gates that are blocked because of the aggressive nature of the sentients on the other end of the connection," Jaktook said.

"I would imagine that alliance members can't count the Colony's invasion as a negative against the Jatouche," Henry proposed.

"No, not for that reason," Pickcit agreed.

* * * *

The meeting broke for a meal, and Harbour requested a private room for her team. The Jatouche had consulted Zystal about foods that could be served to humans and had received his recommendations.

"While I find the discussion about gates interesting, Harbour, it appears that we're headed home soon," Idrian said, tentatively testing a juice drink. "It's evident that we've little to offer the Jatouche."

"I agree with you, Idrian, if we're only considering material things," Harbour replied.

"What else is there?" Dottie asked.

"Elevation," Jessie replied enigmatically. The stares of the delegates prompted him to explain, "The Jatouche feel they're trapped in the lower echelons of the alliance through no fault of their own."

"There is a means of helping them with that problem," Harbour added.

"Explore the Colony dome," Devon supplied. He'd reached the same conclusion.

"How do you expect us to do that based on what we've heard about these incredibly nasty creatures?" Idrian asked. "We don't have a single shock stick among us."

"I don't have the answers, Idrian," Harbour replied. "Whatever we do, it would have to be done in concert with the Jatouche."

Harbour finished the last of her green and stood up from the table.

"Where are you going?" Dottie asked.

"To see Tacticnok," Harbour replied over her shoulder, as she left the room.

Harbour's conversation with Tacticnok was brief. It was Harbour speaking and the royal daughter staring open-mouthed at her.

"This request is far beyond the scope of what I could approve, Envoy," Tacticnok said, when Harbour finished.

"How soon can we meet with your father?" Harbour asked.

"I will see," Tacticnok replied. She stepped back into the room where Jaktook, Pickcit, Tiknock, and she had been enjoying a meal. On a desk comm unit, she contacted her father's apartment, spoke to a senior servant, and requested an immediate appointment with His Excellency.

There was time for everyone to finish their meals before they met with Rictook. The formalities of the envoy's presentation completed, the audience assembled in the royal apartment, except for Roknick, who hadn't reappeared.

When everyone was either seated or stretched out on a pallet, as was the ruler, Rictook said, "The quickness of your deliberations either bodes poorly for your negotiations or I'm about to be taken by surprise."

"Your Excellency, early conversations have confirmed that there is no opportunity for trade," Tacticnok announced.

"Sad words," Rictook replied. "Perhaps, in time, we'll know each other better. Trade can begin slowly as opportunities are found."

"What is your definition of slowly, Your Excellency?" Harbour requested.

"This can occur over the course of many annuals and even generations," Rictook replied.

"I think we can offer value to the Jatouche today," Harbour said.

"I'm listening," Rictook replied.

Tacticnok had noted the slightest twitch of the tip of her father's tail. After meeting the envoy, he was as anxious as she to find value in a relationship with the humans.

"The Colony dome," Harbour said, "We'll investigate it for you."

Rictook and the master advisors were stunned by the proposal.

"Why would you offer to do this?" Rictook asked.

"How many alliance gates connect to the Colony dome?" Jessie asked, looking toward Tiknock.

"The total number of Colony gates is five, and alliance members connect to three," Tiknock replied.

"That response implies that other alliance members have barred the Colony from entering their domes," Jessie riposted.

"That's correct," Tiknock replied.

"It appears the Jatouche have an opportunity that they haven't investigated," Harbour said quietly. She couldn't believe she was proposing this idea, but she was loath to return to Pyre empty-handed.

"I would like to hear you frame this request in a more specific manner," Rictook requested.

"One moment, Your Excellency, while I consult with my advisor," Harbour replied. She motioned to Jessie, removed her ear wig, and stepped to the rear of the room.

Harbour and Jessie held their ear wigs in their hands, while they chatted.

"What are you thinking?" Jessie asked. He meant to get a sense of Harbour's direction and was caught off guard by her throaty laugh.

Harbour bent her head close to Jessie's, and whispered, "I'm not thinking. I'm flailing around in the dark here, and I need help."

"Okay," Jessie allowed, "then what's the endgame?" He had to admit he was stalling by drawing out the conversation. Part of the reason was to give him time to think, and another part was that Harbour was leaning close, and her warm breath was soft in his ear.

"I want you to help me negotiate a deal. Think of this as a business contract," Harbour requested.

"That I can do," Jessie replied. "One piece of advice: Don't try to close the deal until we have more specifics. Use this meeting to allow both sides to bring up their concerns and objections."

"Understood," Harbour said, deliberately leaning close enough for her lips to brush Jessie's ear.

"To be succinct, Your Excellency," Jessie said, when Harbour and he resumed their seats. "The Jatouche would hire us to act as your explorers."

"For what purpose?" Pickcit asked.

"To help the Jatouche discover other sentient races that they could present to the alliance," Harbour replied.

"You would risk your lives for the purpose of elevating the Jatouche within the alliance?" Rictook asked, incredulous at the thought.

Henry partially raised a hand to be noticed. When recognized, he stood and said, "Your Excellency, every Pyrean spacer and many stationers risk their lives each day to earn a living. Except for the wealthy aboard our station or those who live on the planet, life is hard and it's dangerous. Your technology offers Pyreans a better way of life. Risking our lives for the Jatouche offers us a bigger payday."

The translation app did its best to handle Henry's last word.

The Jatouche remained quiet, while they processed the implications of the proposal.

"Your Excellency," Pickcit said, "There is one obvious problem with this idea. The Jatouche would not be credited with the discoveries, unless a notable citizen of our race accompanied the Pyreans."

Tacticnok took a breath to speak, but the raised fingers of her father's right hand stilled her. With those three digits and knowing what she was about to propose, His Excellency Rictook forbade his daughter from accompanying the Pyreans.

"I would go with the humans," Jaktook announced.

Tacticnok's heart skipped a beat. She couldn't be prouder of Jaktook volunteering, but she worried for his life.

"Your Excellency, I applaud Jaktook's courage," Tiknock said, "but I believe our young dome administrator doesn't have the standing that would convince the alliance members that we were instrumental in the exploration and discoveries."

Tiknock's words were addressed to Rictook, but by the end of his remarks, he was looking at Tacticnok, who understood the master's implication.

Tacticnok stood. She waited while her father determined whether he would let her speak. The moment passed, and her father signaled his approval.

"This request is long overdue, Your Excellency," Tacticnok said. "For service rendered to date and for those expected in the annuals to come, I recommend the elevation of Dome Administrator Jaktook to the position of Advisor to Her Royal Highness Tacticnok."

Rictook glanced toward his masters, who were nodding in agreement with the request. He waved a hand toward Jaktook, who rose from his pallet. "Do you wish to accept this appointment, Jaktook?" Rictook asked.

"I'm concerned whether I'm worthy, Your Excellency," Jaktook replied.

"The royal daughter believes you're ready. Do you doubt her opinion?" Rictook asked. For those who knew the ruler, the small amount of mirth in his eyes was detectable.

"We do not always agree, Your Excellency. In this case, we differ in our opinions," Jaktook replied. He stood resolutely, as if he was prepared to defend his statements.

For the first time in the presence of humans, Rictook flashed his teeth. "An excellent reply for an advisor. Whether you believe you're ready or not, Jaktook, the royal daughter and I are in agreement. I hereby proclaim that Dome Administrator Jaktook is promoted to the position of Advisor to Her Highness Tacticnok."

Jaktook was stunned, and it was only by catching the hand motions of Tiknock that he recovered enough to sit down.

"Envoy, if and when you explore in the name of the Jatouche, you must wait a sufficient period of time until our newest advisor has regained his wits," Rictook said. For a second time, the ruler flashed his teeth. His remark elicited a round of chuckles from the Pyreans, who were gazing at an astonished Jaktook.

"Does this enterprise have your approval, Your Excellency?" Tacticnok asked.

"I wait to hear the details of this plan before I go that far," Rictook replied, "but I'll tell you that I'm intrigued."

"In order for Pyreans to work with the Jatouche," Jessie said, "we would need to discuss compensation, Your Excellency."

Rictook's bushy eyebrows rose in anticipation, and he glanced toward Pickcit, the master economist.

"What are you asking for in trade for your exploration?" Pickcit asked. Several thoughts went through the master's mind, examining parameters such as length of time, number of domes, species discovered, and races recommended to the alliance.

Jessie looked at Harbour. It wasn't time to specify details, and he wanted her to make the type of point that she excelled at.

Harbour quietly exhaled and then stood. "With regard to payment, I would ask these two questions for your consideration," Harbour said, her eyes traveling across the Jatouche. "What are the lives of those who would undertake this perilous course of action worth? And what is it worth to the Jatouche to have their alliance status elevated?"

The Jatouche were shocked by the envoy's brutally blunt questions.

Rictook replied with equanimity. "I presume these aren't rhetorical questions," he said.

"No, they're not," Harbour replied.

Rictook nodded slowly. It was obvious that he didn't think they were rhetorical, but he had to be sure. "In my long life, I admit to never having heard the likes of these questions," he said. "It will take time and consultations with my advisors to formulate answers."

Knowing her father well, Tacticnok rose and gestured toward the exit of the apartment. Harbour and she left together, with the remainder of the group following.

Round Two

Tacticnok led the company to the original negotiations room for a second round of discussions. While the group took a few moments to refresh themselves, whispers escaped the royal apartment and circulated across Na-Tikkook to Rissness and to the medical station.

In an incredibly short period of time, word was carried to other worlds, as individuals traveled via the gates, even while the envoy's party was mapping out a plan with the advisors and Tacticnok. Before two Jatouche cycles had elapsed, every alliance race was aware of the Pyreans' proposal to investigate the Colony's domes and beyond for the Jatouche.

In the negotiations room, Jaktook was heartily congratulated by Harbour, Jessie, and the master advisors. He still appeared to be in a daze, and Tiknock whispered to him, "Focus, we will need your acumen."

There was an uncertain moment for Jaktook, when he stood in front of Tacticnok. He was at a loss for words. Tacticnok gripped one of his hands and squeezed. Then she took a seat to begin the discussions.

It was Harbour who offered Jaktook the advice he most needed. "No one understands what you're feeling more than me," she told him. "One moment, I was the empath leader, and the next, I was the captain of the Pyreans' greatest ship. Now, I'm the envoy responsible for the fate of Pyre's future."

"How do you cope?" Jaktook asked quietly.

"I put my fears aside. They do me no good," Harbour replied. "Then I think about what I'd like to happen, regardless of what others think about my ideas. Finally, I act on my thoughts."

"That seems so much to consider," Jaktook protested.

"Worrying about that will mire you in confusion," Harbour replied. "Her Highness needs your advice, your thoughts, not what you think she might want to hear."

Jaktook considered the envoy's words, and they sunk into his consciousness. His posture changed, and he nodded his agreement to her. In a brief exchange, they gripped each other's hands.

When everyone was ready, Jessie asked, "What is known about the Colony's gates?"

"No alliance race has seen the Colony's dome," Tiknock replied. "We do know that the Colony has at least three gates. One of the Colony's gates couples to our gate number five. Two other Colony gates link to alliance member gates."

"I suppose those two are guarded like yours?" Devon asked.

"Yes," Tacticnok replied. "The three alliance members who connect to the Colony's dome regularly pass messages about Colony incursions. We're especially sensitive to any new methods that the Colony species employ."

"It seems paramount to learn if the Colony has more than three gates," Henry said. "There's the possibility that the Colony might have spread to other worlds."

"Is that possible?" Dottie asked.

"Assuredly," Tiknock replied.

"The Colony has had hundreds of annuals to seek an opportunity to expand," Jaktook explained. "If they possess more than three gates, there are endless possibilities of meeting and conquering other species and occupying empty domes."

"I understand that domes are not located on the planets. Is that correct?" Aurelia asked.

"That's been the case across the alliance," Tiknock replied.

"Then the Colony would have to build a shuttle to reach the planet from the dome. Could they do that?" Aurelia added.

"This idea has been discussed many times," Tiknock replied. "Considering the length of time since the Colony first broached our gate, it's conceivable that they could have designed and assembled a shuttle that could reach a planet."

"I would like to know how the Colony is viewed in the eyes of the alliance," Devon said.

Harbour thought it was an odd change in the conversation, and she was curious to hear Devon pursue the line of questioning.

"They're considered incorrigible," Pickcit replied.

"Which means what?" Devon asked.

"In alliance terminology, their species are deemed sentient but not ever worthy of admission to the alliance," Pickcit replied.

"In the fight with the Colony in your dome, you killed a good number of them?" Devon pursued. "How did the alliance view that action?"

"It was considered an act of defense," Pickcit explained.

"And if we journey to the Colony dome and kill some of them there?" Devon asked.

It struck Harbour what Devon had been driving at, and she waited for the response from the Jatouche.

"You would be considered aggressive, and therefore classified as incorrigible," Tacticnok replied.

"Well, that puts a different twist on it," Henry said into the quiet.

Harbour glanced at Jessie, mentally urging him to redirect the conversation, but he appeared to be mired in thought.

It was Devon who was able to keep the discussion going forward. He said, "If lethal force can't be used, the Jatouche must have a choice of technologies that could keep the explorer team safe."

Devon's comment energized the Jatouche, and several began speaking at once.

Tacticnok raised a hand off her leg. It was in imitation of her father and was immediately successful in bringing order to the group. She announced, "I request my new advisor, Jaktook, comb through Jatouche technology for every form of nonlethal technology that could be used to defend the explorers. And, Master Tiknock, I request you support Jaktook and make this project your priority."

"It will be my pleasure, Your Highness," Tiknock replied.

Tacticnok said, "I wish to hear the strategies that might be employed to explore the gates." She'd directed the comment at Harbour and Jessie, but the remark was designed to engage her advisors to consider options in concert with the Pyreans.

Jaktook responded first. He said, "If we discover only three gates, there's no reason to go farther. We reset the console and return."

"Who resets the console?" Tacticnok asked.

"I do," Jaktook replied.

"Unacceptable," Tacticnok shot back. "As it is, the alliance will frown at this action. If we demonstrate a reckless disregard for our representative, a royal advisor, they might believe we're unworthy of our membership."

The Jatouche masters knew Tacticnok's objection was thin, but they also knew why she was attempting to make it.

"I thought you might say that, Your Highness," Jaktook replied. "I spoke to Kractik before this meeting started. She's anxious to go with us, and she's more proficient on a console than I am. The explorer team would defend her, while she resets the console."

Tacticnok nodded her acceptance of the arrangement. That a female Jatouche would be a member of the exploratory team appealed to her.

"And if you find more than three gates?" Pickcit asked.

"Then the team's challenge begins," Jaktook replied. "We'll have identified the gate to Rissness, but we won't know which of the others lead to the two alliance races. This will be where our exploration begins."

"Your next dome must be warned of your coming," Tiknock said. "Recognize that you might be alerting the Colony to your arrival."

"Couldn't we take a set of cubes with recordings made at the Rissness dome?" Harbour asked. "We'd send our message through the gate. We would rely on a visual of two species. Most important, the Colony species wouldn't be in the recording."

"Then what?" Devon asked.

"I'm thinking that we'd have to wait until we receive a return message," Harbour replied.

"That's a lot of exposure time in the Colony dome," Devon remarked.

"True," Jessie agreed. He seemed on the verge of a thought, and Harbour signaled the group to hold their comments.

"Jaktook," Jessie said, "You're probably thinking of supporting our defense against the Colony's bites by employing specialized suits."

"That was one option I was considering," Jaktook replied.

"And that's good," Jessie remarked, "but we could be overwhelmed if we don't have offensive tactics. I'm not a biologist or anything like that, but you've all these incredible medical services personnel."

"Yes?" Jaktook replied. It was more a question than a statement. He wasn't sure what the advisor was implying.

"I think we should ask the creative individuals at Rissness Station how they would repel or neutralize species such as the Colony."

"That's a clever idea," Jaktook enthused.

"We must consider all senses," Tiknock added. "It will be important to develop a series of defensive and offensive tactics."

"Why?" Harbour asked.

"If you find more than three gates within the Colony's dome, your exploration will create an ever-increasing challenge in your passage in and out of their dome," Tiknock explained. "It will be difficult for you to transport much equipment with you. You'll need to be mobile. Hopefully, you'll discover an uninhabited dome, which will allow you to rest and plan. However, your greatest obstacle will be return passages through the Colony dome. Assuming you encounter the Colony, which I believe will be a near certainty, whatever you do to defend yourself on the first passage through their dome more than likely will not work on your return."

"I accept Tiknock's reasoning," Pickcit said. "It would be false to think of this species, either because of their appearance or their aggressive behavior, as less than capable. They are truly sentient. You must not underestimate their cleverness in preventing your subsequent passages through their dome."

* * * *

The Pyreans' strategy meetings ran for three days. Every conceivable option of gate configurations was explored. Within each diagrammed pattern, the group considered who they might meet. The question was always whether to invite individuals through the gates if they'd mastered the dome but had blocked the Colony. Then there was the odder option of a Colony gate connecting to an unoccupied dome that connected to a sentient's dome.

"Our proposal to His Excellency will not be complete if we don't identify who will be doing the exploring," Harbour stated to her envoy team, when the strategy meetings neared completion.

"Well, I can give you my answer right now. It won't be me," Dottie said. "Yes, I'm afraid to go, but more important, I know my limits. I would be of no use to you. The moment I saw one of these creatures, I would freeze in horror."

"It's the same for me," Idrian said. "I'm afraid to go. It's that simple."

"I'll go," Devon said definitively, "but I intend to be well-versed in Jatouche technology. I want the odds in our favor so that if we go, we can return."

"I would like to say that you can count me in," Henry said, "but I'm concerned that I'll be a burden to the team. However, if the Jatouche would see fit to lend me their medical services and the team could wait a couple of months, I think I could put Devon to shame." He grinned and tapped Devon's leg.

"I bet you would, Captain," Devon replied good-naturedly.

Jessie and Harbour stared quietly at each other, and the other Pyreans wondered what the two of them were thinking. Jessie broke first. "Of course, I'm going," he said. "Now, tell me that you intend to go."

"Yes," Harbour replied, keeping her focus on Jessie. She could detect his complex swirl of emotions — frustration, confusion, and fear.

"There's no need to have an envoy on the exploration team," Jessie argued.

"I won't be going as an envoy," Harbour retorted. "I'll be acting as security."

"You want to carry some of our offensive or defensive equipment?" Devon asked.

"I'm a weapon," Harbour declared. It was a chilling statement for some members of the team to hear.

"In that case, two empaths are better than one," Aurelia said defiantly.

"You've spent your life training empaths how to help others, Harbour," Jessie argued. "You employ gentle emotions to calm humans and now Jatouche. But what makes you think that you can employ your powers against the Colony?"

Rather than answer, Harbour walked across the room to a desk comm unit, called Tacticnok, and asked her to join them. She sat down and waited silently.

"Envoy, do you have a request?" asked Tacticnok, when she arrived.

"Yes, Your Highness, do you have life-threatening species on this planet?" Harbour asked.

"Several, Envoy. Early generations of Jatouche were forced to build strong enclaves to protect the populations," Tacticnok replied.

"Have you ever hunted any of them?" Jessie asked.

"We're not an aggressive species, as you've probably noted," Tacticnok replied, with a shrug of apology. "Our preference has always been defense. After the Gasnarian attack, we did create beam weapons for our soldiers, but they're not used against any of our native species."

"I would like you to set up a confrontation with your most predacious species," Harbour requested.

"Please clarify what you mean by confrontation," Tacticnok asked, with concern.

"The creature must be free to see and attack me," Harbour replied.

"For what reason?" Tacticnok asked, shocked by the request.

"We're testing an empath's ability to deal with an aggressive species," Harbour replied to a wide-eyed royal daughter.

* * * *

Days later, Tacticnok notified Harbour that the test she had requested was ready. The envoy party loaded into a vehicle that soon left the densely populated areas behind and entered the planet's lush forests. When the team exited the car, they were surrounded by soldiers.

"Envoy, it's important to do exactly as you're directed by our soldiers," Tacticnok said. "They are tasked with keeping your party and me safe."

The group wound along a newly cut trail to a rough clearing. A three-meter, clear cube sat on the ground. It had sliding doors on opposite sides.

"You will enter here, Envoy," Tacticnok said, indicating the door on their side of the cube. "You will stand near the door on the other side, but you will not step into the doorway or across it. Is that understood?"

Harbour would have asked a question, but the fierceness in Tacticnok's voice kept her quiet. She'd asked for a confrontation with a hazardous creature. It occurred to her that she might be facing a more insidious predator than she could have imagined.

"You will be using your powers against a Rik-tik," Tacticnok explained. "Don't be fooled by its appearance. It depends on camouflage to lure its prey close. It has incredible speed for a short distance and a lethal tongue."

"Then you expect it to charge me," Harbour surmised.

"Yes, you'll excite it by clapping your hands like this," Tacticnok said, demonstrating a staccato tempo but refraining from striking her palms together.

"And if I fail to halt its charge?" Harbour asked.

"The front of the cube has a monitoring apparatus that will shut the entrance if the Rik-tik approaches too closely," Tacticnok said. "Every precaution has been taken. If you wish, we can return to the royal residence now. There is no need to proceed with this demonstration."

Harbour stared evenly at Tacticnok, who replied, "As you wish, Envoy," and gestured toward the entrance.

Waves of fear and frustration swept over Harbour, and she turned to locate the source. Jessie stood with his arms tightly folded and his face distorted. Harbour walked over to him, gripped his arms, and whispered in his ear, "Have faith in their precautions and in me." At the same time, she used the opportunity to open her gates and flood Jessie's mind with the serenity she knew she needed to face the creature.

"You be careful," Jessie whispered in a choked voice.

At the cube's entrance, Aurelia held out her hand. She said, "We should discover our power when we're coupled."

Harbour hesitated, but she couldn't deny the logic of the suggestion. She nodded and gripped the young empath's hand. Harbour paused in the cube's center. She signaled to Tacticnok to close the entrance, turned to Aurelia, and opened her gates wide.

Aurelia sensed the enormous power coiling in Harbour's mind, and she sought to do the same. She hadn't unleashed this much emotional force since she'd attacked Dimitri Belosov in self-defense. For a moment, she faltered, the memories of that time frightening her. Then she stuffed those memories deep and pulled on her mental strength. When she reopened her gates, she felt an incredible merging with Harbour. It was if their waves were in synchronicity, reinforcing each other's strength.

Harbour smiled at Aurelia. The young woman appeared to be a sympathetic copy of her. Harbour led Aurelia to the other door. She said, "We'll try to calm the creature first," and Aurelia nodded.

The empaths stared across the clearing. There was only one object to be seen, and it resembled a segment of a tree trunk.

Aurelia glanced at Harbour, who nodded toward the object. In turn, Aurelia accepted it as the target, without argument.

With Harbour's free hand, she signed to Jessie, who told Tacticnok that the envoy wished the doorway opened. When the glass panel slid aside, Harbour released Aurelia's hand and clapped briskly and loudly. Then she quickly regained Aurelia's hand and restored the link with her.

The empaths watched the log rise up on a series of short legs. It rotated a few degrees to focus on the cube. When the creature didn't charge, Harbour chose not to break her bond with Aurelia. Instead, she stamped her feet, imitating the rhythm Tacticnok had showed her.

Suddenly, the Rik-tik surged forward. Its multiple pairs of legs lending it incredible speed.

Harbour felt Aurelia's hand fiercely grip her own, but the young woman stood her ground. Harbour focused her power on the entity, hoping to calm it.

Unfortunately, the empaths weren't provided enough time to test their technique. The cube's monitoring apparatus detected the swift advance of the Rik-tik and triggered the clear panel, which immediately slammed shut.

The Rik-tik slid to a stop directly in front of the cube, but not before its long tongue shot out. The appendage's meter-long tip was flat and serrated on the sides. It resembled bone, and it struck the clear panel with a resounding thwack. Failing to penetrate the barrier seemed to infuriate the creature. It continued to strike the panel multiple times, creating fine cracks in the material until it relented and scurried away into the forest.

"Close your gates," Harbour ordered. The sudden loss of Aurelia's power was disconcerting.

The rear door opened, and Tacticnok and Jessie hurried into the cube.

"Everyone okay?" Jessie asked.

"We're fine," Harbour replied, with a slight smile, attempting to project an air of confidence, although she didn't feel that way.

Tacticnok listened politely, although she was intent on examining the cracks in the panel. She was annoyed that the material had not withstood the force of the Rik-tik's tongue.

"Is the experiment completed?" asked Tacticnok, which annoyed Jessie. He assumed that it was finished.

"No," Aurelia declared. She looked at Harbour and said, "We need to try a different tactic. Something aggressive."

"What did you sense?" Harbour asked Aurelia.

"I felt white-hot rage," Aurelia replied.

"Me too," Harbour agreed. "It's no wonder that we weren't able to calm the creature."

Tacticnok whistled shrilly and several senior Jatouche came running. She issued a series of orders. Immediately, there was a concentration of activity around the face of the cube. Engineers worked on replacing the damaged panel, and soldiers, who were laden with beams weapons and energy packs, took up a protective ring. When the new panel was ready, the soldiers and engineers retreated.

"Your experiment may continue," Tacticnok announced. When Jessie hesitated, Tacticnok said politely, "Advisor, I would appreciate your escort from the cube."

Jessie gave in to the adamancy of the females, and he gallantly swept his hand toward the cube's rear entrance. Tacticnok flashed her teeth at him and led the way.

"Get ready, Envoy. This forest is full of Rik-tik. Another one will be here soon," Tacticnok called out before the entrance door slid closed behind Jessie and her.

Four soldiers occupied the center of the clearing. Three of them held metal tools borrowed from the engineers. They banged them in individual rhythms. The noise was hellacious. A fourth soldier held up a device with a small monitor. Watching its output, he constantly called to the others.

At one point, the soldier monitoring the area waved his arm excitedly, and all four abandoned the clearing at a run. Soon, various sized Rik-tiks crawled into the clearing. They blared their challenges at one another and used their stout bodies like rams. As they slammed sideways into one another, their bodies made heavy, hollow sounds, and they grunted with each impact. The fights scared off the smallest of the Rik-tiks, and the clearing was left to two, four-meter long behemoths.

Harbour and Aurelia joined hands. Each found something to power their fear, things they would never want to share with another. Gates were opened, and the combined emotional intensity swelled. Harbour signed, and a Jatouche engineer triggered the panel in front of the empaths.

When Harbour stamped her feet, the Rik-tiks swung her way. But instead of charging, they stood on their short legs and grunted. Harbour and Aurelia poured their crushing anxieties into the creatures. Slowly, step by step, the Rik-tiks retreated. Then they turned around and hurried into the forest.

Immediately, the engineer closed the clear panel in front of the empaths and opened the cube's entrance. Tacticnok and Jessie discovered Harbour and Aurelia holding hands and grinning at each other.

"Had I not seen this display, I would have found the story unbelievable," Tacticnok said in wonder.

"My apologies for doubting you, Harbour," Jessie said quietly.

Before Harbour could answer, Tacticnok asked, "Does our material prevent the transmission of your abilities, Envoy? I could feel nothing from where I stood."

"I've the ability to direct my sending," Harbour explained.

"And you, as well, Aurelia?" Tacticnok asked.

"Yes and no, Your Highness." Aurelia replied. "I'm getting better at directing my power, but in this case, I acted like a generator fueling a directional antenna. When empaths touch, we have the ability to twine our power, and this can take several forms."

"An amazing capability," Tacticnok enthused. "Is the experiment complete, Envoy?"

"Yes, Your Highness," Harbour replied, "and I would say it was a success."

Tacticnok and Aurelia led the way out, and Harbour walked beside Jessie. She slipped her hand into his and lightly squeezed it before letting go.

-18-
Presentation

After weeks of work, Harbour and Tacticnok considered they had the critical pieces of the exploration plan and were ready to present it to Rictook. The groups met the ruler in the salon of his apartment.

When Tacticnok entered the room, she was surprised to find Roknick in attendance. The master strategist hadn't been part of their meetings since he'd challenged her and she'd sent him to her father. Her anger spiked. The last thing she needed was the senior advisor disrupting the presentation.

Everyone had occupied a pallet, and Tacticnok sought to head off a confrontation with Roknick. She said, "Your Excellency, we've had the value of the advisors' input in devising our concept, except for that of Master Roknick. He's offered the envoy and her delegates no observations. Surely, as the master strategist, he's considered the problem from many angles."

Rictook was careful not to let the weary sigh he felt escape. He'd hoped to prevent this debacle, but Roknick had insisted he'd a right to attend the meeting. In Rictook's opinion, the advisor's long history of service warranted the granting of that right.

Roknick wore a scowl. He'd expected to hear the envoy's presentation and then pick it apart until he'd exposed every weakness. Failing that, he had a secret, dark hope. The sudden challenge by the royal daughter was completely unexpected. As a strategist, he had to appreciate that she'd outmaneuvered him.

"I believe that Master Roknick is hoping for one of two things to happen," Tacticnok said. "Either he intends to sabotage this meeting or he has hopes the Pyreans' visit to the Colony's dome will result in their deaths."

The audience, including Rictook, was shocked by the royal daughter's forceful accusation. Rictook's long decades of rule allowed him to keep his expression neutral. This was his daughter's challenge, and he sincerely hoped that she was capable of winning it.

"I deny that," Roknick declared.

"What do you say, Envoy?" Tacticnok asked. "Does our master strategist lie?"

Roknick's horrified glance at Harbour echoed the incredulity rippling through the audience.

Tacticnok knew that Harbour and the other empaths had skills that were beyond Jatouche comprehension. Having witnessed the turning aside of two large Rik-tiks, she was depending on those unknown abilities.

Harbour and Jessie exchanged stunned glances. The royal daughter was in a political fight, and her choice of weapons was a Pyrean empath.

"Your Highness, this is an internal matter. It's not my place to interfere," Harbour protested.

"I'm the eldest daughter of the Jatouche ruler, His Excellency Rictook," Tacticnok stated firmly. "I ask the Pyrean envoy if Master Roknick can be counted on to truthfully advise the royal family and represent the best interests of our citizens."

Harbour felt Tacticnok's tactics block her into a corner from which there was no escape. She did make a final attempt. "Your Highness," she said, "I can't read another's thoughts. I can only sense their emotions."

"Then I ask you, Envoy, what did you detect from Master Roknick?" Tacticnok pressed.

Harbour sensed Tacticnok's fury, and she was forced to make a political decision of her own. For the sake of Pyre's future, she decided to throw in with the royal daughter.

"Fear," Harbour admitted. "When you accused Master Roknick of being present to disrupt our presentation and, failing that, wishing for our deaths, he evinced great fear."

"And how do you interpret that, Envoy?" Tacticnok pressed.

"Please, Your Highness, your species is foreign to us," Harbour protested a final time. "That makes it difficult to interpret your emotions."

Tacticnok, who had kept her attention focused on Roknick, turned her gaze on Harbour. There was sympathy in the daughter's eyes for a brief moment. Then the unrelenting stare returned.

"We've spent a long time with you here and at Pyre, Envoy," Tacticnok said. "You know us well. I ask you to explain what you felt."

Relenting, Harbour said, "I believe Master Roknick was shocked that you uncovered his intentions. That led him to fear reprisals."

"Just so," Tacticnok agreed. "Your Excellency, I ask that you remove Master Roknick from this meeting. Furthermore, I request that you excuse him from service. What we're attempting to accomplish with the Pyreans has tremendous consequences for the Jatouche. We can't afford individuals to disrupt this relationship by furthering their personal agendas at the expense of our citizens."

Rictook regarded the master advisor with sad eyes, and Roknick knew that he'd expended what remained of the ruler's favor. The advisor stood, bowed his head, and left the meeting.

There was a moment of silence. Harbour felt guilty, and she glanced at Jessie.

Rictook surveyed the audience, trying to determine the best way of reviving the attendees' enthusiasm, which they'd shown when they first entered the apartment. He had to admit his misjudgment in allowing Roknick to attend. On the other hand, it merely advanced the confrontation with his daughter that would have eventually taken place.

"Envoy," Rictook requested, and Harbour stood, "I apologize for the part you were compelled to play in this clash of wills." Then Rictook's gaze targeted his daughter.

Tacticnok was relishing her victory over Roknick. Belatedly, her father's words made her realize what she'd failed to focus on. She might have been the one to request Captain Harbour as the Pyrean envoy, but it was done with her father's permission. More important, Harbour was presented to Rictook, the Jatouche ruler, for approval.

Tacticnok rose and deeply bowed her head to Harbour. "His Excellency is gracious to offer you his apology," she said, "but I invoked this confrontation. It wasn't my intention to involve you, Envoy, and for that you have my sincere regret."

The royal daughter turned her attention toward her father, as she said, "However, in an effort to protect what I see as a most valuable relationship with your species, Envoy, I'll do whatever is necessary to remove every impediment."

Rictook's lips trembled with effort, as he fought to keep from baring his teeth. The fierceness his daughter portrayed was a necessary ingredient in a successful ruler. It brought him a small measure of peace that he had desperately sought about her eventual ascension. With a subtle motion of his hand, Rictook bade his daughter sit. It wasn't the lift and settling of a few fingers. It was an upturned hand. It was a gracious offer to assume a rightful seat.

"I wait to hear your exploration strategy," Rictook requested. He was amused that the presentation was made by Advisors Jaktook and Cinders. The two males projected on a monitor the scenarios they'd analyzed, and the actions they expected the team to take. They traded off the narration, as if they'd worked together for decades. This gave Rictook an inkling of the bonds made by the intravertor team while they worked beside the humans at Pyre.

At one point, Tacticnok, who had been studiously observing her father, saw his attention waver. He was growing tired. She signaled Jaktook, who'd been speaking, to quiet. "Do you have any questions thus far, Your Excellency?" she asked.

Rictook stirred. "I must admit that I expected a shorter summary of your plan," he said. "That you've thought through your strategy to this depth gives me hope for success if you can counter the Colony's actions. At this point, I do have one question. If you meet non-alliance sentients, who're occupying their domes, how will you communicate with them?"

Tacticnok said, "I've spoken to Jakkock, Your Excellency. While he's willing to join the team, his mate is expecting soon, and I've excused him from joining the team. He told me that if a race has learned the console, a translation app can be swiftly built, and Jaktook has those abilities."

"And if they're present and haven't deciphered the Messinants glyphs?" Rictook asked.

"It would be the same learning process that the Pyreans experienced over a matter of cycles," Tacticnok replied, "and we wouldn't possess those skills or have the luxury of that amount of time."

"Curiosity coupled with a peaceful reception served you well at the Triton dome," Rictook commented. "Let's hope you enjoy that type of reception wherever you journey." He knew full well that wouldn't be the case. The alliance had experienced a significant number of encounters that had resulted in the demise of the initial teams before communication was established.

Idrian and Dottie shared a quiet exchange. Rictook's pronouncement had struck home. Many Pyreans and especially Pyre's leaders had decried Jessie and Harbour's discoveries at the Triton dome. The unknowns of terrifying aliens and deadly infections had led to unreasoning fear. Yet, if it hadn't been for their responses to Tacticnok's invitations, none of them would be sitting here on comfortable pallets in a monarch's apartment, which was situated on a beautifully green planet — one with breathable air.

"Should we continue the presentation later, Your Excellency?" Tacticnok asked, concerned for her father's failing health.

"How much have we seen?" Rictook asked.

Jaktook briefly dipped his head in apology and said, "About one third, Your Excellency."

At that, Rictook finally bared his teeth before he said, "There is no means by which I can judge the thoroughness of your preparations. Suffice it to say, you've surpassed my expectations. I give my consent to your enterprise."

The audience took a moment to quietly celebrate, murmuring to one another and clasping nearby hands.

"Envoy, you asked two difficult questions of me," Rictook said, "and I'm prepared to answer them. As to the value of a Pyrean life, there is no quantification. The Jatouche regard each sentient as irreplaceable, and, as the ruler of this world, it's my duty to safeguard my citizens and the lives of alliance members who visit us. If I were to make a personal judgment, I wouldn't permit this plan to go forward."

Rictook took a moment to compose his thoughts, and Harbour detected a shift in his emotional state. Sadness swept through him.

"However, as the ruler of this world, I'm responsible for the future of my citizens too," Rictook continued, "and what you offer is an incredible temptation for the Jatouche. I recognize that Pyreans lead a harsh existence and are accustomed to risk, and I credit that you're volunteering to do this for both our races. My daughters, one of whom will rule in my place, urge me to support your proposal, but I'd like to give you this final opportunity to rescind your offer."

"Your Excellency, I recognize that this decision has weighed heavily on your conscience. I feel that," Harbour replied, letting the ruler know that she was employing her power in a passive manner. "But this is a matter of survival for Pyreans, and the volunteers are well aware of the risks."

"It was as I thought," Rictook said. "My advisors have put together an offer that encompasses the possible results from your exploration. It gives credit to each phase of discovery, recruitment, and membership of a sentient race. Each phase rewards the Pyreans in technology and material goods. However, for your first foray to the Colony dome and regardless of your success, the Jatouche pledge to supply intravertor parts to the Pyreans at whatever rate you can build and deploy the devices until such time as your planet's surface is openly habitable."

The Pyreans exchanged glances of disbelief. For the possible sacrifice of a few, if it came to that, there was a real opportunity to claim the planet's surface for generations to come.

When the Pyreans' surprise subsided, Rictook continued. "Envoy, I do offer your team an unexpected resource. It might or might not be to your liking, but that will be your decision. I received a request from Mangoth of the Logar. He wished an audience with you. He waits at Rissness for your arrival."

"Did Mangoth indicate what he wanted?" Harbour asked.

It was Rictook's turn to be surprised. "Envoy, Mangoth is a Crocian. The Jatouche are not in the habit of questioning the Crocians."

The audience with Rictook ended shortly after delivery of the ruler's message about Mangoth, and the envoy team retired with Tacticnok and the advisors to an engineering laboratory.

The engineers chittered excitedly among themselves when their guests arrived. For all of them, this had been their first challenge to design and construct weapons against Colony species. It made no difference to them that they were defensive designs.

Over the course of hours, the exploration team tried on new suits, armored against the strike of the Colony species. They tested stun weapons, gas bombs, electronic sound generators, and other tech designed to temporarily impair the Colony biologically.

"What's that?" Aurelia asked, examining a compact ball of ultrafine mesh with a small nipple.

Jaktook signaled an engineer, who picked up the ball, flipped the nipple over, and threw the ball. The ball expanded in a quiet rush of air into a round net. The engineer's eyes were bright with excitement in expectation of the Pyreans' approval, except the humans were confounded.

"What does it do?" Aurelia asked.

"The net is designed to cover a platform and extend over its edge," Jaktook explained.

"And so?" Devon prompted.

"According to the Messinants, individuals or cargo must remain within the platform's limits" Jaktook replied.

"So you've been able to test this mesh on platform activation and this other gear against the Colony?" Jessie asked, seeking confirmation.

The air of enthusiasm drained from the engineers, and their crestfallen faces turned toward Jaktook.

"These are theoretical designs and untested constructions," Jaktook explained. "They're based on the historical recordings of the fights during the Colony's incursions."

"Theoretical, untested," Devon repeated, shaking his head in dismay. "We won't have all day to test these, one by one, on the Colony until we find one that works."

"Maybe that's where the envoy and I can play a part," Aurelia enthused. "Our combined powers might be our initial defense. It would give the team a chance to try out the equipment."

"Whatever we attempt to do," Jaktook said, "It's of paramount importance that we protect Kractik and allow her to reach and program the console. Without that step, we aren't journeying anywhere, either returning to Rissness or accessing another gate."

"It'll be imperative to select a few strategies and have a shorthand method of communicating quickly which one we want to employ," Devon volunteered.

"Agreed," Jessie returned, and Devon and he put their heads together to devise some simple actions and their triggers. When they updated the team, several changes were made until the tactics were complete.

Finally, there were no more preparations to make. Tacticnok thought that discussions should continue on some minutiae, and she was surprised to find the envoy's servants packing her duffels.

"Isn't this premature?" Tacticnok asked.

"I've learned from a wonderful spacer by the name of Dingles that there is a thing such as too much planning," Harbour replied. "We have our strategies, our tactics, and our tools. It's time to find out what we face."

Tacticnok accepted the inevitable, saying, "I'll arrange a shuttle for you."

"Jaktook has ordered one," Harbour replied. She detected a sharp spike of angst from the royal daughter. "Tacticnok, the team is ready, and I think Jaktook didn't want to prolong his goodbye," she said gently.

"It feels as if I'm no longer in control of what I've begun," Tacticnok said wistfully.

"Dingles, the spacer I mentioned, told me that to be a respected captain I had to trust my crew," Harbour said. "You've taken enormous steps to create a relationship with Pyreans, and my envoy party has found a means of enabling a basis for exchange. Now, it's time for you to let this exploration team see what it can accomplish."

Tacticnok nodded her acceptance, but Harbour could sense that her emotional pain had failed to substantially subside.

Having cued the team and the royal servants, arrangements proceeded with alacrity. In a short amount of time, individuals and baggage were aboard the shuttle.

The Pyreans luxuriated in the newly installed seats that suited their proportions. The Rissness console had provided the dimensions of each traveler, and the Jatouche had been able to incorporate features that allowed adjustments to each Pyrean.

Tacticnok and Jaktook sat together, and humans heard their conversation range from murmurs to arguments. Jessie, who was seated next to Harbour, glanced questioningly at her.

"Tacticnok is upset that Jaktook is on the team," Harbour explained. "She accepts the reason for why it is he must go, but she's still unhappy about it."

"I completely understand her reaction," Jessie replied. He added a scowl, in case Harbour didn't catch his point. In reply, she laughed softly and detected Jessie's instant emotional shift from annoyance to affection. She'd felt that shift many times. Something about her laughter triggered an instant and tender reaction in Jessie.

Jessie glanced around, as if to signal a desire to change the conversation. He asked, "Are Dottie and Idrian still committed to their plan?"

"Yes," Harbour replied. "They intend to wait at Rissness with Henry for a few days to see what happens. If we don't return, they will journey to Triton and have the Jatouche console operator call one of your ships for pickup."

"Hmm," Jessie murmured.

Harbour chuckled, more to feel Jessie's emotional emanations than anything else. "That's a terse comment even for you," she teased.

"I don't like the idea of them reaching Pyre first and being the ones to control the information, even with Henry there," Jessie groused.

Harbour noted that Jessie's usually unflappable persona was becoming more mercurial, and she had a good idea as to why. He was still opposed to Aurelia and her accompanying the team.

What Harbour had come to realize was that Jessie's objection to Aurelia and her taking part in the exploration didn't stem from some misguided need to protect women or from a belief that females shouldn't participate in dangerous assignments. A person had only to recognize that two of Jessie's three captains were women. No, it was the fact that these two particular women, both empaths, had gotten past Jessie's emotional armor, and he was struggling to deal with that.

"The three of them can tell their stories, and when we return to Pyre, we'll tell ours," Harbour said. "And whose tale do you think will be more mesmerizing?" she asked rhetorically, grinning conspiratorially at Jessie.

-19-
Mangoth

The party exited their shuttle at Rissness, worked their way through the tunnels, and entered the dome. Harbour's envoy status attracted the courtesies of every alien she passed. It intrigued her how each individual could easily pay her respect without losing focus on where they were walking or what they were doing. *There must be so many worlds and so many envoys*, she thought.

Jaktook walked beside Tacticnok with an element of pride. He proudly displayed his advisor's medallion, which was similar in shape to Harbour's but broadcast a different message.

On the platform deck, the Pyreans watched a heavy-bodied Crocian waddle toward them on a pair of thick, squat hind legs. The massive scaled alien stopped in front of Jaktook, who introduced himself and then Tacticnok. The alien tipped his massive head toward the royal daughter. When Jaktook gestured to Harbour, the alien dropped his head in deference.

"Envoy Harbour, I'm Mangoth of the Logar," the alien announced. "As you can see, the Jatouche have completed their repairs on me. My beauty has been restored." He turned his head from side to side, and the dome's light glistened off his scales, producing tiny prisms of refracted light. "You'll not be averse to being seen in my presence," Mangoth added.

"Yes, you appear magnificent, Mangoth," Harbour said, giving Jessie a bewildered look. The alien's long jaw loomed over her head. A muscular tail protruded from the rear of its sheath, and its folded hands ended in blunt, black claws.

"I've met three of your kind, Envoy. They appealed to me, and I've chosen to support your endeavor," Mangoth announced.

"How do you know what we intend to do, Mangoth?" Jessie asked.

Mangoth's snout turned toward Jessie, and his eyes studied the captain. He'd heard the brief announcement of the envoy's advisor from Jessie's medallion. "I see impertinence runs through your race, Envoy."

"Yes, it does," Harbour acknowledged sternly, "and my advisor asked you a question."

Mangoth's roar had the domes' visitors pausing in their steps before hurrying on their way. "I had hoped the three I met were indicative of your kind, Envoy, and I'm pleased to see my hope realized. We'll make fine comrades."

"And the answer to my advisor's question, Mangoth?" Harbour persisted.

"We're Crocians, one of the original members of the alliance," Mangoth stated. "As such, we're exalted. It behooves our race to know the machinations of the other members. We've watched three species struggle with their gate connections to the Colony and wondered when they would find a means of dealing with the incorrigible sentients. Through our sources, we learned of your proposal, Envoy."

"I appreciate your offer, Mangoth, but we've made special arrangements for our deployment through the gates," Harbour said respectfully.

Mangoth's head snapped back in surprise. The possibility of the envoy refusing his offer had never occurred to him. After all, he was Crocian. He realized he had made a grievous error, assuming he was dealing with a lesser race, and it had produced unintended consequences. He adopted the manners of dealing with an exalted alliance member.

"I wish to hear your concerns, Envoy," Mangoth said politely.

Harbour signed to Jessie, requesting he reply.

"We have armored suits against the Colony," Jessie pointed out.

"I wear mine," Mangoth pronounced, tapping a heavy claw against his scaled hide.

"Our suits are fitted with respirators in case we have to deploy gas," Jessie argued.

"What is the gas intended to do?" Mangoth asked.

"Put the Colony species to sleep," Jessie replied.

"For how long?" Mangoth asked.

"We don't know if the gas will work, much less how long it will work," Jessie said.

"Let me be more precise," Mangoth riposted. "How long is the gas active?"

Jessie looked at Jaktook, who replied, "In our experiments, the gas dissipated within nine gik-kicks."

"Again, this is not a problem," Mangoth replied. "Crocians are capable of holding their breaths for several times this long."

"But the gas can get into your nostrils, Mangoth, and affect you," Jessie contended.

Mangoth stepped toward Jessie. He leaned forward until his snout's end was directly in front of Jessie's face.

Every fiber in Jessie's being screamed for him to shrink away from the horrendous vision of teeth and scales that swam before his eyes. He was staring at Mangoth's dual nostrils, when two bulbs of tissue from inside the openings folded down and slammed the nostrils closed.

"Impressive," Jessie managed to say. He watched the nostrils open and the snout recede. A shudder went through him, which the gleam in Mangoth's eyes told him the alien had witnessed.

Seeking to regain a little dignity, Jessie expressed his final objection, saying, "There are strictures against killing the Colony species."

"There's no need to teach me the alliance's codes, Advisor," Mangoth declared. To a lesser race, he would have roared his defiance at such an insulting insinuation, but his need was greater than his pride.

Harbour sensed Jessie's frustration, and she signed to him to cease.

"I want to know the reason that you wish to journey with this team," Harbour said.

"Will you accompany your humans, Envoy?" Mangoth asked.

"Yes," Harbour replied.

"Then you will have need of my protection," Mangoth said.

Harbour detected an element of anxiety from the Crocian. "Now, I would know the real reason," she said, her voice hard.

"So it's true! You're a special human, who's capable of reading sentients," Mangoth declared. But his triumphant discovery quickly turned to discomfort. There was no deceiving the envoy. "I seek a mate," he admitted.

"A mate?" Harbour repeated. To her, aliens not only appeared different but their social norms were difficult to understand.

"Yes, a mate," Mangoth acknowledged. "I've lost four consecutive challenges to win a female. It was my thought that by journeying with your team and supporting your efforts that I would win honor for myself."

"There are two conditions that you'd have to accept if I were to agree to you joining us," Harbour said.

"I would hear them," Mangoth replied anxiously.

"I'm the leader of this exploration team, and Advisor Cinders is my second," Harbour said.

"Agreed," Mangoth replied. "And the other?"

"Credit for discoveries of new races, regardless of their status, belongs to the Jatouche," Harbour replied.

Mangoth's eyes focused on Jaktook and then on Tacticnok. When he addressed Harbour, he said, "You give the Jatouche the opportunity to accrue great honor. Why?"

"Her Highness displayed courage and acumen when she chose to visit the Gasnarian dome after we had activated it," Harbour said, which garnered a complimentary nod from Tacticnok. "She has requested her father, His Excellency Rictook, be generous to us when there was no reason to do so."

Mangoth regarded Tacticnok. "Untypical for the Jatouche," the enormous scaled alien acknowledged.

"We're grateful for the assistance of the Jatouche, and we intend to repay them," Harbour finished. She knew that she hadn't spoken the entire truth. What she had said to Mangoth is what she wanted the Crocian to communicate to the alliance members.

"Your terms are acceptable," Mangoth said. He had thought joining the exploration was purely to help his status within his race, but the nascent, yet strong, relationship between the Pyreans and Jatouche intrigued him.

Harbour glanced questioningly at Jessie, who burst out laughing and slapped the alien's shoulder. "I say we let Mangoth come. The least we can do is to help him get a female."

Mangoth would have considered the advisor's strike a challenge, but the human's words and demeanor implied an attempt at camaraderie. So, he allowed the slight to pass, but not without dropping his jaw and tipping his head toward Jessie. He hoped the close display of his teeth would balance the advisor's affront.

"My advisor accepts you, Mangoth of the Logar," Harbour announced. "Therefore, I accept you, but hear me. If you violate Advisor Cinder's orders or mine, your association with our team will be immediately forfeited."

"You would strand me on some distant dome?" Mangoth asked.

Harbour snapped her fingers in front of Mangoth's snout, and announced, "In an instant."

The exploration team didn't expect Mangoth's response. The massive alien tipped his snout upward and roared. The bellow seemed to shake the air of the dome. When his roar died, he stared hard at Harbour and said, "Despite your bland appearance, Envoy, you're more akin to Crocians than my fellow citizens would believe. I look forward to our shared experience."

The team members hoisted their bags and headed to the dome's lower level to prepare for their journey.

As Mangoth hoisted a pack that molded closely to his back, he whispered to Jessie, "Are all human females as strong-willed as the envoy?"

"No," Jessie replied.

"That's unfortunate," Mangoth said. He waited for the entire team to precede him down the ramp, but two human delegates were fixed in place and staring wide-eyed at him. So, he ignored them and followed the others.

In a third-level room, Jatouche soldiers opened crates and laid out the armored suits and other equipment for the exploration team.

Dottie slowly approached Harbour and said, "Idrian and I don't want to impede your preparations, Harbour. We're going to say goodbye now and wish you good luck." Dottie hesitated, searching for the right words, and continued. "I find this whole alien and alliance thing daunting. How you've navigated it, I'll never know. But, one thing for certain. I'll be telling every stationer who'll listen what you've accomplished for Pyre."

Dottie hugged Harbour and then went down the line of Pyreans. At Jaktook, she held out her hand and managed not to recoil at the touch of the padded palm.

Idrian was much more formal and had little to say.

When it was Henry's turn to say goodbye, Harbour could sense the captain's regret. She hugged Henry and flooded him with a buoyant emotion. "We each must do what we can, Henry," she whispered. "You keep an eye on Dottie and Idrian. Keep them out of trouble."

Soon after the Pyreans' goodbyes were completed, a soldier led the three humans away.

The Pyreans donned their newly made suits, which incorporated oxygen tanks and carbon-dioxide filters to extend the tank's time. Jaktook broke out his suit and soldiers helped him into it.

From his pack, Mangoth pulled a flexible bag that neatly fit over his head. He touched a mechanism at the throat and the bag conformed to his head. Essentially, it allowed a personal and unique helmet design. The Crocian strapped a bottle to his chest and attached it by hose to his flex-helmet to test it before he removed the contraption.

"You seem to have come prepared," Jessie commented to Mangoth.

"It pays to anticipate," Mangoth remarked.

The Jatouche defensive equipment was uncrated, and Jaktook reviewed the operating characteristics of each piece with everyone, but primarily for Mangoth's benefit. When the gear was to be shared, Mangoth plucked the mesh roll from the pile. Belatedly, he eyed Harbour, who gave her assent.

Careful, Mangoth thought, *do not doubt that this one will leave you stranded if you fail to play your part well.*

When the preparations were complete, Tacticnok addressed the group. "I've been asked to request this one thing of the team, although I'll tell you that personally I won't hold you to it. Master Tiknock hopes you'll collect a venom specimen and preserve it."

The Pyreans eyed one another, doubt marking their faces.

"With all due respect, Your Highness," Jessie replied, "we'd hoped not to get that close."

"Most understandable," Tacticnok commented.

"Envoy, we've no concept of the Colony dome's position relative to its star, which means we can't advise you of your potential arrival time," Jaktook said. "We have a choice of eating and resting or going now."

Harbour glanced at the row of faces who were her team members. She could detect their anxiousness. There would be little appetite for food and none for sleep. "We go now," she said, snatching up her helmet, duffel, and a weapon off the sleeping platform.

Led by the soldiers, Pyreans, Jatouche, and the Crocian trooped out of the dorm room. Lagging behind, Tacticnok slipped her hand into Jaktook's and squeezed. With no one watching, she nuzzled her cheek against his. "Return to me, Advisor, I've need of your counsel for many annuals to come," she said softly.

Momentarily at a loss for words, Jaktook could do little more than flash his teeth. Then he hurried to catch the team.

On the Rissness deck, preparations for the team's launch were underway. Soldiers ringed platform number five, the Colony gate. A console operator stood by to cancel the defensive array.

Before the team entered the weapon's emplacement, Jaktook had a final instruction. "It's imperative that we adopt the habit of ascending and descending the platforms together. We don't want to take the chance of being separated by the Colony's ability, or any other race's ability for that matter, to signal a far platform's operation."

When everyone nodded, Jaktook said, "Ready, Your Highness."

Tacticnok signaled a commander, who ordered the soldiers on alert and the canceling of the weapons emplacement. In turn, the commander signaled Tacticnok when all was ready.

"Take your places," Jaktook said, and the team, consisting of Harbour, Jessie, Devon, Aurelia, Jaktook, Kractik, and Mangoth, surrounded the platform. "Ascend," Jaktook ordered.

The team stepped onto the platform, while Jaktook and Kractik, who were loaded with suits and gear, chose to hop with both legs. Instantly, the console operator engaged the gate and sent the team toward a meeting with the insidious Colony species.

-20-
The Colony

The platform's slash of light dimmed, and the exploration team came face-to-face with the Colony species. The daunting scene froze the explorers in place.

The Colony members were shocked too. They appeared as still life, while they regarded the interlopers. Two huge individuals, red and black, were nearly five meters long. Three meters of their length were on the deck, and two were hoisted in the air. The heads ended in large pincers and contained multifaceted eyes. With strident hisses, they broke from their reverie and raced toward the exploration team on their numerous pairs of legs.

"Fear," Harbour yelled, grabbing Aurelia's hand.

The empaths didn't need to delve into their psyches to generate the required emotion. The entities scuttling toward them provided all the motivation they needed. It was fortunate that the empaths' position on the platform kept the other team members clear of their targets. Otherwise, their team members would have been curled on the platform, mewling in despair.

When the empaths' power hit the two red and black, alien sentients, they screeched and abruptly halted. But they didn't retreat. It created a mental stalemate. The empaths pushed fear into the minds of the Colony species, and the red-blacks hissed their frustration and struggled against the emotional pressure.

The exploration team took advantage of the momentary lull in the action to examine their surroundings.

"Five platforms, and we're in the central one," Jaktook noted, which was as expected. This data had been recorded in the archives by the journeys of the first Jatouche to visit this dome before the Colony achieved space travel. He knew that one of the most important aspects of their exploration was to map the gates and their connections.

"Why are crates on that far platform?" Devon asked.

"Not good," Mangoth supplied.

A second Colony species, smaller than the two, red-black giants and entirely gray, were unmoving, as they observed the new arrivals. Several were on the platform that Devon had pointed out. Others had been moving crates from the ramp toward that platform, and two individuals hovered over the console.

Jessie realized Harbour and Aurelia were fully engrossed in holding the red-black sentients at bay. It fell to him to make the call. The smaller, gray sentients pushing the crates toward platform number one worried him.

"Kractik, we want to go through gate one," Jessie ordered. "Mangoth, protect her. Harbour and Aurelia, focus only on these two monsters. The rest of us have to clear platform one of any of the gray entities. Everybody stay out of the empaths' paths. Now go."

Kractik slung her bag over her shoulder and yipped in surprise, when Mangoth snatched her up. He wouldn't be as quick as her, but his actions assured her safety.

Mangoth's meaty backhand cleared several of the smaller Colony species out of the way, including the two at the console. During the entire time, Mangoth never set Kractik down. He merely leaned her over the console's station number one.

Despite Kractik's initial astonishment at being carried, she appreciated not having her feet on the deck among the Colony species. The gray entities, with their segmented bodies, many pairs of legs, and dark eyes, could loom high above her to say nothing of the dominant red-black pair.

Harbour and Aurelia could sense the ferocious animosity that poured off the red-blacks that they had stopped. As the anger of the huge sentients grew, the empaths felt their persuasion lose ground, and Harbour mentally urged the others to hurry.

Devon was first to gain platform one. Three of the grays attacked him. The first clamped down on his upper right arm with its pincers, trying to pierce the Pyrean's armored suit. Devon could feel the enormous pressure on his arm, and he reflexively punched the entity between its faceted eyes. The pincers opened, and the gray slithered off the platform.

Jessie caught the tail of one gray who had targeted Devon. He yanked on it and was surprised to have the creature curl on itself and attack him. The gray didn't get an opportunity to sink its pincers into Jessie, who delivered a booted kick to its head. Immediately, Jessie dragged the inert form off the platform.

The third gray had pinned Devon to the deck, and its pincers were stabbing again and again, seeking a vulnerable opening. Jaktook saw his opportunity, and he swung his bag of defensive weaponry against the entity's head. The gray was stunned long enough for Devon to free an arm and smack it hard. He felt the entity's weight slide off him and rose to see Jessie pulling it free.

"Ready," Kractik yelled.

Unfortunately, the exploration team was in a slight conundrum. Harbour and Aurelia were transfixed on the red-blacks. Mangoth was swatting attacking grays, who were trying to regain control of the console. He'd placed Kractik on his shoulders so that he had both arms free. And Jessie and Devon were defending the platform, kicking at any grays who attempted to slither aboard.

Jaktook stood on platform one's pile of crates and yelled out the grays' positions when they tried to outflank the Pyreans. Hurriedly, he unpacked one of his weapons. It was the audio generator.

Master Tiknock had argued that the upraised Colony species would still possess aspects of their early predecessors, common insects. His research had shown that certain audio frequencies debilitated insects and caused them to scurry away.

Jaktook activated the generator's compact power source, pointed it at the red-black entities, and pulled the trigger. Ear-splitting screeches issued from the two entities and they curled into tight balls.

Jessie saw the red-blacks fall, and he yelled, "Now, Kractik."

Mangoth backhanded one and then another gray. Then he swung Kractik over the console. The little Jatouche tapped the programmed icon, and Mangoth tucked her under an arm. He waddled as quickly to the platform as he could move his bulk.

Harbour and Aurelia leapt off their platform, but a gray intercepted them. The women launched kicks, which bowled the entity over. They made platform one just ahead of Mangoth and Kractik.

"Behind us," Jaktook yelled. A gray was partially on and off the platform, which activated the dome's safety features. If Kractik's countdown finished and the platform wasn't cleared, the program would have to be reset. Jaktook chose to pull his generator off the red-blacks and direct it at the gray. The entity recoiled, as if struck, and fell to the deck.

Moments later, the platform's blue light shot upwards and the exploration team was launched to an unknown destination.

* * * *

"Oh, for the love of Pyre," Devon moaned, when the light faded.

The team found themselves on gate three of a three-platform dome, and they were surrounded by a horde of grays, who were prepared to unload the crates from the Colony dome.

"Jaktook, the audio generator," Jessie yelled.

Jaktook slung the device off his shoulder, but the team stood in the firing path. Jessie chose not to utter a warning to Jaktook, as he snatched up the Jatouche and hoisted him high overhead. Jessie turned in a circle, while Jaktook directed the weapon's cone at the grays, who were attacking them from all sides.

A few judicious kicks and punches from the team kept some of them at bay until the audio frequencies of Jaktook's device struck them. Soon, the entire deck of grays was curled in tight balls on the deck. Thankfully, not a single, giant red-black was among them.

"What now?" Mangoth asked. He still carried Kractik under his arm. "Stay, go back, or go forward?" he added.

Jessie was intrigued by the Colony transporting crates to this dome. It's why he'd chosen this particular direction, while they were in the Colony's dome. The crates had signified that the gate didn't lead to an alliance member.

"We stay," Jessie said sharply. "We need to know why the Colony is moving equipment here."

"Should we hide in a dorm room?" Jaktook asked from above Jessie's head. He continued to direct the generator's output at the entities on the deck.

"We could be trapped there," Devon replied. "I don't recommend that course of action."

"After we get the answers to your questions, Advisor, do we go forward or back?" Mangoth asked again.

"Depends on the answer to the questions," Jessie retorted.

"Then let us get you answers," Mangoth replied. He set Kractik down. "Stay with the envoy," he admonished her. Then he plucked Jaktook out of Jessie's hands and set the Jatouche on his shoulders. "Spray away," he commanded Jaktook.

Mangoth stepped down from the platform and headed for the ramp. He hoped to find unpacked crates on the second level that might speak to what was being transported.

Jessie kept pace with Mangoth. Kractik was sandwiched between Harbour and Aurelia, who followed close behind Jessie. Devon walked nearly backward, keeping an eye on their rear. He was happy to see that the grays didn't instantly recover. They remained curled up in tight balls.

On the ramp, the team ran into more grays, but Jaktook's generator quickly vanquished them. What surprised the team was that no crates were found on the lower deck.

"Could they have taken them below?" Aurelia asked.

"Unlikely," Jessie remarked, and he nodded his head toward the dome's exit.

"Agreed," Mangoth said, having caught Jessie's idea.

"Are these suits prepared for vacuum?" Harbour asked, eyeing the exit door. She'd no sooner finished speaking than the interior airlock door opened. Three grays entered the corridor without protection. "It doesn't matter," Harbour remarked, as Jaktook directed his audio signal at the grays.

"Should one or more of us guard this door?" Devon asked, as Jessie and he grabbed the legs of the fallen grays and hauled them clear of the interior doorway.

"Negative," Jessie replied. "We stick together."

The team made their way through the airlock and entered a dimly lit tunnel. It was crudely fashioned of curved metal plating and had a flat deck, which gave it the appearance of a temporary structure. Traversing its length required Jaktook to clear the way of more grays.

"I'd love to know how long the effect of your generator will last," Devon commented to Jaktook, as the security officer stepped over the curled bodies of two more grays.

"That's my concern too, Devon," the Jatouche answered from his perch on Mangoth.

At the end of the hundreds-meter-long tunnel, the team ran into a formidable hatch. It was entirely unlike the tunnel.

Jessie noticed it was seamed together from many pieces, which explained how it had been transported through the gate. He'd expected an activation plate beside the hatch, but there was none visible.

"Down here," Kractik said, pointing to an indented plate set to the left of the hatch. "Different species," she quipped, flashing her teeth.

"Ready?" Jessie asked.

The explorers took up positions, and Jessie kicked the indent with his foot. The hatch slid upward, and the team walked carefully into a giant gallery. A dome stretched high overhead and was a hundred meters across. A deep cavity had been drilled in the middle of it, and manufacturing equipment ringed the dome's periphery.

The din of noise kept any of the Colony species from noticing the team until several grays turned their way to exit the dome. Before Jaktook could stun them, they let out defiant screeches. Then a multitude of grays and tens of red-blacks turned their way.

"Kractik, data record," Jaktook ordered.

The console operator hurriedly dug out her portable recorder. Jessie turned around and snatched Kractik up to place her on his shoulders, where she had a clear view of the construction.

"Too many," Jaktook ground out, as he swung his generator wildly at the onslaught of red-blacks and grays.

"Time to go, Advisor," Mangoth growled. He didn't relish being pinned to the deck by the weight of a horde of Colony sentients, while they took their time peeling off his helmet and seeking an opening to inject their venom, possibly through his eye sockets.

"Agreed," Jessie yelled.

Aurelia whirled around and located the plate for the hatch, which had closed behind them. She kicked it with her foot. Rather than wait for it to fully open, she threw her duffel and equipment load under the rising hatch and rolled under it. That was a mistake. Four grays rose up in front of her, hissing their indignation. Aurelia opened her gates and unleashed the fear that the creatures had generated in her. They halted in mid-sway, rearing back on their long frames.

Harbour's baggage struck Aurelia in the back of the legs. When she crab-walked under the rising hatch, she joined Aurelia in keeping the grays occupied. Devon quickly followed.

Jessie and Mangoth eyed each other, and Jessie tossed his head toward the hatch. "Backing up," Jessie warned Kractik. The hatch was two-thirds of the way up, when Jessie slipped Kractik off his shoulders. She scooted under and Jessie followed.

Mangoth set Jaktook down, and gently pushed the Jatouche toward the hatch. Then he bent his head and shoulders to clear the hatch.

Immediately, Devon hit the kick plate, and Jaktook kept the Colony sentients at bay, while the hatch closed. The team could hear the angry hisses of the red-blacks and grays on the other side.

Mangoth hoisted Jaktook into position and tapped the empaths on their shoulders. Harbour and Aurelia ceased their sending, and Mangoth strode forward. Jaktook was bringing his generator to bear, when Mangoth smacked the four hissing grays aside.

The team retraced their steps. Mangoth waddled quickly down the length of the tunnel, while Jaktook incapacitated their adversaries.

As the team navigated the tunnel, Jessie called out, "We go back."

"Agreed," Harbour said. "We must analyze what we've found."

The far end of the tunnel and the dome's corridor were crowded with grays. The number was so great that the team had difficulty picking their way around and over the spiraled bodies, quivering from the ultrasonic waves of the generator.

Devon carried Kractik on his shoulders. He walked at the group's rear, and the two of them searched for red-blacks and grays approaching from behind.

At the ramp, the team discovered grays had piled crates in a blockade to prevent them from returning to the platform. Mangoth set Jaktook down and bade the team stand aside. Then he grabbed crate after crate and threw them off the side of the ramp. Several popped open from the impact, and without being told, Devon kneeled so that Kractik could record their contents.

When Mangoth had created an opening in the barrier, he hoisted Jaktook up. The team made their way to the deck to discover the grays had continued to transfer crates and equipment from the Colony's dome to this one. Every platform was piled with material in such a fashion as to prevent the gates from being activated.

In addition to grays, tens of red-blacks dotted the deck. Pincers click-clacked, opening and closing, sounding the specie's defiance.

A tableau was created. The Colony entities waited for the team, which stood at the top of the ramp, to make their move. Jaktook had turned off his audio generator's power source to conserve energy. He eyed the reserve indicator.

"Envoy, Jessie, I've less than nine percent of power for my device," Jaktook announced quietly.

"How long will that last?" Jessie asked.

"Perhaps twelve or thirteen of your units at the rate I've been using it," Jaktook replied.

"Then we better make this quick," Jessie said. "Give me Jaktook," he said to Mangoth, who transferred the little Jatouche.

"I will clear platform three," Mangoth announced firmly.

"Devon, keep Kractik and stay with me," Jessie ordered. "We'll take the side of the platform facing the console. Harbour, Aurelia protect the backside of the platform."

"Kractik, ready a cube," Jaktook said, as he switched on his audio generator.

"Everybody ready?" Jessie asked. When he received nods all around, including a finger sign from Jaktook in front of his face, which he didn't recognize, he said quietly, "Now."

When the team moved, their adversaries did too. The dome's deck became a mêlée, as the red-blacks and grays desperately tried to reach the team, who strove to gain platform three.

Harbour and Aurelia ran in advance of Mangoth, freezing many entities in place. Often Mangoth would reach over the top of the empaths and smack the hissing antagonists aside.

Devon used his equipment bag and swung it like a club to keep the attackers at bay, and Jaktook did his best to debilitate the closest foes.

When Mangoth reached the platform, he grabbed the nearest crate and threw it. Jessie watched the heavy item sail over his head and crush two grays. He recalled the remonstrations to take all precautions to prevent injury to the Colony species until he suddenly remembered that they weren't in the Colony's dome. The red-blacks and grays were interlopers here just as they were.

The team could hear Mangoth's grunts as he hoisted crates and equipment off the platform. He wasn't pitching the material willy-nilly. He was creating a barrage, lifting items overhead, picking targets, and launching his weapons.

"I'm getting low, Jessie," Jaktook said in warning.

"Mangoth, clear a path to the console," Jessie yelled.

"I hear you, Advisor," Mangoth grunted, and the next crate that sailed overhead caught a red-black in the head.

"Your path to the console is clear," Mangoth roared.

A clear path was an exaggeration. Mangoth did eliminate most of the adversaries between the platform and the console, but now the path was a jumble of broken and unconscious bodies and strewn crates and equipment.

"We're going," Devon cried out.

Jessie whirled around to see that the lieutenant and the console operator had divested themselves of their equipment. It lay on the platform. Kractik clung to Devon's back. Her sharp nails were dug into the mesh armor of his suit.

Devon was running like a madman, straight across the piles of bodies and equipment without regard to what or who he stepped on. Pincers snapped at Devon's legs as he passed.

The Colony species turned their attention from the platform to prevent the console's operation.

Reaching the console, Devon planted both hands on the near edge, twisted his body, and kicked his booted feet to the side. He caught a gray in the head, who was defending the console, and knocked that one into a second gray. The maneuver opened up the console. Kractik leapt from Devon's back and hurriedly set gate three for operation.

"Done," she announced.

Devon turned his back to Kractik, and she jumped on. He'd picked up a heavy bar of metal that had broken off equipment that Mangoth had tossed, and he swung it viciously. Unlike Jessie, he'd not thought of the fact that the Colony had invaded this dome. Right now, he didn't care about the restrictions. He wanted to live, and the hissing and clicking enemy wanted him dead.

At one point, a red-black interceded, and Devon barely had time to reverse his swing and connect with the attacker's head. Despite the terrorizing moment, he wanted to laugh. With each swing and connection of his bar, he heard Kractik spit her defiance. There was nothing the diminutive Jatouche could do to physically combat the Colony species, but she was going to declare with all her strength that she didn't fear them.

Devon was close to the gate, when Kractik screamed, "Devon, jump for the platform."

Kractik's voice was so shrill that Devon obeyed out of desperation. He dropped his tool and dove. Remembering to keep his body within the boundaries of the platform, he landed on his belly, twisted to the side, and curled his legs up. A split second later, the gate activated.

The team's nerves were on edge. When the blue light faded in the Colony's dome, they regrouped and stood ready to repel the red-blacks and grays. Instead, the deck was only partially occupied.

"Most of them must be at the other dome," Aurelia marveled.

"Descend," Jaktook ordered, and the team hurriedly stepped off the platform. "Mangoth, deploy the net," he added.

Mangoth pulled the mesh from his pack, activated the net, and tossed it neatly onto the middle of platform one. It bloomed, covering the entire surface and cascading down the sides.

"Good toss," Jessie admitted.

"Kractik, hand a cube to Devon," Jaktook ordered. "Jessie, protect Kractik. Devon, place the cube on gate three. Mangoth, carry me to the ramp. Go."

Mangoth placed Jaktook on his shoulders. He detoured toward the console, swatting the few grays aside to give Jessie and Kractik access to the console. Then he hurried to the head of the ramp. More attackers were clambering up, and Jaktook used the last of his generator's power to fell them.

"The cube is sent," Kractik announced.

"Time to go," Jaktook yelled.

Mangoth didn't need any other inducement. He turned and lumbered for the third platform. Kractik tapped the activation panel, and she scampered for the platform, leaving Jessie to hurry after her.

"Would they have time to receive your message, Jaktook?" Harbour belatedly asked, just before the gate activated.

The Rissness dome soldiers spotted the cube an instant before the automated weaponry vaporized it. An officer called over his comm to deactivate the defensive emplacement, and in the next instant the team appeared.

"Descend," Jaktook ordered. "Clear the gate area."

The moment the team slipped between the emplacement walls, the officer reactivated the weaponry.

"I thought we were going to deploy the mesh, Advisor Jaktook," the officer queried.

"Already used it," Mangoth said.

The officer regarded Jaktook sitting comfortably atop Mangoth's shoulders. The odd arrangement caused the dome's visitors to stop and stare in surprise. It was unthinkable that a Crocian would demean his status by carrying a Jatouche above him. And a Jatouche ordering other races was no less a foreign concept.

The officer and dome visitors took in the explorers' armored mesh suits, which showed nicks, dents, and tears. Even stranger were the body fluids that marked the suits of many of them. But most arresting were the harrowed faces of the team.

"Where is Her Highness?" Jaktook asked.

"She is with our guests on level three," the officer replied.

"Take us there," Jaktook ordered.

Mangoth lifted the Jatouche off his shoulders and set him on the deck, and Jaktook quipped, "And I was just getting used to riding."

"No, you were enjoying the lofty view that belongs to Crocians," Mangoth riposted. The deep rumbling that accompanied his retort was a sound that the Pyreans hadn't heard before, but the gleam in Mangoth's eyes cued them that it was his manner of laughing.

The team joined the flow of alliance members down the ramp. Their appearance drew stares until they were able to descend to the third level.

The officer tapped a glyph and opened a door. Then he stood aside.

Henry was the first to spot the team, and he remarked, "That was quick. A dead end?" His next words died on his lips, when he took in the expressions on the teams' faces, and he softly exhaled, "Oh, for the love of Pyre."

"Your Highness," Jaktook said, "we've encountered unusual circumstances. We've collected data, which we need to analyze. Afterwards, we'll require the advice of your father and his masters."

"I'll have the shuttle readied for Na-Tikkook," Tacticnok announced, but she didn't move. She was busy taking in the state of the explorers. They had been gone but for a short while, yet they appeared disheveled, fight worn, and, most of all, harried.

"Which is closer, Rissness Station or Na-Tikkook?" Harbour asked.

"By far, Rissness Station," Jaktook replied.

While Harbour ordered her thoughts, Jessie asked, "Mangoth, will you stay with the team?"

"These events have surpassed my simple reasons for joining the team, Advisor. This has become a grave alliance matter," Mangoth replied. "I will stay."

"Good," Jessie replied. "We need you."

"What, Advisor, no strike on my shoulder in approval?" Mangoth jested.

"I would have, Mangoth, but you're wearing a bit of Colony sentient there," Jessie riposted.

Tacticnok, Henry, Dottie, and Idrian watched Mangoth pick off a bit of shell with flesh attached to its underside. The former two individuals blanched. Dottie gagged, covered her mouth, and ran for the facilities, and Idrian turned a shade of green. As Mangoth passed him to deposit the piece of tissue in the recycler, he quipped to Idrian, "A becoming color, Delegate."

"What's the status of the Pyreans at Rissness Station?" Harbour asked Tacticnok.

"As of my latest report, which is a few cycles old, all but two of the twenty were repaired," Tacticnok replied. "I didn't inquire as to the time frame for those individuals. Should I?"

"Please," Harbour said.

"I need to clean up," Devon announced.

"Agreed," Kractik added. The two of them were covered with body fluids, and the scent was overpowering.

"And I'm starved," Jessie added, to which Mangoth grunted in affirmation.

"And I'm dizzy," Aurelia said.

Harbour caught Aurelia's arm and lowered her to the pallet that Dottie had vacated. "Tacticnok, we need my crate with the ingredients for greens. Aurelia and I are depleted. Everyone needs access to their own facilities. Then we need to eat and talk."

Harbour's orders were rapid fire, and they galvanized the royal daughter. She called the officer on duty, relaying the requests. Soldiers led the team members, except for the empaths to other rooms. They stood by to take the suits and equipment for cleaning. Several soldiers recoiled at the mess that coated many items.

Kractik carefully removed her recorder and kept it with her. It was too precious to let it out of her sight.

Soldiers opened and laid out the items Harbour requested to make greens. She hurriedly set up the Jatouche blender with its power source, rapidly added the ingredients, and mixed a large batch. She poured two cups for Aurelia and her. They were small, and Aurelia finished hers before Harbour had taken much more than a mouthful.

"Here," Harbour said, exchanging cups with the young empath. She poured two more, handed Aurelia a third, and downed hers. It took several more rations for Harbour to feel her headache fade and for Aurelia's color to return.

"Facilities," Harbour ordered Aurelia. She was pleased to see the young woman rise under her own power. Nonetheless, she kept a close eye on her.

Aurelia made for the room's exit, but Harbour steered her toward their room's facilities. She pounded on the door, calling out, "Dottie, vacate the premises."

The door slid open. Dottie stood in the entrance, her face wan and pale.

"The soldiers will find an alternate room for you to lie down and rest," Harbour remarked, and Dottie pushed past her.

Harbour glanced toward Tacticnok, who issued the necessary orders.

In the facilities, Harbour helped Aurelia strip out of her suit. While Aurelia stepped into the mister cabinet for a wash, Harbour rid herself of her suit.

"If a pale, hairless alien makes you gag, hide your eyes," Harbour yelled out to Tacticnok. Her remark elicited a giggle from Aurelia. Harbour triggered the facilities' door, dumped the suits outside, and slid the door quickly behind her, but not before catching Tacticnok's bared teeth.

We'll all need our sense of humor before this is over, Harbour thought.

"There's room for two," Aurelia said from the cabinet.

Gratefully, Harbour joined her. She couldn't wait to rinse off the stink of sweat, fear, and fluids. The latter had splashed her face, when she mistakenly opened her helmet's visor. She had mentally created a list of changes for the Jatouche engineers and surmised that her list was probably half that of Jessie's.

While Harbour and Aurelia were enjoying the mister, Tacticnok piled clean skins and deck shoes inside the facilities. Having stopped to absorb greens, the empaths were the last to join the team in a larger dorm room.

Kractik cradled her recorder in one hand, while she greedily spooned paste with another. "Who knew near-death experiences could make you so hungry?" she commented.

Devon managed a brief mumble around a mouthful of paste but hoisted a utensil in agreement.

Mangoth had four portions of the paste in front of him. A wide, flat tongue issued from his mouth, and with one motion he swiped the plate clean. As fast as he consumed them, Tacticnok placed others in front of him. She paused in serving him to bring two plates for Harbour and Aurelia.

When everyone was satiated, Tacticnok cleared the table.

"Your attention to our needs, Your Highness, is appreciated," Mangoth said.

"It's nothing of the sort, Mangoth. This team looked like they would take forever to get food. I merely hastened the point at which I could hear the story," Tacticnok replied.

Mangoth started to roar, but a huge belch escaped him. After a second, smaller burp caused those around him to chuckle, he added a rumble of pleasure to the mix.

Harbour glanced around. Henry and Idrian had joined them, but Dottie was nowhere in sight. She assumed the woman wasn't coming.

"This is the entire team's story, but I'll start it," Harbour remarked. "The rest of you should jump in to fill out what I'm missing."

Tacticnok was fascinated and distressed by the tale that unfolded. There were many facets of the story that were difficult to process. At one point, she asked for clarification, "You're saying that you ... you ... eliminated the sentients, not merely knocked them down."

"I think the word you're looking for is killed, Your Highness," Devon said.

"Your concern is understandable, Your Highness," Mangoth added. "I'm a witness to these events. None of our adversaries were eliminated within the Colony dome, during both passages. It was at the second dome where we fought to defend our lives against the invading Colony."

"Were many eliminated?" Tacticnok asked.

"As many as it took to get clear of that dome and by any means at hand," Jessie stated. "Personally, I haven't been so proud of a team since my crew accidentally activated the Triton dome, trapping us."

"And without the efforts of Pyreans, Jatouche, and the assets of a Crocian, we wouldn't be alive to bring back this incredible discovery," Jaktook opined.

The team continued telling their story until they'd exhausted the facts and themselves. As the tale wound down, eyelids began to droop.

"Rest," Tacticnok said, "I'll make arrangements for the shuttle to Rissness Station."

Harbour nodded in approval, as she collapsed on a pallet. Except for Henry and Idrian, who exited the room with Tacticnok, the others quickly imitated Harbour.

"You better not snore," Jessie challenged Mangoth, who had the pallet next to him.

In reply, Mangoth lifted his snout and displayed his plugged nostrils to Jessie. But, as Jessie later, much later, discovered, a Crocian doesn't snore but rumbles. But this time, Jessie was too tired to be disturbed by anything, as he quickly fell into a deep slumber.

* * * *

It became Tacticnok's responsibility to wake the weary team members. The shuttle was ready, and it couldn't occupy one of the Rissness transport slots forever. There was a constant demand for the four tubes and often the shuttles carried exalted members of the alliance.

Tacticnok's concerns about the explorers' reaction to being disturbed were unwarranted. The eyes of the Pyrean empaths and the Crocian popped open before she could creep across the room. Their reactions underlined her citizens' insularity. The Jatouche knew a great deal about the medical aspects of every alliance race, but they knew little about their intimate behavioral and social mannerisms.

"Everyone, up," Harbour ordered crisply into the stillness, and instantly the others struggled awake.

"We must board the shuttle soon, Envoy," Tacticnok said. "I let you rest as long as I could."

Jessie was about to ask about their gear, when soldiers entered the room and began packing their equipment. It didn't take long before a troop of soldiers stood in the corridor with the team's suits, equipment, and duffels.

Forgoing the morning's amenities, Tacticnok led the way, with Jaktook beside her. They picked up the other three delegates at the end of the corridor and ascended the ramp to the second level and the dome's exit.

"Your Highness, I must send a message," Mangoth said. His tone was polite but firm.

Tacticnok gazed at Mangoth and checked her chronometer. There remained a small window of time. "Kractik, assist Mangoth to send a cube and procure an officer to expedite your travel to the shuttle."

"Yes, Your Highness," Kractik replied. She glanced at Mangoth and then hurried for the ramp to the deck.

At the console, Kractik used the controls for gate five. She set up a cube and cued Mangoth when she was ready. Kractik expected Mangoth to update family, friends, or the Logar clan head. Instead, he addressed his message to the Norloth, the supreme Crocian body. He delivered a terse summary of the Pyrean–Jatouche arrangement, the exploration team, and its exploits through the Colony dome to an unknown location.

When Mangoth finished, he said, "It's a priority message, Kractik."

Mangoth's request required Kractik to add a code to the cube. On arrival at each platform, the cube would flash continuously, requiring console operators to immediately recover the cube, read the priority destination, and send it on its way.

"Ready, Mangoth?" Kractik asked. She'd handed the cube off to an assistant operator to deploy. Mangoth assented, and Kractik hurried for the ramp. An officer met her and the threesome used the soldier's access level to speed through the tunnels.

The team's transport was the premier shuttle reserved for Tacticnok's use. The humans settled into the recently installed seats, which had been exclusively crafted for them.

Mangoth spotted an expansive seat with a cutout for his tail. He rumbled softly as he inserted his thick tail into the seat's slot and sunk into the generous padding.

"Your generosity toward my magnificent bulk is appreciated, Your Highness," Mangoth said.

"Your efforts on our behalf are appreciated Mangoth of the Logar, and we like to demonstrate our appreciation," Tacticnok replied, flashing her teeth. "Were the arrangements for your message satisfactory?" she asked.

"It was a priority to the Crocian Norloth," Mangoth replied.

Tacticnok was taken aback. Her question was meant to be polite conversation.

"There are priority cubes?" Jessie asked, from the seat across the aisle from Mangoth.

"There are many classification codes for cubes," Tacticnok replied.

Jessie and Harbour stored that little gem of information for later.

"A priority message, you say," Tacticnok queried.

"Yes, Your Highness, a message to the Crocian Norloth," Mangoth said. "After reviewing my report, I would expect the Norloth to contact the Tsargit."

"Who are these individuals or organizations?" Harbour asked. She was seated next to Jessie.

"The Norloth leads the Crocians. It comprises the leader of each clan," Mangoth replied, "and the Tsargit governs the alliance."

"Oh," Harbour muttered quietly. She exchanged glances with Jessie. What seemed to have started out as a simple exploratory mission for them was escalating out of control, and the question was: What role would the Pyreans play in the future?

Soon after launch, the team was asleep again.

Dottie regarded the explorers and whispered quietly to Henry, "They're sleeping so hard, but they weren't gone that long."

"The challenge was extraordinarily physical, and it was also mentally exhausting," Henry replied. "Emergencies aboard a mining ship produce the same results. Brief periods of overwhelming anxiety and adrenaline followed by a desperate need to sleep and regain equilibrium."

-22-
Messages

After landing aboard Rissness Station, Harbour notified the Pyreans, who had finished their rejuvenation. They were relaxing in a dorm room, while they waited for the final two to complete their repairs. Her message was that Captain Cinders and she had arrived aboard the station and would speak to them later.

Tacticnok commandeered a data center and instructed the operator to display the images that Kractik had captured.

After the poor operator experienced a few moments of the Colony species rushing toward the team, she was too overwrought to exercise precise control of her fingers.

"Kractik, please relieve our operator," Jaktook requested, and as soon as the support individual was replaced, she hurried from the data center.

The team carefully examined every scene. The Pyreans were shocked at the detail that was available, even when Kractik enlarged the images multiple times.

"I reach only one conclusion," Jessie said, when the review of the newly constructed external dome was completed.

"It's the same for me," Jaktook added.

"A shuttle," Mangoth concluded, and Jaktook and Jessie agreed.

"The Colony must have been working on this project for a long time," Henry said. "Think of the effort that was expended to move everything in small crates from their home planet to their satellite and then to this second dome."

"The better question to ask ourselves is why?" Harbour posed.

"The Colony has to have discovered something valuable about the planet," Dottie suggested.

"If the planet has sentients, more than likely they haven't achieved spaceflight," Jessie said. "That would mean the Colony thinks they can overrun them."

"Expansion for what purpose?" Idrian asked. "It's difficult to move goods through the gates. I think that's a concept the Messinants incorporated into their grand plan."

"What if the Colony has consumed their planet?" Aurelia suggested.

"That's a distinct possibility," Henry acknowledged, "especially if they exhausted resources by overpopulation or there was some environmental catastrophe."

"Kractik, display the imagery of the crates that broke open," Jaktook requested.

"You had time to stop and open crates?" Dottie asked. She'd been horrified by the images of the nightmarish creatures, most certainly the red-black ones.

"It wasn't necessary," Jaktook remarked, flashing his teeth at Mangoth.

"Quite unnecessary," Mangoth remarked, with a rumble.

While Kractik loaded the next recordings, Henry said, "I wonder how far the Colony has gotten? We see the dome and the shuttle tube but nothing of the shuttle."

"Ready," Kractik announced.

Jaktook nodded, and Kractik ran through the scenes of the crates' interiors.

Jessie and Henry, the most experienced of the Pyrean spacers, looked at Mangoth and Jaktook for explanations. The pieces of shiny metal that were exposed meant nothing to them.

"Engine components," Mangoth concluded.

"Or generators," Jaktook added.

"That would suggest there's a shuttle's aft end framework in that tube," Jessie hypothesized.

"That's a fair conclusion, Advisor," Mangoth said.

After the viewing finished, the group was escorted to a dorm room, with extensive conference space. They took a few moments to eat and use the facilities.

Seated around a large table, Aurelia said, "I was just thinking. I know the Colony species look and act ferocious, but they're sentients, right?"

"Undoubtedly," Mangoth agreed.

"We used our empaths' power and a sonic weapon on them," Aurelia continued, "and I was wondering what we'd do if the roles were reversed."

Mangoth harrumphed and said, "The young one reminds us that we've not given due consideration to our adversaries."

"And here I'd been planning to make the audio generator my first defensive tool," Jaktook lamented.

"It might still be useful," Jessie commiserated. "Keep it handy."

"Think about what Aurelia is saying," Devon pursued. "Aboard the station, we found criminals often employed one of two options in response to new security procedures we implemented. They either demonstrably negated them or created a surreptitious means of circumventing them ... aggressive and passive, offense and defense."

"Hmm," Jessie mused, "meaning, in this case, we could have an audio generator tested on us or they might be wearing hearing protective gear. I did see membranes, of a sort, on the sides of their heads.

"Based on our experience with these sentients, I would suggest the Colony will choose the more aggressive response," Mangoth said. "Our suits should be prepared for a sonic attack."

"Our suits?" Jessie queried, offering Mangoth a wry grin.

"I might have been hasty believing that my natural gifts were all the protection I needed against the Colony," Mangoth replied to Jessie. "In which case, Advisor Jaktook, I'm requesting a suit for myself. However, I've suggestions for my version, which my teammates might wish to hear."

"Each of us probably has thoughts for version two," Devon said, getting a round of verbal agreement from everyone.

Jessie regarded Harbour, who appeared lost in thought. He tapped her knee under the table to draw her attention.

"Hmm," Harbour murmured, "sorry ... this feels all wrong." Suddenly, she understood what was bothering her and became galvanized. "Kractik, contact Rissness. I want to know the status of gate five."

Kractik leapt from the table and placed a call to Rissness Station control. She requested the information in Tacticnok's name.

"Okay, what are we missing?" Jessie asked Harbour.

"Think back to the plumerase attack at the YIPS," Harbour explained. "We were caught off guard because we couldn't perceive of our adversaries being that devious and that insidious. I think we're making the same mistake here."

The comm console buzzed and Kractik answered. "Envoy, gate five is offline," she announced," and there is a priority cube for Delegate Mangoth of the Logar."

Everyone skipped over Kractik's first statement and focused on the second.

"When did you become a delegate?" Jessie asked, as Mangoth rose from the table to hear the message.

"Apparently recently, Advisor," Mangoth replied.

Kractik handed Mangoth a headset, and the group heard him request the cube's message be relayed via an officer.

"Did you expect the gate would be offline?" Devon asked Harbour.

"I thought it was likely," Harbour replied. "What Aurelia said made a great deal of sense to me. I think the Colony is ambitious, and we're not giving them enough credit. I don't have any idea about their intentions, except to build a shuttle, as you surmise. What I do believe is that they'll work harder to prevent another incursion by us, and I think they'll hasten their efforts in the unknown secondary dome."

Mangoth replaced the headset. He faced the group, and, despite his alien features, the Pyreans thought he didn't look any too happy.

"I've been delegated to the Tsargit," Mangoth said.

"Can they do that without asking your permission?" Henry asked.

"The Tsargit never asks," Mangoth replied. "However, there is a potentially bright outlook. If I survive this duty, I will have my pick of a mate." Mangoth had attempted a cheery note, but his demeanor was one of an individual who had received a death sentence.

"What have they requested you do?" Harbour asked.

"The Tsargit believes the issue warrants further investigation and requests more detailed information," Mangoth replied. "I'm to assist your efforts, Envoy, to determine the Colony's intentions."

Jaktook snorted. "Typical Tsargit response," he said. "Study the issue to death until the events have passed and a decision is moot."

"There is opportunity for you, Envoy, and your citizens," Mangoth said. "The Tsargit offers the exploration team remuneration for their efforts."

"Define remuneration?" Jessie requested.

"It would be whatever you request, within reason," Mangoth supplied. "We should be thankful the Tsargit didn't decry our use of deadly force at the unknown dome."

"And if they had?" Henry asked.

"They would have ordered the Jatouche to end their relationship with humans," Mangoth replied.

Harbour glanced toward Tacticnok and Jaktook. They wore disgusted expressions. Obviously, they believed the Tsargit's dominance over the alliance members was too invasive.

"I'm not sure I care for the Tsargit," Harbour said quietly. "What if we, the Pyreans, chose not to further our exploration?"

Mangoth's jaw dropped open as if the concept was too incredulous to conceive. Then he bellowed to the overhead. The idea of sentients ignoring the Tsargit delighted him.

* * * *

Harbour wanted time to think. The team had valuable ideas about new suits, equipment, and second-generation weapons with which to take on the Colony. However, the broader question was: What direction should she take as envoy?

It seemed an appropriate time to visit the Pyreans who had undergone repair, and a guide led Harbour and Jessie to visit them. Meanwhile, Tacticnok sent a lengthy message to her father, updating him on events.

At the Pyreans' room, the door slid aside, and Harbour and Jessie stepped across the threshold.

Olivia Harden glanced up and a cry of, "Envoy Harbour," escaped her lips. She hurried to get a hug from Harbour, who had thrown open her arms. After a warm embrace, Harbour held Olivia at arm's length and carefully examined her face.

"Careful, Envoy," Bryan Forshaw said. "She's still embarrassed by her fresh looks."

"Bryan," Harbour said, enthusiastically greeting him. "And where's handsome Pete?" she asked.

"Here, Envoy," Pete said, winding through the group from the rear of the room.

"Looking pretty, Pete," Harbour teased, noticing the lack of scarring on his face, neck, and hands.

The eighteen Pyreans, who had recently been repaired, were anxious to greet Harbour and Jessie. When it was a young woman's turn, she rushed forward and embraced Harbour. "Thank you," she said, over and over. "I'm Tracy," the young woman said, stepping back. "This is my brother, Dillon," she added, gesturing toward a young man near her age.

Each of the eighteen ecstatically displayed their new limbs and chatted about the complete recoveries from their injuries. The gratitude that poured off every man and woman in the room threatened to overwhelm Harbour. In response, she tightened her gates.

"I understand Captain Flannigan's first mate, Nelson Barber, is here," Jessie said.

"Nelson's one of the two still undergoing repair," Tracy said. "Medical services spent some time stabilizing him before they could deal with his injuries."

"So, all twenty of you are safe?" Harbour asked.

"We're all safe, Captain," Dillon replied, "thanks to your efforts and those of the Jatouche."

"You're welcome," Harbour said. She opened her gates and sent a wave of contentment flooding through the room.

Tracy's smile was in full bloom from Harbour's power, when she asked, "Did you come to Rissness Station to visit us?"

Harbour regarded Jessie, and he signed, "It's your choice."

"Sit," Harbour invited the eighteen and the three engineers, "and we'll tell you what's been happening."

Harbour chose to share in detail their consultations at Na-Tikkook, and Jessie wondered about her strategy. It became apparent when Harbour spoke about the domes and the Colony. The spacers and the engineers began speaking all at once, talking over one another. Harbour laughed at their enthusiasm. Then she quieted them and entertained their questions, one by one.

The questions intrigued Jessie. These individuals were adept at solving problems. Their lives often depended on their ability to tackle obstacles and solve them swiftly and efficiently. Now, Harbour had laid the greatest challenge in their laps that they'd ever heard, and they were eager to pit their wits against it.

"If we presume that these Colonists —" an older spacer said at one point, addressing Harbour.

"Colony," Jessie corrected. "The collection of species is known as the Colony."

"Thank you, Captain," the spacer said. "It sounds as if the Colony is a devious lot, and from what you're telling us, the forward hatch, the direct route, has been closed to you. Are there any more hatches on this ship of yours, Captain?"

Jessie interrupted. "Some more corrections. In the presence of the Jatouche or other alliance members, I'm Advisor Cinders, and this," he added, indicating Harbour, "is the Pyrean Envoy."

"I'm confused. Do we salute, tip a cap, or bow?" a female spacer asked, which tickled the group.

"You'll see the alliance members tip their heads to Envoy Harbour," Jessie explained. "Me, they just pass by."

The group chuckled appreciably at Jessie's humor. He understood that these men and women liked their routines. They depended on them. The change in titles combined with the unusual nature of the alliance members had an unsettling effect on them.

"Back to what you were saying about another hatch," Harbour interrupted. "We know that the Colony dome has five gates. As you've heard, one gate connects to Rissness. According to Jaktook, two of the five gates connect to alliance members who've built defenses against the Colony's incursions. We've journeyed through one of the two unidentified gates. The destination of the other one is unknown to us ... to any alliance race for that matter."

"That leads me to my next two questions," the older spacer said. "Is it possible to reach the Colony dome via the two gates that connect to the other alliance members? Next, if it's possible, do you think the Colony would have negated their access?"

"We'd have to ask Her Highness Tacticnok about permission," Harbour replied. "From what I understand, alliance members travel freely through the gates. However, we aren't alliance members."

"You said that Mangoth has been requested to support you," Bryan said.

"Yes, the Tsargit has drafted him as a delegate," Harbour replied. "By the way, he remembers you three fondly," she added, pointing to the engineers."

"Don't know why," Pete remarked. "We spent most of the time insulting him."

"I think he enjoyed your challenge," Harbour said.

"What are you intending to do, Envoy?" Bryan asked.

"Good question, Bryan," Harbour replied.

-23-
Decisions

When Harbour and Jessie left the dorm room of the repaired Pyreans and engineers, she requested a private space from their guide. The medical tech took them to a small room. It was well appointed and had a view of the stars.

The guide touched a key pad on a chair, and its structure and cushions underwent a series of shape changes. She manipulated the other chair in the same manner.

"We haven't programmed this room for humans, Envoy," the guide apologized. "This format is the closest approximation for your structure."

Harbour smiled at the Jatouche and said, "They'll do fine. How do I get in touch with you when we're finished?"

"That will be unnecessary, Envoy. I'll be waiting outside for you and will take you wherever you wish to go on station," the Jatouche replied.

The door closed behind the guide, and Harbour sank into the comfortable chair with a sigh.

Jessie gazed out the one-meter diameter, round viewport. "I work among the stars, but I never get tired of looking at them," he said in wonder. "So, Envoy Harbour, why are we in this intimate little setting?"

"Take a seat, Advisor Cinders," Harbour replied, with a tired smile. "I have need of your counsel."

Harbour waited until Jessie settled into the other chair. Then she said, "I've never had to make life-and-death decisions like this."

"Didn't you make one when you decided to accept Rictook's offer to investigate the Colony dome?" Jessie asked.

"Hmm ... I suppose I did," Harbour murmured. "It didn't seem like one, at the time."

"That's understandable," Jessie replied gently. "We see this many times on our ships. Newbies hear the warnings, and most of them survive their first emergencies. Occasionally, they don't. But for those who do make it through, suddenly, all the warnings, the dos and don'ts, become real."

"You're saying that even if you'd warned me of the potential danger, I wouldn't have heard you," Harbour accused. The words sounded harsher to her ears than she intended.

Jessie rose abruptly and walked back to the viewport. Staring at the stars, as a shuttle cut across the scene, he said, "I've dedicated my entire spacer life to taking care of my captain, then my ship, and then my company. I've been successful in my endeavors, but I've led an isolated life. When Aurelia hid on my ship, everything changed for me."

Harbour wasn't sure how Jessie's confession related to their discussion, but this didn't seem the time to ask.

"Since you and I've become involved, I see the future differently and that goes for my role in it," Jessie continued. "Right now, I'm thinking of Pyre ... of our small group of humans, who've been hanging on to a hot piece of rock for nearly three hundred years. We deserve something better."

"My problem is that I'm the newbie who's survived her first life-threatening encounter," Harbour said. "I see death no matter which way I decide to go. If our exploration continues, it will be sooner but for only a few of us. If I decide to go home, the deaths will come slowly, but surely, and be more numerous. Pyreans will die unnecessarily without the support from the Jatouche, which we might have had."

Jessie turned around and leaned against the viewport. He wore a grin. "In each stage of my life, I thought the job I had, at the time, was the toughest one. It didn't matter whether it was as a newbie, an officer, a captain, or a company owner. Right now, I'm tickled that I'm the lowly advisor and not the envoy."

Harbour wanted to be angry at Jessie, but she couldn't. Instead, she laughed. In that moment of release, her gates slipped open, and she inundated Jessie with her affection for him.

"Well, Advisor, do your job," Harbour challenged, a broad smile on her face. "Tell me what you think."

"I say we've got an opportunity to do more for Pyre than anyone in our history, and I say we take it," Jessie replied. The wry grin faded, and his expression turned grave. Moments later, his face softened, and he momentarily ducked his head before he looked Harbour in the eye and said, "Yes, I'm voting for continuing our exploration. But, personally, I'm choosing to go wherever you go. The things you do give my life meaning."

Harbour stared at Jessie, tears forming in her eyes. She blinked them back, stood, and crossed to face him. She studied his face. Then she leaned in, placed a gentle kiss on his lips, and in a husky voice said, "Come with me, Advisor. I've an idea."

* * * *

In the corridor, Harbour said to the guide, "I need a room that can accommodate about thirty-five individuals for a conference. It should comfortably seat Jatouche, a Crocian, and Pyreans."

"That can be arranged, Envoy," the guide replied.

"It must be able to display recorder material that a console operator captured," Harbour added. "Then I need you to request Her Highness bring the explorer and delegate group to that room. In addition, I need the Pyreans from the dorm room we visited."

"If you'll wait in this room, Envoy, I'll make the arrangements," the guide offered.

"Thinking thirty or more heads are better than two?" Jessie asked, when they returned to the small room.

"Another lesson from Dingles," Harbour replied. "I can hear him saying now, 'You don't have to think of everything, Captain, just ask us what you want. We'll figure it out.'"

"Captain Mitch 'Dingles' Bassiter," Jessie said, shaking his head in disbelief. "I never thought to hear that title applied to Dingles, when I had to put him on station. Have you ever had a bad rescue?"

Harbour thought through all the individuals who she'd accepted from security incarceration. "None that stayed with us aboard the *Belle*," she said. "A good percentage returned to the JOS. I didn't keep track of them after they left. So, I don't know what happened to them."

"Makes sense," Jessie said. "I've never seen my people more contented since you and I hooked up."

"Yes, I still consider you my best rescue," Harbour replied. She gave Jessie a wink. It seemed to halt the retort that was on his lips.

They sat quietly with their thoughts after that exchange until a soft tap at the door. The Jatouche guide opened it and said, "All preparations are complete, Envoy."

"Time to be adventurous, Envoy," Jessie whispered to Harbour.

They were led to a room that functioned as a medical conference center. The chairs were similar to those in the small room, and medical techs stood by to program them for individuals.

Tacticnok, Jaktook, Kractik, and Mangoth, followed by Harbour's delegates, were the first to arrive. The Jatouche and the Crocian adjusted their chairs at the middle of the three-quarter circle. Techs adjusted the chairs for the Pyreans.

The group directed expectant expressions at Harbour, but she stared quietly at the room's entrance. A few minutes later, the repaired Pyreans and the engineers filed into the room.

Mangoth let loose a roar, and the engineers yelled in a chorus, "Mangoth." The Crocian hurriedly left his seat to greet the threesome.

Harbour directed the Pyreans to take places around the circle, and Mangoth and the engineers soon joined them.

"It's my intention to explore the viability of furnishing the Tsargit with the information they've requested Delegate Mangoth obtain, and I want this group to help me with that," Harbour said. "But to make sure that we're working from the same information, I want to have the newcomers see what we're up against."

When Dottie realized what Harbour intended to show the group, she said, "You'll excuse me, Envoy."

Harbour nodded her understanding and noted that Idrian accompanied Dottie from the room.

"Kractik, if you would?" Harbour requested.

The Jatouche console operator used the medical display equipment to run her recorder's program. She played the scenes taken in the dome and of the broken, open crates, and Harbour verbally annotated what they were witnessing.

"Biggest bugs I've ever seen," a spacer murmured, when the viewing ended.

"You'll notice that these sentients, who you refer to as bugs, are the ones transporting, piece by piece, the material to construct an external tunnel, a dome, a shuttle silo, and, apparently, a shuttle," Henry stated sternly.

The spacer tipped his head, accepting the reprimand.

"Their bites are poisonous, right?" a spacer asked.

"Deadly," Jaktook replied. "During the Colony's first incursion into the Rissness dome, none of the alliance members who were bitten survived."

Harbour quickly shifted the subject. "You've seen our adversaries. They're ferocious, deadly, and clever. However, we're a pretty smart group too."

The Pyreans cheered Harbour's statement, which surprised the Jatouche, and Mangoth's deep chortle joined the cheering.

"Envoy," Tacticnok said after the noise died down. "It might be instructive to speak to why you're interested in exploring this opportunity."

Harbour acknowledged the point. "Her Highness reminds me that there is more at work here that you should know."

Harbour proceeded to lay out the offers to Pyre and, specifically, the explorers from the Jatouche ruler, Rictook, and the Tsargit. When she finished, there was absolute quiet from the Pyreans. They eyed one another. More intravertors, more repaired injured, and more technical support sounded too good to be true.

"Envoy Harbour," Bryan said, raising his hand. "Is there the possibility of some of us joining the exploration?"

Harbour smiled broadly. "I certainly think so, Bryan, but first I want to discuss the strategy. I'm not willing to commit us to this investigation, if we don't think there's any chance of us succeeding."

"Your Highness, Jaktook, and Mangoth, this question is for you," Harbour said. "We know Rissness gate five, which leads to the Colony's dome, is offline. Our newcomers are aware that two of the Colony's gates connect to other alliance members. Is there a manner of testing the other alliance members' gates, which connect to the Colony's dome, without alerting the Colony members?"

To Harbour's surprise, the three individuals regarded one another and then turned to Kractik.

The console operator's eyes unfocused, while she reviewed everything she'd learned about the Messinants console. What frightened Kractik was that it appeared that the Colony had become more adept at console manipulation than the alliance members.

Finally, Kractik said, "There are several means by which we can test the links between the alliance and the Colony gates, but I believe that every manner of contact will be detected."

"Then, if we wish to attempt another journey to the dome, which has the external construction, we must attempt the passage only once," Jaktook announced, "and we must be ready for every eventuality."

"The corollary to that pronouncement," Mangoth said, "is that there'll be no going back the way we came. Once the Colony realizes what we've done, they'll block every gate until they defeat us."

"Envoy, doesn't that make it likely that we'd be trapped in this unknown dome after we got there?" Dillon asked.

Tracy's fingers tightened under the table. She'd asked her brother to remain quiet during the discussion. His habit was to challenge everything from a negative point of view. But, in this case, he actually had a good question.

"The alliance has studied the domes for several millennia," Jaktook explained. "At the present time, member-to-member connections represent only about two-thirds of the entire gates possessed by the alliance."

"I don't get it," Pete said. "Wouldn't the gates always be built in entangled pairs? That would mean they all lead somewhere."

"This is politics, not science, Pete," Jessie said. "Alliance members wait for a new race on the other end of a gate to become versed in the Messinants console before contacting them."

When Pete frowned, Harbour intercepted his question. "Yes, Pete, we were an exception, thanks to Her Highness." She swung a hand toward Jaktook to indicate he should continue.

"The alliance has no way of knowing the number of domes that extend beyond the third of member gates that haven't established links," Jaktook said. "We knew the Colony dome had five gates, and we've just discovered one of those gates leads to a dome with three gates. You can ask yourself how many domes and gates are yet to be identified."

"Jaktook, you're saying that a member race might visit a dome," Tracy posited, "and find no one home. And, if they discovered the dome had other gates, they wouldn't explore those connections?"

"There isn't much reason," Tacticnok interjected. "The Messinants chose to locate the gates offsite from a planet. For trade to take place, each race must be able to travel from their planet to their dome."

"Except, in this case, the Colony isn't waiting for those circumstances to occur, Your Highness," Mangoth pointed out.

"Did you finish your point, Jaktook?" Harbour asked.

"Thank you, no, Envoy," Jaktook replied. "It's this: We suspect there are many unidentified domes and gates. I believe that we will find a means of reaching a member race by exploring one or the other of the two gates at the unknown dome. It will only be a matter of time."

"How much time?" Dillon asked.

"I'd think it would be a matter of numbers," Jessie said. "The more people who explore the gates, the sooner a connection might be found."

"Not what I'd call a specific answer," Dillon mumbled.

"You'll have to excuse my brother," Tracy said in exasperation. "He doesn't realize that the exploration party is about volunteers, and with his attitude, there isn't much chance of him being invited."

Dillon glared at his sister, and the laughter circling the table only added to his pique.

"Speaking of which," Harbour said, "this is about volunteers. I seriously suggest that those of you with dependents return to Pyre."

"Is the original team going to make another try?" Olivia asked. She looked at each explorer, who either nodded or stared quietly back at her. "Hmm," she said. Then, looking around at her fellow engineers and the eighteen, she added, "They've faced the Colony, and they're going back."

"Let's discuss the specifics of what we'll encounter," Devon said. "Jaktook, how many levels can be accessed in a dome?"

"To my knowledge, only the deck and two levels below have been accessed," Jaktook replied.

"Why did you qualify it?" Jessie asked.

"The Colony has already exhibited an understanding of the consoles that exceeds our knowledge," Kractik interjected. "It's possible that they've discovered the means to penetrate below a dome's third level."

"Earlier, Jaktook made a good point about the passage through the Colony dome," Devon continued. "The complication is that we've got to take enough individuals to secure the construction dome, and that means multiple transfers through the Colony's dome."

"True, Devon," Kractik said. "It would require defending the console, while I made as many transfers as we had explorers and equipment."

"And those arriving first in the construction dome would have to defend that platform while the reinforcements arrived," Jessie concluded. "By the way, I'm tired of calling this place the unknown or construction dome. Every dome we visit after this one will be unknown."

"Our target will be alpha dome," Devon said. "From the Colony dome, we'll arrive at gate alpha-three."

"Works for me," Jessie replied.

"For the newcomers," Harbour said, "it must be stressed that deadly force can't be applied against the sentients in the Colony dome, but that doesn't hold true for those in the alpha dome."

"Wait," Pete called out. "We can't kill them until we catch them outside their own dome? Who made up this stupid rule?"

"The Tsargit," Mangoth replied, "and as their delegate, I'm required to report any infractions of this rule."

"Oh," Pete said quietly.

After the meeting with all parties, Harbour spoke to Tacticnok, who passed on the envoy's request to Jaktook. He made arrangements for the entire group to be housed together in one of the better-appointed facilities within Rissness Station.

When a guide ushered the individuals into the spacious room, the Pyreans halted in their steps. In contrast, Jaktook and Kractik quietly accepted the amenities. However, it was Mangoth, who swaggered into the space and declared, "Now this befits a Tsargit delegate."

"This is to make us feel good before we get killed," Dillon grumped.

Tracy rounded on him, and the heat in her face made her brother hold up his hands in apology.

"What part of 'you don't have to go' don't you get, newbie?" Pete growled. He'd delivered his message from behind Dillon into the spacer's ear. It caused the young man to flinch.

Tracy grinned at Pete, who winked in return.

"She's too young for you, Pete," Olivia admonished, having caught the exchange.

"I know that," Pete said. "Now that I'm repaired, I need to get back into practice. Besides, Dillon's right about one thing. There's a good chance that some, maybe many, of us are going to die during this exploration."

"Then you're going?" Olivia asked.

"Yes, aren't you?" Pete returned.

Bryan joined his fellow engineers. He'd heard the last part of the conversation. "She's going," he said.

Pete looked at Olivia, who flicked her eyebrows up.

"Why not say so?" Pete asked.

"I might want to go, but we've got an obstacle to clear," Olivia replied.

"What?" Pete asked.

"Not what, who ... Envoy Harbour," Bryan interjected.

"Why wouldn't she want us to go?" Pete objected.

"The intravertors," Olivia replied. "The Jatouche will send parts with the first Pyreans to return to Triton."

"Then we need a plan," Pete said, and the others agreed with him.

Once the group was settled into their new space, which was ringed with private sleeping quarters, Jaktook led a series of discussions about the type of equipment they needed and any changes to the suits.

In the initial meeting, Kractik was the first to pipe up. "I want Jatouche suits to have armor on the top of the hands but the palms must allow the nails to protrude."

Jaktook agreed, which is why Olivia wondered about the request. Jaktook eased her mind by saying, "There's no need for this change on Pyrean suits. More than once, Kractik and I were either carried or rode on the backs of our companions."

"And I, for one, prefer to ride than be carried," Kractik added.

"What am I missing here?" Dillon asked.

"Think of facing adversaries, who are ten times your length, young human, and you'll understand," Mangoth said. "The view becomes more harrowing the closer you are to the deck. We're not journeying anywhere if we lose our console operator. And, lest you forget, we must protect the one advisor who gives the Jatouche credit for the exploration. So, I admonish all of you who travel with us to do your utmost to protect these two key individuals."

Kractik's small hand patted Mangoth's thick, scaled forearm, "I did enjoy the view from your shoulders. It was a novel experience," she said. In reply, Mangoth loosed a deep rumble of satisfaction.

"That reminds me," Jaktook said. "I'm adding hand and foot straps to the back of every non-Jatouche suit." He eyed the group and added, "Be prepared to feel our impact on your backs for safety's sake."

"Who do *we* jump on to?" a spacer asked. It was meant in jest, but he wore a worried expression.

"My advice is to keep your wits about you, move quickly, and use your weapons and equipment wisely," Devon said.

"Well said," Mangoth added.

"We need to be able to trigger a shift in the visor's tint," Aurelia said. "In our last outing, there was a need in the alpha's tunnel and dome to lighten it. We must be able to manipulate it without using our hands."

"I was looking at your defensive weapons list," Henry said. "Did you deploy the gas at any time?"

"No," Jaktook replied. "And in retrospect, there wouldn't have been time. It was in an equipment bag, and we were too busy defending ourselves."

"This makes a great argument for more individuals in the exploration party," Henry continued. "You need specialized individuals, who are dedicated to deploying one or two pieces of equipment or weaponry. Carrying critical items in your bags won't work. That's like sailing in space and leaving your vac suit packed in a bay."

"Jaktook, consider attaching smaller weapons or tools to our thighs and forearms," Devon said. "Heavier items can be slung over the shoulder where they can be easily accessed."

"And no bags or duffels," Aurelia added. "Whatever else we need has to be carried in a backpack like Mangoth uses. And Envoy Harbour's and my packs need to carry the makings of greens. We're employing our full power for considerable periods of time. If we don't replenish ourselves, we'll be useless."

"And I'll need multiple mesh nets," Mangoth supplied. "They're light. If we vacuum pack them instead of rolling, I can carry twenty or more."

Later, Harbour, Jessie, and Tacticnok joined the group, and Jaktook updated them on the discussions.

When Jaktook finished, Jessie said, "I didn't hear anyone mention energy weapons, such as the ones the Jatouche soldiers use."

Tacticnok delicately cleared her throat before she said, "It is against Tsargit policy to supply non-alliance sentients with advanced weaponry."

"Putting aside the question of whether we have access to these types of weapons or not," Harbour said. "We're limited as to who can use them.

We can't have a newcomer, Pyrean or Jatouche, carry that type of weapon. The first time they encounter a pincer-clacking red-black, they'll be spraying the entire dome's deck in fire."

A brief argument broke out among the group arguing the merits of taking an energy weapon and deploying it. The veteran explorers recalled their reactions to the onslaught of the Colony species, and they knew Harbour's concern about the weapon in the hands of a newbie explorer was correct.

"All arguments aside," Harbour added into the noise, "there's still a case to be made for taking an energy weapon."

"The Tsargit is aware of our actions at alpha dome after receiving Mangoth's cube," Devon said. He eyed Mangoth, who tipped his long muzzle in assent. "Then if the Tsargit was to single out anyone for remonstration, or worse, it might as well be me who carries the energy weapon. After Mangoth, I killed more of the Colony sentients than anyone. Therefore, if it's decided to allow us this type of weapon, I suggest you let me carry it. Adding a few more Colony dead to my total to save our butts can't make my situation any worse."

"You don't fool me, Devon," Mangoth said, baring his massive rows of teeth. "You wish the energy weapon because your count of the dead was less than mine, and that's the only way you can compete with my magnificent attributes."

"Yes, you found me out, Mangoth," Devon replied, pretending sadness. "Your beauty, strength, and natural gifts are too much for me."

Mangoth bellowed his pleasure at Devon's response. He couldn't remember when he'd enjoyed the company of two species, as much as he had this team of Pyreans and Jatouche, and he would never have considered the latter race if it weren't for the humans.

"I can easily solve this argument," Mangoth said. "The Jatouche can't give Pyreans an energy weapon. They don't have the authorization. However, as a Tsargit delegate, I do. I'm officially requesting you, Your Highness, to supply Pyrean Devon Higgins with an energy weapon and train him in its operation."

"I hear Delegate Mangoth's request, and I'm pleased to fulfill it," Tacticnok replied.

"Just don't shoot me, Devon," Mangoth said, his rumbling hinting at his mirth.

Harbour gently rapped the table to draw everyone's attention. "There is a greater question to settle before we go much further," she said. "I wish to hear from the newcomers. Who wishes to return to Pyre and who wishes to go with the team?"

"I'm going," Tracy piped up.

"No, you're not," Dillon growled under his breath.

"And, Envoy Harbour, may I request that you refuse my brother's offer to join the team if he makes one?" Tracy added.

Harbour took note of the emotion roiling off Dillon. It was a mix of anger, embarrassment, and deep concern, probably for his sister.

"What do you say, Dillon?" Harbour asked.

"I'd rather go home, but my sister is dead set on going," Dillon replied, "which means I'm going too. If nothing else, I'm going to see if I can keep her from being eaten."

"There's no indication that the Colony species eat sentients, Dillon," Mangoth interjected. "They appear to bite and let the victims die from their venom."

"Wonderful," Dillon grumbled.

After the initial rush of Tracy and Dillon, the room was quiet. The veteran explorers regarded one another, surprised that there weren't more volunteers. Harbour took it upon herself to ask the Pyreans to raise their hands if they were returning to Pyre. Slowly every Pyrean, who'd been recently repaired, except for Tracy and Dillon, raised their hands. Harbour detected waves of self-recrimination.

"There is no need for embarrassment," Harbour said gently. "I know many of you have partners and children to support, and I wish you well in your endeavors after you return."

Harbour's words hadn't lessened the intensity of the returnees' shame. In addition, she detected the veterans' discomfort. They felt abandoned by the abdication of so many fellow humans. *Forgive me, Rictook, for not heeding your admonishment,* she thought before she sent her support across the company.

Aurelia felt Harbour's power, and she added hers. Both empaths attempted to direct their emotional waves away from the Jatouche. They were partially successful.

While on Pyre, none of the newly repaired ever had a reason or the coin to visit an empath. Since completing their repairs at Rissness Station, they'd multiple opportunities to receive the ministrations of empaths.

Eyes closed and minds relaxed into the sending. The Jatouche slouched in their seats, and soft sounds escaped their short muzzles.

"Delightful," Mangoth said, as he luxuriated in the sensation.

Harbour signed to Aurelia, and the empaths eased off their power.

"Without doubt, I broke a promise to His Excellency Rictook," Harbour said to Tacticnok. "For that, I apologize."

"For what?" Tacticnok asked, recovering from the pleasant feeling. "Didn't you specify, Envoy, that you wouldn't withhold your power when there was a critical situation? From the expressions on this group's faces, I believe I witnessed a dire need. In my opinion, there's no reason to report this incident."

A round of quiet laughter accompanied Tacticnok's words. For many years afterwards, the returnees would suffer bouts of guilt and regret, but for now their pain had been eased.

Harbour was surprised that the engineers hadn't raised their hands, expressing their intention to return to Pyre. Bryan was seated near her, and she opened her senses to detect his mood. Disconcertingly, she received little sensation from him. Then it dawned on her. The engineers were intimately aware of her powers, and they'd chosen to hide their emotions. *You're probably solving intricate math or engineering problems in your heads,* she thought.

When the meeting concluded, Harbour requested to speak to the engineers, and the foursome adjourned to a small conference room.

"You don't think you're needed on the YIPS?" Harbour asked, without preamble.

Bryan and Pete glanced quickly at Olivia. She'd been right on two counts. Harbour would object to their joining the exploration team, and her primary concern would be for the intravertors.

"The purpose of engineers is to design, fabricate, and test to ensure the results meet design specifications," Olivia lectured. "The purpose of techs is to carry out the engineer's prototype instructions and document their steps. The purpose of the documentation is to enable engineers to examine where errors were introduced when results don't meet specifications. Having finally achieved the desired results, the techs are able to repeat the process ad infinitum."

Harbour laughed and held up her hands in surrender. "Point taken," she said. "The first intravertor was a success, and the YIPS has the engineers, techs, and documentation to manufacture and assemble the others."

"Several problems remain," Bryan said, "which have nothing to do with us. The Jatouche are going to be sending intravertor parts as fast as we consume them, right?"

"Correct," Harbour replied.

"If you're here, who's going to drive the fundraising?" Olivia asked.

"My delegates, although they don't know that yet," Harbour replied, holding a finger to her lips and requesting their secrecy.

"Another point, Envoy," Pete said. "The *Belle*'s shuttle isn't made to launch the intravertor. Yes, it was overhauled nicely after the first launch, but successive deployments will wreak incremental havoc on its systems. One day, there'll be a catastrophic failure, and we'll lose an intravertor, a shuttle, and two fine people."

"What do you propose as an alternative?" Harbour asked.

The engineers dived into a host of mechanisms by which intravertors could be delivered to a platform and launched from there. They explored various means with which to ensure an accurate delivery to the planet, spreading successive units across the surface. This was necessary, they explained, because the YIPS and the JOS kept geosynchronous orbits.

At one point, Harbour said, "Enough. I lost you somewhere after the explanation about a new platform and geosynchronous orbits. I'm going to have you meet with Advisor Cinders and Captain Stamerson. You can sell your ideas to them."

The engineers smiled and stood up to leave.

"Not so fast," Harbour said sharply, and indicated the engineers should regain their seats. "We haven't covered the final point. Why do you think you should travel with the exploratory team?"

When Bryan and Pete looked at Olivia, Harbour did too.

"What do the Jatouche, the Crocian, or you, for that matter, know about Colony engineering?" Olivia asked.

"I presume that's a rhetorical question," Harbour replied, her eyes narrowing.

"Yes, well ..." Olivia stammered under Harbour's gaze, "you've got some good people, but I count two empaths, a captain, a dome administrator, a security officer, a console operator, an alien delegate, and two newbies. Where's your engineering acumen?"

"Another good point," Harbour admitted. "I dearly want to say no to you three, but you're right. We'll need your help."

The engineers briefly celebrated their win, but Harbour cut it short. "Understand me," she said harshly. "You'll have to be trained to defend yourselves like the rest of us. Using your engineering skills will come only after we've made it to the alpha dome and secured it."

-25-
Destinations

The final two members of the twenty, Nelson Barber and Jacob Deering, completed their repairs two days after Harbour spoke to the engineers about joining the team. Harbour met with the first mate and the mining tech to update them on the events that had transpired. When Harbour finished, she fully expected the men to request to join the delegates and the sixteen repaired who would soon be leaving for Triton.

"Tell me more about the Colony," Nelson requested.

"Yeah, Envoy, I want to know more too," Jacob said.

"Are you sure?" Harbour asked.

"Captain Flannigan owns a single ship," Nelson said, "I've been his first mate for nine years. He intends to sell his ship when he retires. I make a decent living, but I can't afford to buy his vessel. Seems to me, the only way I'll get ahead will be earning a reward for joining the exploration."

Harbour wasn't pleased to hear that Nelson lacked an altruistic motive. Yet, in the next moment, she chastised herself for mentally passing judgment on the man. There was no doubt the explorers needed him. He was a trained and disciplined ship's officer.

"How about you, Jacob?" Harbour asked.

"It's kind of the same thing for me, Envoy," Jacob said. "I'm a senior mining tech, but I don't have the aptitude to become an engineer. I'll probably never make enough coin to comfortably retire aboard the JOS. So I'm interested in an alternative."

"Okay then. Let me show you what you'll be encountering," Harbour said. "Come with me."

Harbour requested their guide lead them to a data center and call Kractik. Harbour watched the Pyreans' eyes track the small Jatouche, as she set up the recorder's replay. It occurred to her that the two men had been unconscious during their transport to Rissness Station. Since waking, they'd had a series of face-to-face encounters with aliens, and it showed in their focused stares.

Harbour opened her gates to sense the men's emotions while they watched the recordings. Nelson evinced surprise and brief moments of fear, which he controlled. Jacob, on the other hand, wasn't as calm, but eventually he suppressed his deep angst too.

"Well?" asked Harbour, when the viewing finished.

"A scary lot," Nelson commented.

"Too scary?" Harbour asked.

"Depends," Nelson replied. "Are we going empty-handed?"

"Everyone will be armed with either offensive or defensive weapons," Harbour replied.

"Do we have a choice?" Jacob asked.

"No," Harbour replied. "There are complicated rules that govern what we can do in the Colony's dome versus anytime we encounter the Colony in other domes."

"That's confusing," Jacob said.

"This part of the galaxy has many sentient races. They've been gate travelers for longer than humans have been in space," Harbour explained. "They've many rules, and we're subject to them all."

"What's the hierarchy of the team?" Nelson asked. "There are Pyreans, Jatouche, and the ... uh —"

"Crocian," Harbour supplied, "who, by the way, is a Tsargit delegate."

"A what?" Jacob queried.

"There's much you've got to learn if you travel with us," Harbour said. "For now, let's deal with the immediate concerns. I lead the exploration. My second in command is Advisor Cinders. Any questions on that subject?"

"None, Envoy," the two spacers echoed in unison.

"Good," Harbour replied. "Now, are you still interested in going with us?"

"Aye, Envoy," were the replies.

* * * *

There was no longer a reason to delay the return of the three delegates or the sixteen repaired Pyreans to Triton. Tacticnok had seen to the stocking of intravertor material at Rissness and was prepared to ship three sets of parts with the returnees.

Harbour chose to have a final private conversation with the delegates before they returned, and the foursome met in a private room.

"I'll remind you that you're elected or appointed delegates," Harbour said in her opening remarks. "That holds true whether you're here or at Pyre."

"What are you driving at?" Idrian asked, suspicious of Harbour's motives.

"Just this," Harbour replied. "This delegation journeyed to Na-Tikkook to broker a deal with the Jatouche. A deal has been struck. Now, it must be implemented. The explorers have their duty, and you have yours."

"Could you be more specific, Envoy?" Dottie asked deferentially.

"First, Captain Stamerson, I'm making you the Assistant Envoy," Harbour stated. "You'll be responsible for two things: Ensuring my objectives are met and replacing the delegates if they fail to assist you in accomplishing those objectives."

"Thank you for your faith in me, Envoy," Henry replied, with a wry smile. "I'll be happy to see to the fulfillment of your wishes," he added, eyeing the other two delegates.

"What are we supposed to be doing?" Dottie pursued.

Harbour pulled out her comm unit, which she hadn't used in a while, and sent copies of her notes to the delegates. "You have received the agreement, as I understand it," Harbour replied. "They're reminders for you, but you were present during Rictook's pronouncements. What do you think I want?"

"Twenty Pyreans need to be recruited and delivered to Triton for repairs, at the specified interval," Henry answered quickly.

"That will be a costly hire," Idrian said. He was waiting for Harbour's response, but she stared at him instead. "Therefore, the delegates must find a means of procuring the coin for the transport," he belatedly finished.

"Start thinking in greater terms," Harbour said.

"We'll be sending groups of people for repair on a regular basis," Dottie said suddenly. "Pyre needs a passenger shuttle with cargo space, which will be dedicated to transport to Triton."

"Now, you're thinking," Harbour said, and Dottie beamed.

"More cost," Idrian added.

Harbour ignored him and waited for the delegates to continue.

"We're going to have intravertor parts. We need more coin for the Pyrean Green fund," Henry supplied.

"Yes, you will," Harbour agreed. "Henry has been taking part in a discussion with Jessie and our three engineers. They've ideas about deployment of the intravertors that won't involve risking the *Belle*'s shuttle. Henry, I task you with informing Captain Dingles that he's forbidden to use his ship's shuttle."

"Aye, Envoy," Henry replied smartly.

"These projects will cost an enormous amount of coin," Idrian insisted. "Ordering a transport shuttle for Triton, absorbing its cost of operations, assembling intravertors, and constructing a new means of delivering them."

"Yes, it will," Harbour replied calmly, "and you're the delegates who are in charge of making it happen. That is unless you'd rather take my place and face the Colony, in which case, I'd enjoy returning to Pyre without acquiring any deadly injections."

Dottie paled, Idrian scowled, and Henry chuckled.

"You have my instructions; make them happen," Harbour ordered. She could hear a captain's authoritative tone in her voice, and she thought Dingles would be proud of her. "Gather your gear," she added, "you're on a shuttle to the Rissness dome."

Tacticnok accompanied the Pyrean returnees to Rissness to ensure that they were escorted on their journey to Triton by a console operator, two soldiers, and crew to help transfer the intravertor crates.

After Harbour saw the returnees off from Rissness Station, she gathered the remaining individuals. They numbered fourteen.

"I've been speaking to Jaktook about the size of our team," Harbour said. "He has some advice for us."

"Our number is too great to journey through a gate as one group," Jaktook said. "Yes, we could squeeze tightly together, but we'd be unprepared to defend ourselves on the other side. I'm recommending two teams."

"That would require a console operator accompany each team," Jessie interjected.

"Agreed, Advisor," Jaktook replied, "and I remind you that I'm a dome administrator. While I might not know the console's depth, as well as Kractik does, I'm fully capable of managing basic platform operations, programming cubes, and facilitating console communications."

"Good to know," Jessie replied, tipping his head in acknowledgment of Jaktook's skills.

"I've considered Jaktook's idea, and it's suggested to me that we need to balance the teams," Harbour said. "Team number one will be led by me and will comprise Devon, Mangoth, Kractik, Olivia, Pete, and Jacob. Advisor Cinders is in charge of team two, and he'll lead Aurelia, Jaktook, Bryan, Nelson, Tracy, and Dillon."

A good many Pyreans had questions on their minds, but Jessie silenced them when he firmly replied, "Aye, aye, Envoy."

Jaktook listened to a call on his ear wig. "Envoy, Jatouche engineers are ready to meet with your teams."

"Good timing," Harbour replied. "Take us to them, please."

The extended team was strapped into cars and rode toward the central axis. From there, the vehicles journeyed most of the station's length. When the cars reached the programmed level, they exited the tube and moved outward until a location was reached where station's spin imitated Na-Tikkook gravity.

The guide led the teams to a large bare space. It was an empty bay. Thirty-two Jatouche engineers and techs waited for them, and they were dwarfed by the stack of open crates, which were covered with a host of suits, equipment, and odd-looking devices.

Jaktook had an intimate and lengthy conversation with the head engineer. When finished, he turned to Harbour and said, "They had orders from Tacticnok to deliver material that would cover every eventuality of contact with the Colony."

Harbour surveyed the Jatouche technical individuals, the stack of crates, and the amount of displayed equipment. "There's enough here to outfit five or six teams," she said laughing. "We're in their hands," she added.

Jaktook relayed to the head engineer the envoy's request, and the Jatouche technicians swarmed forward. They led each team member to piles of vac suit equipment and helped them try on various combinations.

When an explorer expressed concerns about some small detail, the technicians would hurry to the side of the bay, where a line of machines waited. They would operate on the piece of suit or fabricate a new one. Step by step, each team member got exactly what they wanted.

Harbour took in the satisfied expressions and the emotional glow of her team members, "Well done," she said to the lead engineer, who flashed his teeth in a broad manner. "Our packs next, please," she ordered, and the process was repeated until the explorers were pleased with the results.

"It's time for weapons," Harbour requested. "I want them displayed on the deck."

The engineers and techs lugged mounds of equipment in front of Harbour and lined them up. Then one by one they reviewed the intended purpose of each item, classifying it as offensive or defensive and its potential level of incapacitation.

"Recall, Envoy," Jaktook said. "Other than the audio generator, none of these claims can be verified."

Harbour glanced at the lead Jatouche engineer, who ducked his head and nodded twice in agreement.

"Envoy," Mangoth said, pointing to the pile of mesh nets.

"Agreed," Harbour replied, and Mangoth stripped off his pack, made room for the nets, and stuffed in as many as he could carry.

"Devon, the energy weapon," Harbour said.

Devon stepped forward, but an engineer held up his small hands.

"Training first," Jaktook explained.

"Make it happen," Harbour said firmly.

The lead engineer communicated to several of his support staff. They scooped up suits, the weapon, and Devon and made for the bay's exit.

Over the next few hours, Harbour, Jessie, Jaktook, and Mangoth consulted carefully about which weapons should be taken and who should carry them. They made an effort to share the offensive and defensive weapons evenly among the teams.

"I'd prefer an offensive weapon, Envoy," Jacob objected, when he was assigned his device.

"What was your reaction, spacer, when you saw the recordings of the Colony species attacking us?" Jessie asked harshly.

"They didn't bother me," Jacob replied, before he remembered who had been seated next to him. He glanced at Harbour, whose narrowed eyes held his gaze. "Maybe a little," he clarified, but Harbour's expression added a frown. "Okay, maybe a lot," he admitted.

"That's why you can't carry a deadly weapon, Jacob," Jessie said.

"Listen up, newcomers," Jessie announced in his captain's voice. "One glance at a hissing red-black racing toward you will be enough to make you soil your skins. We know this, and we sympathize. You're likely to fire a deadly weapon at the attacker out of fear, but if we're in the Colony's dome, you'll place your team in jeopardy by breaking a Tsargit rule of conduct."

"Imagine the reverse situation," Harbour added. "Devon has left to learn how to fire an energy weapon. Due to heavy energy pack and firing tube, that's the only device he'll carry. When he reaches the Colony dome, he'll be defenseless. My team must protect him."

The division of weapons was completed, and Harbour thanked the Jatouche technical team for their efforts and told them that she would relay her appreciation to Her Highness. That comment garnered an enormous display of Jatouche teeth.

"Explorers, please divest yourselves of weapons, packs, and suits in discreet piles," Jaktook instructed. "They will be transported for you."

"Anything else?" Harbour asked Jaktook. When the Jatouche advisor shook his head, Harbour announced to the teams, "Pack up your personal gear. It will be stored at the Rissness dome."

"I'll order Her Highness' shuttle," Jaktook said, as he removed his gear.

The teams packed up, caught the shuttle, and transferred to the dome. The Jatouche took care of the transport of their equipment. Soon after they arrived, Tacticnok and Devon joined them in a third-level dorm room.

"Successful trial, Devon?" Jessie asked.

"Oh, yes," Devon replied. "We took a transport to Rissness and rode a vehicle across the moon's surface. The engineer demonstrated the weapon for me." Devon smiled, as he recalled the event, "They built it for me. So, they kept the energy pack on the back of the vehicle. It was too bulky for them to wear."

"How did it work?" Pete asked.

"I'm informed this is a modified energy weapon," Devon replied. "Apparently, the ones carried by the Jatouche soldiers allow variable controls. The engineers decided I'll have a single need. My weapon has a limited range, due to the beam's focus, and a moderate energy output. Nonetheless, at four meters, I was able to hole a piece of rubble."

"So, it's a deadly weapon?" Jacob asked.

"Well, yes and no," Devon replied. "The engineers and I talked about the use of the weapon in light of the Tsargit strictures. There is the idea that I could use the beam to wound, if my aim was lucky."

"What do you mean lucky?" Harbour asked.

"Where do you shoot a red-black or gray to wound them?" Devon retorted.

"Point taken," Harbour replied.

After a brief rest, a knock at the door announced the arrival of a Jatouche tech crew. They set up a small, dark box with its own controller. They handed the controller to Mangoth and exited.

"This is the information provided in response to our request to journey to the Colony dome via an alternative path, Envoy," Mangoth said. He operated the controller, and the small box projected a three-dimensional display of an enormous star chart. A blue line linked several stars. Then it separated into yellow and green lines. Where those two lines terminated, two red lines led to the same location.

"All paths lead to the Colony," Jessie remarked.

"True, Advisor," Mangoth replied. "The blue line ends at Veklock and the green at Norsitch."

"Which path do you advise we take, Mangoth?" Harbour asked.

"I've no opinion as to which direction will give us the greatest opportunity for success, Envoy, I'm sorry to say," Mangoth replied.

"Regardless of the direction your teams take, Envoy," Tacticnok said, "Be aware that I've communicated your intentions to the Tsargit, and they've instructed Veklock and Norsitch to fulfill any request you make."

"So, which way do we go?" Aurelia asked, gazing at Mangoth, Tacticnok, and Jaktook, who she thought would have significant knowledge of the alliance members. Unfortunately, no one replied.

"What's the history of these two members with the Colony?" Devon asked.

"According to Tsargit records," Jaktook began, "the Veklocks had a single incursion from the Colony, while the Norsitchians have repelled the Colony multiple times since the first attack."

"What's the conjecture about why there was only the one time for the Veklocks?" Jessie asked.

When Jaktook shrugged, Mangoth said, "The Veklocks are an aero-capable race."

Jessie frowned at Harbour, thinking there was a glitch in the translation app.

"The Veklocks can fly," Jaktook interjected.

"They were once capable of traversing the air for long distances," Mangoth continued. "When the Messinants uplifted them, their bodies underwent severe changes. They became heavier, and their flight limbs were shortened. The combinative effect limited their aero capability to lifting themselves off the ground for a brief spell."

"So, when the Colony attacked, the Veklocks escaped by launching themselves off the deck," Devon supplied.

"Just so," Mangoth replied. "To the Colony's detriment, the Veklocks retained one aspect of their ancient heritage … heavy, sharp beaks. They descended on their foes from above, striking with their beaks and killing them."

"Do the Jatouche have anything that could allow us to hover?" Aurelia asked hopefully.

"This could be developed, given time," Tacticnok commented.

"Time is something we don't have," Harbour responded. "The Colony knows we've made one pass through their dome. More important, they know we've discovered their secret. The question becomes: How great is their secret?"

"Is Mangoth's information an answer as to direction?" Devon asked.

"I believe so," Jessie replied. "A one-time incursion by the Colony, and no reverse attacks by the Veklocks. And, don't forget, the Colony doesn't know of the Tsargit injunction."

"Eat, refresh yourselves, and rest," Harbour ordered. "We leave soon."

-26-
Alpha Dome

Sleep eluded the explorers, but they did get some rest. They lay awake on their pallets in the dorm's dim light, which edged the joints between the walls and the overhead.

Jessie occupied the pallet next to Harbour. She sensed his elevated concern and turned her head to find Jessie staring at her.

When Harbour sighed, Jessie announced in a firm voice, "Everyone up. Time to go."

The first time the explorers journeyed to the Colony dome, few were aware of their purpose. This time, the explorers were greeted by a throng of Jatouche soldiers and citizens, in addition to aliens of all sizes and shapes. They dipped their heads to the explorers, as they passed.

"Nice send-off," Aurelia commented quietly to Jessie.

It occurred to Jessie that the throng might have been saluting the brave, who they didn't expect to return, but he kept the thought to himself.

"First team up," Harbour said. She was joined on the platform by Mangoth, Devon, Kractik, Olivia, Pete, and Jacob.

When team one was ready, Harbour looked at Jessie. "See you and your team at the Veklock dome," she said.

Jessie nodded, and Harbour pointed at the Rissness console operator. Team one vanished in a flash of blue light, and Jessie felt his heart squeezed. A hand slipped into his, pressed it lightly, and withdrew. Aurelia had sensed his discomfort.

Team two, with Jessie, Aurelia, Jaktook, Bryan, Nelson, Tracy, and Dillon, gained the platform and was sent on its way to follow Harbour's group.

At each dome, Harbour's medallion announced her status, which demanded the console operator's attention. Mangoth, who had memorized their route, called out their destination, and a console operator would point to the correct platform.

An operator discovered that no sooner had he, she, or it sent the team on their way than a second group arrived behind them. Without much exchange, the operator would point to the desired platform and would send team two through the gate, chasing team one.

To the Pyreans, the aliens they briefly witnessed throughout their journey presented a dizzying array of lifeforms. They might have paid more attention to the bizarre sights, but a shared thought continued to intrude. With each gate, they got closer and closer to their final location, the Veklocks' dome. From there, the next journey would land them in the midst of deadly adversaries.

Many gates later, Mangoth announced, "Envoy, this is the Veklock dome."

The Crocian's statement was unnecessary. Team one looked at a collection of sentients. The majority had thin necks, ruffled in plumage. Their large eyes framed pointed beaks, and their heads had a habit of turning sharply. They wore tunics, which allowed the wings Mangoth had described to remain visible.

Harbour's team stepped off the platform, and the Veklocks tipped their beaks to honor her presence.

Swiftly behind the first team came the second group. When the two teams mingled, Jessie remarked quietly to Harbour, "I might have accumulated enough odd visions to fuel my nightmares for a lifetime."

"And we might have had the same impact on many more races," Harbour replied.

"Rest or keep going?" Jessie asked Harbour.

Harbour examined the faces of her teams and tasted their emotions. They appeared a little tired after the numerous journeys, but they were anxious. Attempting to rest would be a waste of time.

"We go on," Harbour announced.

"We require the Colony gate," Mangoth called to the Veklock operators.

Beaks turned toward one another in consternation. A Veklock, who appeared to be a dome supervisor, made a comm call. In response, a crew ran up the ramp. They hurried to gate two. It was covered in a transparent globe.

"Clever," Jaktook commented, as he watched the crew activate a controller at the base of the globe. It separated the structure into four sections, which slid away from the platform.

"We must get the formula for this material," Kractik said. "It allows the beam to merge with the dome without hindering the transmission."

"And traps the Colony journeyers," Devon added.

The Veklock dome supervisor indicated the now accessible platform.

"Remember the injunction against killing in the Colony dome," Harbour said. "However, Devon, if it means saving our lives, then do what you have to do. Worst-case scenario, we admit our transgression, go home to Pyre, and make the most of our overheated little planet."

Harbour could taste the rising fear, "Do your best everyone. That's all I can ask," she added.

"Team one on the platform," Devon called out.

Harbour turned toward Aurelia. She leaned her forehead against the young woman's. "Be safe," she whispered. Then she turned toward Jessie and gripped his hands.

"See you in alpha dome," Jessie said. His smile was weak and hesitant.

"I *will* see you there," Harbour replied, making it sound like an order. Then she kissed him firmly and climbed on the platform.

Helmets were donned and sealed. After looking around at her team, Harbour signaled the console operator.

* * * *

The platform light cleared. Red-blacks and grays rose up hissing at the arrival of the intruders into their dome.

Harbour radiated fear with all the intensity she could muster. It caused the Colony sentients to hesitate briefly, but without Aurelia's combined power, her sending didn't defeat their rage. Watching the red-blacks shake off her mental barrage made her worry for Aurelia's effectiveness on the other team.

Pete could see the Colony species writhing in anger and knew that Harbour wasn't going to defeat them. He nudged Harbour in the shoulder, and she shut her gates, as he stepped around her.

At the platform's edge, Pete held up his sprayer, triggered it, and swung it in an ever-widening arc, as he walked around the perimeter.

The gas, designed by the Jatouche medical services units, filled the dome. The advance of the hissing red-blacks and grays slowed and then ceased. They wavered, as if swaying to some unheard music. Then they collapsed to the deck.

"Hurry, Kractik," Harbour urged.

Kractik leapt from the platform and raced to the console, and Mangoth lumbered after her.

The team noted they'd arrived at gate five. Their target was gate one, clear across the deck. They jumped from the platform and made their way across the twitching bodies of the Colony sentients.

"They're not entirely out," Olivia warned.

"Hurry," Harbour replied.

Kractik was still setting the transfer for gate one when the dome's air-clearing process kicked on. This had happened in the Triton dome. After sitting unpowered for centuries, its activation had initiated a whirling column that sucked the dust from the dome's surfaces. In this case, the Colony dome was clearing the gas. Unfortunately, the only explorers who had seen this process were Jessie and Aurelia, and they were on the other team.

The group hesitated, as the fierce air column swept around them, and Harbour broke through their quandary with a shout of, "Now, on the platform."

Galvanized, the group raced for gate one.

"Go," Kractik urged Mangoth, shoving on his hip.

The Crocian hesitated, but realized the dilemma. Protecting Kractik wasn't the immediate concern. It was speed. He waddled toward the platform, and the diminutive Jatouche raced past him.

Gaining gate one, Kractik loudly counted down the timing until initiation. She'd shortened the delay period, and Mangoth could see that he might be late. In a final burst of speed, his heart hammering at the thought of being left behind, he bounded on to the platform as the gate lit.

* * * *

Team two arrived in the Colony dome in time to see the blue light of gate one spear the dome.

"They deployed the gas," Jessie cried out over the comm to be heard over the swirling torrent of air. "Hurry," he yelled.

Jaktook made for the console, and Jessie ran behind him. While the Jatouche advisor frantically set gate one, the dome's sweep of the gas shut down. In an effort to complete the console process as quickly as possible, Jaktook, unlike Kractik, chose the standard delay.

Jaktook nodded to Jessie, and they turned to make for gate one. In front of them, a gray rose up, blocking their path. It wobbled, swaying from side to side. Jessie shoved at its body, and the gray toppled over.

"The gas is still affecting their senses," Jaktook yelled.

As the pair made their way toward gate one, more aggressors rose up in front of them. Each one was a little more conscious and less under the influence of the gas. Finally a red-black hissed and lunged at Jessie. Its heavy pincers threatened to close on him, and Jessie stuck the weapon he carried into the grasping mandibles. The strength of the red-black shocked him, as the attacker tore the weapon from his grasp and hurled it across the dome.

Jessie snatched Jaktook and retraced his steps.

"The gate," Jaktook called out. "We won't make it."

The rest of the team was at gate one, fighting to hold off the aggressors, who woke up near them.

"Reset the gate," Aurelia yelled out. When Jessie hesitated, she stepped off the platform and swung her weapon into the body of a swaying gray.

Nelson followed Aurelia, and Jessie could see their intentions. They were going to carve a path for Jaktook and him.

"Reset," Jessie ordered. He'd swung Jaktook over his shoulder and was grateful to feel the Jatouche's weight settle on his back. A gray rose up, and Jessie planted a boot in its midsection. Punching and kicking grays, Jessie fought his way back to the console.

Jaktook clambered off Jessie's back and hurriedly reset the gate. When he reached the delay menu, he asked, "How long?"

Jessie eyed the team, who were fighting aggressively to reach them. But with every second, more Colony members scuttled up the ramp, and none of these had been affected by the gas.

"Forty," Jessie replied, and he counted off three numbers to give Jaktook an idea of the timing.

Dillon saw a red-black rise up behind his sister. With no time to warn her, he swung his weapon around to embed the entity in a sticky web. But the red-black was swifter. Its heavy pincers grabbed Dillon around the neck, shook him, and tossed his body away. The young spacer died from a broken neck.

Tracy screamed her brother's name and fired her weapon at the red-black. It was the same tool her brother had carried. The net landed over the red-black's head and wrapped around the upper body. Exposed to the air, its sticky filaments instantly shrunk and dried. The attacker hissed its anger and fell to the deck. Its lower legs clawed at the filaments in an effort to extricate itself from the webbing.

Tracy sobbed, as she pulled another canister from her belt, split open her launcher, and loaded another shot. She pushed to the forefront of the team and fired on two grays, ensnaring both of them. She kicked them over and reloaded.

Jessie climbed on the console, which horrified Jaktook. However, he didn't hesitate a moment to grasp the hand that was held out to him. With the added height, Jessie was better able to fend off the grays, but he watched two red-blacks making their way toward them.

Jaktook unloaded his audio generator, powered it up, and triggered it at the sentients, attacking from the ramp.

Jessie received a burst of unrecognizable sounds in his ear wig. He figured the little Jatouche was swearing because none of the Colony members were curling up in agony as they had before. That's when Jessie noted small patches on the sides of their heads. "Protective pads over their membranes," Jessie shouted, pointing to the side of a gray's head before he kicked it.

As the team closed on Jessie, he grabbed Jaktook and swung him up behind him. The Jatouche dropped the nozzle of his generator and snatched at the straps on Jessie's suit. Jessie launched them off the console at the two grays, who stood between them and the team. He knocked them down with his weight.

"Roll away," Tracy called out.

Jaktook jumped free, and Jessie squirmed out of the way of snapping pincers, as Tracy embedded the two grays in a net.

The team retraced their steps to the platform, leaping over entangled or unconscious foes. Several oozed body fluids from cracked segments where the team had struck them. The group regained the platform, and Aurelia stepped forward to halt a red-black with her power. It hesitated and hissed its displeasure.

Tracy spared a final glance at her brother's inert body, and then the gate fired.

* * * *

Team one appeared in the alpha dome. The view was similar, except no red-blacks were in evidence. However, the rules had changed for the explorers.

Devon stepped to the forefront of the platform and powered his beam weapon. A gray reared up in front of him, and Devon fired in reflex. A holed drilled through the gray's head, giving it the appearance of a third eye, and it slumped to the deck.

"So much for a wounding shot," Devon remarked.

Immediately, another gray took the first one's place, and Devon managed to hit it in the midsection. When that didn't faze the sentient, he shot it in the head.

The remainder of the grays held back when they saw two of their members drop inertly to the deck.

"Off the platform," Harbour ordered. The team jumped down, and Harbour directed them. "Everyone, wave your arms toward the ramp. Devon, stay at our front and threaten them with your weapon."

Reluctant at first, the grays accepted that they were being offered an escape route. They dropped to the deck to utilize their entire leg pairs, scurrying across the deck and down the ramp.

A flare of light signaled the operation of the gate that led to the Colony dome. Jacob looked over his shoulder. "Team two has arrived," he announced on the comm, happy not to see a mass of squirming Colony sentients. When he counted only six individuals, he gulped, and returned to waving his arms. It didn't seem the time to distract the envoy.

"Kractik, the console," Harbour ordered. "Get ready to close the wedge."

Kractik edged slowly toward the console, keeping close to Mangoth, as the grays backed away.

A few foolhardy attackers tried circling behind team one, Pete tapped Devon on the shoulder, and the lieutenant aimed his weapon their way. The grays received the message loud and clear. They backed away and headed toward the ramp.

Jessie's team recognized the tactic being employed and joined in the process, waving their arms at every Colony sentient in sight. The explorers carefully circled every platform to ensure no grays hid there. When the final Colony sentient slipped down the ramp, Kractik tapped the console panel, and a wedge in the deck slid closed.

"This isn't permanent, Envoy," Kractik announced. "If the sentients trigger the plate at the bottom of the ramp, the wedge will open."

"Devon stand guard at the ramp," Harbour said. "If the wedge opens, wait until you see an attacker and then put a shot in a tail section. Then Kractik can close it again."

"Understood, Envoy," Devon replied.

"Mangoth, deploy a net over platform three. I don't want any of the Colony following us," Harbour requested. She turned to speak to the other team. The scene that greeted her stole her breath away. Aurelia was hugging a figure she couldn't identify. From across the deck, she could sense the waves of grief that poured off team two, and Aurelia's efforts to soothe them. The count was six explorers, and Harbour hurried to them. When she saw Jessie, relief flooded through her. Then she identified that it was Dillon who was missing, and Aurelia was hugging Tracy.

"What happened?" Harbour asked Jessie. He signed for a separate comm channel and Harbour complied.

"The dome swept the gas out, and the Colony members rapidly revived," Jessie replied, "and reinforcements flooded up from below deck. It was a fight to get free from the onslaught. Jaktook and I were trapped at the console, and the team came to our rescue. I don't know exactly what happened to Dillon. I'd kicked a gray, and out of the corner of my eye, I saw him fly across the deck, about three meters in the air."

"Should we go back for him?" Harbour asked.

"His helmet looked like it was turned around," Jessie replied. "I think a red-black broke his neck. Even if Dillon wasn't dead, which I highly doubt, the Colony has him now."

Harbour shuddered. She hated that she hoped Dillon was dead. She didn't want to think about him in the clutches of these insidious sentients.

"I'm all right," Tracy said, pushing away from Aurelia. She didn't want to admit that the young empath's ministrations had done a great deal to lessen her pain. The emotion that ruled her was white hot anger, a lot of it. She stalked toward the console to get free of her team. Standing next to Kractik, she said to Devon, "If you ever want to give someone else a turn with that weapon, you let me know. I'd be happy to take it off your hands."

Devon nodded without replying. He'd seen angry family members before. Shortly after losing a loved one through a tragic accident or murder, they looked for justice, if not vengeance, and they didn't care how it was obtained.

"What now?" Jessie asked Harbour.

In response, Harbour called, "Mangoth, I need you."

"Yes, Envoy," Mangoth said, hurrying to gain Harbour's side.

"The Tsargit tasked you with providing evidence of the Colony's operation here," Harbour said to Mangoth. "We're on the deck, and our adversaries are trapped below ... and so are the tunnel and the newly constructed dome. How do we collect your proof?"

When Mangoth hesitated, Jaktook piped up. "The console, Envoy, will provide us with proof of the Colony's presence and activities. A download to our cubes will identity the alpha dome as an unidentified location to the Tsargit."

"Take care of it," Harbour ordered.

Jaktook ran to the console and chatted with Kractik. The console operator doffed her pack and dug out four cubes. She searched through the console's records, working backward to find the moment the Colony first arrived. Kractik pointed out the image's date to Jaktook and spoke of the most recent recording date. The difference surprised Jaktook, but there wasn't time to dwell on it, and he requested Kractik hurry.

Kractik programmed an activities download from the console. She set her first cube in position and tapped the menu item. When the console signaled the cube was full, she replaced it. The records required three cubes before the download was complete.

"Envoy, Mangoth," Jaktook called. When the two individuals reached the console, Jaktook handed the cubes to Mangoth. "Delegate Mangoth, I present you with the proof the Tsargit requested of the Colony's incursion into this dome."

"Your efforts are appreciated, Advisor Jaktook," Mangoth replied in formal tones. "The Tsargit will be made aware of the Jatouche and Pyrean's efforts to assist me."

"Envoy, look here," Jaktook requested. He made a brief request to Kractik, who queried the console.

An image popped up above the panel, and Harbour asked, "What should I be noting?"

"Wait," Jaktook managed to say before the image changed.

Harbour watched a series of recordings from the dome's overhead point of view. A consistent theme became evident. "The Colony is flowing out of this dome through gate one," Harbour said.

"So it appears, Envoy," Kractik replied.

Mangoth studied the image of the Colony sentients frozen in the panel's projection. Gate one held a load of crates, and Colony sentients were draped over them.

"The Tsargit won't be pleased," Mangoth said, with a deep sigh. "They've set the guidelines for alliance members for millennia, and they've failed to consider the ramifications of ignoring rogue sentients who don't wish to abide by their restrictions."

"Did the Colony travel through gate two?" Harbour asked.

"Not at any time, Envoy," Kractik replied. "I queried the console for that very thing."

Harbour wanted to ask Kractik if she was sure, but she considered that it would be an absurd question. Instead, she said, "Looks like we'll be taking gate two," Harbour announced to the teams. "Mangoth has what we came here to get. Now, we have to find a way home."

"My team will go first," Jessie said to Harbour. "You'll need Devon to hold the ramp."

Harbour agreed with Jessie's suggestion, and team two mounted platform two. They readied their weapons, and Jessie cued Kractik, who sent them on their way.

"Everyone but Kractik and Devon mount the platform," Harbour called out, and her team hurried to obey. When they were ready, Harbour said, "Short delay, Kractik. Then the two of you run."

Kractik set the gate's activation. When she initiated the program, she yelled, "Now, Devon," then the two of them raced each other to get to the gate first. It was a tie — Devon's legs were longer, but Kractik had the shorter distance to travel. Within a count of three after gaining the platform, the gate activated.

-27-
Beta Dome

"Welcome to beta dome," Nelson quipped, when the gate's light faded on team two.

The explorers arrived with weapons drawn only to face an empty deck. Through the blue glow of the dome, they could see the night sky.

"No crates, no debris," Bryan remarked. "No sign of occupation."

"Clear the platform," Jessie ordered.

The team jumped down and waited anxiously for their fellow explorers. When Harbour's team arrived, they immediately cleared the platform, and Mangoth spread a net over it.

"The wedge is closed," Jaktook noted. "That's a good indication that this dome has been vacant since the Messinants left it."

"Nonetheless, we should check below," Mangoth offered.

"Agreed," Jessie added.

The team had rehearsed these movements before. Jaktook and Kractik occupied the console. Devon took up a forward position directly facing the ramp. Tracy was on his flank. She wore an evil grin. The rest of the team members were arrayed beside and behind them.

Kractik initiated the console, which appeared to have been dormant. She activated the needed panel, touched off the wedge, and called out, "Opening."

After a half hour of investigating every room on the second level, the team finally admitted that beta dome was safe. No one was here but them, and they were probably the first sentients to set foot in the dome after the Messinants.

The company retired to one of the larger dorm rooms. They stripped off their gear and suits, used the facilities, and sat desultorily eating their paste.

Jessie finished his plate and pushed it forward. A mild burp escaped his mouth, and he apologized.

"So the action is not appreciated by humans?" Mangoth asked Jessie.

"No, but it happens to all of us," Jessie replied.

"Unfortunate," Mangoth said. "It's expected in my culture."

There was subdued chuckling from several of the team members.

"I see that we have two choices," Jessie said. "We can either fight our way through the alpha and Colony domes to reach Rissness, or we can search for an alternate route home."

Kractik gently cleared her throat. "I'm sorry to disagree with you, Advisor," she said. "We've only one choice. Before we retired I checked the status of this dome's four gates. We journeyed from alpha dome to arrive at beta gate one. That gate is now offline."

"The Colony is probably using my net to block the gate," Mangoth growled.

"Undoubtedly, Delegate," Kractik replied. Turning to Harbour, she said, "The other three gates are active and unobstructed."

"That this dome has four gates bodes well for the possibility of our success, Envoy," Jaktook added.

"As I was saying, we have a clear choice before us," Jessie quipped, amending his earlier remark in disgust.

"Too bad," Tracy said harshly. "I would have voted for taking the direct route home."

No one replied to Tracy's comment. It was clear that, at this moment, she didn't care if she survived the journey through the alpha and Colony domes or not. She wanted revenge.

Devon was instructed that the beam weapon had a means to lockout unauthorized users. He hadn't thought to employ it, but he made a mental note to do so before he left the dorm room again.

"Expectations must be properly set, Jaktook," Mangoth said soberly.

Jaktook tipped his head in acknowledgment of the delegate's statement. He gazed at Harbour and Jessie. Then he said, "That beta dome has four gates and is unoccupied indicates that potentially there is a complex web of gates beyond our three choices. Consider that beta gate one leads to alpha gate three, which leads to the Colony gate one, which leads to Rissness, which connects to the alliance."

"To be more specific," Kractik added, "we'll start with three choices, which will lead us to other domes with more choices."

"And until we reach an alliance member, these domes will be undocumented, and we'll have no way of knowing which gate to take," Bryan reasoned.

"We'll have to explore them one at a time and track them," Olivia noted.

"That will be critical," Jaktook agreed.

Pete held up a finger for attention, "Do we have a method of doing that?" he asked.

"I can query each console, Pete," Kractik replied. "That will give us a precise locator for our position."

"How?" Bryan asked.

"Every dome has a unique identifier, which is contained in the console," Jaktook explained.

"Then we can map our journeys, if we have an application to record it," Olivia said.

Kractik flashed her teeth. "After my first visit to Triton, I desired to be a dome investigator for the Tsargit one day. At the time, it was a lofty thought, far above my standing. However, I chose to prepare myself for the role, in case an opportunity was afforded me. One of the tools of the investigator is an application that maps the domes. Journeyers use a simpler version to navigate through the alliance domes. However, my app is more robust. It allows me to add new domes, name them, detail their gates, and display the linked gates."

"Excellent," Olivia said joyously, clasping the Jatouche on the shoulder.

"If we are able to return to the alliance, the Tsargit will hear of your cleverness and foresight, Kractik," Mangoth said.

This time, Kractik flashed her teeth so wide it resembled a snarl.

"I've a question," Aurelia said. "We can map our progress. That's great. But what I want to know is how do we protect ourselves during our journey through each gate?"

"Good point," Pete agreed, looking at Jaktook.

"The cubes," Jaktook said. "We record visuals of us and send the cube ahead. That will announce us."

"There are some holes in that thinking," Pete replied. "Say the receivers have recently discovered the dome but can't operate the console. They're surprised by the appearance of a cube. Their response is to let the cube sit on the platform forever, waiting for it to do something."

"Or sentients have discovered the console, are learning to operate it, and are able to view the cube," Bryan suggested, "but they're an aggressive species, and we walk into an assault."

"Or there's no one there," Olivia added, "and the cube sits there as in Pete's scenario."

"I retract my suggestion," Jaktook said in a desultorily fashion.

There was quiet, while the team mulled over a means of effectively communicating with whoever might be on the other end of a gate pair. Jessie regarded Aurelia, and said, "I think the answer to your question is that we can't. We'll have to take our chances."

"But we'll arrive with our weapons displayed. We have to," Harbour objected.

"Who's to say they're weapons if we don't portray them as such?" Mangoth asked.

"True," Harbour agreed, seeing his point. "They could be the tools of explorers. In which case, we have to take care to keep them at our sides and not point them at dome inhabitants."

* * * *

Sleep came quickly for most of the team. Nerves and muscles were heavily stressed, resulting in mental and physical exhaustion.

Harbour and Aurelia bracketed Tracy's pallet. The girl had pushed off their ministrations several times. But, as she slumbered, her dreams haunted her, and she whimpered in her sleep.

The two empaths turned on their sides to face Tracy and lent her emotional support for hours before they too succumbed.

In the morning, by the explorers' chronometers, they assembled on the deck, fed and rested.

"Do we use logic or chance?" Jessie asked, gazing at the three gate choices.

"Mangoth and Jaktook said that this might be a long process," Olivia reminded Jessie. "I vote for logic. We came in on gate one. We should start with gate two and map our way along the journey."

"I concur," Kractik piped up.

Harbour chose to take up Olivia's suggestion. "Kractik, set the console to activate gate two."

The company departed in two teams. The next dome was mercifully anticlimactic. It was unoccupied. Kractik addressed the console for its ID, mapped the gates, and the teams, who had arrived on gate three, left on gate one.

And so it went for days and days. The teams jumped from dome to dome, recording their passage and mapping the gates. Following their chronometers, whether the sky was bright or dark, they rested at the end of a ten-hour period.

After the third day of travel, Mangoth remarked, "I find it hard to comprehend the number of unoccupied domes."

"Agreed," Jaktook replied. "I wish I'd carried my scope. I want to examine the nearby planets to look for burgeoning civilizations."

"There is the possibility," Bryan offered, "that we're journeying through some of the newest domes constructed by the Messinants. Their experiments, which were designed to uplift the species on these planets, might not have matured yet."

"That's a possibility, Bryan," Jaktook offered.

"It also means that alpha domes' gate one and two represent open territories for the Colony," Devon said. "Maybe that's why they're expanding in gate one's direction."

"That's a salient point, Devon," Jessie acknowledged. "It would indicate that the Colony members explored the routes from alpha gate one in depth, realized the opportunity, and developed a plan to usurp those worlds."

"And that means the Colony intends to invade the planets and wipe out any developing cultures," Harbour said.

"That makes our return to the alliance all that more imperative," Mangoth said. "The Tsargit must be warned of the Colony's intentions."

After journeying through a gate on the eleventh day, Harbour's team arrived in a dome with a single platform. The deck was crowded with individuals studying the console and the glyphs on the deck. The flash of the platform had frozen them in a tableau.

"Send us back, Kractik," Harbour whispered. "Everyone else stay still."

Kractik eased off the platform and wound her way past several green-skinned, round-bodied sentients. Their huge, bulging eyes stared at her. At the console, she had to point to it to get an individual to step aside. She accessed the controls for their gate, brought up the menu, chose the delay mode, and set the time. All the while, one of the sentients studied her every movement.

When Kractik finished, she made her way back to the platform, threading through the staring throng. She gained the platform, and then the team was gone. They carried latent images of a stunned young race, which had just had an eye-opening demonstration of the dome's purpose.

Kractik was overjoyed to share the news with Jaktook that after all their travels they'd finally encountered a new race who'd achieved space travel. "And I suppose I advanced their understanding of the dome's operation by half an annual," Kractik remarked.

"The bad news is that if this race begins exploring the domes, the first species they encounter might be the Colony," Jessie said. His pronouncement put a damper on the explorers' excitement.

The first time the team returned to beta dome, the sight of Mangoth's net lying across gate one told them immediately where they'd arrived. There was a brief bit of laughter about the irony that they had returned to the starting point after twenty-one cycles of travel.

They rested and ate in a familiar dorm room before starting out again. The routine repeated, and the teams lapsed into a daze, traveling through empty dome after empty dome.

Their second return to the beta dome produced no laughter. Instead, feelings of despair rolled off everyone, which Harbour and Aurelia sensed. They'd been journeying for thirty-eight days and were emotionally exhausted by the lack of progress.

With few words among them, they trooped down the ramp to the second level and the prior occupied room. After cleanup and food, they lay on their pallets, a despondent group of individuals. Even Harbour and Empath couldn't muster sufficient sympathy to alleviate the mental suffering of their team members.

Jessie's imagination produced an image of the team as a pack of vermin running through a maze of pipes aboard a huge station. Lacking knowledge, the creatures were never aware of the greater structure in which they roamed. Instead, they were doomed to traverse familiar paths until their lives ran out. He hardly recognized that he complained out loud, "One dome looks like another. If I was a Messinant, how would I know where I was without querying a console and carrying a map? For a highly advanced race, that seems a tedious method."

"Perhaps the console updated the Messinants, as they arrived," Jaktook suggested.

"With what?" Jessie asked, rolling over and propping up on an elbow.

"I would assume —" Kractik started to say before she stopped, thought, and said, "Perhaps I should find out."

When Kractik rose off her pallet and shuffled wearily toward the door, a sigh escaped Jaktook. He crawled off his pallet and followed her. The pair worked on the console for a few hours, without making much progress before Jaktook called a halt to their work. They retired to join the others who were fast asleep.

The next day, the team relaxed on the deck, while Kractik, Jaktook, and Mangoth poured over the console menus. The morning passed without success, and the team took a break to eat and use the facilities.

After a meal, Kractik returned to the console. Jaktook and Mangoth lounged with the rest of the team. They'd acknowledged that her console knowledge far exceeded theirs.

During this time, the engineers, Olivia, Pete, and Bryan, held a private conversation, discussing the problem. Eventually, Nelson, Tracy, Jacob, and Aurelia joined them, ostensibly to help but really wanting to be part of a discussion to relieve the boredom.

"Kractik has been over the panels and menus an inordinate number of times during her lifetime's experience, and she's found no means of getting a master display of the domes," Pete objected.

"What if the Messinants provided other means of communicating with the console?" Bryan asked.

"Such as?" Olivia asked.

"Voice requests," Bryan replied.

The engineers strolled over to the console, the others following, and posed their question to Kractik.

"Consoles' don't respond to voice commands," Kractik replied to the question. "We believe the Messinants expected the races, those which achieved full sentience and space travel, would be moving between domes. That would require the consoles carry every possible language. In addition, the Messinants left before many races matured. Language updates wouldn't have been possible."

"You're searching for maps, right?" Aurelia asked.

"Yes," Kractik replied.

"What about searching for stars?" Aurelia suggested.

"How would that help us?" Kractik asked.

Jessie had wandered over with the rest of the team, and he'd caught Aurelia's questions. "Perhaps a star map might be annotated with the domes," Jessie added.

"Would we still understand where we are in the star display?" Jaktook asked.

"Less conversation," Harbour said firmly. "Search for a star map, Kractik."

"Yes, Envoy," Kractik replied with alacrity.

Kractik knew of a deep submenu on a rarely used panel. The general opinion of the alliance members had been that many of the submenu's glyphs produced readings that were used by the Messinants to monitor the dome's operational statuses.

As the menu's items moved past their eyes, Jessie requested Kractik halt. "Start from the top, Kractik, and translate the glyphs for us."

"Yes, Advisor," Kractik replied.

Harbour and Aurelia detected a glimmer of hope from the console operator, and the two empaths exchanged brief glances. It was Harbour's thought that Kractik was energized by the input of Pyreans, who didn't know the consoles and were liable to ask questions outside the accepted norms.

Kractik would translate a glyph, and the team would mull it over. If there were no questions, she would move on. Unfortunately, there was no interest from the group in pursuing the relevant submenus based on her translations. Eventually, she reached the end of the menu.

"This is not a well-understood glyph," Kractik said. "We believe it means end or final."

"What does it display?" Jessie asked.

"There isn't one," Jaktook replied. "This is one of the consoles' mysteries."

"What happens when you select it?" Aurelia asked.

"Nothing," Kractik replied, touching the panel. "You get a projection with nothing in it."

"Odd," Aurelia commented. She reached out a finger and touched the projection. A yellow dot was left floating in the midst of the projection, when she withdrew her hand. After a short period of time, the projection blinked off.

"What happened?" Olivia asked.

"We don't know," Jaktook replied. "The menu item creates a projection, and a digit can write inside it."

"I assume you've tried to write all sorts of things in there," Bryan said.

"If the statements of the oldest races are to be accepted," Mangoth said. "Every glyph etched on the walls and decks has been tried."

"Is the meaning of every glyph known?" Harbour asked.

"Not nearly," Mangoth replied. "When it comes to understanding the Messinants, we're woefully ignorant. If we were comparing the domes to ships, the alliance races would be considered the cargo crews, nothing more."

Star Map

The explorers retired to eat and rest. Kractik lay awake on her pallet and chose to slip out of the darkened room. Her excitement alerted Aurelia, who followed her, and their passage incited Olivia's curiosity.

At the console, Kractik initiated the odd menu item, with its empty projection, and stared at it.

"How many menus and submenus have an empty projection?" Olivia asked.

"Only a few," Kractik replied.

"In other words, most of the console's operations are display driven, so they can be easily mastered," Aurelia suggested. "Not that Pyreans have figured the thing out," she muttered.

"In time, you would have," Kractik said, patting Aurelia's forearm. "Of that, I've no doubt."

"If I saw an empty screen on my comm unit, I would expect to enter a request for an item or a query," Olivia mused.

"A query would take multiple glyphs," Kractik explained. "Based on the number of glyphs in a dome, a two-glyph request has a possible fifty million combinations. Three glyphs in a query would represent an unbelievable three hundred and forty billion combinations."

"That's supposing you considered every glyph as a potential entry," Olivia said. "I think that we're probably dealing with a set of fewer than a hundred."

"But which hundred?" Aurelia remarked.

Olivia visualized the extensive number of queries she'd written in her lifetime. She tried to narrow them down to their basics. Finally, she said, "Assuming we're building a query, we need an action word. What glyphs in the basic console menus can be interpreted as locate, display, or show?"

Kractik took Olivia and Aurelia through the menu again, pointing to relevant glyphs and interpreting them for the Pyrean women.

Olivia halted Kractik, looked at Aurelia, and said, "We should have brought our comm units. I left mine in my personal gear at Rissness. I wonder if one of the others has theirs."

"No need to wonder, I have mine," Aurelia replied, with a bright smile. She skipped down the ramp, slipped into the dorm room, silently dug through her pack, retrieved the comm unit, and eased out.

Good luck, Harbour thought, having been woken by Aurelia's bubbling enthusiasm.

Kractik repeated her initial lesson, and Aurelia captured an image of the glyph and annotated its meaning. "That's all the glyphs that indicate an action," Kractik said, when she finished.

"We need a set of nouns," Aurelia said excitedly. Her gates were leaking, and Kractik and Olivia were caught up in the young empath's desire to resolve their dilemma.

"Nouns, nouns," Olivia muttered.

"Star or stars," Kractik volunteered.

"Map," Aurelia added.

The threesome built a list of over thirty keywords that they thought could form their request. Kractik repeated her exercise, going through the menus and submenus and pointing out the useful glyphs.

"We have twenty-one action symbols and thirty-eight subjects," Aurelia summarized.

Kractik frowned, while considering the challenge. She said, "Inferring your intended approach, I don't expect this to be a two-glyph query. I would think three or more glyphs would be required to make your request sufficiently clear."

"I'd agree with that," Olivia said.

"But if we start with a verb and use two nouns, that would give us slightly less than thirty thousand combinations," Aurelia said, her elation rising.

Kractik's eyes rolled up in her head, and Olivia caught the Jatouche before she slumped to the deck.

"Aurelia," Olivia admonished.

"I'm sorry," Aurelia replied, slowly curtailing her sending.

Moments later, Kractik awakened and flashed her teeth. "If we're to wander these domes forever, I'll require you put me to sleep every night in just this fashion."

Aurelia smiled sheepishly and said, "I can do that for a friend."

"I was about to explain, before Kractik was put on the deck," Olivia said, eyeing Aurelia, "that your calculation assumes two things. One: That you understand the syntax. Meaning, does the action word come first? Two: Do two nouns follow the verb? If those two assumptions are incorrect, then the possible combinations get enormously larger."

"What if we don't follow a process of trying all possible combinations in some kind of logical order?" Aurelia insisted.

"As opposed to what?" Olivia asked.

"We know what we want to ask. But let's also think about what the Messinants might have asked the console. Then we'll select the most relevant combinations and try them first," Aurelia suggested.

"I believe the first idea might have value," Kractik replied. "As for guessing what the Messinants requested, I've no hope of imagining that."

The threesome tried Aurelia's idea for hours until Kractik loosed a wide and long yawn.

"Time to call it quits and get some rest," Olivia said. "Otherwise, we'll be out of sync with the rest of the team."

They retired, and soon afterwards, Olivia and Kractik were deep asleep. Not so for Aurelia. She lay awake, thinking of the glyphs and the needed query. When sleep didn't come, she slipped out again.

Rather than start with the empty projection, Aurelia lay on a platform. She stared at the light blue glow of the dome overhead and let her mind wander. The glyphs and their meanings drifted through her thoughts. When she felt she had some clarity, she approached the console, pulled up the empty projection, and began entering combinations.

Unlike the threesome's earlier thoughts, Aurelia felt she had only a few dozen key query combinations, and she entered them in every variation of order. The final entry failed to produce a result, and she pounded her fists in frustration on the console.

Aurelia slid to the deck and sat with her back against the console. *I don't think I'm going to be a source of good cheer, in the future, Kractik,* she thought. Disappointment ruling Aurelia's emotions, she rolled onto her knees and reached for the console's lip to pull her up. Her eyes focused on an elaborate glyph on the console's face. She'd never noticed this symbol on the other consoles but presumed she'd never looked for it either.

Running a finger over the complex symbol, Aurelia whispered, "Do you identify this dome?" She stayed on her knees, tracing the glyph over and over again. The process soothed her and allowed her to focus on the query again. Aloud she asked, "If I were Messinants, what would I want to know?" and then she answered herself. "I'd want to know where I am in relation to this place."

Aurelia stood up, activated the projection, and said to herself, "You're a spacer. You travel the galaxy. How do you think about where you are and where you want to go?" It hit her that the concept of verbs and nouns had confused the threesome. "Map isn't only a thing; it's also a request," she whispered.

After drawing the glyph for map, Aurelia added the complicated glyph on the console's face. She said quietly, "And this is the dome where I am."

The projection had always faded if the user paused for any length of time. This time, it remained, as if waiting for the user to finish the query. Aurelia was exhilarated. She knew she was on the right track.

"What am I missing? Map the dome ... to what ... or how?" Aurelia asked, continuing to talk to herself. She searched her list of keywords, thinking she might have missed a word for network or something that indicated the entire conglomeration of domes.

Aurelia's finger was scrolling down the list, and it hesitated over a word. "Could it be that simple?" she asked. Carefully, she drew the symbol for stars. Immediately, the projection disappeared. Aurelia had a brief moment to be disappointed. Then the dome's constant blue glow winked out, and she panicked.

"Now you've done it, Aurelia," she whispered harshly, hanging her head in her hands. "Try explaining this to Harbour. Worse, think of telling Jessie." She closed her eyes and tilted her head back to calm herself. The training of the senior empaths kicked in, and she slowed her breathing and centered herself. When she opened her eyes, she focused on the dome, and her mouth fell open.

Aurelia turned from the console, ran down the ramp, and raced to the dorm room. On entering, she smacked the light plate to full, and yelled, "On the deck, everyone." To her consternation, the team jumped off their pallets and snatched up their weapons.

"No, no," Aurelia cried, waving her hands in negation. "We're not under attack. Come on," she yelled and raced out of the room.

The group dropped their weapons, slipped on boots, and hurried after Aurelia. When they reached the deck, they found Aurelia facing them, with hands on hips, and an ecstatic expression on her face.

The young empath didn't have to say a word. The darkened dome spoke for her.

Gazing upward, Jessie whispered, "Oh, for the love of Pyre."

"While the meaning of your words is unclear, Advisor," Mangoth said quietly, "the sentiment is understood."

Aurelia burned with desire to explain what had happened, but she chose to luxuriate in the sense of awe that flooded off the group.

"A star map," Jaktook said in wonder.

"Not just a star map," Jessie corrected. "Notice the tiny yellow rings around a portion of the stars."

"Domes?" Mangoth suggested.

"What else could they mean?" Jessie asked.

As the group walked to the middle of the deck to wonder at the magnificent image of stars that the dome displayed, Nelson asked, "Could we be seeing the night sky beyond? In other words, could Aurelia have just reduced the intensity of the dome's light?"

There was a sudden chill that passed over the group, including Aurelia. A darkened dome meant that the gates might be inoperable.

Kractik hurried to the console. "The gates are offline," she said.

"Set gate three for a timed delay, Kractik, and activate it," Jaktook ordered.

As Kractik activated panels, the star field display disappeared, and its blue glow reappeared. "The gates are active," Kractik reported, shutting down gate three's countdown.

There was a collective sigh of relief, and Aurelia felt vindicated. From Harbour, Aurelia received a hug, a flood of emotional approval, and a whisper of, "I'm so proud of you."

"You can repeat what you did, Aurelia, can't you?" Pete asked.

"Sure. Do you want to see?" Aurelia asked, and laughed at the reaction of the company, which had literally crowded her toward the console.

"I didn't do this by myself," Aurelia explained. "It began with Kractik, Olivia, and me. We started with the assumption that the projection was waiting for a query. Rather than attempt all combinations of glyphs, which we were assured the alliance races had been trying, we narrowed the list to key terms that we thought would be used to express our question. Kractik explored the menus, and we recorded the relevant glyphs and their meanings on my comm unit."

Kractik eyed Jaktook. It was against Tsargit decree to teach non-alliance races the meaning of glyphs. This prohibition had been broken several times by the Jatouche with Pyreans, but none so blatantly as to allow the Pyreans to record the information. In response, Jaktook flashed his teeth broadly at Kractik, and she relaxed.

"But we didn't get anywhere," Olivia pointed out.

"Right, the three of us went back to the room, but I couldn't sleep," Aurelia explained. "So I came up here to try again. I got frustrated, and while I was wallowing in my disappointment, I saw this glyph." She pointed at the face of the console.

"Which means what?" Harbour asked, looking at Jaktook.

"It's unknown," Jaktook replied. "That symbol is found nowhere else in the dome, and the console operation instructions don't refer to it. Incidentally, it's the most complex glyph, by far."

"Because it's not a single thing," Devon said.

When the groups turned to him, Devon explained, "I watched a vid from the JOS library. It was on ancient Earth cultures. In several cases, early societies laid one symbol on top of another to add meaning to the first symbol."

"It's a unique identifier," Kractik proposed.

"That's what I thought," Aurelia continued. "To me, it represents where we are in space. This dome, this body, this system."

"This star," Nelson added, and Aurelia nodded enthusiastically.

"So my query was," Aurelia said, as she activated the projection and began to draw. "Map ... as a request, not a noun ... this dome's location ... to the stars." When she completed her entries, the dome darkened and the star map appeared.

"I was watching the star field beyond the dome before this display appeared," Bryan said. "It isn't the same one. The dome is definitely responding to Aurelia's query."

A joyous outpouring of celebratory noise followed Bryan's announcement. Pyreans and Jatouche were hugging, and the Crocian was clasping forearms.

"We've established that this is a representation from the console to Aurelia's query about where we are," Jacob said, "And we believe the yellow-ringed stars signify dome locations. But how do we orient ourselves to this map?"

Jacob's question dampened enthusiasm again, as the explorers examined the extensive display. The field held tens of thousands of bright stars, and many more dim ones. In contrast, the highlighted ones were a mere few hundred.

"We need orientation," Nelson said softly. Jessie eyed him, and Nelson answered, "I was a navigator before I made first mate."

"Our navigation apps," Jessie exclaimed, and the two men disappeared down the ramp, as fast as they could.

"If they return with their comm units, I'm going to be upset," Olivia exclaimed. "We were told to leave our personal things behind. Am I the only one who complied?" She looked around, and the Pyreans navel-gazed or winced under her glare. "Thanks, everyone," she said in frustration.

As Olivia expected, Jessie and Nelson returned with their comm units, whose screens projected their navigation apps.

"This isn't going to be easy," Nelson said. "We have the one viewpoint, which is from Crimsa, Pyre's star. It'll require that we continually rotate our viewpoints though an entire sphere's orientation to align with some small portion of this display."

"But we know that we're on this map," Harbour argued. "Triton has an active dome. So we must be up here somewhere."

"It will take patience," Mangoth said, eyeing the dense star map.

"We have to cut down the field somehow. Search it quadrant by quadrant," Bryan said. "Otherwise, we'll be looking all over the place, and we'll have to hand off the process so that our eyes and brains can recuperate.

It was Jaktook's turn to run from the ramp and disappear below. He returned with a small device, which he set on a platform. "This is a survey tool," he explained. "I thought we might have needed it at the alpha dome to record the new construction. It projects a beam and records the pattern, giving engineers an accurate concept of scale."

Jaktook pointed it at the bottom edge of the dome's image, overlapping one of the highlighted stars. He reduced its intensity and adjusted its shape until it formed a square. Then he tapped on its tiny panel and produced a crosshatch pattern.

"Excellent," Mangoth said. "We can assign the grid's starting point and the direction the survey must take. Each individual must supply the location of the next grid to their replacement."

"I can make it easier," Jaktook said, and tiny symbols appeared in the upper right hand corner of each grid.

Pete walked close to the projection to view the symbols. "These don't mean anything to us," Pete complained.

"Understandable, Pete," Jaktook replied. "These are Jatouche characters. But you can better indicate the grid you completed by finger-drawing the symbol."

Pete agreed that was a better idea than trying to count off squares across and up the block to convey the next grid.

"Is this where we want to start?" Jacob asked. He meant it simply as an alternative point to Jaktook's indiscriminate setup of his device.

The group looked at Jacob, considered his request, and turned to gaze at Aurelia.

"What?" the young empath asked in surprise.

"I believe we think of you as our lucky piece," Jessie said, "and your choice of a starting point might prove more fortunate than any one of ours."

"No, no," Aurelia objected. "All I did was solve a puzzle. This ..." she said, swinging her arms at the huge star field, "isn't a puzzle. It's a humongous undertaking, and I'm not going to be responsible for starting us off in the wrong quadrant."

"Then I propose we accept Jaktook's starting point," Harbour said. "It does include a ringed star. Who knows? That could be where we're located."

* * * *

Harbour was wrong about the ringed star being their location. They searched the first block without success. When it came time to shift the pattern, an earnest discussion broke out, but it was quickly settled by Nelson's logic.

"Jaktook has told me that his tool can track the previous positions of the grids and align as necessary," Nelson stated. "We know that Crimsa has a dome. If we're to continue to assume that these ringed-stars represent domes, which is logical, then one of them must be Crimsa. I say we swing the grid pattern around the dome's base to that star." He pointed at a yellow-ringed star nearly halfway around the circumference of the base.

"I'm in agreement," Jaktook said. "These are the only two stars that fit our requirements within the pattern's projection height. When we finish with the second star, I'll raise the projection up the height of the block and rotate it until we include another ringed-star. We'll continue around the display without missing one of the objects of our search."

No one had a better idea. So, Jaktook programmed his device and swung the tool around. He compensated the beam's size for the change in distance and aligned it with the dome's bottom.

"I do love advanced technology," Bryan whispered.

"Do you celebrate personal events in your lifetime?" Jaktook asked Bryan quietly.

"Some people celebrate the day of their birth," Bryan replied.

"And when does this day occur for you?" Jaktook asked.

Bryan winked conspiratorially at the Jatouche, and said, "Today."

Jaktook flashed his teeth and then chuckled. "How opportune!" he riposted.

The days passed. Jaktook's surveyor tool marched around the dome shifting around and up to the next yellow-ringed star.

The navigation apps had been copied to every comm unit, and the Jatouche and the Crocian were taught to manipulate them, although Mangoth, with his heavy clawed hands, found it difficult.

At any one time, two individuals worked on the square of the grid containing the ringed star. It helped to guarantee a mistake wasn't made in trying to match Crimsa's view of neighboring stars.

Pallets were laid on a platform to make the searchers more comfortable.

Over half the yellow-highlighted stars had been searched, when Kractik blinked in surprise. She'd rotated the navigation view of Crimsa through most of the angles and had nearly missed the subtle similarities to the grid square she was viewing.

"Tracy, two hundred and twenty-eight degrees rotation, one hundred and fourteen degrees declination," Kractik whispered urgently. She didn't want to get the others excited if she was in error.

"It's similar, but the alignment isn't quite exact," Tracy said. She'd struggled with the application, but she'd kept quiet. The thought of lying around for days on end, while others were occupied with the search, was unthinkable to her.

"My comm unit is at arm's length, and I'm at twenty-eight percent magnification," Kractik whispered.

Tracy adjusted her comm unit's image scale, crawled over to Kractik, eyed the Jatouche's shorter arm, and held her device at the same length. Then the young Pyrean let out a shriek and hugged Kractik.

"We found it," Tracy yelled, which brought the others running. "Well, to be honest, Kractik found it, and I've confirmed it."

Immediately, Jessie and Nelson activated their comm units, and Kractik read off the orientation.

"Squat down over here," Tracy said, indicating the pallets. She added details about the magnification and the short-arm's length to hold their devices.

"Good job, you two," Jessie congratulated. "That's Crimsa's star."

"Agreed," Nelson added.

"Now that we know where we are," Devon asked, "how do we use this star map to navigate to where we want to go? Which, by the way, is where?"

"I've been saving this piece of information," Mangoth said. "You might have noticed that the colored rings have tiny filaments in the upright position."

"I saw those," Olivia said. "There are four of them on our star. Do they indicate gates?"

"They do," Mangoth agreed. "And I know this because I've found only one of the ringed-stars with six filaments, and I've been searching the display the entire time it's been present. We head there." Mangoth had stretched out a thick, scaled arm and pointed at a star nearly opposite Crimsa on the dome's display.

"Why there?" Jessie asked.

"Because that is the one dome that I can guarantee is an alliance member. It's my home world. The Crocians have six gates," Mangoth announced proudly.

"If we do as Mangoth suggests, "Jaktook said, "we should encounter an alliance member before then and can be directed to Rissness."

"That was my thought," Mangoth said, his massive snout nodding in agreement.

Kractik stared at the Pyreans' ringed star and said, "Crimsa has a single gate, which connects to Rissness, but we don't know which of these ringed stars that would be. I would suppose it's a nearby star, but we can't be sure. I would suggest that we stay away from this area so that we don't accidentally arrive at the Colony's dome."

"An excellent point, Kractik," Harbour agreed.

"As to your questions, Devon," Nelson said, "the method isn't going to be pretty. We lay out our intended path toward the Crocian star in this display. We pick a gate in this dome and start our journey. When we arrive at the next dome, we query the console, and we see if we ended up at the star we wanted. If not, we go back and try another gate until we reach the correct star. We keep doing that until we reach an alliance member or encounter the wrong race."

"There's nothing simpler?" Devon asked. He eyed the knowledgeable individuals for confirmation — Mangoth, Jaktook, and Kractik. None of them offered an alternative method.

"When do we start?" Devon asked.

"Now," Pete said, "I'm tired of this dome. I want to visit a different one."

Despite Mangoth's alien nature, he was the first to catch the joke and roared to the overhead.

Harbour waited for the laughter to die down. "There'll be one addition to Nelson's methods," she said. "Aurelia will enter the query each time. It seems obvious the Messinants used a hand, digit, or what-have-you to write in the projection, and Aurelia imitates their style."

"Agreed," Jaktook said.

-29-
Homeward

Harbour and Jessie shuffled the teams. Having encountered few sentients in their journey to return to Rissness, Harbour had Jessie, Aurelia, and Nelson join her team in exchange for Devon, Pete, and Jacob.

Nelson's prediction was accurate. Their journey wasn't pretty. They rarely chose the correct gate the first time, which meant they had to reverse course and try again. However, they made progress, slowly but surely.

Their routine became a well-worn habit. They'd arrive in the new dome with weapons ready, but held at their sides. In an empty dome, Kractik and Aurelia would hurry excitedly to the console. After Kractik ensured the console was online, Aurelia would enter the query.

The dome would display the star map, and Jessie and Nelson would examine their navigation applications and recorded images from the beta dome's display to track their progress. If they were successful, they would wait until the second team joined them, and they would choose the next gate. If they weren't, they returned to the previous dome and selected another gate.

Jaktook monitored his chronometer to determine the timing to send his group after team one, when they didn't return. It was always a nerve-racking period for him, having never been responsible for a group of humans.

Occasionally, the teams spotted evidence of habitation, but they didn't encounter sentients. The items at various domes amounted to recording devices, a large telescope, a few crates, and, in each case, deck wedges opened. In those circumstances, the conclusion among the explorers was that young races had discovered the domes and had yet to comprehend a console's operation.

The first time a recording device was seen, Kractik commented, "I believe we just educated a second race about the purpose of the domes."

"I think our journey is going to deliver that lesson to a good many more races," Harbour riposted.

With each hard-won successful step, the team grew closer to their target star, the home of the Crocians, and hope grew. Weeks earlier, evenings had been punctuated by quiet — a meal, small talk, and sleep. Now the explorers talked of returning home and the tales they'd tell.

Often, Harbour and Jessie spent some time on deck alone. The subjects ranged from the leadership problems of Pyre to what the Tsargit reward might mean. On the latter subject, Harbour was of the opinion that the reward would belong to the citizenry of Pyre, and Jessie argued against that idea.

"Harbour," he said, "those gifts, whatever they might be, should be substantial, if I understand Mangoth correctly. And if they are, then that's leverage. Or do you want to enrich the commandant and the dome council at stationers' and spacers' expense? The Jatouche and Tsargit rewards would be your opportunity to shift the status quo."

"You're referring to the *Belle*'s stolen documents," Harbour replied.

"Absolutely," Jessie exclaimed. "Earth and the original colonists signed on to a different concept of government than the one we have now. Their dreams were hijacked. This is the perfect time to return it to them."

"We could become outcasts if the downsiders and the commandant banded against us and the stationers didn't take sides, or worse, took our opponents' sides," Harbour warned.

"That's a possibility," Jessie agreed. "We'd have to have a plan and be careful executing it."

"Talk to me, my Advisor," Harbour said, grinning.

That had been Harbour and Jessie's discussion on the last night of their intrepid exploration. The next morning, they reviewed their progress on the dome's projection. When they were ready, Harbour's team mounted the platform of the next gate to try, and Jaktook sent team one on its way.

The explorers' arrival in the new dome was a spectacle for all. Instead of an empty dome or a singular group of aliens, the deck was a hub of activity of many species. Or it had been a hive of energetic motion until the sentients took note of the weapons in the hands of the arrivals and hesitated.

Jessie growled softly but sternly, "Weapons behind you. We're safe."

"An alliance dome," Kractik whispered.

It was the medallions broadcasting the status of an envoy, an advisor, and a delegate that calmed the crowd. With tips of their heads or crowns to the exalted group, the sentients went about their business.

"Descend," Harbour ordered to clear the gate for the second team.

When Jaktook's team arrived, the Pyreans and he were overjoyed by the sight.

Jaktook flashed his teeth at Harbour, who was smiling at him.

"We made it," Tracy said, tears forming in her eyes, which expressed every explorer's sentiment.

A tall individual, with a coat of spotted fur, a short snout, and sharp canines, hurried from the console toward the group. She bowed her head to Harbour and Mangoth.

"There's no need for alarm," the sentient said, observing the armored suits and various odd and imposing tools the visitors carried. "I'm Shevena, the dome administrator, Envoy and Delegate. We were made aware of your explorations, but I'm surprised that you came by way of this gate. We know the sentients on the other end have not achieved space travel. Your arrival from that direction is quite unexpected."

The explorers broke out into laughter, some weeping tears of joy.

"Your pardon, Shevena," Harbour said. "This is the first alliance dome we've reached since we left Rissness, a third of an annual ago."

Shevena's short jaw loosened, and she frowned, as she considered the possibilities. "Did you remain at a dome for an extended period of time?" she asked.

"You might say, Shevena, that we took the long way home," Mangoth said enigmatically. "And now, we'd like to be sent along the shortest path to Rissness."

"Immediately, Delegate Mangoth," Shevena replied. "Gate two," she added, indicating the platform. She returned swiftly to the console and spoke to the operator, who temporarily took gate two offline to accommodate the priority request. As soon as the first group mounted, the operator activated the gate and sent them on their way. In quick succession, the other explorers followed.

Fifteen journeys later, the blue light of the gate faded, and Harbour's team gazed at another busy dome, but this one had Jatouche operators. Kractik and Aurelia slipped a hand into each of Harbour's and squeezed.

"Let's give the others a chance to enjoy this moment," Harbour said. She continued to hold the hands of the young females, as she stepped off the platform.

The second team arrived and took a moment to take in the view. Then they broke into laughter and cheers.

"Come on," Harbour said to her group. Then she walked slowly toward the ramp.

Word spread, and techs and soldiers came running to strip the explorers of their gear. The entire entourage made their way to the dome's third level, taking over the same dorm room that they'd occupied months ago. They sorted out their personal gear and left for other rooms to use the facilities before returning to share a meal with their fellow journeyers.

When Jaktook had a private moment with Harbour, he asked, "Should I send a console operator to Triton to notify your associates of your safe return?"

Harbour thought and said, "No, Jaktook. We'll be returning to Pyre soon."

"Understood, Envoy," Jaktook said. "I spoke briefly to Her Highness and told her that I expected you to leave for Triton soon. She said she commiserated with your desire to return home."

"Tell Her Highness that she's most considerate," Harbour replied. "Most important, Jaktook, Her Highness will want to accept some level of guilt for the loss of an explorer. Tell her from me that she must not do that. Pyreans chose to go, and we knew the dangers."

"I will tell her, Harbour," Jaktook said, gently touching Harbour's forearm, "but I doubt she'll listen to me."

"Then you tell her that if she wallows in self-pity I'll return and discipline her severely," Harbour said, maintaining a straight face.

Jaktook flashed his teeth and shot back, "If I told her that, she'd probably pretend to accept responsibility to the extent that you'd be enticed to return."

Harbour laughed at that thought, helped herself to a meal from the dispenser, and joined the others at the tables.

When the teams fell onto their pallets, they slept deeply. In the corridor, per Harbour's request, soldiers rotated duty to prevent the explorers from being disturbed with messages.

They'd arrived at Rissness in the early afternoon, Pyre time, and slept for more than half a day. It was an indication of the extraordinary stress each individual had suffered for an extended period.

On waking, Mangoth was the first to depart. "I must make a lengthy report to the Tsargit," he told the group, "and they will need to study our data in depth."

"Before you leave, Mangoth, I'd like to make copies of your three cubes," Jaktook requested.

"Certainly, Jaktook, please do it quickly. I must be on my way," Mangoth replied. He turned to Jessie and said, "Advisor, any time you wish to explore the galaxy's domes, I'll expect a message from you. I wouldn't want to be left out."

"That I'll do, Mangoth," Jessie replied. "I wouldn't want to go exploring without a magnificent fellow such as you."

Mangoth roared his amusement and said, "In truth, Jessie, I'm far from being the most magnificent of my kind."

Harbour, who had been listening to the exchange, said quietly, "You are to us, Mangoth."

Mangoth regarded his fellow explorers. "The events surrounding our journey will remain with me for my lifetime," he said. "You've been most honorable and trustworthy companions. A Crocian could ask for none better." He tipped his snout to Harbour and Jessie. Then Jaktook and he made their way to the deck's console to copy the cubes.

While the explorers were enjoying a second meal, Jaktook returned with his cubes.

"Will you join us?" asked Harbour, when she saw Jaktook hesitate.

"A shuttle leaves soon for Na-Tikkook," Jaktook replied. "I wish to catch it, and speak to Her Highness as soon as possible. I believe my audience will include His Excellency and the master advisors."

"Please give His Excellency my regards, Jaktook," Harbour said. She rose from the table, bent down, and embraced the little Jatouche. While she held him, she sent the gentlest touch of warmth and heard his sigh. Standing up, she added, "Beloved friend, we will see each other again someday."

"I'll make sure of that," Jaktook said. "See them safely home, Kractik," he ordered, and then he said his farewells to the group and left.

"There's nothing to keep us," Harbour said. "All weapons are to be left behind. We take only our personal gear."

"Seriously?" Devon asked, eyeing his beam weapon, which elicited a round of laughter.

Yet, Harbour didn't sense levity or mirth from Devon, which gave her a moment of pause, and in addition, Tracy was another individual not laughing.

Personal gear was grabbed, and soldiers gathered the teams' vac suits. Jessie noted that the soldiers also packed for them the specialized Jatouche armored versions, and he signed to Harbour to take note of it.

The teams left in their latest order. After arriving in the Triton dome, Aurelia waited until the second team arrived. Then she ran to the console, opened the empty projection submenu, and entered the query. When the dome darkened and displayed the star map with ringed-stars indicating the locations of Messinants' domes, she turned a self-satisfied smile on the group.

"Show off," Olivia quipped, ending her comment with a wry smile.

Jessie decided to test his console abilities by accessing the comm panel, projecting the ship choices, and selecting the *Belle*. He smiled at Aurelia, sharing their mutual pleasure at discovering the workings of the consoles of the ancient race of Messinants. Aurelia grinned in reply.

Harbour stepped beside Jessie for the call.

Beatrice "Birdie" Andrews was on comm duty on the *Honora Belle*'s bridge. She nearly jumped out of her seat when she saw Harbour and Jessie's faces on the comm monitor. She yelled, "They're back," without accepting the call. Then she realized her error and tapped the panel to connect the call.

"Captains ... I mean, Envoy, Advisor, you're back," Birdie declared happily.

"You sound like you missed us," Jessie teased.

"You've no idea," Birdie replied, her voice suddenly serious. "There's a lot going on, and you're needed."

Harbour and Jessie glanced at each other, nearly missing Birdie say, "Let me comm Captain Bassiter."

"Captain Bassiter?" queried Harbour, a smile on her face.

"The crew refuses to address him as Captain Dingles," Birdie replied. "They said it doesn't suit the captain of Pyre's most prestigious ship."

Harbour's smile widened. A few years ago, the *Belle* had held station over Pyre without getting underway for centuries. Now refurbished, outfitted, and supplying much-needed slush for the YIPS, the crew was proclaiming her ascension.

"Here's the captain," Birdie announced, right before Dingles' face appeared in the console's projection.

"I hear it's now Captain Bassiter," Harbour said. She was overjoyed to see the aging spacer and was careful to keep her power under control lest she overwhelm Jessie.

"Only in public, Envoy Harbour," Dingles replied.

"I think it's appropriate, Captain," Harbour stated. "Did you move into the captain's quarters?"

"Negative, Envoy," Dingles replied evenly.

Despite the separation, Harbour could detect the stress in Dingles' voice, and she began to wonder what had transpired in her absence.

"See that you and Nadine occupy those quarters before I board your ship again, Captain," Harbour ordered. "Your promotion to the position of captain of the *Honora Belle* is hereby made permanent."

"You're not returning to the *Belle*?" Dingles asked. The tone of his voice wavered ever so slightly.

"My returns will only be for visits, Captain," Harbour replied. She kept her tone firm to impress on Dingles the importance of the leadership change.

"Big doings at Na-Tikkook?" Dingles asked.

Harbour's eyes bored into the projection, seeking to lock with Dingles. Then she said, "Big doings in the galaxy." She could hear Birdie in the background say, "Oh, for the love of Pyre and elsewhere."

"Captain Bassiter, we need a ride," Jessie said.

"The *Belle* is making for the YIPS. We're on the opposite side of Pyre from you, Captain," Dingles replied. "Your ships are at the YIPS and the JOS."

"Send the *Spryte*, Captain," Jessie said. "Tell Captain Tulafono that she can leave a number of crew behind so that we can have some empty berths."

"Aye, aye, Captain," Dingles replied. "One ship and berths for eleven coming up."

"That's berths for ten," Harbour corrected. She saw the furrowing of Dingles' face, and she could guess at the questions forming in his mind, but he chose to keep them to himself.

"Understood, Envoy," Dingles replied quietly.

Harbour signed to Jessie, and he said, "Triton out," ending the call.

"My work is done, Envoy, if you have no more need of me," Kractik said.

"We'll be fine, Kractik. I think we know our way around a dome or two," Harbour replied.

The little Jatouche flashed her teeth wide at the humorous remark.

Before Harbour could thank Kractik, Aurelia knelt in front of the Jatouche and enfolded her in her arms. "I'll miss you," Aurelia whispered, sending the smallest amount of warmth Kractik's way.

Kractik's eyes fluttered, and she quipped, "And I'll miss that ... and you," she added, with a display of her teeth. When Aurelia released her, Kractik spent some time with each explorer, sharing her thoughts with them. At Tracy, Kractik held the spacer's hands in silence. There was nothing she thought she could say that would ease the pain of a beloved sibling's death.

At the console, Kractik set the delay for her journey through the gate. With Jessie and Aurelia hovering over her, she canceled the settings and slowly set them again. Then Jessie stepped in and set them for Kractik.

"Activate, Advisor," Kractik said, gathering her pack and hurrying for the platform. She leapt onto it, waved her hand, and was gone.

There were a few moments, while everyone gathered their thoughts. They were nearly home, but it would be a couple of weeks before they saw some familiar faces.

"Well, I don't know about anybody else, but I can't wait to dig into another plate of paste," Devon quipped. He picked up his gear and led the way to the third level and the more expansive dorm room.

-30-
New Futures

Before the *Spryte* reached Triton, Jaktook was in the company of Rictook, Tacticnok, and the master advisors, including Roknick, to Jaktook's disappointment.

At Rissness, Jaktook had played his copies of the cubes on the console and recorded the alpha dome's events on a Jatouche device. They were being viewed in Rictook's royal apartment.

"This was a foolish undertaking," Roknick commented, during the initial viewing.

"Foolish would have been to fail to present the Tsargit with the proof they requested," Tacticnok shot back. "Foolish would have been to remain ignorant of the Colony's expansion to other worlds." She'd kept her eye on her father's hands, but they lay still on his lap.

Jaktook anticipated he would be required to stop and start the playback to answer questions. The reception was mixed — astonishment, curiosity, worry, and anger were evident.

At one point, Jaktook chose to freeze the display. "I respectfully request everyone take note of this image," he said. "You've been viewing the platforms at alpha dome. It was named that by our Pyrean friends, as it was the first dome journeyed to after leaving the Colony dome."

Jaktook used his device control to highlight platform three on the right. "This is the gate through which we arrived from the Colony's dome." Circling platform two, he added, "This is the gate by which we would leave to journey to beta dome."

"What is the significance of this terminology?" Master Scientist Tiknock asked.

"A Pyrean engineer explained that it is an ancient Earth custom of naming things in sequence rather than using numerals," Jaktook replied. "I thought it odd, but when we started referring to gates as alpha one, two, or three, it made sense to me."

"There are crates and sentients on alpha one," Pickcit, the master economist, exclaimed.

"Yes, there are," Jaktook agreed. "As you watch the rest of the recorded information, you'll witness the extent of the Colony's operations."

"How far do you think the Colony has penetrated in the direction of alpha one?" Rictook asked.

The ruler was normally silent during these types of meetings. It was his custom to listen to the interplay between the advisors and his daughter. That he was asking questions this early in the meeting indicated the subject's seriousness.

"There's no way of knowing, Your Excellency," Jaktook replied. "However, there was no sign of the Colony's activity past alpha gate two from which we journeyed."

"I require your estimation, Advisor," Rictook replied.

It was not only a royal command, but Rictook had evoked Jaktook's title. Half an annual ago, this kind of demand might have rattled Jaktook but facing the Colony sentients and striving to reach home again had hardened him. He organized his thoughts, not caring how long his audience waited. It was an important question that Rictook chose to ask.

"The Colony is intensely aggressive, as we're all aware, Your Excellency," Jaktook began. "I'm trying to imagine their reactions when they first ventured out through three of their gates and met the Norsitchians, the Veklocks, and the Jatouche."

"And they were repulsed by every alliance member," Tacticnok interjected.

"And rightfully so," Roknick added. "They attacked us."

Rictook's fingers rose, and his audience quieted. Then a finger indicated Jaktook.

"My point is that a race, which met such defiance, would not take well to being denied three of their five gates," Jaktook continued. "It's my thought that they had explored all five of the gates in a short period. Colony gate one led to the alpha dome, which they found empty."

"And domes beyond alpha," Tiknock said.

"Welcoming domes, unlike those of the alliance members," Jaktook agreed.

"You keep speaking as if the Colony had a right to attack us," Roknick declared.

"And you speak from a lack of imagination, Master Roknick," Jaktook shot back. "You weren't on this exploration. You haven't tried to understand the Colony's motivation, which is the height of lunacy. While the alliance has ignored the Colony, choosing a defensive posture, these species focused their anger and drive to explore the domes of other worlds. Hear my words, Master Roknick. Someday, the Tsargit and every alliance race will face the Colony."

"Not with the limited access of the gates," Roknick riposted. He felt sure that he had the superior argument, despite Jaktook's searing outburst.

"Your shortsightedness is amazing, Master Roknick," Jaktook replied. "It's obvious the Colony has a superior knowledge of the consoles compared to the alliance. They've already demonstrated that, and if it weren't for the inventiveness of the Pyreans, you wouldn't even be aware of the events I'm showing you. The Colony knows that the domes have limitations. What do you think they're going to do about that?"

"There's nothing they can do. They don't know where the alliance domes sit within the galaxy," Roknick replied smugly.

"I do. The Pyrean, Aurelia, showed us," Jaktook replied. His lips rippled up, exposing his teeth in a manner of superiority. "If we know, there's a good chance the Colony knows or will know someday. Given time, they might well be visiting alliance worlds in ships. Ships with weapons."

The audience was stunned. Even Roknick, whose jaw hung open, was at a loss for words.

"What will the Tsargit hear from their delegate?" Rictook asked.

"My data is a copy of what Delegate Mangoth carries, Your Excellency," Jaktook replied. "We had many evenings after our numerous journeys to discuss what we'd seen. The two of us came to the same conclusions. I've no doubt that Mangoth will be informing the Tsargit, as I've tried to do this group today."

"The delegate's delivery will cause consternation in the Tsargit," Rictook commented. "But they won't be quick to move on this, not that they ever had that capability."

"Your Excellency," Pickcit said, "I'd like to point out that Jaktook and Kractik's efforts with the exploration party will draw favorable attention from the Tsargit to the Jatouche. Taken with the discovery of the Colony's expansion and a dome's star map, our race will certainly be elevated among the alliance members. It might even culminate in a seat on the Tsargit."

"If these things come to pass, credit must be given to the one person who started us down this path," Rictook said. His tired eyes shone with pride, as they settled on his daughter.

Tacticnok watched Jaktook turn to her and dip his head in obeisance, which she found embarrassing and irritating at the same time. She couldn't imagine the dangers the explorers encountered or the depression they battled in their attempt to return home. If the two of them were alone, she would have been bowing to him. *Honoring my mate,* she thought, which stunned her.

"What of the Pyreans?" Rictook asked, switching subjects.

"In what manner do you ask, Your Excellency?" Jaktook asked.

When Rictook didn't reply, Jaktook assumed it was an open question. "They were extraordinary, Your Excellency. They were never defeated by the obstacles we encountered. I saw Dillon Shaver defend his sibling and lose his life for his bravery. I saw two females stand with Kractik for hours on end to understand Messinants glyphs and solve one of the mysteries of the empty projections. Aurelia, the young empath, writes as the Messinants did, and the console accepted her glyphs. It resulted in the dome's display of the star map, which we used to navigate home. Of all the races I've met, they're the ones that I'd advise the Jatouche make allies."

"I must ask," Tacticnok interjected. "What was it like to journey with a Crocian?"

Jaktook's head dipped, while he recalled the tumultuous moments with Mangoth. "I can say that the view from the top of a Crocian is an unusual perspective and to ride one's shoulders and feel his power is unforgettable."

"You rode a Crocian?" Rictook asked. His aging lips curled back, and he flashed his teeth. It was a rare expression from the ruler, during an audience.

Jaktook's eyes displayed the mirth he felt. "All things considered, Your Excellency, Mangoth's a most magnificent individual," he said.

Despite the presence of two royal family members, Jaktook couldn't help the wave of emotions that swept through him. The journey's tensions had been with him for days and nights on end, and the subsequent relief of making it home was only beginning to be felt. One moment, he was laughing uncontrollably. Then he was hiccupping. Then he was ducking his head and hiding his eyes.

Roknick was aghast at the display, but he saw that the others were sympathetic to what Jaktook had endured and his need for a moment of release.

"I beg your pardon, Your Excellency," Jaktook said, when he gained control.

"This lack of discipline does not give a ruler confidence in the opinion of such an individual," Rictook said sternly, "Her Highness deserves better, but I'll forgive you this once, Master Jaktook."

Jaktook had focused on the rebuke. He barely heard the final two words. When they sunk in, he looked around him for the reactions of others. The title of master was bestowed on those with great experience and acumen. Tacticnok, Tiknock, and Pickcit were pleased for him, and Roknick was agitated.

Jaktook drew breath to say he didn't deserve the honor, but Rictook's fingers rose and halted the words in his throat.

"Do you think your ruler unwise?" Rictook asked.

The question took Jaktook aback. Before he could formulate an answer, Rictook mercifully moved on.

"I don't make my pronouncements lightly, Master Jaktook," Rictook said. "These old eyes have rarely witnessed so much courage and daring from a Jatouche. Of course, I'm not referring to you facing the Colony, exploring the galaxy through the domes, or solving the console's riddles. I'm referring to you riding a Crocian."

Rictook's teeth flashed in a wide display, and he issued a series of strangled chuckles, as his body tried to give expression to the delight he felt. Here was a young Jatouche, who thought as did his daughter, and fortune providing, he would be with her for her long life.

* * * *

The Pyrean explorers went to sleep knowing the *Spryte* would make station over Triton soon. They'd tracked the ship's progress via the console's comm panel, which displayed the potential contacts. There was only one vessel closing on their moon.

In the early hours of the morning, Harbour woke as Jessie slipped out of the room. Lately, he'd done this frequently, staying up on deck for hours. Tonight, Harbour was determined to understand the problem that Jessie was keeping to himself. She donned her deck shoes and padded softly after him. She found Jessie sitting on the edge of the platform staring at the stars, which were barely visible through the dome's glow.

"You know you're preventing anyone coming through from the other side," Harbour teased.

"Why would anyone want to come to Pyre?" Jessie asked.

Harbour was taken aback by the despondency in Jessie's voice and the conflicting emotions rolling off him. This wasn't like him. Worse, she depended on his strength, and it appeared to be ebbing. She opened her gates wide and relied on her years of empathetic training, intending to treat Jessie as a client who needed her help.

Briefly, fear bloomed in Harbour's heart. She was afraid of not being of use to him. She resorted to a breathing technique to regain her calm and rid herself of negative emotions. When she was ready, she sat beside Jessie. He had a faraway gaze, as if he was among the stars instead of sitting next to her.

"What's on your mind, Jessie?" Harbour asked.

"Many things," Jessie replied.

"Can you tell me one of them?" Harbour encouraged.

Jessie's gaze shifted to Harbour and then the console. He'd spent the time on deck trying to understand the depression that had gripped him since returning to Pyre. It made no sense to him.

"I'm wondering what to do next," Jessie said.

There was a lengthy pause from Jessie, and Harbour waited him out. A long sigh escaped him, which Harbour thought indicated that he'd come to a decision.

"If I return to the captaincy of the *Spryte*, I'd have to demote Ituau, which would reverse her promotions and possibly a hiring or two," Jessie complained.

"Is that what you want to do ... take over as ship's captain?" Harbour asked.

"Not really, but I'm not trained to do anything else," Jessie replied.

"I don't know ... I thought you did a great job as my advisor," Harbour said. She noted the shift in Jessie. His emotional mix turned positive, hopeful, and he fingered the medallion he wore.

"Do you expect to return to Na-Tikkook?" Jessie asked, his voice showing a spark of energy.

"Not immediately," Harbour replied, and Jessie deflated.

At that point, Harbour dismissed her training. An empath-client relationship was of no use. This was personal. She stared at Jessie until he returned her gaze. Then she said, "Do you expect me to continue the job of envoy by myself? You're the one who said I should make the most of the Jatouche and Tsargit rewards."

"Yes, but you don't need me for that," Jessie said quietly.

"Okay, if that's what you want, Jessie," Harbour said, keeping her voice evenly modulated, as if it was of no concern to her what he chose to do. "I would ask one final favor of you, as my advisor."

"Certainly, name it," Jessie said, sitting upright.

"Outline for me the steps I need to take to make the best use of the rewards and implement the essence of the *Belle*'s stolen documents," Harbour requested sweetly.

For a moment, Jessie's mouth fell open, and then he laughed. Harbour felt the emotional energy course through him and radiate outward. This was Jessie back from the dead and depressed.

"Yeah," Jessie said, nodding his head and chuckling, "I think that would take a little more than an outline. Looks like you're in need of an advisor for a bit longer."

"That's what I thought," Harbour acknowledged, reaching across to grip Jessie's hand. As much as she wanted to share what she felt, she knew it was the wrong time to do so.

-31-
Intravertor Status

Henry, Idrian, and Dottie had returned to Pyre months ago, and like Henry, Dottie was frustrated by the lack of success in the endeavors that Harbour had charged them to complete. Adding to her annoyance, Idrian was refusing to take her calls.

At the regular Starlight cantina meeting, Dottie eyed her fellow patrons, Hans Riesling, Oster Simian, and Trent Pederson. "None of you have contributed?" she asked incredulously.

"And you have?" Trent retorted.

"Of course, I have," Dottie shot back. "What is with the three of you? You supported the deployment of the first intravertor, but you won't continue to fund the effort. That doesn't make sense to me."

"Things have gotten much more complicated," Oster said, in a placating tone. "We're not dealing with a governor anymore. The domes' council has taken a hard position on the question of access to the surface."

"You need to understand what that means, Dottie," Hans interjected. "What good is clearing Pyre's air, if stationers and spacers are denied access to the surface? We're up here, and they're down there."

"Downsiders don't have a right to do that," Dottie said hotly.

"Calm down, Dottie," Oster said, his hands motioning her to be quiet. "No, legally we can't be denied access to the surface, but the families can withhold their coin."

"And we can't build intravertors without their contributions. The families have a heck of a lot more coin than we do," Hans added.

Dottie considered her companion's remarks. They were disappointing to hear, but she respected them for their honesty.

"Let's face it, Dottie," Trent said. "Harbour might have started something that can't be finished. It would have been better if she stuck to being the empath leader and left the *Belle* on station over Pyre."

Dottie turned her gaze on Trent, and it blazed. In surprise, Trent leaned back in his chair.

"I'll say this once and only once," said Dottie, her voice low and hard. "I never want to hear any of you utter another disparaging remark about Envoy Harbour or any empath, for that matter. That woman and her team of explorers undertook enormous risks for all of Pyre. You would have wailed like children and wet your skins if you saw even the images of the horrendous, venomous aliens they faced. You sit here safe and secure aboard this station, while you pass judgment on something you know nothing about."

With that, Dottie stood up, said good night, and left.

Trent looked at his fellow investors for sympathy but found none in their gazes.

"You do realize that you insulted the envoy to the face of one of her delegates," Oster said to Trent.

Suddenly, the entire Starlight cantina was abuzz. Word passed from table to table, often aided by the servers.

"The envoy and her people are back," a server said to Dottie's investor friends. "They're one short."

"Somebody stay behind?" Oster asked.

"Doesn't sound like that," the server said. "Word is the explorers might have lost one."

Hans looked at Trent, and said, "I think you'd better start working on your apology."

"And make it a good one," Oster added. "Or we might decide it's better to have a delegate in our midst than a fellow investor."

Trent drew breath to object, but reason ruled, and he shut his mouth.

* * * *

Jessie readied the comm panel, when the console indicated the *Spryte* had closed on Triton. The team knew how to make a call and could choose whether it should be audio only or include visuals. Aurelia's detailed recording of the glyphs and their meanings were proving to be extremely valuable.

"You've got quite a list growing there," Jessie had commented to Aurelia, when he saw her adding to her list.

"This might become my new career," Aurelia quipped. "We can't be admitted to the alliance or form a true partnership with the Jatouche until we learn the console. I say there's no time like the present."

"You have to be there to test the glyphs of each panel," Harbour pointed out.

"That's no problem. I can eat paste for a long while," Aurelia replied, which elicited groans from most of the explorers.

"I wonder if we can tap into the dome's energy sources to power a cold locker and a cooker," Olivia mused.

"We'd probably blow a power connector," Pete grumbled.

Despite Pete's comment, the engineers had gotten gleams in their eyes, and Harbour and Aurelia sensed their excitement.

When the conversation wound down, Jessie tapped the panel icon for the nearby ship.

"Captain, incoming message," Nate Mikado, the *Spryte*'s first mate called out.

Ituau had hung around the bridge, as the ship decelerated to take up station. There was no means of connecting to the dome's console, so they'd had to wait until they were called.

Nate punched the comm icon on his panel to accept the call, and the faces of Harbour and Jessie appeared.

"Captains," Ituau and Nate called out enthusiastically, all decorum aside.

The pair's delight had Jessie and Harbour grinning.

Ituau was the first to recover, quickly adding, "Sorry, Envoy Harbour and Captain Cinders."

Harbour signed to Jessie to respond. "It's wonderful to see the two of you again," he said. "But, let me correct your address. I might be the owner of the company, but you will address me as Advisor Cinders in public."

When Ituau frowned, Jessie continued, "That means my final company promotion remains, Captain Tulafono."

"Are you sure?" Ituau asked. Jessie stared at her out of the bridge monitor until the reason for his firm gaze jogged her thoughts. "I mean ... are you sure, Advisor Cinders?" she rephrased.

Jessie minutely tipped his head in acknowledgment of Ituau's correct response.

Ituau straightened her broad shoulders. Jessie's pronouncement had relieved her of the stress that had been building ever since she'd received the message from Dingles to sail for Triton.

"I understand we have ten to board, Advisor," Ituau said.

"Correct, and three crates of intravertor parts," Jessie replied.

"We'll be down shortly, Cap ... Advisor," Ituau replied.

Jessie ended the call, and Ituau regarded Nate. "These new titles are going to take some time to adopt."

"I understand the challenge," Nate replied. "It took us a while to think of you as captain." He'd spoken while standing in the bridge's hatchway. That enabled him to drop his remarks and make a fast escape.

The explorers had been grateful for the appearance of the first delivery of intravertor parts. It had ended the tedium. Aurelia and the engineers broke from studying the console glyphs to help clear the platform. Minutes later, a second pile appeared on the platform.

When the final shipment arrived, a huge pile of crates spilled across the deck. Olivia regarded the size of the piles, and said, "I think we've enough parts to build three more devices."

Jessie looked at Harbour for orders, and she laughed. "Envoy," she said, pointing to her chest.

Jessie had grinned in response and ordered the explorers to start carrying crates to the second level and stage them in the corridor next to the dome's exit. "I'd like them stacked outside, but I wish to reserve our air tanks," he'd said.

* * * *

In three days' time after the *Spryte* made Triton, the explorers and the cargo were aboard the mining ship and inbound for Pyre.

Harbour waited until they closed the distance to the JOS to prevent comm lag. Then she called Henry.

"Envoy, I was pleased to hear of your return, and I'm sorry about Dillon," Henry said.

"Dillon was a tragic loss, but we're lucky that we didn't lose more of us. The journey was that risky," Harbour replied. "I'll save our story until we dock at the JOS. Right now, I'm interested in hearing about the delegates' progress."

"I wish I had good news for you, Envoy," Henry replied. "Initially, we made good headway. The arrival of the three sets of intravertor parts with us generated enthusiasm from the stationers and the spacers. The Pyrean Green fund received a swell of contributions. The problem was that the coin amounts were modest. We didn't receive any of the significant donations that we received last time."

"How far did you get on the buildout of the convertors?" Harbour asked.

Briefly, there was silence on the comm. Then Henry said, "Regretfully, Envoy, only two devices are complete. The third is barely begun."

"And the deployment efforts?" Harbour asked.

"Nothing," Henry replied, in a desultory manner. "I'm not you, Envoy. Without your presence, we haven't garnered the major supporters. Worse, the commandant refuses to commit station resources to build a deployment platform."

"By your comments, I take it that there's no progress on a JOS–Triton passenger shuttle," Harbour suggested.

"That's the strange thing, Envoy," Henry replied. "I've heard that the architect, who designed the *Belle*'s new shuttle, has received a commission for a heavy passenger shuttle."

"Who's paying for that?" Harbour asked.

"No information on that, but I've an idea," Henry replied.

"Dorelyn and the dome council," Harbour supplied.

"That's my guess," Henry acknowledged.

"Has the commandant offered a reason for his failure to support the launch platform?" Harbour inquired.

Henry pitched his voice high to imitate the commandant, and said, "It's under consideration."

"Under consideration for months?" Harbour shot back, incredulity textured her voice.

"Perhaps the commandant needs some persuasion," Henry proffered. He waited for Harbour's reply, which was slow in coming. When it did arrive, it was totally unexpected.

"Perhaps we need a new commandant," Harbour said "We'll talk more when I make the station, Captain." Then she ended the comm.

"Did you expect anything different?" Jessie asked.

Harbour had made the call from the *Spryte*'s captain's quarters, which Ituau had relinquished, and Jessie had heard every word.

"Actually, I didn't have any expectations," Harbour said. "It's easier that way ... no disappointments."

"I'll have to try to adopt that technique," Jessie said.

"No major contributors and nothing from the commandant," Harbour mused.

"I can understand Emerson Strattleford's reluctance," Jessie suggested. "He's probably on Dorelyn's payroll, which means he's taking her orders."

"So what's her agenda?" Harbour asked.

"If I had to guess, I'd say the dome council wants a land deal before they commit their resources," Jessie volunteered.

"Then why commission the long-range shuttle before they get their agreement?" Harbour asked.

"You need to allow a long lead time before a shuttle can be delivered," Jessie explained. "The first step is the architect's design. You can get that for a relatively small amount of coin."

"Hmm," Harbour mumbled. Then she added, "I didn't get involved in the order of the *Belle*'s shuttle. Danny Thompson took care of everything. I just paid the invoices."

"No wonder everyone likes working for you," Jessie remarked.

"And what's wrong with our wealthy stationers?" Harbour asked.

"Leadership," Jessie offered.

"As my advisor, I expect more qualified answers," Harbour said. She sent him a small amount of warmth to ensure he knew she was teasing.

Jessie took no umbrage from Harbour's ministration. In fact, he rather enjoyed it. There were multiple times during their explorations that Harbour and Aurelia used their powers to keep the teams' spirits up. His exposure to the empaths had slowly changed his mind about their abilities. The value of power came down to who wielded it and for what reasons.

"The wealthy stationers are investors. They're not going to contribute large amounts of coin, if they don't see any long-term value in it," Jessie explained.

"But the intravertors will change the face of Pyre," Harbour insisted.

"You're thinking of the end result. Investors must consider the stability of the steps to get there," Jessie argued. "If they don't have confidence in those processes being completed successfully, then they won't see a reason to commit the funds."

"You're saying that without major contributions from the downsiders and the commandant withholding JOS construction funds, the station investors don't have confidence in the eventual deployment of the intravertors," Harbour reasoned.

"You have it in one," Jessie agreed.

"So where's the weak link?" Harbour asked.

Jessie considered Harbour's question. Political maneuvering wasn't his forte. However, finance and contract negotiations were his strengths, which caused him to consider the problem from that point of view.

"I think all things center on the commandant," Jessie said. "We won't be able to negotiate with Dorelyn and the domes' council. They'll be adamant about what they want, and we won't be able to accept their terms. The question is: How much coin is the commandant controlling? He's not released that information in years."

"Isn't he required to do that?" Harbour asked.

"The previous commandant did that as a matter of course on an annual basis," Jessie said. "Emerson continued that policy for a few years. Then it became once every two or three years. Finally, it stopped. The problem is there's no requirement to disclose the station's finances."

Harbour thought for a moment and then snatched up her comm unit.

"Captain Tulafono, when is the next commandant's meeting?" Harbour asked.

"The commandant has moved his monthly meeting, Envoy," Ituau replied. "It now falls on the start of the third week of the month."

"Interesting," Harbour commented. "Any reason given why he changed the timing of the meeting?"

"None, Envoy, and he didn't make a general announcement about the change," Ituau replied.

"Will we arrive at the JOS in time to attend the meeting?" Harbour asked. She could hear Ituau questioning her navigator, Jeremy Kinsman.

"Affirmative, Envoy, you should have two days to spare," Ituau replied.

"And the status of the *Belle*, Captain?" Jessie asked.

"According to Captain Bassiter, the ship emptied her tanks at the YIPS and is making for the JOS to procure supplies," Ituau said.

Harbour muted the comm unit and glanced at Jessie.

"What are you thinking?" Jessie asked.

"I'm thinking we should attend the meeting and ask some direct questions of Emerson," Harbour replied.

"We'll need the audience to support us," Jessie cautioned.

Harbour nodded, took the comm unit off mute, and said, "Captain, request Captain Bassiter hold the *Belle* at the JOS for our arrival. Communicate to him that we intend to join the commandant's party."

"Certainly, Envoy," Ituau replied, a wide grin spreading across her face. "Do I understand that I should be encouraged to mention your attendance at the meeting to others ... purely in passing, of course?"

"A subject like that is sure to come up in passing, Captain," Harbour replied, in a conspiratorial tone.

"It stands to reason," Ituau replied, and Harbour ended the comm.

"It's a shame that first mates aren't welcome at the meeting," Nate commented. "I'd love to attend this one."

"Me too," Jeremy added.

"You going, Captain?" Nate asked.

"You'd better believe I'll be there. I'd give up my share of this slush haul if that's what it took to attend," Ituau remarked.

-32-
Emerson's Meeting

The *Spryte* made the JOS but halted a few hundred kilometers out. It took up station close to the *Belle*.

Harbour and her fellow explorers took a shuttle to the colony ship. She'd asked the team to accompany her and stay aboard the *Belle* until she attended the commandant's meeting. There were a few questions, but everyone agreed to cooperate.

Dingles and a large contingent of the ship waited outside the *Belle*'s bay for Harbour and her people to disembark. In the corridor, there was a concerted effort to swiftly free the shuttle's passengers from their vac suits. As soon as the suits were doffed, Harbour, Aurelia, and the nearby empaths lit like beacons, spreading their joy. The Pyreans were doused in waves of celebratory emotions. It was a dizzying moment for all.

Slowly, Harbour and her explorers extricated themselves and followed Dingles to the ship's bow. The cabins of the ship's officer row were refurbished in anticipation of the team's return. Each person was allotted an individual cabin, and they marveled at the accommodations.

"If I knew I was risking my neck for something like this," Jacob said, admiring the spaciousness and rich appointments, "I might not have griped so much."

"Wait until you get a look at the cantina," Pete said, bumping Jacob's arm with an elbow.

While the team members waited in their cabins to receive their gear and unpack, Harbour and Jessie accompanied Dingles to the captain's quarters.

Harbour was delighted to see Nadine, who was standing next to a prepared dining table and holding forth a tall green. Harbour accepted the green, set it on the table, and hugged her friend.

"Enjoying your new quarters?" Harbour asked.

"They're wonderful, but I feel like I don't belong," Nadine whispered.

"You keep our captain in line," Harbour replied, holding Nadine's hands, "and you'll have more than earned these quarters." She threw a quick grin Dingles' way, before she snatched up her green and downed half of it.

"I'd love to chat, but tomorrow is the commandant's meeting," Harbour said to Dingles.

"And there's been some last-minute maneuvering, Harbour," Dingles said.

"Like what?" Jessie asked, as Nadine guided him to a seat at the table.

"The commandant is holding the meeting in the auditorium again," Dingles replied. He was self-conscious, as he sat at the head of the table, the captain's rightful position, but a quick touch by Harbour calmed him. "This time, a table and some chairs will be on the stage."

"He's trying to control the meeting," Jessie surmised. "Unless you arrive early, Harbour, there won't be a seat at the table for you."

"I intend to join the meeting after it's in progress," Harbour replied.

"There's more," Dingles added. "According to our security sources, the commandant will have officers posted around the stage, in the wings, and the steps. He's chosen young ones who don't have strong allegiances to senior staff."

"Has the word been spread?" Harbour asked.

"Same as last time, Harbour," Nadine replied. "The odd word here and there aboard the JOS. Every stationer and spacer probably knows by now that you'll be attending the meeting."

"Good," Harbour replied.

Nadine cued the servers, and they entered and served dinner.

Harbour picked up the subtle transmissions of an untrained empath and focused on a young girl of about fourteen, who was helping Yasmin. When the servers exited, Harbour focused her gaze on Nadine, who said, "We picked her and three others off the JOS a few days ago."

"Empaths," Harbour explained to Jessie, when she saw his forehead furrow.

"Their power is nothing exceptional, like Aurelia's and Sasha's, but they're strong, above average, I'd say," Nadine explained.

After dinner, Harbour, Jessie, and Dingles retired to the study, and Dingles shared the *Belle*'s accounting with them.

"So, you haven't distributed the funds from the general account?" Harbour asked, examining the monitor over Dingles' shoulder.

"Actually, we have," Dingles replied.

"How many tanks did you fill compared to the last haul?" Jessie asked.

Dingles grinned at Jessie. "Thirty percent," he said. He regarded Harbour and Jessie for a moment, his face quiet and serious. "When you left, the other captains and I felt we were handed a great responsibility, and we were determined to not let you down."

Jessie smiled, and Harbour said to him, "I think we should get our rear ends back to Na-Tikkook. They do better without us."

"Any accidents?" Jessie asked.

"A few minor ones," Dingles admitted. "We were pushing the limits, but it's not like we had to force the crews. More than once, a captain had to restrict a crew member to quarters for staying on duty past the safety limit."

"Slow it up," Harbour said to Dingles. "Do you hear me?"

"Aye, Envoy," Dingles replied.

"May I?" Jessie asked, pointing to the monitor.

When Dingles slipped his comm unit out, Jessie plugged his device into the dock, and he accessed his company accounts.

Harbour and Dingles retired to the couch to chat.

"Where's the cap?" Harbour asked, pointing to Dingles' head.

"In the sleeping quarters, waiting for my retirement or demotion," Dingles replied with a sad face. "Nadine has declared it undignified for a captain to wear."

Harbour smiled and patted his knee in commiseration.

"What's the plan?" Dingles asked.

"Short term, get the intravertors planted; long term, use the alliance to help Pyre," Harbour said simply.

Dingles mouth fell open. "What happened to my newbie captain?" he said in astonishment.

"Much more than I could ever explain, Dingles," Harbour replied.

While Harbour and Dingles conversed, Jessie found the YIPS deposit to his company. As expected, it was a significant increase over the last haul. He managed the distributions to captains and crew, including bonuses for the captains. Completing his accounting requirements, he pulled his comm unit free and joined the others.

"What about you —" Dingles started to ask Jessie.

"Advisor Cinders," Jessie replied, "as if you hadn't already heard."

Dingles grinned. "Not all rumors are true. Just checking, Advisor Cinders." He released a sigh and took a sip of his after-dinner drink.

"You seem rather self-satisfied," Harbour remarked to Dingles.

"It's strange, isn't it?" Dingles mused. "I thought my life was over when I contracted space dementia, and a few years later, I'm cured of it, have a wonderful empath for a woman, and I'm the captain of the *Belle*. But that's not the best part," he added, sitting upright. "You two are back, and you're keeping your new titles. That means there's much more to come, and I can't wait." He raised his glass to them, and toasted, "To tomorrow."

"To tomorrow," Harbour and Jessie echoed, as they hoisted their glasses.

* * * *

Harbour spent the evening collecting the latest information on the commandant and the council's positions. Early the next morning, she rose, donned her best set of skins and deck shoes. She joined Dingles, Nadine, and Jessie for morning meal. There was little conversation, and the food was consumed quickly. At the end of the meal, they waited while Harbour finished a second tall glass of greens, and they exchanged concerned glances.

"Ready," Harbour announced, her glass clinking, as she set it on the table.

In the bay, Harbour greeted Claudia Manning, the *Belle*'s shuttle copilot, and hugged Danny Thompson, the pilot. She led the delegates, Jessie, Aurelia and Devon, plus Dingles aboard the shuttle.

Devon eyed the comfortable seating, and remarked, "This reminds me of Tacticnok's shuttle ... after they replaced the seats for us."

"Yes, and if we had a couple of hundred more years, we might even be able to build shuttles that could sail like the Jatouche," Jessie remarked. He didn't mean it to sound as disheartening as it came out, and he signed an apology to Harbour.

"Stick with me, Advisor, the envoy will make it all better," Harbour teased, and she heard soft laughter from the others.

As the group disembarked onto the JOS terminal arm, Harbour tarried at the shuttle's hatch and waited for Danny to join Claudia and her.

"Say goodbye to those prosthetics, Danny," Harbour said quietly, when it was just the three of them. "You're among the next twenty to journey to Rissness."

Danny frowned and started to object, but Claudia said forcefully, "Thank you, Envoy. I'll make sure he's ready."

Harbour smiled at Claudia, and then she eased her gates open and sent her power over both pilots.

"Oh, for the love of Pyre," Claudia said, in a slow exhale, as she watched Harbour disappear down the arm's ramp. "I can't believe that's what you've been getting all this time."

"Afraid so," Danny replied, a smile plastered on his face.

"I knew there was a reason to hang with you besides your charming personality," Claudia replied. She gave Danny a quick kiss on the cheek. They both knew that Danny displayed his gruff side, more times than either cared to admit.

After catching the ring's cap to transition to the station, Harbour discovered a group of individuals waiting for her. They were composed of well-to-do stationers and captains. In front of the group stood Dottie.

"Thought you might need some moral support, Envoy," Dottie announced proudly.

Harbour could sense the enthusiasm issuing from Dottie. "Thank you, Delegate Franks. Your courtesy is much appreciated."

Harbour led the way to the auditorium. Along her route, she collected more of the station's investors and many more captains, including Henry Stamerson. She would have thought these individuals would have been seated in the auditorium already. Then it occurred to her that they were demonstrating their support by entering with her.

At the twin doors to the auditorium, two security officers stood with shock sticks in their hands.

"Sorry, we've orders to not admit anyone after the meeting has started," one of the officers said.

Devon, who had donned his lieutenant's uniform, closed on the officer until he was nose to nose with him.

"I can appreciate that you're following orders," Devon said to the youthful officer, "but the envoy has business in there."

Faster than the eye could follow, Devon snatched the officer's shock stick.

"Do I need to take yours?" he asked the other officer, who timidly extended his stick toward Devon.

"Put these away," Devon said, returning the weapon, "and step aside."

As soon as a path was cleared, Devon hit the access plate, the doors slid aside, and Harbour marched through.

On stage, Emerson spotted Harbour and her entourage. Blood colored his neck at the failure of his officers to keep them out. Then he saw Devon next to Harbour, and realized how they'd gained entry. He stood up, intending to stop them from hijacking his agenda.

"This meeting is in progress, Captain," Emerson announced, his voice rising. "Please take seats, while this table conducts its business."

"It's Envoy Harbour to you, Commandant," Harbour replied forcefully.

Dorelyn touched Emerson's hand and he sat down. "Your trip is over," Dorelyn said to Harbour. "The title no longer applies."

"Is that what you heard from your representative?" Harbour asked, indicating Idrian, who sat next to Dorelyn. "Oh ... but your delegate didn't stick around for the hard part, did he? So he wouldn't have the latest information, would he?"

The audience tittered and chuckled at the insinuation.

"Two others returned with me," Idrian complained.

"Yes, that would be these two delegates," Harbour said, looking around to locate Henry and Dottie and then placing her hands on their shoulders. "A mature woman and a retired captain, and a captain, I might add, who did volunteer to explore with us. However, the team judged him unable to take on the challenges we faced. As it was, we lost one of our youngest and strongest, Dillon Shaver. He died defending his sister."

Harbour signed to Jessie to hold back the group, and she stepped down the center aisle toward the stage.

"Through my teams' efforts, we've secured rewards from the Jatouche and the Tsargit, the alliance governing body," she announced loudly.

There were audible gasps from the audience, and conversations erupted. Emerson called for order, but his efforts were largely ineffective.

Harbour partially raised her arms, and the audience immediately quieted.

"In what form are these rewards?" Rufus, who sat next to Idrian, asked.

"Some of these you know," Harbour replied. "The repair of our injured and the supply of intravertor parts, which were promised by Her Highness Tacticnok. In addition, His Excellency offered us rewards for discovering details about the unexplored domes, details which would elevate the Jatouche in the eyes of the alliance."

"And did you?" Emerson asked.

"You've no idea what we discovered," Jessie shouted from the back of the auditorium. "Let me say simply that the Jatouche couldn't be happier."

"In what form are these rewards?" Dorelyn asked. She hoped to hear that they might be of little value. In which case, she could undermine Harbour's credibility with the audience.

"In whatever form we'd like," Harbour replied.

"We get to choose?" Dorelyn asked, indicating those at the table.

"We?" Harbour asked. "I don't remember seeing you fighting beside us to repel the Colony sentients, five-meter-long, squirming insectoids with deadly pincers."

The audience was aghast at the thought that such aliens existed. Again Harbour quickly silenced them.

"The Jatouche and the Tsargit reward those who accepted the risks," Harbour added. "That would be the explorers, eleven Pyreans, two Jatouche, and one magnificent Crocian."

Jessie, Aurelia, and Devon exchanged smiles at the reference to Mangoth.

"And what do you intend to ask the Jatouche and the Tsargit for in regard to these rewards?" Emerson asked.

"I'm glad you asked that question, Commandant," Harbour replied. "I must admit that my team and I were surprised to learn that so little progress had been made on the intravertors and a launch platform. Furthermore, we've discovered the station isn't funding a long-range passenger shuttle to reach Triton, the council is underwriting it."

The captains rose out of their seats and shouted their indignation at Emerson. Owning and crewing Pyre's ships were the exclusive business of spacers. It was the means by which the topsiders kept the balance of power with the downsiders. Allowing the council to build the first JOS to Triton passenger shuttle was a betrayal by the commandant, who had to know this was underway.

When Harbour regained control of the audience, Dorelyn announced in a clear, strong voice, "There is nothing in the station's articles that precludes the domes from building ships, and the commandant was right to allow us to engage a ship's architect."

"And while we're talking about the commandant," Harbour shouted, before the audience could erupt, "I would like to ask Commandant Strattleford why he's not supported the completion of the present intravertors nor begun work on a deployment platform."

"These aspects are still under review," Emerson stated officiously.

"For months?" Harbour shot back. "Who are the people reviewing these projects? What's taking them so long to communicate to topsiders their decisions? And how much coin is in the capital construction account?"

"These are official matters, Envoy, and not for public announcements," Emerson replied. He hated using Harbour's title, but he didn't want to rile the investors and captains any further.

"Whose side are you on, Commandant ... ours or theirs?" Harbour asked, with heat, pointing to the three family heads sitting with Emerson.

"That accusation is uncalled for," Dorelyn fired back, while Emerson sat stunned by the accusation.

"Because you've chosen to reply for the commandant, Dorelyn," Harbour said, the controlled anger in her voice evident, "I'm putting the council on notice. Your hardline stance of insisting on property rights in exchange for your funding of intravertor deployment is unacceptable. It's the opinions of the explorers, which I share, that we won't unconditionally distribute the rewards we've earned."

"That's not why you were elected, "Rufus snarled.

"You forget, Rufus Stewart, I wasn't elected," Harbour riposted. "I was chosen by Her Highness Tacticnok. The explorers are prepared to make Pyre's needs the focus of the Jatouche and Tsargit gifts, providing our conditions are met."

"We don't even know what the rewards will be," Idrian objected. "How can we judge the worth of your conditions without knowing what we might receive?"

"You can't know," Harbour replied, "and I don't care if you have to make decisions in the dark. That's what the families have been doing to stationers and spacers since they erected the first dome and established the El. If you want to share in the largesse that will be coming our way, then the families need to contribute to the Pyrean Green fund and enable the completion of the intravertors, the building of a deployment platform, and the construction of a JOS–Triton shuttle."

Emerson had regained his equilibrium, and he announced forcefully and in a higher octave, "These are not proposals you can make to this group in this meeting, Envoy. Submit your requests in writing to my office. They'll be considered in due time."

Harbour laughed loudly and rudely. Her warm contralto voice had an effect on many in the audience. "Thank you, Commandant. You reminded me of my final point."

"And that is?" Emerson asked, walking into Harbour's trap.

"For refusing to reveal the station's accounting and failing to fund the intravertor projects, I suggest to this audience and all topsiders that we need a new commandant."

"You can't do that," Emerson shouted indignantly, his voice breaking.

"On the contrary, Commandant Strattleford," Henry shouted over the din. "It's in the station's articles. It's just never been done before ... until now."

Those who heard Henry laughed in delight.

Emerson tried shouting at Harbour, but he was speaking to her back. She marched out of the auditorium, with her people following close behind. To Emerson's dismay, much of the audience filed out too. Apparently they'd been present just to see the contest between those seated at the table and Harbour.

"Where to now?" Jessie asked Harbour quietly. She signed L-I-A-M, and Jessie nodded.

Harbour stopped in the middle of the station's prestigious central corridor, and said to her followers, "I thank you for your support. If you're wondering if I was serious about electing a different commandant ... I am." Her comment elicited cheers. "I've private business to conduct. So, I'm inviting you to go about your business and share the discussion that took place in the auditorium."

As the group dispersed, many took a moment to thank Harbour for her support of stationers and spacers. Her people waited patiently for orders. When Harbour's small team was alone, she said, "Lieutenant, Aurelia, you're with Advisor Cinders and me. Captain Bassiter, let the *Belle*'s complement know that they're free to visit the JOS."

Jessie spotted his captains standing at the rear of the group, and he walked over to them to speak privately. "Downtime for the crew on the JOS or the *Belle*," he said. "For the time being, I want all ships kept local."

When Jessie dismissed the captains, Ituau lingered. "Yes?" Jessie asked.

"I received my captain's sharing," Ituau said, "and I'm stunned."

"You earned it, Captain," Jessie replied, "but I'll warn you that the envoy learned there were injuries and wasn't too happy about the report." He was pleased to see Ituau, who had a history as a free-wheeling individual on downtime, taken aback by this pronouncement. "You might share that with the other captains," Jessie added and returned to Harbour's side.

33

Candidates

Harbour led the foursome, and Jessie soon recognized the route. They weren't headed toward security administration.

"I take it that Major Finian wasn't at the auditorium," Jessie remarked to Devon.

"He wasn't allowed to attend, by order of the commandant," Devon said in disgust.

At the hatch to the Miner's Pit, Jessie smacked the door activator and looked up at the security monitor. Moments later, the hatch swung open, and Maggie May swept out to give Jessie a fierce hug. "Thought I wouldn't see your ugly butt again," she said in a husky voice.

"When did you see my butt?" Jessie teased.

"It doesn't matter. I've seen it, and it isn't pretty," Aurelia commented.

"Looks like you and I have been spared the sight," Harbour remarked to Devon.

"Thank goodness for small mercies," Devon quipped.

"Enough about my butt, thank you," Jessie said, stepping past Maggie to enter the Pit.

"Major Finian?" Harbour asked Maggie.

"Already here, Envoy," Maggie replied. "I want to say that was a fine thing you did for those twenty spacers, and I'm sorry to hear about Dillon."

Maggie noticed the pain that crossed Harbour's face at the mention of Dillon, and she quickly changed the subject. "Well, don't stand out here in the corridor, Envoy. Come on in."

The Pit wasn't open yet, and Liam sat at a table by himself. He rose and greeted the foursome, saving a strong hug for Devon.

"Good to see you again," Liam said to Devon.

"Even better to make it home," Devon replied.

Liam took in Devon's mannerisms. His lieutenant's demeanor exuded a level of assurance and self-confidence that he hadn't seen previously.

Maggie delivered water and fruit drinks to the new guests. "Courtesy of the *Belle*," Maggie remarked in answer to quizzical expressions. As another surprise, she set two greens before Harbour and Aurelia, adding, "Courtesy of Nadine and Yasmin."

The foursome took a moment to enjoy their drinks. Then Liam opened the conversation. "I'm sorry I missed the meeting."

"You didn't," Devon said, patting his breast pocket. "I recorded Harbour's interaction with Emerson and the table."

Aurelia smiled broadly, and she hefted her comm unit. "So did I, and from what I saw, just about everyone else did too."

"That will prevent the rumor mill from distorting what took place," Jessie commented. "Those recordings will be flashed to a lot of comm units. People can hear the exchange for themselves."

"Well, Envoy, I'm here," Liam said, changing the conversation, "but I don't know why."

Devon couldn't help the chuckle that escaped. Harbour's comments to Emerson gave him a clue about what was coming.

"We know the commandant moved from the pay of one governor to another," Harbour said. "More than likely, he's now receiving coin from one of the family heads."

"Dorelyn," Liam said.

"You're still recording?" Devon asked, and Liam nodded.

"What have you heard?" Jessie eagerly inquired.

Liam hoisted his fruit drink and finished it. Setting the glass on the table, he said, "Emerson has realized that he holds the upper hand on the council, and he's been squeezing them for greater and greater monthly payments. First, it was to hide the station's license to construct the shuttle. Then, it was to withhold the station's funds for the intravertors, while the council pushed for an agreement to get a major share of the surface."

"Can't we use these recordings?" Aurelia asked.

Liam stared quietly at the young spacer and empath. She represented a fractious part of Pyrean politics. But what he didn't know is why she was invited to sit at the table.

Harbour could sense the emotions that had risen in Liam, and they weren't positive, regarding Aurelia. However, before she could fashion a response, Devon spoke up.

"Let me set you straight on one thing, Major," Devon said, with authority. "You should regard any of Harbour's explorers through a unique lens. They've lived through events that you can't imagine. They've risked their lives and faced the possibility of being trapped in a complex of domes that offered little possibility of ever returning home."

"Does that include you?" Liam asked.

"I must admit it does, Major," Devon replied, holding Liam in a steady gaze.

"Enough," Harbour said firmly. "I've my reasons for wanting Aurelia with me. She's a delegate and an explorer. That's all that need be said."

Turning to Aurelia, Harbour added, "The recordings were obtained illegally. If they're produced as evidence, the Review Board can't consider them. Worse, the commandant would have grounds to dismiss the individuals involved in making those recordings."

"Which would be Devon, me, and others," Liam explained. "And my apology for doubting your presence."

"Not a problem, Major. Most people don't know what to do with me," Aurelia replied. She detected a sudden shift in Devon's emotions in response to her comments, and she deliberately didn't look at the lieutenant. There was no doubt in her mind that Harbour had sensed Devon's surge in interest.

"We're at the same place we were before you left, Harbour," Liam said, spreading his hands in supplication. "We know that the commandant is dealing with the downsiders, and we can't show what we've got. So, I ask again: Why are we meeting?"

"How would you like to be the new commandant?" Harbour asked. She opened her gates wide to judge Liam's emotional reaction. Aurelia was sitting next to Liam, and Harbour expected to compare her reading with Aurelia's, later.

Liam's reactions were as Harbour supposed they would be. He stared at her in surprise, while he processed her question. Internally, he was a mix of emotions that fluctuated wildly.

Liam took his eyes off Harbour and swung them to Devon, Jessie, and even Aurelia. They didn't react or signal their thoughts, which told him that they knew this coming. *I missed one heck of a meeting,* Liam thought.

"Let me state the obvious. We already have a commandant. How do you intend to remove him?" Liam asked.

"Henry Stamerson researched the station's articles. A plebiscite involving topsiders can be taken to elect a commandant at any time. No cause is required," Harbour replied.

"Has this ever been done?" Liam asked.

"Not according to the records that Henry reviewed," Harbour replied.

"If you hold this plebiscite or election, Emerson will surely run," Liam said, "and I can guarantee you that the families will spend an enormous amount of coin to keep him in place."

"More than likely, the families might enter a candidate of their choice to run against the commandant if they think he might not win," Jessie added.

"Which is why we need a strong candidate of our own," Harbour remarked, locking eyes with Liam.

Liam leaned back in his chair, folding his arms over his midriff. "How would this work?" he asked.

Harbour's anxiousness eased. The first barrier had been crossed. Liam hadn't rejected the idea out of hand.

"According to Henry, ten percent of the topsider population must sign a petition to hold the plebiscite," Harbour said.

"We'd have to knock on a lot of cabin doors, and that would expose us," Liam opined.

"You would stay out of it for the time being," Harbour replied. "I push for the plebiscite. I provide a site where the comm signatures can accrue. When we reach the ten percent threshold, the Review Board declares the election request valid. They set the timing, establish the election site to ensure spacer votes are recorded too, and announce the winner."

"And if I was interested in running?" Liam asked.

"When the Review Board announces the plebiscite will go forward, many prominent individuals will pronounce you as their candidate," Harbour replied.

"But not you," Liam suggested.

"Too polarizing," Harbour responded. "However, I've the signature of every eligible voter aboard the *Belle* already signed up on the site. We just haven't published it yet."

"How many is that?" Devon asked.

"Four percent of the topsider population," Harbour replied. In response to the surprised faces, she added, "We've been growing ever since the *Belle* started sailing."

"And it helps that the colony ship has become the greatest profit-generating ship in the history of Pyre," Jessie added, with a self-satisfied smile.

"My advisor likes everyone to note that hauling slush aboard the *Belle* was his idea," Harbour said. She couldn't help but send a small wave of pleasure Jessie's way. His idea had transformed her life and those aboard the *Belle* in extraordinary ways.

"We started this conversation, discussing the recordings," Liam offered.

"Yes, we did," Harbour replied. "Keep them safe. They might become necessary if the families move against us in a manner that overwhelms our efforts."

They heard Maggie's comm unit buzz. "Opening time," she announced.

"Better not keep hungry spacers waiting," Jessie warned.

"I say we order," Harbour suggested. "Anyone hungry?"

* * * *

Dorelyn, Idrian, Rufus, and Emerson retired to a private room that the council maintained for their visits aboard the JOS.

"Why couldn't those creatures the Jatouche fear have eaten that woman?" Rufus growled.

"My thought is that Harbour is probably indigestible," Idrian remarked.

"Drop your animosity toward Harbour," Dorelyn scolded. "It does us no good. We must focus on the challenge she laid down."

"Do you think she's serious about a new commandant?" Emerson asked.

Dorelyn schooled her face. More than anything she'd like to see Emerson exit a hatch on a terminal arm without a ship docked on the other side. She couldn't imagine how he'd gained the commandant's position. Then again, she considered it was with the help of Markos Andropov, who held the domes' governorship position for so many decades. *Markos was the type to prefer an idiot*, she thought.

"Yes, she's serious," Dorelyn stated evenly, "and she wouldn't have suggested it unless she knew it was possible. I have to give the woman credit. She's taken on a staggering amount of responsibility and power, and she's wielded it effectively. We've underestimated her."

Dorelyn stared into the distance for a moment, and then added, "But that can be corrected."

"Emerson, your job is to visit with Captain Stamerson," Dorelyn ordered. "By the captain's comment, he knows the processes this election must follow. We must have the details. That means every line of the articles, which govern the rules to request an election, to nominate candidates, to safeguard the voting ... everything."

"Certainly," Emerson agreed, relieved that the council appeared to be backing him. "What else?"

"That's all," Dorelyn replied. "You may go."

Emerson hesitated but then got up and left. His ears were burning at being dismissed like an errant child. It was his growing retirement fund that kept him silent.

"Are we backing that fool?" asked Rufus, when the door slid shut behind Emerson.

"Wrong question," Dorelyn instructed. "The right question is: What's the best path to take to ensure we win? It might be by supporting Emerson. Then again, it might be by recruiting another candidate, without Emerson's knowledge."

"Is the idea of eliminating the opposition candidate off the table?" Rufus asked.

Dorelyn considered the question, finally saying, "No, but it's a last resort, and if we decide to move in that direction, we'll have to ensure that it appears as an accident."

"The only way to prevent blame falling on us is with a catastrophic accident. That will entail the loss of more than a few stationers and spacers. Possibly a terminal arm's emergency decompression," Rufus said.

"Possibly," Dorelyn commented quietly. "Let's focus on our first steps. Who do we have that's vulnerable, someone we can control, and would make an appealing candidate?"

"Can we consider stationers and spacers?" Idrian asked.

"No spacers," Dorelyn relied swiftly. "They don't have widespread appeal, except for maybe Cinders." She chuckled at her own joke, and Idrian and Rufus were smart enough to politely smile.

"We've several to choose from," Rufus remarked.

"And do they all possess respectable standings among stationers?" Dorelyn inquired.

"Some do; some don't," Rufus said, shrugging.

Dorelyn's eyes narrowed at Rufus, and he gritted his teeth. He hated Dorelyn's silent remonstrations. In hindsight, he knew he should have thought before he opened his mouth.

"I want the two of you to put your heads together and get me a list of potential candidates," Dorelyn requested. "I want details on them. I'll speak to my security chief and get his input."

"Are we taking this to the council?" Idrian asked.

"Not yet," Dorelyn replied. "If we inform them prematurely, we'll be inundated by their suggestions for candidates. You can be sure they'll be ones who're beholding to them. I want to craft our list and present it to them. They can choose one of our candidates," she finished, a cruel smile twisting her lips.

When Dorelyn dismissed Idrian and Rufus, the two men strolled down a retail corridor, discussing the conversation they'd had with Dorelyn.

"You know what she's going to do, right?" Idrian asked.

"Yeah, we'll produce this list, but she'll maneuver the council to back her choice," Rufus replied. "Then she'll be the one to suborn the candidate. The end result will be that she'll own the commandant."

"Exactly," Idrian agreed. "We'll be right back where we started. Instead of a governor controlling the domes, it'll be Dorelyn, with the weight of the families behind her."

"The good news is that she only serves for three years," Rufus pointed out.

"Which means Dorelyn has three years to find a way to make herself the permanent head of the council," Idrian riposted.

Rufus walked and considered Idrian's prediction for the council's future. He hated that at every turn others had the power over the domes. It would never be him, and he knew it ... he wasn't clever enough.

"If Dorelyn ends up getting the council's choice, her choice, elected as commandant, the council will probably give her permanent control," Rufus admitted.

"And there's not much we can do about it," Idrian said. "Unless you want to contemplate a different order of things."

Rufus latched on to Idrian's arm to halt their walk. "What are you suggesting?" he asked.

"Not here. Not in the open," Idrian said, and continued walking.

34

Intrigues

The conversation between Idrian and Rufus waited until they returned downside. They were seated in Idrian's office, when Rufus said testily, "I've been waiting two days to hear you explain yourself."

"Look at our situation, Rufus," Idrian pleaded. "We spent decades under Andropov, and the families got the leftovers from his table. Then we got Panoy, who wasn't any better."

"And she was replaced by Gaylan, who is turning out to be the same thing. I get it," Rufus interrupted. "So, tell me something I don't know."

Idrian hesitated. The thoughts he wanted to share were incendiary, and he was under no illusion that Rufus was his friend. Family heads didn't have friends. They had allies, and often those allies became enemies.

"Look, Idrian," Rufus interjected, "I know you've got reservations about sharing dangerous ideas with me, and it's not like we've always agreed. But on the subject of dome rule, you and I are probably thinking the same thing. We're on a wheel that's going round and round, and we can't see a way to get off."

Idrian mused about Rufus' comments. He decided to disclose a portion of what he'd been thinking but not everything.

"Here's something I want you to consider, Rufus," Idrian said. "What if the council's candidate loses? And what if Dorelyn is unable to eliminate the contender, who's backed by our opponents?"

"Do you think that's possible?" Rufus asked.

"All things are possible, when you consider the existence of unseen forces," Idrian replied enigmatically.

Rufus stroked his chin, considering where Idrian was headed. To his annoyance, he didn't see it. "Go on," he finally said.

Idrian waited. He needed there to be a discussion in which Rufus committed to the conversation.

"Okay," Rufus blew out. "Dorelyn ... we, the family heads, lose control of the commandant position, which means we'd lose sway over key topsider issues."

"True," Idrian agreed.

"So who's in control? Who's the new commandant beholden to?" Rufus demanded.

"Good questions," Idrian replied. "Maybe he or she isn't in anyone's pocket."

The idea of a commandant not under anyone's influence seemed foreign to Rufus. Then, like a bolt, it hit him where he'd seen that concept before and what Idrian had been leading him toward.

"We're talking about the *Belle's* documents," Rufus declared. "But then, how does that help us, if someday there's an elected president and elected representatives?"

"Maybe it does, and maybe it doesn't," Idrian replied, shrugging his shoulders. It was all he was prepared to say at this time.

* * * *

Dorelyn finished updating her security chief on the commandant's meeting. She was pleased to hear that he'd already obtained a copy of the numerous recordings floating around the JOS. When he left her office, Dorelyn called for Sika, her administrative assistant.

A mid-thirties woman entered Dorelyn's office. She was blonde, with a slight build, and she was pretty but in an unassuming way.

"Sit, Sika," Dorelyn said, indicating a chair. "It's my guess that Envoy Harbour is serious about pushing for the election of a new commandant. This presents us with several problems. We'll back the commandant and maybe an alternate candidate, but there's always the possibility the opposition could win. You need to prepare contingencies."

"What type and for whom?" Sika asked.

"If we see that the opposition's candidate is likely to win, he or she needs to have an accident," Dorelyn said. "One that can't be traced to us."

"Is collateral damage acceptable?" Sika asked. She sat demurely on the edge of her seat. No one would suspect her of the skills she possessed.

"I would say that's acceptable," Dorelyn replied.

"Who else?" Sika asked.

"If by some fluke, the opposition wins and their candidate attains the commandant's position, it might be necessary to clean up our prior relationships. They'll know too much," Dorelyn said. "That's all," she added, indicating the door.

Sika silently exited the room.

A small chill went down Dorelyn's spine. Unless you were facing Sika, you were never aware of her approach.

* * * *

Before the Miner's Pit opened for the day, Maggie cracked the hatch. "You two don't have anywhere else private to meet?" she asked Liam and Devon.

"Nowhere safe, like here, Maggie," Devon said, blowing Maggie a kiss.

"Get in here before you're seen," Maggie said, laughing. "Serve yourself. I'm in the back, recording inventory."

Devon got water from the bar for the two of them and sat across the table from Liam.

"Well, we've got privacy," Liam said. It had been Devon who'd requested the private meeting and suggested the Pit.

"I want to talk about the commandant recordings. I think I've got a way to use them," Devon said quietly.

"I don't have any ideas. So, I'm anxious to hear yours," Liam replied.

"You know I don't have any family and few friends," Devon explained. "I've always been a bit of a loner. But something happened during my journey through the gates. My companions were an astounding group ... Pyreans, Jatouche, and a Crocian."

"Not to mention Aurelia," Liam interjected. In reply to the lift of Devon's single eyebrow, he said, "I'd have thought she was a little young for you. She's eight years your junior. Then again, I don't know who a good partner would be for one of the most powerful empaths to ever exist."

"You forget Harbour and Jessie," Devon remarked.

"Are they —" Liam started to ask.

"No," Devon quickly denied. "I think they orbit each other like twin stars. Gravity keeps them entwined, but it's possible that they might never meet."

"We'd all better find safe places to hide if they collide," Liam remarked. "Does Aurelia know how you feel about her?"

Devon frowned at Liam, as if he'd asked the silliest of questions.

"Oh, right, empath," Liam quickly said. "Sorry, not thinking. Then I take it you two haven't talked things out."

Devon managed to offer a shrug to his friend.

"Don't you think you should?" Liam asked. "Or would you rather admire her from afar?" He'd never had a younger brother and wondered if he was offering the right advice to Devon.

When Devon gave Liam a second shrug, the major shook his head in astonishment. "Oh, for the love of Pyre, Devon. You fought giant creatures, and you can't summon the courage to talk to Aurelia about your feelings?"

"I know. It's ridiculous, isn't it?" Devon admitted.

"That's one word for it," Liam replied. "Okay, enough about your nonexistent love life. Let's get back to your idea about the recordings."

"It's simple," Devon said. "I resign and then release the recordings. I take the blame for everything."

Liam regarded his subordinate and wondered again about the experiences Devon had endured as an explorer.

"I can tell you, Devon, that it won't work," Liam said.

"Why not?" Devon demanded.

"After you confess, you'll be up before the Review Board," Liam explained. "It won't take long for the prosecution to poke holes in your defense."

"I'd keep my mouth shut," Devon protested.

"You're not thinking, Devon," Liam said gently. "First, you couldn't use any of the recent recordings. They were made during the time you were gone, and the data proves it. Second, the Review Board would know that you had help, and there'd be a hunt for your accomplices. Then there's your sentencing. If Aurelia cares about you, how do you think she'd feel, knowing you were going to be incarcerated for a long time?"

Liam could see that he was getting through to Devon, but it occurred to him that his lieutenant wasn't long for security services.

"Then again," Liam continued, "you probably wouldn't have to worry about doing any serious time. At first, Aurelia would probably mope about. Then, she'd get angry and influence Sasha. One moment you'd be in your cell, and the next you'd be walking free, passing the lot of us cowering under our desks and enduring visions of some nasty terrors. As a result, Aurelia and Sasha would share your criminal legacy."

"You're good at drawing bleak pictures, Major," Devon commented.

"Glad you see it that way, Lieutenant," Liam replied, adopting a more erect posture. "We've got to be smarter than our adversaries, not dumber."

"Speaking of smart, Major, you need to be careful," Devon warned. "And I mean in everything you do ... where you go, where you eat, who you're with —"

"No need to tell me," Liam interrupted. "That's something I've been thinking about ever since Harbour proposed that I run for commandant. After I'm announced as a candidate, my life will be in danger. I don't have any illusions about that."

"Well, Harbour is ahead of us," Devon said. "You're to have two constant companions."

"I don't want to put other people in harm's way," Liam replied. But after he thought about it, he asked, "Who?"

"Aurelia and me," Devon replied, smiling.

Liam laughed, "I bet you objected vociferously to that."

"My first thought was that Harbour was playing with us," Devon admitted, "But then I realized that I'm a logical companion to the new candidate. People would expect you to have an escort."

"And Aurelia?" Liam asked.

"You're really not good at this, are you?" Devon riposted.

"At what?" Liam retorted.

"At empaths, Major. Aurelia would be our early warning system," Devon explained. "You and I might allow an attacker to pass us by, and he or she could hit us from behind, but people can't hide their emotions from her."

"Is she that good?" Liam asked. He waved his hands to forestall Devon's reply. "I know she's powerful, but you're talking about scanning hundreds of people an hour."

"I watched Harbour and Aurelia link up and keep an entire deck full of the Colony ... five-meter long, serpent-like, venomous sentients at bay. They were weaving in the air and hissing, angry that they couldn't overcome the fear that those two empaths were projecting," Devon related. "As long as I live, I'll never forget that sight. It was magnificent."

Liam watched Devon fade into his memories, and where it was a supposition before, now he knew for sure that his lieutenant wasn't long for the job.

"I still think it's a bad idea to put others in the way of an assassin's attack," Liam said.

"No problem, Major, you can explain your reasoning to Envoy Harbour," Devon replied, ending his statement with a wicked smile.

"I think I'd rather take on those aliens you fought," Liam grumbled, and Devon laughed in sympathy.

* * * *

Henry ate his dinner and stopped briefly to check on the status of the Pyrean Green fund. Its growth had slowed to a trickle. The one thing in the fund's favor was that the YIPS manager, Evan Pendleton, had agreed to store the two completed intravertors, the partially constructed one, and the pile of new crates for free.

It had been Henry's hope that Harbour's challenge to Emerson would result in the commandant seeing the wisdom of giving up his relationship with the families. Unfortunately, it appeared that Emerson lacked the moral fiber.

Henry picked up his comm unit and called the *Belle*, requesting Harbour.

"Evening, Henry," Harbour. She was in her cabin's study, relaxing with Jessie after dinner with Dingles and Nadine.

"I'm ready, Harbour," Henry said. "I've prepared an announcement about the plebiscite and attached a link to the station's articles for further information. In my message, I explain the required signature count to authorize the challenge of the commandant. The only thing I'm missing is the link to your site."

"One moment, Henry," Harbour said. She switched from comm mode to the site that two of her techs had prepared, copied the link, and sent it to Henry.

"Got it," Henry said. He opened the link to verify it and laughed. "That will certainly make a point," he added. There was only one signature on the site. It was Harbour's.

"The moment others begin signing up, we'll start mixing in the signatures from the *Belle*," Harbour explained. "I want to create an air of momentum."

"Have you thought of running, Harbour?" Henry asked.

Harbour had her device in speaker mode, and Jessie covered his laugh.

"I've got other things I want to do," Harbour replied.

"With aliens and such, I imagine," Henry suggested.

"And such," Harbour said quietly. "Good evening, Henry," she added, closing her device.

Henry sent his message to the officer on duty in security, who quickly posted it to both stations and all ships. He spent the rest of the evening on the couch with his wife, watching a vid that she'd selected. They'd seen it before, but it was one of their favorites from the colony ship's library.

Before Henry retired, he decided to check the signature site, not that he was expecting any progress in this short period of time. To his shock, there were over a thousand signatures. Shaking his head, he went to bed.

After morning meal, Henry couldn't resist checking the site again. The signature count was five thousand plus. He sat there for fifteen minutes, and watched the number tick up every few seconds. He picked up his comm device and called Harbour.

"I thought you were going to add your signatures a few at a time," Henry inquired without preamble.

"Good morning to you, Henry," Harbour replied. She was still wet from her shower.

"Have you seen the signature site?" Henry asked.

"You launched it late last evening, Henry. Why would I check it?" Harbour asked.

"We've collected more than five thousand, three hundred signatures, including the *Belle*'s," Henry explained.

"That would be difficult to do, Henry. I've left orders for the techs to add the first hundred later today," Harbour replied.

"Oh, for the love of Pyre, Harbour. We're speeding toward the required ten percent without your signatures," Henry said, his amazement evident.

Harbour set her comm unit down and dried off while she thought. "Henry, don't announce that the plebiscite has obtained the required number of signatures when it gets to the ten percent."

"That's going to be self-evident soon," Henry said.

"I know, Henry. I'll have the techs accelerate the addition of our signatures, but I want the populace to get an idea of the general mood."

"When do you want it announced?" Henry asked.

"When it slows, Henry, and call me before you do that," Harbour requested.

The signatures that Harbour, Jessie, and Henry expected would take weeks to collect took only three days. Thirty-four percent of topsiders had connected their comm units and added their signatures to the site.

During a dinner hour, Henry sent a message to security. The plebiscite was official. Within Henry's announcement, he laid out the requirements for the candidates, who had to collect at least one thousand signatures to be placed on the ballot.

-35-
Campaigns

The morning after Captain Stamerson's announcement, topsiders and downsiders were talking about nothing else but the plebiscite. Everyone waited to see who would qualify. There were the usual assorted characters, who visited cantinas or hung out in well-trod corridors soliciting signatures. Only two of these were eventually successful in achieving the minimum number of signatures and barely at that.

However, the first candidate to qualify was Emerson. He easily collected the requisite number. Yet, his delight at seeing his name alone on the site's candidate list was short lived. Within three days, another name appeared, and Emerson had to wonder: Who was Rod Fortis? He researched the name and discovered the man had nothing to recommend him for the commandant's position.

Rod Fortis was an investor, who had made one too many bad investments. He was in danger of being ousted from his luxury cabin and faced the ignominy of moving inward to a retirement cabin. Then, he'd received a visit from a person who chose to remain anonymous.

"Good morning," a man said, after Rod opened the door to his cabin. "I think I can help you with your financial difficulties. May we talk?"

Rod hesitated. The stranger disturbed him, but his lack of coin bothered him more. "Come in," he finally said. After offering the man some water and a seat, he asked, "Who are you?"

"That will be revealed in good time," the stranger said. "The first question for you is: Are you interested in having a patron, someone who will pay you a great deal of coin to do their bidding?"

"That depends on what they want me to do," Rod replied. At which point the stranger rose, wished Rod a good morning, and made for the door.

"Wait," Rod called out. "What's this about?"

When Rod faced the stranger, who patiently waited for a decision, Rod chose to ignore his principles and opt for a comfortable life.

"Yes, I'm interested," Rod said. "How much coin are we talking about?"

Dorelyn's number two in security returned to his seat on the couch and laid out the monthly payments that would be available to Rod.

"And what do I have to do for these funds? And when do the payments start?" Rod inquired.

"You're going to run for the commandant's seat," Nevis replied.

"But I'm not remotely qualified for the position," Rod objected.

"That doesn't matter. Your patron will advise you on the large and small issues until you grow into the job," Nevis replied.

"I don't think I can generate a thousand signatures," Rod complained.

Nevis shook his head. "It will be done for you. Your responsibility is to campaign. Talking points will be provided for you."

"And the coin?" Rod asked.

"We know your assets have dwindled considerably," Nevis replied, "and we're prepared to deposit fifty thousand today and ten thousand more each month until the election is held."

"What if I don't win?" Rod asked.

"At that point, our association will end," Nevis replied.

Rod got up from his chair. It was early in the morning, but he poured himself a drink and slugged it down. Many pieces had fallen together, while the stranger and he talked. That they knew of his financial condition and were willing to part with a good amount of coin to buy his participation said the man represented a family head, maybe the council.

When Rod imagined selling off his furnishings, which he loved, to fit in a cabin a fifth the size of his present one, his decision was made. If he was broke, there would be no more visits to the sumptuous cantinas, no more hobnobbing with other investors. Then he imagined himself wearing the commandant's uniform and the respect he'd receive.

Rod turned around to face the stranger, and said, "Done."

Nevis smiled. It appeared genuine, but then again, he was practiced at deception. He pulled out his comm unit, and with a few quick taps, he announced, "You're now fifty thousand in coin richer, Rod Fortis."

Then Nevis handed Rod a second comm unit. "We'll be in touch exclusively via this device. You will not have any further conversation with me, and you will never have communication with your patron. All exchanges with us will be through messages. Is that clear?"

"Yes," Rod replied. "And if I win the election, what about the payments?"

"They'll continue on a monthly basis. The amount will remain ten thousand. However, if certain goals, which are judged to be important, are met, there will be bonuses. Good morning," Nevis said, and casually exited the cabin.

Rod's mouth felt dry. He poured himself another drink, but that didn't seem to help. "What have I done?" he muttered. Then he snatched up his comm unit and checked his primary account. It no longer showed the paltry two thousand in coin. It was a hefty fifty-two thousand, and much of the angst he'd been feeling disappeared. "What you've done," he said, answering his own question, "is chosen to be rich rather than poor."

Nevis waited until he was in a secure location. Then he made a brief call to his security chief. "It's done," was all he said before he ended the connection.

* * * *

It was another meeting, before hours, at the Miner's Pit. Harbour, Jessie, Liam, Devon, and Aurelia sat around the table sipping on fruit drinks and greens.

"Rod Fortis," Liam said. "An odd choice."

"What do you know about him?" Jessie asked.

"A man born to privileged parents. He inherited his wealth, and then he squandered it over time," Liam summarized.

"Why does this qualify him for the commandant's position?" Aurelia asked.

"It doesn't," Devon replied. "But he generated the requisite number of signatures in a short period of time."

"The families," Aurelia concluded.

"Undoubtedly," Liam said.

"Dorelyn is covering the council's position," Jessie surmised. "She's backing two candidates."

"Are we sure that she's supporting Emerson?" Harbour asked.

"If I were her, I would," Jessie replied.

"So we have two serious competitors and two individuals, who will absorb a few percent of the votes," Harbour stated. "You still with us, Liam?" she asked.

"I must admit that the one thing that's convinced me to be a candidate in this election is the slate of competitors," Liam said. "I can do a better job for topsiders with my eyes closed than any one of these individuals."

Liam's audience chuckled at his indignant attitude toward his competition.

"I do have one thing that I wish to discuss," Liam said to Harbour. "That would be the companions that you're proposing to escort me." He tipped his head in Devon and Aurelia's direction to emphasize his subject.

When Harbour lifted an eyebrow in invitation, Liam said, "I don't know how effective they might be in protecting me, and I don't want anyone hurt if they're called on to do so."

"Your concerns are noted," Harbour said, "but I don't want to waste my time gathering support for a candidate who can't make it to the election. So, if you're running and you want our help, then you'll accept their protection."

Liam gazed at the faces of his audience.

"He's unconvinced," Aurelia said, focusing her attention on Liam.

"Stop that," Liam said indignantly.

"Get used to it," Jessie shot back. "Her powers might be the difference between Devon and you surviving an attack or getting killed."

"Let me remind you about the plumerase attack on Olivia, Pete, and Drigtik," Harbour said. "If the families were prepared to take that risk to delay the intravertor's deployment, what would they do to keep control of the station by owning the commandant?"

"I want to add another note to Harbour's remarks, Liam," Jessie said. "In general, Pyreans don't have any concept of what's entailed in fighting for their lives. Their experience with violence is minimal. During our exploration, Devon and Aurelia encountered a level of desperation in trying to survive that you can't imagine. If there is an attack, I expect you'll employ your security training."

"What's wrong with that?" Liam interrupted.

"Nothing. That's entirely appropriate," Jessie replied. "However, it might not be aggressive enough to save you." He swung a finger at Devon and Aurelia, and added, "They'll provide the appropriate response."

"I take it that all immediate concerns are satisfied," Harbour asked, focusing on Liam.

"Let's do it," Liam replied, with a resigned sigh.

By the end of the day, Liam's name appeared on the candidate list. The race for the commandant's position now numbered five, and it would remain that way until the election. Voting could take place up to five days before the election to allow spacers to register their choices, as far away as the inner belt. However, their votes wouldn't be revealed until the poll site closed.

* * * *

"What's the latest?" Dorelyn asked Idrian and Rufus, who sat in her office.

Idrian prefaced his remarks with, "These are the conjectures of my security forces, who are embedded on station, and the reports of my informants. Effectively, we can discount two of the candidates."

"Who's backing those two idiots?" Dorelyn asked.

"One is supported by a fringe group of xenophobes. They want nothing to do with aliens," Rufus replied. "My sources say the other is a hardliner against the domes, but his positions are considered too extreme."

"Continue," Dorelyn directed Idrian.

"Sentiments are about even for Strattleford and Fortis," Idrian said.

When Dorelyn's eyebrows furrowed, Rufus interjected, "My sources concur."

"Unfortunately, mine do too," Dorelyn added. "Odd, isn't it? The incumbent has this extensive history, and a new candidate with no experience runs even with him."

"It's the pressure we applied to Emerson to withhold the funds for the intravertors," Idrian replied. "My sources report that topsiders, especially stationers, are angry about that."

"Is there any indication of the division of topsider sentiments for our three front runners?" Dorelyn asked.

"About thirty percent for each of our men, and about forty percent for Finian," Idrian replied.

"What I don't understand is why Finian isn't running away with this?" Rufus asked.

"I've had my people digging into him," Dorelyn commented. "Unfortunately, they've not found anything embarrassing, which I find unbelievable. The prevailing attitude of Finian's nonsupporters is they think he might be Emerson's man. In their minds, they might be trading like for like, if he was elected."

"I would have thought Finian's arrest of Andropov and rescuing the empaths would have counted for more," Rufus countered.

"Actually, I would have thought so too," Dorelyn said. She sat quietly considering the reports. "Essentially, we've an even race," she finally said.

"Have you investigated the possibility that Finian could be bought?" Idrian asked.

Dorelyn stared at Idrian and Rufus, deciding whether to share what she knew. It wasn't that she trusted them. It was whether informing them was in her interest or not. She decided it was.

"Despite the easily obtained information that it's the investors, captains, and general populace who are behind Finian, it's Harbour who's supporting him," Dorelyn said. She carefully watched her associates to judge their reactions. Rufus showed surprise, but it seemed artificial, and Idrian hadn't indicated much more than raised eyebrows. Her conclusion was that both of them knew and hadn't shared, but this wasn't unexpected.

"Then we can be sure that Finian will never be suborned," Idrian commented.

Dorelyn nodded, but Rufus frowned. In Rufus' world, everyone could be bought. It was only a matter of finding their weakness.

"Empath," Idrian said, tapping his temple.

"Oh, right," Rufus admitted, peeved that he'd revealed his failure to consider what Harbour's support meant.

"Do you think Harbour will come out in favor of Finian, at some time?" Idrian asked. "And if she does, will it help or hurt Finian?"

"I think Harbour is asking herself those very questions," Dorelyn said, smiling at the thought that Harbour was faced with the same difficult decisions that occupied her.

"If Harbour is behind Finian, so is Cinders, and that means Finian has the spacer vote," Rufus said.

"We never had them," Dorelyn remarked, "but they're a small percentage of topsiders. No, our focus isn't going to be on impugning or suborning Finian. If we try to besmirch him, that will offer Harbour the perfect opportunity to announce her support."

"If we combine the numbers for Strattleford and Fortis, we'd have sixty percent of the vote," Idrian proposed.

"I was thinking the same thing," Dorelyn replied. "What concerns me is whether the stationers see the remaining two men in the same light. My suspicions are that they don't. If we cut one of our candidates loose, we run the risk of dividing those supporters in unequal proportions between the final two men to our detriment. In that case, we won't have achieved our goal."

When the conversation appeared to conclude, Idrian pulled out his comm device. "There is something I think you should see," he said, setting up his device to play a recording. "This is Tracy Shaver, the explorer who lost her brother. Yesterday, she was in a cantina, and she got angry at one of our paid Emerson supporters. Listen to her response."

The replay started, and Dorelyn saw a young girl, anger etched across her face, say, "My brother, a spacer and recent recipient of Jatouche medical treatment, died to earn the rewards that we're receiving. And the commandant, in his wonderful wisdom, is withholding the funds to put those gifts to work. But here you stand, spouting the commandant's wise governance of our future. I say Strattleford doesn't serve the people of Pyre, he's serving himself. In which case, I say we need a different commandant."

Idrian let the recording continue, and Dorelyn could hear the enthusiastic applause that Tracy's tirade generated.

"That cantina is frequented by retired spacers and stationers," Idrian commented.

"Was this recorded by one of our people?" Dorelyn asked.

"I wish it was, but no. It was taken by a bystander, and it's making the rounds," Idrian said, closing the comm unit and sitting back.

Dorelyn shook her head and enumerated Tracy's assets as a spokesperson. "Young girl, attractive, passionate, an explorer, and a dead brother, and she's making a compelling argument."

When Dorelyn dismissed her associates, she called for Sika.

"I think our competition might win unless we eliminate their candidate," Dorelyn said. "What progress have you made in your plans?"

"None," Sika admitted. She sat on the edge of her seat and delivered her pronouncement in the same tone of voice she'd use to request a glass of water.

Dorelyn prided herself on having mastered control of her anger, which was legendary when she was much younger. Now, she invariably employed subtler means to communicate to her associates that her enmity was brewing. Yet, here sat the one person to whom she hoped she never communicated any kind of emotional frustration — Sika.

Sika had come to Dorelyn's attention at the time she had inherited control of the family. The girl, only a late teenager, had been caught eliminating one of Dorelyn's security officers.

"Why did you kill him?" Dorelyn had asked. She was curious as to why the girl would do such a stupid thing. She had to know that she couldn't get away with the murder.

"He was rude to me, and then he hit me. No one hits me," Sika said.

"And if I ordered these two men to kill you and dump your body outside the dome?" Dorelyn proposed.

Sika carefully sized up the officers on either side of her. They severely outmassed the slender girl.

"I would kill one and hurt or kill the other before he could take me," Sika stated quietly.

"How?" Dorelyn demanded, but Sika stared at her, as if she'd never asked the question. Then Dorelyn said, "Show me."

The teenager, who wasn't restrained, leapt onto the man to her right and bit deeply into his neck, tearing out an artery. She threw herself to the opposite side of the security officer, as he screamed and grabbed at his bleeding throat. As Sika's feet hit the floor, she pushed the man she'd attacked into his fellow officer. In the mêlée, she pulled the shock stick from the first man's belt.

The second officer had his hands full fending off his partner to get to the girl. In those split seconds, Sika came for him. She jammed the shock stick under his chin and held it there, burning it into the man's flesh while she drove him to the floor. During the entire time, Sika's face hadn't shown any emotion. When the two officers were down, dead or dying, she spit out the piece of flesh in her mouth onto Dorelyn's expensive rug. Then she stood there, blood dripping down her chin and the shock stick in her hand.

"Would you like to work for me?" Dorelyn had asked.

"Does it include food and a bed?" Sika asked.

"That and more," Dorelyn replied.

"Then okay. Can I eat now? I'm hungry," Sika said.

"Let's get you cleaned up first," Dorelyn replied, leading the girl toward her office's facilities.

That encounter was nearly twenty years ago. Sika's social skills had developed to a point where she could blend into any environment, even though every gesture was fabricated, and her techniques, which she employed against Dorelyn's enemies, had become flawless.

"Elaborate," Dorelyn requested of Sika's one-word answer.

"Major Liam Finian presents limited exposure," Sika explained. "He delegates well, which means that the vast majority of his time is spent at security administration or with his family. The opportunity for a catastrophic accident, which would divert suspicion from us, is limited."

"What is the opportunity to entice him out of his comfort zones?" Dorelyn asked.

"Also limited, but there is a further development," Sika stated.

"Explain," Dorelyn requested.

"When Major Finian leaves the office or home, he has two constant companions, Lieutenant Devon Higgins and Delegate Aurelia Garmenti," Sika replied.

"An odd pair," Dorelyn commented.

"No, smart," Sika replied.

"Explain," Dorelyn asked.

"The empath tends to walk forward of the men. She can sense the emotions of others. The lieutenant's demeanor has changed since his return. His walk is no longer casual and unrestrained. He's intense, wary." Sika had delivered her information in her usual monotone.

"Summation," Dorelyn requested. Sika's estimation of Liam's companions underlined Harbour's subtle maneuvering. Her earlier admiration of the woman was quickly turning into frustration.

"Probability of a catastrophic accident is near zero. A direct attack would have to occur during the day, with multiple attackers, which defeats your request for deniability. The option remains to eliminate the entire family in the evening," Sika replied.

"Can that latter scenario be performed in a manner that looks entirely accidental?" Dorelyn asked.

"That probability is also extremely low," Sika replied.

"Thank you, Sika," Dorelyn said, and Sika slipped noiselessly out of her office.

-36-
Attack

Half the days between the plebiscite's announcement and voting day had passed. Candidates were visiting cantinas, putting out messages on the station's media channels, and finding ways to influence voters. Emerson and Rod were proving to be much better at pushing their agendas than Liam, who was the most reserved of the three men.

Reports to Dorelyn showed the council's two contenders were still equal in influence among voters, and they were slowly closing the gap on Major Finian.

Harbour had her own sources, and they were telling her the same things that Dorelyn heard. She was plagued by the thought that they had an unreleased treasure trove of Emerson's recordings with the governors and Dorelyn. Unfortunately, every idea she proposed to Jessie to make them public, he shot down.

During one discussion, Harbour had grown extremely frustrated and shouted, "You're my advisor. You come up with an idea and stop saying mine are idiotic."

Jessie was shocked by Harbour's outburst. It was unlike Harbour, and he chose to reply calmly. "I've never called your ideas idiotic, Harbour. I've only tried to point out the ramifications of each of your scenarios. In each case, there are devastating consequences to exposing those recordings. And as to why I haven't made any fabulous suggestions, it's because I don't have any and it's not for lack of trying."

"I can't believe we might lose," Harbour complained, throwing herself dejectedly into a chair.

"I admit the trend looks bad, and with the time to go before the election, this could turn into a tossup," Jessie admitted.

Jessie watched Harbour gather herself. She folded her legs, as Aurelia had done, indicating she intended to focus herself. He sat back in anticipation. To his way of thinking, a calm empath was much better than an upset one.

Harbour relaxed her mind and examined their challenge, as if it was a client's problem. She dissected the issues, attempting to see what lurked behind the obvious manifestations. She smiled, opened her eyes, and caught Jessie's noticeable exhalation.

"I'm better," Harbour said apologetically. "You needn't have worried. I might get angry, but it wouldn't cause me to project my power uncontrollably."

"I wasn't worried for myself," Jessie said, sitting forward on the edge of his seat. "You're the architect of this scheme. It won't work if you aren't thinking calmly and deliberately. What made you smile?"

"We think the council is backing Emerson and Rod, correct?" Harbour asked. When Jessie tipped his head in agreement, she said, "If the council is getting the same information we are, what do you think they'll want to do?"

Jessie sat back in his chair. This had been one of questions bothering him. He couldn't see them backing both men and hoping that one of them beat Liam. "I think Dorelyn will convince the council to smear one of their candidates and boost the other," Jessie replied.

"And how do you think topsiders would shift their votes?" Harbour asked.

Jessie offered a small shrug before he said, "I wouldn't know. I guess it would depend on how they denigrated the one candidate and boosted the other."

Then a thought struck Jessie, and he said, "No. Dorelyn would cut Emerson loose, and she'd do it in such a way that it besmirched the existing security structure. In that way, she would drive Emerson's supporters to Rod."

"That's what made me smile," Harbour remarked. "Instead of railing against our seeming misfortune, I tried seeing our challenge dispassionately and viewing it from the council's perspective."

"Any other thoughts?" Jessie asked.

"Yes. We have to move before Dorelyn does," Harbour said. "Once she smears security, we'll never recover those voters."

"So what's the plan, Envoy?" Jessie asked, smiling.

"We announce our support for Liam," Harbour supplied.

"I thought you wanted to remain in the background," Jessie said.

It was Harbour's turn to shrug. "When we started, I thought it was a good idea. Now I'm convinced that we have to beat Dorelyn to whatever action she's planning to cut her candidates from two to one."

Harbour picked up her comm unit, "Birdie, I need a Pyre-wide broadcast."

"Certainly, Envoy," Birdie replied. "When do you want to schedule it?"

"Give me five minutes to prepare, then Advisor Cinders and I will be on the bridge," Harbour replied.

Birdie set up the comm board, accessing the app that she hadn't used in half a year. Then she made a quick call to Dingles, who told her to route a signal to his comm unit so that he could watch real time.

Harbour and Jessie entered the *Belle*'s bridge, and Birdie reported that she'd sent a Pyre-wide message announcing the upcoming transmission. "I take it that it'll be full signal, Envoy," Birdie said, eyeing Harbour's decorative skins.

"Only the best for our citizens," Harbour replied, which made Birdie snicker.

Harbour and Jessie took up positions in front of the vid pickup. Birdie watched for Harbour's hand signal. When she received it, she initiated the broadcast and cued Harbour.

"Citizens of Pyre, specifically stationers and spacers, you face an important decision in a few weeks," Harbour said. "It's one that will greatly affect the future of the planet and its surroundings. I want you to know that I initiated this plebiscite, with the approval of the Review Board. I believe that we need to take a bold new direction to ensure the viability of our society. We can't depend on living in space anymore. We must have the planet's surface to support our growing population, and we have the means to do that. Maybe not tomorrow, but someday."

Out of sight of the pickup, Harbour signed to Jessie, who took over the message. "In case you're not aware, the envoy and I requested the three delegates, who first returned to Triton, to ensure the completion of the three intravertors that accompanied them. In addition, they were to initiate the building of a launch platform and a JOS to Triton passenger shuttle. Whether we like it or not, humans aren't alone in this galaxy. There's a marvelous collection of sentients out there, and we've earned their respect. The envoy and her team returned with three more intravertor parts."

Jessie passed the broadcast to Harbour, who said, "But what's the status of these plans? Six sets of intravertor parts, and only two constructed, no platform, and the needed shuttle is being constructed by the domes' council. Is this what you expect of a commandant? I don't. I want someone in charge who believes the planet's surface needs to be recovered for future generations of Pyreans. This person should have integrity and respect for stationers, spacers, and downsiders ... except maybe the family heads."

Harbour could hear the chuckles of the bridge crew.

"What you might not know," Jessie continued, "is that the alien alliance is governed by entities who call themselves the Tsargit. For what the envoy and her explorers accomplished, during their journey, the Tsargit has announced their own rewards for us. These are in addition to those offered by the Jatouche. And while this aid is welcomed, we need to demonstrate to these alien cultures that Pyreans are capable of helping themselves."

Harbour concluded the broadcast. "We tell you these things so that you understand we believe only one candidate embraces this future vision of Pyre. That's Major Liam Finian. We hope you'll join us in electing Major Finian as the new commandant."

Birdie ended the transmission and turned in her seat to stare at Harbour. "The things you don't know," she said softly, and received a wink from Harbour before Jessie and she exited the bridge.

* * * *

Alone in her office, Dorelyn was able to give vent to her frustration. She'd watched the *Belle's* broadcast, which was transferred down the El's diamond-threaded cable and carried throughout the domes. It didn't take long for her comm device to signal her of incoming calls. Every member of the council wanted to speak with her. To her disgust, the family heads forced her to meet with them.

"Yes, I agree we've been outmaneuvered," Dorelyn admitted to the council members. "But it's a temporary setback. We've not lost, and we've got one response that Envoy Harbour can't prevent or overcome."

"What's that?" Lise Panoy asked.

"I'm not prepared to share the details yet," Dorelyn replied. "However, I can tell you that it involves cutting our candidate count from two to one. It will be done in such a way that we'll shift the voters away from Major Liam."

"That's your intention anyway," Lise remarked.

Dorelyn fielded other questions, intentionally ignoring Lise, until she'd exhausted the council's inquiries. Afterwards, she met with Idrian and Rufus. They threesome sat quietly together, mulling over recent events.

"I think we can't wait," Idrian said, breaking the silence. "The longer we delay, the more time the voters have to consider Harbour's broadcast."

"I agree with Idrian," Rufus added. "We've got to throw our support behind Rod Fortis."

"What's the plan?" Idrian asked.

A cruel smile decorated Dorelyn's face, and she said, "We start by exposing Emerson's liaison with Andropov and Panoy." Her opening made Idrian and Rufus smile in reply. They liked the idea of curtailing Lise's influence.

"Next, we follow that message with information that Finian has always operated in league with Strattleford," Dorelyn continued.

"But the citizenry knows that it was Finian who arrested Andropov," Rufus objected.

"That's the beauty of it," Dorelyn chuckled. She was enjoying the opportunity to best Harbour. "The final part of the plan is to leak a rumor that Strattleford and Finian had a falling out with Andropov. Then they conspired with Lise to replace him and support her for the governorship."

"I love it," Rufus crowed.

"That's inspired," Idrian admitted. "When does this begin?"

"I can initiate the first part in a few days, after I put the right people in place to drive the message," Dorelyn replied. "We can't afford to start this and have it sputter out."

"Are we offering proof?" Rufus asked.

"I've obtained image copies of Emerson's account, the one containing our monthly deposits," Dorelyn replied. "They were captured off a monitor to ensure there's no record of data transfer, no evidence of a breach. They cover a few years of time, during which Andropov and Panoy paid him. You can see Emerson's name, the dates, and the monthly deposits."

"Will that be enough?" Rufus asked.

"That's why your people will be aboard the station," Idrian supplied, nodding his head in appreciation of the plan.

Dorelyn's self-satisfied smile spoke for itself.

* * * *

Emerson heard Harbour's announcement. At first he was furious, and then he was frightened. For weeks he couldn't understand how an unqualified investor, who had wasted his inheritance, could capture as much attention as he had.

Try as hard as Emerson could, he hadn't identified who backed Fortis. That, in itself, was an answer. If they were that well-hidden, it was the council or, more specifically, it was Dorelyn. He could understand that she was being careful to protect the families' influence over topsider issues, but nonetheless, he felt betrayed.

Just when he thought that the race could be won, Harbour had thrown her influence behind the major. It was all he could do not to stalk into Finian's office and scream at him. He knew it would make him look foolish, and more than likely, Liam would record his outburst.

The more he ruminated on losing the commandant's position, the more agitated he became. Too frequently, he was yelling at staff, despite knowing it was affecting his chance of winning.

To add insult to injury, Lieutenant Higgins had taken to escorting the major everywhere, as if he was an exalted person. Worse, when the major left the office with the lieutenant, the empath joined them. He could never quell his deep-seated anger at Aurelia Garmenti. In his mind, she was the reason that his long-standing, stable relationship with Markos Andropov was undone.

* * * *

Every evening after seeing Liam home, Devon and Aurelia retired to a small cabin inward. It was rented for them by Harbour. The compact space contained a kitchenette, two reading chairs, a pair of stacked bunks, and a compact facility.

The pair would purchase food to eat in their cabin. After a quick shower, they would tuck in for the night to be ready for Liam. He was an early riser.

Devon would climb into the upper bunk, and Aurelia would take the lower. They'd chat in the dark, during which time Aurelia would open her gates. Her experience with men had run the extremes. Downside it was the dark, ugly moods of Dimitri, who had molested her. Topside, Aurelia had found safety on Jessie's ships. She was respected and accepted as a fellow spacer by the crews.

Returning to the station presented Aurelia with the many varieties of emotions that men offered her. Tempted as she was to close her gates, she had to keep them open to protect Liam, and she did her best to ignore the distasteful things she sensed.

Devon was different. Lying below him, with her senses open, Aurelia thought of Devon as a cleansing shower after a long stint in a vac suit — warm water washing away the sweat and grime — gentle and refreshing.

This evening, as Aurelia lay there, she asked, "You haven't had much experience with empaths, have you?"

"No, Harbour and you are my first," Devon supplied, and Aurelia had to suppress a giggle.

"But you've never expressed fear of us," Aurelia said. "Why not? Most every stationer does."

"I've never been frightened of you, if that's what you're asking," Devon replied.

"And Harbour?" Aurelia pursued.

"When we met, it was obvious that Harbour meant a great deal to you. That's all I needed to know," Devon supplied.

As with every evening, Aurelia noted that her questioning hadn't produced strong emotional swings in Devon. He was matter-of-fact in his conversations with her, comfortable discussing any subject.

Tonight, Aurelia chose to bring up a subject that had been bothering her. "I'm concerned for Liam, now that Harbour has come out in support of him."

"I am too," Devon replied. "Try not to take any unnecessary risks."

"Good night," Aurelia said, smiling. In contrast to most subjects, Devon had broadcasted his fear with his last remark. His heightened emotional state indicated what he felt for her.

The next morning, Devon and Aurelia met Liam at his cabin door.

Liam had acquiesced to their new routine and had stopped objecting. Previously, as a matter of habit, he'd preferred using the back passageways to reach security administration. Instead, his companions led him through the station's broadest corridors, where people were more likely to greet him.

Aurelia walked in front of the men, smiling and greeting stationers and spacers. Despite his reticence, Devon attempted to do the same thing. He considered it a small price to pay to see his friend elected.

It wasn't difficult to initiate conversations for Liam. Investors were eager to talk to the major and hear his views on station expansion, commerce, and the intravertor deployment. Young men were eager to talk to Aurelia, and women of all ages wanted to talk to Devon. Once Devon and Aurelia were engaged, they'd introduce Liam to them.

After a lengthy spate of conversations in the station's promenade corridor, Liam remarked, "You two are more popular than I am."

"Only briefly," Devon replied.

"Yes," Aurelia agreed. "They might engage us, but most of them want to know you. They like what Harbour said, and they want to place their trust in you."

"You know this for sure?" Liam asked. When Aurelia squinted her eyes at him, he added, "Of course you do," and he heard Devon chuckle.

In the evening, Devon and Aurelia met Liam outside security and retraced the morning's steps. They exited the busy retail corridor and wound through smaller and smaller passageways toward Liam's cabin.

Aurelia detected a wash of fear and excitement. The passageway was empty, with most doors closed, except for one about six meters ahead.

Devon saw Aurelia tense, and he placed a hand on his shock stick, while Liam chatted on about the stationers he'd just met.

Aurelia felt the excitement spike, and she identified the direction. She had time to yell, "Danger," swinging her arm up to point to the open door, when a figure in an emergency fire suit emerged from the open doorway. He carried a portable electric torch.

Devon drew his shock stick and heaved it with all his might at the figure Aurelia had identified. The stick struck the suited figure in the left shoulder. The electric torch was dropped as the figure grasped his shoulder in pain.

Devon raced forward, lowered his head, and drove his weight into the midriff of the suited figure. The two men rolled deeper into the passageway. Devon fought to get purchase on the assailant, but the slick suit hampered his grip. Worse, the figure was no lightweight. One moment Devon was on top, and the next he was launched over the individual's head with the aid of the attacker's arms and a well-placed boot.

While Devon wrestled with the suited figure, Liam rushed forward, snatched up the torch, and turned it off. Standing even with the open door, he could smell the flammable liquid that was spread across the floor of an abandoned cantina. He was tempted to close the open door via the actuator, but he feared an explosive trigger might be embedded in the switch.

Devon was on his back, fighting to keep the assailant's hands off his throat, when a deck shoe crossed his vision and connected with his attacker's helmet. He felt the hands around his neck loosen. A second kick to the attacker's head rolled the figure off him.

Aurelia had managed to free Devon, but the suited figure was shaking off her kicks and struggling to stand. By the individual's size, she judged him to be a man, and she chose to deliver a well-aimed kick to the crotch, which effectively ended the man's struggles.

Aurelia reached out a hand to help Devon off the deck. "You okay?" she asked, gently touching his bruised neck.

"I think so," Devon said, coughing briefly.

"Good," Aurelia replied. "I'm not done figuring you out yet," she added, running the back of her fingers alongside Devon's cheek.

Aurelia turned to the assailant, who had regurgitated into his helmet. She efficiently unlocked the helmet, swiveled it, and pulled it over the man's head. Her nose wrinkled at the putrid smell.

Devon knelt beside Aurelia. "Roby," he declared in surprise. The man was a known petty criminal. He'd never been involved in something as nefarious as murder.

"Security and emergency services are on their way," Liam said, closing his comm unit.

"You know this man?" Liam asked Devon. He was about to add that Devon should restrain him, but the only thing the man was capable of doing was moaning and cradling his genitals.

"Something's wrong here," Devon said, standing to address Liam. "Roby isn't a professional at this kind of thing. This is a clumsy attempt on your life."

"Well-planned or not, he nearly succeeded," Liam replied. "That old cantina's floor is awash with flammable liquid. We were about to be caught in an explosion and probably burned to death."

Sergeants Cecilia Lindstrom and Miguel Rodriguez rushed around the corner. Liam briefed them, and Cecilia called medical services for the suited figure writhing on the deck.

Several moments later, emergency services arrived, and the sergeants restrained Roby and guided him away from the personnel, who investigated the cantina.

Standing in the next passageway with his protectors, Liam said, "I want to thank you for your efforts this evening. However, you've put me in an awkward situation with Harbour." Then he smiled, and added, "Remember, I was the one who objected to her about your companionship."

"There are more days to go," Aurelia said.

"You're much too young to be such a stark realist," Liam remarked. Immediately, he winced. He mentally kicked himself for failing to recall the horrendous events that had shaped Aurelia's life.

Aurelia laid a hand on Liam's forearm, and said, "Apology accepted."

Liam was dropped at his cabin, and Devon and Aurelia sought a small food stall, bought more than they could eat, and headed to their cabin. After eating and cleaning up, there didn't seem to be an appetite for small talk. Devon lay in his bunk and was close to falling asleep, when he felt the stacked beds shake.

Aurelia climbed up the short ladder to the upper bunk. Silently, she slipped under Devon's blanket and snuggled against him, immersing her mind in Devon's emotions.

When Devon felt Aurelia's head on his shoulder, he folded his arm around her. From that moment, he was too happy to give any thought to the concerns of tomorrow.

-37-
Roby

"What happened?" Dorelyn railed to her security chief. She was livid and losing control of her temper.

The security chief stood his ground and repeated the limited information he possessed.

Dorelyn stared at the man, desperate to take out her anger on someone. When she could manage to speak without yelling, she ground out, "Find out whoever is behind this. I want them buried outside."

The security chief acknowledged his orders and hurried from Dorelyn's presence.

Dorelyn stalked around her office, racking her brain for what family member might have been so incredibly foolish as to attempt to murder Liam Finian. She picked up her comm unit and called Idrian.

"I take it you've heard," said Idrian, when he saw who was calling.

"What do you know?" Dorelyn demanded tersely.

"My source inside security tells me that the man, Roby, is a small-time thief and forger," Idrian supplied. "He tried to ambush the major by flooding an empty space with fuel and igniting it as the major and his companions passed. The idiot was wearing a fire emergency suit to protect himself."

Dorelyn stopped her pacing and leaned against her desk. None of this made sense to her.

"I was ready to see a family head occupy a piece of Pyre's surface," Dorelyn said, working to regain her emotional equilibrium. "This doesn't sound like the work of a professional."

"No, it doesn't," Idrian agreed. "I think a stationer was behind the attack."

"Who?" Dorelyn asked.

It sounded like a rhetorical question to Idrian, and he chose to offer his own reasoning. "Strattleford and Fortis have the most to gain, but a supporter might have hired Roby without either candidate's knowledge."

"Whoever this was, they hurt us badly," Dorelyn said. "Finian will receive a lot of sympathy."

"Perhaps not," Idrian said. "What if we offered the rumor that Finian orchestrated this himself? I mean, it is a sloppy piece of work. If it was supposed to be a real job, how come it wasn't a better setup?"

"I like that," Dorelyn said. "Pass that along to the family heads. Let's see if we can't defeat this surge of concern for the poor major before it can start."

Dorelyn ended the call with Idrian and signaled for Sika. "I have a job for you," she told her assistant, when Sika closed the door to her office.

* * * *

"Where's the commandant?" Devon asked. "I've not seen him all day." Aurelia and he were seated in Liam's office.

"Said he had some personal business," Liam replied. "What's Roby's status?"

"He'll be in medical services for a while," Devon replied. "They're working to reduce the swelling of his genitals, and he's heavily medicated."

Both men glanced toward Aurelia, who announced, "You attack us; you get hurt."

Liam lifted a questioning eyebrow at his lieutenant, and Devon responded with, "Sounds fair to me."

"Did you get an opportunity to interview Roby?" Liam asked.

"I didn't, but the sergeants spoke to him, while he was being taken to medical," Devon replied. "And before you ask, Major, the only thing he said, which he repeated over and over, was that he hated empaths."

Liam was momentarily embarrassed to have Aurelia hear that, but a glance in her direction revealed the slightest of smiles on her face.

"I meant to ask you: What did you pick up?" Devon requested of Aurelia.

"Some fear, but an enormous amount of excitement," Aurelia replied.

"Excitement?" Liam repeated. "That doesn't sound like a cool, calm professional."

"He's not, Major," Devon said. "We've a history of encounters with Roby for a bunch of small things. A pro would have set a remote and ignited the fuel by watching us on a vid cam, as we approached the space."

"Let's face it," Liam riposted, "a pro wouldn't have used that approach. It's too messy and too dangerous. He could have created a fire that grew out of containment and caused an explosive decompression."

Liam considered the disjointed facts and then ordered, "Devon, inform medical services that I want Roby's medication reduced, as quickly as possible. We need to find out who paid Roby. If this election wasn't contentious enough, it's gotten a whole lot worse."

"I can tell you that it wasn't the council or an individual family head," Devon stated. "This was an amateurish attempt."

"Maybe and maybe not," Aurelia interjected. "And maybe it doesn't matter, except in the pursuit of your jobs. Be prepared for the council's spin on this event. They will find a way to make you look bad."

"How?" Liam asked.

"You need to ask someone like Harbour or Jessie to answer that question, Major," Aurelia replied. "Based on my observations, you're not suited for the position of commandant ... not until you can think like your adversaries ... and they will be many."

"Speaking of adversaries, Major," Devon said, "your escorts have been increased. Spacers will lead us and follow us every time you leave your cabin or security ... the envoy's orders."

This time Liam didn't argue. Last night, his wife had harangued him that the commandant's position wasn't worth his life. Unfortunately, he'd never shared with her Emerson's duplicitous nature, which meant she didn't know how important it was to replace him.

* * * *

Sika had been at work aboard the JOS for the past thirty-six hours. She'd obtained a medical services uniform and an ID. In the first use of her disguise, Sika had obtained a sample of Roby's blood. A visit to a source provided her with a solution of blood proteins, and she was required to pay an exorbitant price for the rush request.

On Sika's next trip to medical services, she busied herself with menial jobs, while she waited for her opportunity. Near midday, the number of staff dwindled, as they sought meals. Sika slipped into Roby's room. She was surprised that a security officer hadn't been posted to monitor the assailant.

The vial Sika held contained a thin membrane, which separated two solutions — the blood proteins and a coagulator. She shook the vial harshly, bursting the membrane and combining the solutions. Loading the mixed solution into an injector, Sika pressed it high on Roby's inner thigh in the area of bruised tissue. It would help disguise the injector's telltale mark.

Sika exited medical services and sought out the public facilities she'd prepared. In a stall, she removed a bag that had been concealed above an overhead air duct. She stripped off her uniform, ID, wig, and facial alterations. From her pack, she donned a pair of wildly decorated skins. Then she tucked up her hair and pinned it in place with trans-sticks, a downsider fashion statement. Finally, she applied a garish mist mask to her face. It was a style favored by the dome's well-to-do young. Sika's transformation complete, she threw her paraphernalia into the recycler chute, strode out of the facilities, and sauntered down the primary corridor to catch the next El drop.

When medical services techs received a warning that Roby was in cardiac arrest, Sika was descending toward the domes. The cultured proteins in Roby's blood coagulated as designed and blocked critical arteries that fed the brain and the heart. Despite the best efforts of the staff, Roby succumbed to the blockages.

When Liam heard the news, he immediately ordered an autopsy without consulting Emerson. Theo Formass, the medical services director, called Liam, noting that the commandant's approval wasn't on the request form. Liam tersely replied that Theo should perform the autopsy anyway.

Knowing Roby's death was a critical campaign issue and the commandant and the major were at odds with each other, Theo chose to go forward with the investigation without the requisite authorization.

The following morning, Theo marched into security administration, collected Liam, and headed toward Emerson's office.

Tapping on the doorframe, Theo said, "Commandant Strattleford, I've critical news that you should hear immediately." He noticed Emerson's frown when the commandant spotted Liam behind him, and he added, "As you both are candidates and officers in security, I feel it appropriate that you be apprised of my news together."

When the men were seated, Theo said, "I took it upon myself to conduct an autopsy on Roby." He deliberately did not glance toward Liam and hoped the major wasn't staring at him. He wasn't a man who was good at subterfuge. As his wife frequently warned him, "Theo, you're an open book. Don't even think about lying."

"Why the autopsy?" Emerson asked.

"Roby was too young to suffer such a massive stroke," Theo replied.

"What about his injuries from the struggle with Lieutenant Higgins and the empath?" Emerson suggested. He'd said the word empath, as if he had a bad taste in his mouth.

"His injuries were, no doubt, painful, Commandant, but they weren't life-threatening," Theo explained.

"Go on, Director," Emerson invited.

"During the autopsy, manufactured proteins were discovered in Roby's bloodstream. They were the cause of the blockage in his arteries," Theo reported.

"How were the proteins delivered?" Liam asked. He was controlling his frustration. He'd been anxious to interrogate Roby and discover who had paid him.

"We discovered an injector site high in the groin area. It was obvious that someone meant to disguise it," Theo concluded.

"Do you have a suspect?" Emerson asked.

"I've requested surveillance vids be sent to your sergeants," Theo replied. "We know that there was an unauthorized female, masquerading as staff, but her ID fooled our systems. We're still attempting to discover how that could have happened."

"So there's an attempt on my life and now the perpetrator has been eliminated," Liam summarized, anger biting into his words.

"Curious," Emerson said, delivering an accusatory stare at Liam.

"That's all I have to report. If you'll excuse me," Theo said hastily and hurried from the room. He didn't want to witness an explosive argument between the commandant and the major.

When Liam stood up, Emerson asked, "Don't you have anything to say?"

Liam paused at the door, and replied, "I'm going to catch a killer and find out who's behind the attempt on my life. How about you, Commandant? Are you going to do anything worthwhile?"

Liam could hear the commandant shouting, as he made his way to the sergeants' area.

-38-
Election

Liam marched into the sergeants' area. His arrival was brusque and heads snapped up.

Sergeant Miguel Rodriguez anticipated Liam's questions and hurriedly said, "We heard about Roby, Major, and we've received the vids from medical services."

"And we've run facial recognition on the staffer. No hits, Major, nothing even close," Sergeant Cecilia Lindstrom added.

"Disguised?" Liam asked.

"We did track the woman's movement into a public facility. She went in but never came out," Miguel said. "I think she changed her disguise again."

"And what did facial recognition get on those who came out," Liam asked.

"We're running that now, Major," Cecilia replied. "We started with every individual who exited after she entered. We're at forty minutes."

"The results so far?" Liam inquired.

"Everyone identified but her," Miguel said, pointing to his screen.

"A teenager?" Liam asked incredulously.

"Or a woman meant to appear as a teenager," Cecilia replied. "Who can tell her age under that pile of makeup she's wearing. But the thing that you should take from this is that the assassin knew how dome teenagers appear."

"And walk," Miguel added. He tapped his comm unit's interface, and Liam watched the woman or girl, whoever she was, swinging her arms and sashaying down the corridor, as if she owned the place."

Liam sat down heavily on the edge of Miguel's desk. The sergeants stared at him expectantly, but Liam was struggling with the facts of the case.

"This doesn't make any sense," Liam said, scratching the back of his head.

"Understood, Major," Miguel said sympathetically. "We have a sloppy, amateurish attacker eliminated by a subtle, professional assassin."

"And the first is a stationer, known for petty criminal conduct, and the second is definitely a downsider," Cecilia added.

"So what's the connection between these two?" Liam asked.

"Maybe there isn't one," Devon said from the door. He'd been listening to the exchange, having been alerted by the commandant's yelling. "I heard about Roby's death, and I talked to Theo on his way out."

"So what's your theory?" Liam asked.

"First, you should be aware that Roby's death will be pinned on you," Devon replied. "You killed him to cover up the attempt on your life, which, by the way, you engineered."

The sergeants' mouths were hanging open, and they were staring incredulously at Devon.

"Don't mind the lieutenant," Liam said offhand. "Aurelia and he have been doing that since they started accompanying me through the station. The thing that irks me is that they've been right an extraordinary number of times."

"What *is* your theory, Lieutenant?" Cecilia requested. She was fascinated by this turn in the conversation.

"I think we have different parties involved," Devon explained. His comment elicited confused expressions, and he expounded, "Two different and unconnected parties behind each of these events. That's why this doesn't make sense."

"That still doesn't offer an explanation as to why this woman killed Roby," Miguel said.

"It does if you look at it from a political angle," Devon replied.

* * * *

After the news of Roby's death broke, rumors were rampant, and the wildest and most egregious were fueled by the paid parties. The subject of the attacker's murder dominated every cantina table and bar. Conjectures about who did what to whom were rife.

Dottie listened to her fellow investors, as they sat around their favorite table in the Starlight. Each proffered one or more of the rumors. The most injurious one against the major said he orchestrated his own assassination attempt and then killed Roby, when Roby survived the arrest. A twist on that odious rumor was that it was propagated by the families to smear the major. Still another variation was that stationers were behind the machinations. And the most ludicrous one was that aliens were operating among them, attempting to influence Pyrean politics.

When Dottie's companions were finished espousing their favorite theories, they looked at her to hear which one she preferred. She regarded the men and laughed heartily.

"How did I befriend such intelligent men, but such foolish students of human nature?" she asked. "Don't listen to the rumors, the conjectures. Most of them are lies. Ask yourself which candidate is most trustworthy. Which candidate do you believe will work for the things you want? And, most important, what proof have they given you of their true nature? Who has withheld station funds, while professing support for topsiders? Who arrested Markos Andropov and Giorgio Sestos for kidnapping and imprisoning empaths? And who has no experience in security and has squandered his family's wealth?"

"You make it sound so simple," Trent pressed.

"It is," Dottie replied. "You're the ones making it complex by listening to every rumor and message that's put out. Do we know who's behind each of them? We can guess, but does it matter? Look at the facts, look at their actions, and make your judgments on those." Dottie finished her drink and left.

"She has a point," Hans said. "All you hear are the most titillating rumors. The facts are rarely discussed."

"I think it's obvious who Dottie supports," Oster said, sipping on his drink. "And let's not forget that the envoy supports him."

"But you're assuming that the envoy doesn't have an alternate agenda," Trent objected.

"I don't accept that idea," Oster riposted. "None of us have personal experience with Harbour. We don't know her."

"Except for Dottie," Hans offered.

"And that was my conclusion," Oster said, hoisting his drink to Hans. "Dottie's a delegate. She spent weeks with Harbour, and she believes in the woman and what she's trying to achieve for Pyre. I suggest we stop sharing the rumors and start speaking to the facts."

"I second that," Hans said. Oster and he eyed Trent and waited.

Trent drew breath to offer a final objection, but the hard stares of his comrades halted him. "I'm not sure of the facts," Trent said, compromising, "but I'll stop sharing the rumors."

"Fair enough," Oster allowed, and the men touched glasses to seal their agreement.

* * * *

In the final days, it was obvious to topsiders that the race had dwindled to two men. The rumors against Strattleford and Finian escalated, driving voters away from the commandant, and splitting them between Fortis and Finian. More went to Fortis than Finian.

The common theme among reports from the political manipulators was that Fortis was leading among voters, and Dorelyn congratulated herself and shared the news with the council. However, a subtle maneuver wasn't receiving the attention of the family heads' sources.

In the early morning hours, Danny and Claudia were extraordinarily busy, shuttling *Belle* residents to the JOS. They made seven to eight runs, docking at various terminal arms. Then they reversed the procedure to collect their passengers in the late evening hours. This allowed Harbour to deliver approximately four hundred residents to the JOS every day to campaign for Liam.

The essence of Harbour's plan was that her people were reaching stationers who didn't haunt cantinas, prestigious shops, and sleepholds. A *Belle* tapestry weaver visited shops where she purchased her materials. A metal sculptor dropped by to visit the individuals who reclaimed parts from derelict ships or damaged terminal arms. Spacers visited the vendors who supplied their vac suits, skins, and accessories.

And for the first time ever, empaths used a hastily converted station location to offer their ministrations at tremendously reduced costs. It became an extremely popular spot, as its location spread by word of mouth through the ranks of the less fortunate. The empaths didn't discuss politics. That was against the rules of their service. But the clients knew who helped them, who their leader was, and who their leader supported.

Harbour's plan was a work in progress, and it was difficult to measure its effectiveness. In contrast, the common thought in cantinas was that the election was going to be a tossup between the two leading candidates.

While the individual votes were secret, the count wasn't. It was obvious to topsiders that the turnout was enormous. Visits to a voting location weren't required as in the days of ancient Earth. Only registered comm units were allowed to connect to the voting site, and those connections were checked against the station's records of citizens.

Throughout the day, people asked one another who received their vote. Truthful answers often started arguments, and soon people refused to answer the question.

Spacers had days to register their votes, and an overwhelming ninety-eight percent had accessed the site. By the time the polling site closed, Pyrean topsiders had turned out by ninety-three percent.

Henry and the Review Board had sole access to the voting compilation. Even security administration was locked out. Late in the evening, the news of the election was broadcast. Henry faced the vid pickup, and he was flanked by board members.

"The Review Board has ascertained that voters have been accurately verified by the station's list of citizens," Henry announced. "Furthermore, the board is satisfied that the election process has been run in accordance with the requirements of the station's articles. I would ask the board members to add their assent to what I've announced."

Henry paused for the vid pickup to focus on each member. The individuals took a moment to point out other steps that were taken to ensure the election standards were met. Henry had stressed to his fellow captains that it was critical to educate topsiders on how the election process was crafted and observed. The reason for this was simple. There wasn't a single stationer or spacer alive who had ever participated in an election.

When the auxiliary board members were finished, the vid swung back to Henry. "Here are the final results for the three leading candidates for our commandant," Henry began. "For Commandant Emerson Strattleford, eleven point six percent. For Rod Fortis, thirty-nine point three percent, and for Major Liam Finian, forty-seven point four percent. The Review Board announces that Major Liam Finian is the new commandant."

Liam had invited Devon and Aurelia to listen to the election announcement with his family. When the pronouncement was made, Liam hugged his tearful wife and two children. Then he offered his hand to Devon and Aurelia. "Looks like your days of shadowing me are over," he said.

"Not until Envoy Harbour says so," Aurelia riposted. "I believe we'll be with you for a little while longer."

"And I agree with that decision," Devon added. "Emotions are running high. It would be better to be careful until things get a chance to cool down. Have you thought about what you're going to do tomorrow?"

"Yes, I have," Liam replied. "We're going to visit the other candidates. Words of appreciation and sympathy need to be said."

"And you need Emerson's codes," Devon added.

"Those too," Liam agreed.

＊ ＊ ＊ ＊

Emerson had spent the several days preceding the election in his cabin. He was a disillusioned man. Dorelyn had never announced her decision to withdraw her support from him. In fact, he'd received the latest monthly stipend from her, while reports indicated that his supporters were abandoning him. That's when his suspicions were confirmed. Fortis was a council candidate.

The door chime caught Emerson's attention, and he checked his comm unit, which displayed images from the security cam mounted outside his cabin. The last person he wanted to see stood there. Emerson stared at his comm unit for so long that Liam tapped the door chime again. Emerson sighed and triggered the cabin door aside.

"Did you come to gloat?" Emerson charged.

"No, Emerson, I came to tell you that I won't pursue you for any illegal activity you engaged in during your time as commandant," Liam said.

Emerson's mouth gaped open, and he stared at Devon and Aurelia, who stood beside Liam. Their eyes drilled into his. *They know,* he thought with horror.

"I need your codes, Emerson," Liam politely requested.

The thought crossed Emerson's mind that he'd no longer be addressed as commandant. That was, perhaps, the cruelest cut of all. He accessed his comm unit and sent the list of codes to Liam's device. The moment that happened, the codes disappeared from his unit. It was a security protocol.

Liam checked his device, stored the codes, and asked, "I'll expect you to clear out your office today, or I can have your things sent to you."

"Send them to me," Emerson said. "I don't expect to set foot in security administration ever again."

"It'll be done," Liam acknowledged and exited the cabin. He experienced a moment of satisfaction. Emerson didn't know the evidence against him had been illegally obtained. It was enough for Liam to make the man suspect it had been legal.

Liam had one more stop to make. Navigating a few more corridors placed him in front of Rod Fortis' cabin. Tapping the door panel didn't gain Fortis' attention. The display indicated he was in residence, and Liam was about to give up, when the door slid open. Surprisingly, there was no one there to greet him.

"Rod Fortis," Liam called out.

There was a lengthy pause, and then a voice said, "Here."

Liam advanced into the cabin's salon. It was one of the more luxurious and spacious cabins on station. "Where's here?" Liam asked.

"I don't know," said the slurred voice.

Liam followed the sound to the back of a couch. Rod Fortis lay on the floor, a container resting on his chest. "Offer you a drink, winner," Rod said in slurred speech.

"I'll come back tomorrow," Liam said.

"Be in the same condition then," Rod replied, his eyes rolling about.

"Okay," Liam said quietly, and Rod closed his eyes.

At the door, Liam set the panel for a delayed close, and the threesome exited the cabin.

"Where to now?" Devon asked.

"Security," Liam replied.

-39-
Liam Finian

Liam sat behind his desk in his old office and connected his comm device to the monitor. Then he requested the station's accounts, which hadn't been accessible before now. With a sigh of relief, Liam watched them scroll up on the screen. The codes had been accepted.

"Do you have what you need?" Devon asked.

"Yes, thanks, Devon," Liam replied.

"Aurelia and I are stepping out, but we'll be back in time to accompany you to midday meal," Devon said. "Call us if you have to leave administration."

"Understood. On your way out, send Sergeant Lindstrom to me, please," Liam requested. He studied the figures in the various accounts while he waited.

"You requested me, Commandant?" Cecilia asked from the doorway.

"Congratulations, Sergeant, you're the first to use my title," Liam replied, with a smile.

"Didn't you see the candidates this morning?" Cecilia asked. "I would have thought you'd have heard it from them."

"One was depressed; and one was drunk," Liam replied.

"I won't ask which was which," Cecilia said, and Liam chuckled.

"I want to create a channel dedicated to the station's accounts, Sergeant. I intend to publish certain ones. How's the best way to go about that?" Liam asked.

"We already have the Pyrean Green fund on a stationwide channel, Commandant. Why not shove that site down one level, add a link to it on a cover page, and then add a second link to the published station's accounts?" Cecilia suggested.

"I like it. Set it up, and I'll need to make an announcement before that goes live," Liam said.

"You'll have to send me a link to whichever account you want to display, Commandant. I won't have access to it," Cecilia suggested.

"Come here," Liam requested. "It'll be this one." He pointed at the third item on the monitor. It was the station's reserve account, which was dedicated to JOS and YIPS expansion projects."

"Is that figure correct?" Cecilia asked in awe.

"And how would I know that, Sergeant?" Liam asked in a teasing manner. "I've only been the commandant since yesterday evening."

"Why was the comm ... I mean Emerson ... not putting these funds to use?" Cecilia asked.

"You'd have to ask Emerson, and I don't think he's in a talkative mood," Liam replied. "In addition to adding this account, I need you to separate the Pyrean Green fund into two subaccounts. One should include topsider donations and the other will encapsulate downsider donations. Can that be done?"

"Easily, Commandant, we have the origination source of each transfer," Cecilia replied.

Liam considered what Cecilia was saying. He thought he saw a possible problem. "Sergeant, what if topsiders were working in the domes when the transfer requests were made?"

"Then those individuals would have comm unit IDs that matched their citizens' records," Cecilia replied, smiling. Don't worry, Sir, I'll ensure that the records are carefully separated. What's the purpose of this?"

"Sorry, Sergeant, I'm not ready to announce that yet. Set up the new site with the link I sent you, and the changes I've requested. I'll review everything when you're ready."

"Yes, Commandant," Cecilia said.

"And have Sergeant Rodriquez pack up Emerson's personal things and deliver them to his cabin," Liam requested.

"Should I have the office fumigated too?" Cecilia suggested with a wry smile. But when Liam raised an eyebrow, she hastily added, "Maybe just a thorough cleaning."

"That would be fine," Liam acknowledged.

Cecilia turned to leave but paused in the doorway before saying, "Congratulations, Sir. It'll be a pleasure to work in security again." She flashed him a bright smile and disappeared.

Liam leaned back and considered his next step. Emerson had held up the intravertor process to such a degree that he wasn't sure what to try to tackle first. *Ask, if you don't know,* Liam thought. It was an adage drummed into his head by his mentor.

Selecting Jessie's contact info from his comm unit, Liam made his first call. After a brief exchange of congratulations, Liam explained what he'd found in the station's accounts and what he intended to publish.

"My question is what to do next, Jessie," Liam said. "I have a view of the Pyrean Green account and the station's capital growth fund. But I need advice on how to weigh the avenues available to me, and I can tell you that I've never negotiated contracts or estimated the cost of massive projects."

"That's what friends are for, Liam," Jessie replied, with a laugh. "You're correct. You need hard data and expert advice to be able to make these kinds of decisions, and I can help you gather that information."

"Good to hear, Jessie. Where do we start?" Liam asked.

Jessie quickly organized the topics that he'd have to educate Liam on to help him understand the various critical steps. "First, Liam, are you committed to the construction of the intravertors?"

"Absolutely," Liam replied enthusiastically.

"How about the platform? Will you support its construction?" Jessie asked.

"Is that the best way to deploy the intravertors?" Liam queried, in return.

"Yes, according to the brightest engineers we have. I can have them forward their recommendations to you," Jessie explained. "And you should know that the two *Belle* pilots, who dropped the first intravertor, have refused a repeat performance. They say it's too dangerous."

"Okay, then we need a launch device of some sort," Liam said. Then in an afterthought, he added, "How much is one of those?"

Jessie couldn't help the laughter that erupted out of him. It wasn't that Liam was naïve about these sorts of things. It was that it was refreshing to hear a commandant request information to make critical decisions.

"Liam, you're going to do just fine in this job," Jessie said. "I'll have Evan Pendleton send you the cost proposal for the engineer's concept of a platform and the intravertor construction. You'll also get the engineers' original report on launch mechanisms and deployment concepts. Last item, Liam: What about the JOS–Triton shuttle?"

"You mean the one the council's ordered?" Liam asked.

"Yes," Jessie replied.

"I don't know what to do about that. I'll have to think on that one," Liam said.

"Fair enough," Jessie acknowledged. "I'll get the information over to you this afternoon."

Liam was sure that he heard Jessie correctly about the timing. It dawned on him that he was only catching up to individuals who had been working far in advance of him. "Is this the work of Harbour and you?" Liam asked.

"Liam, there are a good many people who worked to get you elected, and they expended that effort on the assumption you would win. Choosing to believe in that version of the future, they've worked to be ready for when you held the commandant's position," Jessie explained.

Jessie waited for a reply, but the comm remained silent. A check of his unit revealed the connection was solid.

"What are you thinking, Liam?" Jessie asked cautiously.

"I'm thinking I don't want to disappoint a lot of good people," Liam replied in a quiet voice. "What if I'd lost?"

"I suppose we'd have gone with plan B," Jessie replied good-naturedly.

"Which was what?" Liam asked.

"Well there was always immigrating to Na-Tikkook," Jessie said, laughing.

"You're kidding?" Liam shot back.

The fact that Jessie didn't answer his question but politely ended the call frightened Liam. He'd never considered what might have happened if

Strattleford or Fortis won. A shudder went through him, and he could feel the short hairs on his head stand up. *You have your work cut out for you, Liam,* he thought. It was more of a warning than a statement of the obvious.

The next item on Liam's to-do list involved setting expectations with the family heads. That meant a message to the council, and Dorelyn was best suited to carry it for him.

"Congratulations, Commandant Finian, on your election," Dorelyn said politely, when she picked up her comm unit. "I hope we'll be able to establish a stable and profitable working relationship to the benefit of both our societies."

Dorelyn had been caught off balance. She'd expected to eventually receive a call from Liam, but she was surprised that it came so swiftly.

"We only have one society, Dorelyn, and I think it would behoove the council and you to start thinking like that," Liam riposted.

"An interesting perspective, Commandant, but you need to take note of the fact that you've introduced a new tradition into your society ... elections. Now that your citizens have tasted an opportunity to elect a new leader, who knows where that might lead? They might want to request another one in the near future."

"And I'm sure the council will try to influence the next one, like you did this past one," Liam said, an edge to his voice.

"That's conjecture on your part, Commandant," Dorelyn replied tartly. "I thought your organization was supposed to deal in facts."

"Enough bantering, Dorelyn," Liam growled. "I've a message for the council. Soon, I'll be posting an update to the Pyrean Green site. In addition, I'm uncovering the station's capital expenditure account."

"Why are you telling me this?" Dorelyn asked.

"I've separated the Pyrean Green fund into topsider and downsider contributors," Jessie continued. "I'm sure that, unlike last time, the domes' contributions will be paltry. You should inform the council that if they wish to share in the planet's surface, they must match the topsider's portion of the Pyrean Green fund."

"I imagine you're intending to contribute the station's coin to the fund, and that's meant to be part of your threat," Dorelyn accused.

"Yes, it is," Liam replied, in a self-satisfied tone.

"I'll inform the council, Commandant," Dorelyn replied. She was biting her tongue. She wanted to unleash her ire on the new commandant, whom she considered an upstart and undeserving of the post.

"Good day, Dorelyn," Liam said, ending the comm.

* * * *

Aurelia was unsure why Devon had requested they wander the station's wide, premier corridor. After they'd lapped nearly a quarter of the station's circumference in silence, Aurelia asked, "Devon, you're nervous, anxious. Are you anticipating trouble?"

Devon's soft laugher was tense. "Only from you," he replied.

"Ah," Aurelia said under her breath. "We're walking and talking because our assignment with Commandant Finian is coming to an end, and we're about to return to our old jobs."

"Yes," Devon replied. He was struggling with how to approach the subject he wanted to discuss, but, as usual, Aurelia had a habit of speeding ahead of him. *Or maybe I drag my feet too much,* he thought.

"And you don't want that to happen, but you're hesitant to ask what I want. Why is that?" Aurelia asked.

Devon felt as if he was talking to a woman eight years his senior rather than eight years his junior.

"I'm trying not to be overbearing," Devon replied.

Aurelia stared at him and then burst out laughing. It was a light, sparkling sound, and it drew the attention of the corridor's pedestrians, especially because it issued from Aurelia Garmenti. What intrigued the stationers was that they'd considered Aurelia a composed and serious individual, and they couldn't recall hearing her laugh during the many weeks she'd accompanied the major.

Devon's flush of embarrassment swept through Aurelia's mind. Although she'd sensed the emotions of thousands of men whose eyes had roamed over her, she had little experience with relationships. Except for Jessie, who was twice her age and her father figure, she hadn't opened her heart to another, and she'd never accepted a lover.

The pair walked in silence for a while longer, and Aurelia considered the various indicators from Devon that she'd witnessed. He said he wasn't afraid of her, and she knew that to be true. Only now did she realize the number of times that Devon had tended to take a post beside her, when the teams mixed during the journey through the domes.

Aurelia considered that Devon might be worried by her hesitancy to respond to his attempts to get close to her. There had been the one time she crawled into his bunk to sleep next to him. But she'd left the bed early in the morning, while Devon slept, and they'd never talked about it.

"I'm going to talk to Envoy Harbour about working at the dome," Aurelia said, voicing a desire she'd never repeated after the one time at Triton.

"Translating the glyphs," Devon guessed.

"Yes," Aurelia replied.

"You plan on asking anyone to accompany you?" Devon asked.

"I had considered who might be useful to assist me, but I couldn't think of anyone who might be easy to work with and have a facility for translating an alien language," Aurelia replied.

Despite the crowds passing them by, Aurelia kept her gates open and focused on Devon. She could sense his disappointment as she spoke, and it dawned on her that there was a form of cruelty that she hadn't suspected she possessed. *Do you resent men who want to be with you, because of Dimitri's actions?* she asked herself.

That question disturbed Aurelia, and she considered what that would mean for her future. In a sudden decision, she chose to reject that direction and embrace the opportunity the man walking beside her offered.

Aurelia came to a halt, faced Devon, and said, "It's occurred to me that someone who had been through the gates would have a perspective that could be useful. And if that someone was a welcome companion, it would make the time in the dome pleasant," Aurelia said.

"Any idea who that someone might be?" Devon teased.

Aurelia didn't need to sense the change in Devon's emotions. His smile said it all.

"It's still under consideration, but I've narrowed it to a pretty short list," she said, linking her arm in Devon's to continue their walk.

* * * *

In the afternoon, Liam received Jessie's promised information, and he sat glued to his monitor, absorbing the details. He was anxious to review the engineers' recommendations for the intravertors' deployments. The document's opening comments spoke to the hull and engine damage that the *Belle* shuttle suffered, while dropping the first device. This analysis hadn't been widely circulated, and he was astounded by the courage the pilots displayed in ensuring the success of the launch.

"Okay, so no more shuttle drops," Liam mumbled, moving onto the report's analysis of alternate deployment scenarios. The engineers had been quite fanciful with some of their suggestions, but, one by one, they laid out the reasons why these ideas were untenable, either by expense, technology, time, or some combinations of all three.

Eventually, Liam became bogged down in the report's details. Engineering wasn't his forte. To be blunt, he had little knowledge in that science. Halfway into the report, he admitted defeat and jumped to the summary.

The engineers chose a mobile launch platform. Intravertors would be loaded into tubes that would be pointed toward the planet's surface. Compressed gas would launch the devices toward the planet, and gravity would do the rest.

Liam loved the simplicity of the idea. The fact that the platform could be moved across the surface and reused made it seem ideal. He slid a thumb up his comm unit's virtual screen to get to the budget outline.

There he blinked twice and sat back in his chair. The platform was the equivalent of adding two terminal arms to the JOS or installing another foundry line on the YIPS.

When Liam finished his call with Dorelyn, it'd crossed his mind that he might have been too harsh with her, especially about the domes' contributions to the Pyrean Green fund. Now it occurred to him that he missed the opportunity to have been tougher with her. *We're going to need a lot more coin,* he thought.

Pulling up Evan's report on the construction cost of intravertors, Liam jumped to the budget summary, and mentally added the cost of three-and-a-half more intravertors to the expense of the platform. The total was staggering, and Liam wondered if there was that much coin Pyre-wide. The magnitude of what was being attempted struck him. Pyreans were trying to make the planet habitable to support a growing population, but they would be spending coin for decades, if not generations, without an immediate return.

"And you'll be asking for more coin every quarter, as more intravertor parts arrive," Liam said, speaking to his monitor.

Liam pushed back from his desk. He needed to think and decided to take a walk. Passing the sergeants' office, he heard Cecilia call out, "Going out, Commandant?"

Liam stopped and sighed loudly.

"Don't blame Sergeant Lindstrom, Commandant," Miguel said firmly. "None of us want to risk the Envoy's displeasure."

Liam pulled out his comm device to call Devon, but he saw Cecilia had already done that. Within a few minutes, Devon came running through the lobby.

"We're ready, Commandant," Devon said in a rush of breath.

"How long is this supposed to go on?" Liam asked. He meant it to be a simple question, but it came out rather peevishly, which he regretted.

"I would suggest you call Envoy Harbour and register your complaint, Commandant," Devon suggested. "But be prepared to be reminded of the attempt on your life and the elimination of your attacker days later."

Liam regarded Devon, who was trying to suppress a smile. The sergeants' lips were wiggling, as they fought to do the same.

For a moment, Liam regarded the overhead and resigned himself to the imposed regiment. He had too much to worry about to take issue with this one thing, a contest he was sure to lose.

Passing through the lobby, Liam said, "We're taking a walk. I need to think."

In the corridor, a trio of spacers fell in front of them, and the same number followed.

Liam glanced around. "Where's our early warning system?"

"If you're speaking of the woman who saved your life, Commandant, she's busy," Devon replied tersely.

"Sorry, I meant no disrespect, Devon," Liam apologized. He mentally booted himself and acknowledged that he was now the commandant and his remarks carried greater weight.

"Well, perhaps it's for the best, Devon. I've wanted to talk to you," Liam said. "I know that you're not long for security, but I need your experience."

Devon eyed Liam and waited.

"Okay, let me be more specific," Liam continued. "With me moving up and you intending to leave, an officer gap will be formed. I need you to close that. My focus will be trying to put what Harbour and Jessie have started back on track. You know how critical those projects are to Pyre."

Devon's nod told Liam that he'd phrased his need properly. Devon was a strong supporter of the envoy.

"What's your plan?" Devon asked.

"I promote you to major, and I promote Rodriguez and Lindstrom to lieutenants," Liam replied.

"Rodriguez has seniority," Devon argued.

"True, Devon, but while Aurelia and you have been guarding my rear end, I've been doing a lot of thinking," Liam said. "Take a look at the future, the one you and others are pushing us toward. What do you see?"

Lately, Devon had come to enjoy these types of questions. "A green Pyre," he replied, and then he added, "And a need for a security force across the planet."

Liam smiled at Devon. The lieutenant had got it in one.

"One day it's going to be what ... a commandant, a few colonels, a bunch of majors, and multiple security commands?" Devon asked.

"I think something like that," Liam replied.

"Then there's the possibility that Miguel and Cecilia could head separate commands instead of reporting one to the other," Devon suggested. "That means they need to lead their own investigations and work independently of each other."

"You see why I need you?" Liam pushed.

They walked for a while, and Devon steered Liam into the Latched On.

"Are we buying spacer gear?" Liam asked. Devon responded with a small smile and said nothing.

Liam waited patiently, while Devon chatted with Gabriel, the store's owner.

When they left the Latched On, Devon said, "The *Belle* and Jessie's ships will take more than half a year for another rotation to Emperion. I can give you, at least, that much time, but this is a conditional response until I speak to Aurelia."

"I'll take that answer," Liam replied quickly. "Let me know soonest. I want these promotions to happen swiftly."

-40-
Dorelyn Gaylan

Dorelyn convened the council. She chose not to speak with Idrian and Rufus before she addressed the body of family heads.

"I've been asked to deliver a message from the new commandant," Dorelyn began, which immediately grabbed the attendees' attention, especially those of Idrian, Rufus, and Lise Panoy.

Dorelyn carefully reiterated her conversation with Liam. When she finished her recitation, she said, "We've entered a new era, one in which no family head has influence over topsider issues by owning the commandant."

"You assured this body that one of our candidates would win," Lise accused.

"And we *were* winning, according to every report, until the assassination attempt on Finian. Would any of you like to admit to that colossal blunder?" Dorelyn asked. Her eyes swept the council members, and she ended her challenge by staring at Lise.

"You insisted we could recover from that," a family head objected.

"And yet another factor was introduced," Dorelyn replied. "Harbour flooded the station with *Belle* residents, and our agents were late discovering this. The *Belle*'s shuttle arrived in the early morning hours, docking at different terminal arms, and flooded the station with the colony ship's residents. We suspect the purpose of these visits was to influence their contacts in favor of Finian."

"How many residents are we talking about?" Rufus asked.

"According to estimates, the shuttle brought in about four hundred individuals," Dorelyn replied. "You can imagine their influence. These four hundred talked to maybe five to ten stationers, who talked to possibly the same number of friends and acquaintances."

Murmurs circulated among the council members, and Dorelyn could sense their dissatisfaction.

"Let's return to the issue of the commandant's request," Lise said. "How are you advising this council to respond?"

Dorelyn knew Lise was intent on exploiting the negative turn of events under her council's leadership. Lise was chafing under the assignment of the council's choice of security chief to her office, and this was an opportunity for her to turn the tables.

"Let's examine our choices," Dorelyn replied, trying to evade Lise's trap. "One, we can refuse to cooperate. We simply keep our coin in our accounts. Two, we can contribute amounts equal to the topsiders."

"And what's your opinion, Dorelyn?" Lise pursued.

"I think the choice belongs to the council members. The issue should be decided by a vote," Dorelyn replied, sidestepping the question.

Lise sat in the front row of the small auditorium, where the council met. Few could see the sly smile Lise offered Dorelyn at her adroit maneuvering.

"Are you requesting we vote now?" Idrian asked.

"Is there any other discussion on this issue?" Dorelyn asked.

"How much are we talking about?" a family head asked.

"It's unknown," Dorelyn replied. "The commandant didn't say how much of the station's construction account would be contributed to the Pyrean Green fund."

"I'm not comfortable contributing without knowing the final outlay," a family head said, "and I'm not referring to the addition of the station's funds. We're being asked to support a capital expenditure program that is destined to last for years, if not decades. Harbour has secured a Jatouche commitment to supply twelve sets of intravertor parts every year. On top of this, we hear a launch platform will probably be built. We have no idea how much this is going to cost, and you're saying one of our choices is to pay half the bill."

"It would take us a while to gather the information to determine the cost of these projects, and we can challenge Commandant Finian to supply those numbers before we commit to matching the topsiders' funds,"

Dorelyn replied. "But does anyone doubt that we have more reserves than the topsiders?"

"You're missing the council's points, Dorelyn," Lise challenged. "The families could be committing their funds to projects that might last their lifetimes. Projects that offer no financial returns. What if the concept fails and the surface can't be rehabilitated? The families' leverage, which has always been our coin, would be diminished."

"I can't advise you on whether the aliens know what they're doing," Dorelyn replied, reminding the council members of the intravertors' source. "And I doubt any of you know this either. I admit this is the greatest challenge facing the domes since their origination. You'll have to decide for yourselves. I'll procure the requested cost information and present it to you, as soon as possible."

* * * *

"Why weren't we consulted before the meeting?" Rufus asked. Idrian and he sat in the comfortable chairs of Dorelyn's office.

"I needed to determine the mood of the family heads without any influence," Dorelyn replied.

"You think we would have talked out of turn," Rufus accused.

Dorelyn stared coldly at Rufus, who quieted.

"And what did you determine?" Idrian asked.

"That the council members didn't get either message ... the commandant's or mine," Dorelyn replied.

"I think it's worse than that," Idrian said. "The failure to elect one of our candidates to the commandant's post has undermined confidence in the council."

"What?" asked Dorelyn, when she saw Rufus shift uncomfortably in his seat.

"Several family heads approached me after the meeting about an alternative to the council," Rufus replied.

"What were their suggestions?" Idrian asked.

"They didn't have any," Rufus admitted. "They wanted to find out if I still believed in the council —"

"You mean they wanted to know if you still trusted my leadership," Dorelyn interjected.

Rufus nodded guiltily, affirming Dorelyn's conjecture.

"How did you respond?" Idrian asked.

"I told them that they were reacting prematurely, and they should wait until Dorelyn obtained the information from the commandant," Rufus replied.

"That's not what I meant," Idrian objected.

"I know what you meant," Rufus replied defiantly. "That's all I'm going to say."

Dorelyn observed the obstinate expression on Rufus' face. The triumvirate had a fracture in it, which meant the council's dissolution wasn't far behind. She had no idea what would replace it. Certainly, Lise wouldn't have her way. A governorship would never have sway over the domes again. She feared chaos — open competition among the families for influence in the domes and over the topsiders.

After Idrian and Rufus left, Dorelyn sat behind her desk, taking stock of the council, her position, and her family. If the council disassembled, then her family would need allies, and she considered the best mix to support her. In the meantime, to prevent the council's unraveling, she needed to know who ordered the attack on Finian. If she could call out that family head, it would serve to divert the council's anger away from her and toward another.

Making a decision on the latter subject, Dorelyn called Sika into her office. The woman sat primly on her seat. Her fingers were intertwined and rested lightly on her knees, as she awaited orders.

"I have to know who paid Roby, Sika," Dorelyn said.

"Proof?" Sika asked.

"It must be irrefutable proof, a confession, a financial trail, something," Dorelyn replied.

"And then?" Sika asked.

"If there's an intermediate on station, I want them eliminated. Make it invisible," Dorelyn said.

Sika nodded. Invisible was Dorelyn's request to make the death appear accidental. Sika experienced a thrill. This was her favorite assignment. It was the most difficult to perform. When it was successfully completed, she lived on a high for days.

"And if the buyer is a stationer?" Sika asked.

"I doubt any topsider had the fortitude or wherewithal to order this," Dorelyn riposted.

"Roby was an amateur. He was a petty thief and forger. Who would hire this fool?" Sika argued.

Dorelyn halted the response that had been on her tongue. Sika wasn't a woman of many words. Three sentences said that she didn't accept her mistress' analysis.

"If it was a stationer behind this, then it doesn't do me any good to collect proof of their involvement. Eliminate them as you would the intermediate, if they exist," Dorelyn ordered.

Having sent Sika on her errand, Dorelyn experienced a moment of satisfaction. Someone had ruined her carefully laid plans to elect Rod Fortis. Now that someone would pay.

* * * *

Rufus ordered an e-trans, when Idrian and he left Dorelyn's house. He requested the small electric vehicle drive a circuitous route for twenty minutes before it reached its intended destination, Idrian's home. By using his family code, the e-trans was directed to not stop to pick up other passengers.

"What did you say to those who approached you after the meeting?" Idrian asked after they were underway.

"It's not important what I said," Rufus replied. "It's what they said. They're ready to abandon the council."

"How does that help us in the long run?" Idrian complained.

"Think about what you're saying," Rufus argued. "This intravertor project, if it's successful, could be generations away."

"And you're telling me that these family heads are not concerned with the future but the present," Idrian finished for Rufus.

"Yes. And why not?" Rufus shot back.

"If we allow that attitude to dominate our policies, we'll be abdicating a strategic position with regard to the topsiders. Where do you think that will lead us?" Idrian argued.

"I don't know," Rufus replied. He'd sympathized with the council members who had approached him, but the conversation he was having with Idrian was why he wanted to talk to him. At first, he'd wanted to sound Idrian out on his attitude about the council. But, as usual, he was learning much more from Idrian.

"I can tell you," Idrian offered. "The families' powers will be wasted fighting one another for dominance. In a generation or maybe two, the families will have wasted their reserves and will be infirm. After that, it won't be long before the topsiders occupy our domes."

"I don't see that ever happening," Rufus declared.

Idrian glanced at Rufus, who resolutely stared forward. Idrian didn't know whether to laugh or cry at Rufus' refusal to envision the future if the families were locked in protracted battles. But he knew neither emotional option would serve him well.

"Rufus, our populace enjoys the stipends that our families' wealth lavishes upon them," Idrian explained. "If the families' funds are depleted in decades of infighting and those nice stipends dry up, what's to stop our populace from descending into chaos?"

Rufus took his eyes off the ped-path and the approaching dome airlock to regard Idrian. He hated Idrian's questions, which asked him to speculate on a future based on the long-term machinations of the dome's families.

"I'll tell you what I think," Idrian said, acquiescing to Rufus' entrenched silence. "If the families lose control over the populace, station security will descend on our domes in significant numbers to restore order. Then topsider administrators will arrive. They will offer our privileged young and our house staff an opportunity to work on topsider needs or starve. Which do you think they'll choose?"

Rufus turned to Idrian. He did have opinions on more focused questions, such as this one. "We'll lose our staffers in a heartbeat," he said. "As for the privileged young, they'll become a mob. They'll be angry and shouting to get their stipends back."

"Which won't ever return," Idrian added.

The e-trans wandered through an agri-dome before it turned around and headed toward the dome it had just left.

"What do you think we should be doing?" asked Rufus, having decided he needed to hear Idrian's advice.

"Doing? Nothing!" Idrian urged. "We're reacting and maneuvering, when we should be waiting, watching, and learning."

"Are you looking for allies?" Rufus asked. It was the one question he wanted to put to Idrian.

"No, I'm not," Idrian replied forcefully. "But I can tell you that Dorelyn is probably examining every contingency. She'll try to protect the council and her position, but she'll be creating a list of potential allies."

"If she asks you to join her, will you accept?" Rufus pursued. He didn't want an alliance with Dorelyn, and he hated the idea that he'd lose the support of the one family head who'd never tried to undermine him.

The men sat quietly, having voiced their opinions. The e-trans stopped at Idrian's house, and the family head climbed out, waved quickly to Rufus, and headed inside.

Later, Rufus would report his conversation to the three family heads, who'd confronted him.

"Idrian is not choosing allies at this time," Rufus said.

"Do you believe him?" a family head asked.

Rufus glared at the woman. "More than I would believe any other family head," he growled.

"What do you think we should do?" a man asked.

"Idrian suggested it's best to wait and see what develops. I think that's a good idea," Rufus replied. "We'll talk later," he added and departed the group.

-41-
Choices

Aurelia asked Devon to lunch at the Miner's Pit, and he took the opportunity to discuss the conversation he had with Liam. Maggie greeted the pair and found a table in the corner for them after directing three retired spacers to the bar with their drinks.

However, Devon didn't find the courage to broach the subject until after they finished their meal. It did occur to him that Aurelia was sensing every turn of his emotions.

When the dishes were removed, Devon cleared his throat, and Aurelia suppressed a smile. "Liam has asked a favor of me," he began. "He wants me to train the sergeants he plans on promoting."

"You would be a lieutenant training lieutenants?" Aurelia asked. "A ship's captain wouldn't follow that type of practice."

"I'd be promoted to major," Devon said.

"What did you tell him?" Aurelia asked. She kept her emotions from broadcasting. Devon had woken something in her that had been dormant since she was a young teenager, and she worried that it was about to be torn asunder by the opportunity Devon was offered.

"I said that I could give him the length of time for the *Belle* to make one more rotation to Emperion for slush," Devon replied.

Aurelia was quiet, waiting for Devon to continue. He seemed poised to tell her more.

"Here's the thing," Devon said, reaching across the table to lightly grasp Aurelia's hand. "Liam needs my help. If I left now, there would be a huge officer vacuum in security. I can't let that happen. But ... but ... at the same time, I don't want us to be separated. I realize it's selfish on my part, but could you see your way clear to put off your trip to Triton for that amount of time?"

Aurelia laughed softly. It was strained, as if it served to release some pent-up angst.

"I told Liam that I needed to talk to you first before I gave him my answer," Devon added, with a touch of urgency.

"You did, did you?" Aurelia replied. It was a rhetorical question. She could sense Devon's worry, hope, and desire for her. It was a heady mixture. She gave him a warm smile, and said, "I realized that I need some specialized training and some applications developed before I could go to Triton. I wanted to tell you about the delay during lunch. That's why I invited you here."

"Oh," Devon muttered. "I guess I was worried for nothing."

Aurelia felt Devon ease the grip on her hands, and she held tightly to his. "Understand me, Devon. I loved everything you said about us. That you didn't want us to be apart. That you wanted me to wait. If I'd been planning to leave when Jessie's ships sailed, I would have stayed on station, because you asked me to wait for you."

The subtle wrinkles in Devon's forehead and slightly narrowed eyes told Aurelia he was unconvinced. Those indicators helped her make an important connection. Devon and she were a lot alike. Both of them were insular people, slow to trust, and wary of strangers.

Aurelia's eyes beseeched Devon's. Then she closed them, opened her gates, and sent him emotions the like of which had only been shared with her mother and sister when she was young. She didn't project a brief or subtle wave. She pushed and held it. When she opened her eyes, Devon was grinning like an idiot. That he sat in the corner of the room was a plus. It had allowed her to focus on him and prevent her emanations from influencing the other diners.

"Why didn't you say so before?" remarked Devon, a grin still plastered across his face.

"I guess I take a while to warm up," Aurelia replied. "Come," she said, releasing Devon's hands. "We have some planning and work to do. The *Belle* will complete its roundtrip before you know it."

Aurelia couldn't help herself. On the way out of the Pit, she left behind her a trail of smiling customers, as she shared her happiness with others.

The pair parted company at security. Devon headed to Liam's office to tell him the news, and Aurelia informed Devon that she had an appointment.

* * * *

"I'm going to work on station for one rotation of the *Belle*," Aurelia told Harbour, when they met in a JOS business center. "I need to prepare myself ... study how to learn a language and purchase some specialized apps."

"I think that's a great idea, Aurelia," Harbour replied. "You won't forgo your share of the *Belle*'s empath stipend." Harbour heard Aurelia laugh, and asked, "What?"

"You've been keeping funds for me under the *Belle*'s general account to hide my stipends, and Jessie has used his company accounts to do the same thing," Aurelia replied. "The funny thing is I've no idea how much is in either account."

"Let's fix that, shall we?" Harbour replied. Now that Liam was the commandant, Harbour had no fear for the influence of the family heads over JOS security, which might have endangered Aurelia. What made that less likely now was Devon's constant companionship.

Harbour guided Aurelia in creating a financial account via her comm unit, which Jessie had given her years ago. Aurelia showed Harbour when it was ready and sent her the account information. Then Harbour accessed the *Belle*'s general account. She accessed Aurelia's funds and made the transfer.

Aurelia watched her comm unit update its display. "Can this be right?" she asked.

While Aurelia was mesmerized by the coin that had accrued for her during the years, Harbour sent a message to Jessie with Aurelia's account information. She could imagine Jessie's smile, as he transferred Aurelia's crew earnings to her new account.

"Oh, for the love of Pyre," Aurelia whispered.

"Now you have your empath and your crew earnings," Harbour announced happily.

"Thank you, Harbour," Aurelia said, sharing her pleasure empath to empath. "I'll miss you, when you sail."

"No you won't, Aurelia. Jessie and I are staying behind. We've work to do on station," Harbour said.

"The projects," Aurelia guessed.

"Exactly," Harbour replied. "It will take some personal leverage to keep those moving forward."

"Now that I'm learning about coin and expenses, I'll have to find out how much Devon has saved," Aurelia said excitedly.

"I assume Devon's going to accompany you to Triton," Harbour said.

It didn't surprise Aurelia that Harbour had guessed. She knew she was broadcasting.

"What about the lieutenant's job?" Harbour asked.

"That's Major Higgins to you, Envoy," Aurelia announced officiously.

"That would make it even more difficult for him to leave," Harbour remarked.

"It might, if he didn't have an enticing reason to give it up," Aurelia said, with a pleased smile.

Harbour had never detected the level of happiness that Aurelia projected, and she worried that it might be a bubble that could be burst.

"What's the plan?" Harbour asked.

"We wait for one rotation of the *Belle*," Aurelia explained. "I study, and he trains two sergeants, who will be upgraded to lieutenant positions."

It clicked for Harbour. Liam was filling the void that his promotion and Devon's leaving had created. It was a smart move on the part of the new commandant.

"When Jessie's ships return, we request a ride to Triton," Aurelia continued. "I wonder how much it costs to lease a mining ship for a trip to Triton." The new account, with its two immense deposits, had suddenly reminded her that things cost, and some things cost a great deal.

"It'll be free, Delegate Garmenti," Harbour replied, smiling. "Your work on the dome will benefit Pyre, and Devon and you will be compensated for your efforts."

"Wait until Devon hears that," Aurelia replied, grinning. "He's probably worried about giving up his annual stipend to decipher glyphs with me."

"Is anyone else planning to go with you?" Harbour asked.

"No, and I'm not intending to ask others," Aurelia replied.

Harbour examined Aurelia's joyful face. She asked, "Is that smart?"

"It was my being alone with the console that helped me discover the technique of the empty projection," Aurelia replied. "I don't need people looking over my shoulder."

"Except for Devon," Harbour teased.

"Some people are welcome to look over my shoulder," Aurelia riposted.

After Aurelia left, Harbour reviewed her conversation with the young empath and it made her realize a significant mistake on her part. Nelson Barber and Jacob Deering had joined the exploration team in hopes of personally accruing some of the Jatouche rewards. Unfortunately, whatever the Jatouche and Tsargit sent to Pyre probably wouldn't directly benefit these explorers. Only coin in their accounts could do that.

At her desk, Harbour connected her comm unit to the monitor and examined the *Belle*'s general account. Her thought was to reward the explorers, but using the colony ship's funds didn't seem appropriate to her. Instead, she accessed her personal account and nearly fell out of her chair. Funds had been accruing for her for many years, first as an empath, then as their leader, and finally as the captain of the *Belle* and its lucrative slush project.

It was the fact that Harbour rarely needed anything for herself. She was content with what the colony ship provided her. That resulted in the coin mounting up with minimal expenses.

Harbour laughed to herself, as she composed a quick message to Devon, requesting the accounts of the explorers, except for Jessie's. She added that it was a surprise and requested he keep her secret.

Minutes later, Devon supplied her with the information that she'd requested, and Harbour composed a second message to Aurelia, Devon, Olivia, Pete, Bryan, Tracy, Nelson, and Jacob. Before she sent it, she took half of her enormous personal funds and divided it between the eight explorers. It wasn't enough to allow them to retire, but if they invested it wisely for the next decade or two, it would be.

Harbour's message to the eight explorers said, "For services rendered to the citizens of Pyre, I thank you."

Reflecting on her message, Harbour crafted a third one and sent it to Liam and Dorelyn. She detailed what she'd done for the eight explorers and ended with, "I suggest you match my transfer of coin. I'll be watching for your generosity and be anxious to share the goods news with Pyre that the commandant and the council value what these courageous explorers have accomplished."

* * * *

Harbour waited for Liam at the corridor intersection that led to the terminal arm, where the *Belle*'s shuttle was docked. She stood watching the flow of pedestrians in the broad promenade corridor. Everything about Harbour drew the attention of a passerby — her beauty, her striking skins, which outlined her shape, and her alien medallion, which was prominently displayed.

As opposed to years ago, when Harbour would have engendered furtive glances, perhaps even fearful ones, she witnessed stationers nod or smile as they passed, although not all of them. Spacers were another matter. They tipped their caps or touched fingers to brows in a salute to her.

The stationers and spacers weren't the only individuals who had changed. During Corporal Terrell McKenzie's attack on Harbour, his anger and shock stick had overwhelmed her ability to call on her power. The fight with the Colony sentients had sharpened her control and increased her abilities. The thought occurred to her that it had probably done the same thing for Aurelia.

Today, Harbour knew that she needn't fear an assailant or even multiple assailants if she had a moment's notice. Certainly, no normal possessed the mental fortitude of the Colony sentients that Aurelia and she had held at bay.

Liam strode to meet Harbour, and the pair of them joined a short line to share a cap to cross the station's ring. A boy, who was strapped across from Harbour, stared at her medallion. Harbour fingered it and whispered to him, "It's a Jatouche gift that talks to aliens when I meet them."

The boy's eyes widened, and his mouth formed an astonished "o."

The *Belle*'s shuttle was half full, and Liam took his time walking down the center aisle, enjoying the seating's quality. When they were settled, Claudia exited the pilot's cabin to welcome Harbour and Liam aboard.

"Congratulations, Commandant on your election," Claudia said.

"A quick question for you," Liam said. "I understand you believe this shuttle can't be used to make an intravertor delivery. That it was a near escape. Do you believe the platform is the best option, for the future?"

Claudia considered the question, glancing once toward Harbour, whose expression was impassive. "Let me say this, Commandant. Even if every investor, council member, and you were aboard this shuttle, indicating your trust in our ability to make a second delivery. Danny and I would tell you to fly this ship yourselves ... after you bought it," she quickly added. "The platform is the only safe and economical means of delivering the intravertors, especially considering we're going to be seeing a steady stream of them."

"Thank you for your candor, Claudia," Liam, said, dismissing the copilot.

Liam regarded Harbour to check his reaction to the questioning of Claudia.

"My opinion, Liam, is that you're smart to gather as much independent opinion, from those closest to these projects, as you can. Never rely exclusively on reports, accounts, and data."

Exiting the bay into the colony ship's corridor, Harbour and Liam were met by Dingles.

"Welcome aboard, Commandant," Dingles greeted Liam, "I believe this is your first trip to the *Belle*."

"It is, Captain," Liam said, furrowing his brow, as he examined the tight corridor and the garish piping running close overhead.

"She wasn't built for elegance, Commandant," Dingles remarked. "Our upgrade funds have been spent on the ship's engines, systems, tanks, hydroponics, and cabins. Oh, let's not forget that we possess the finest cantina in this solar system."

"That, I'm interested in seeing," Liam replied, smiling and erasing the frown.

"This way, Envoy and Commandant. Your table is set in the captain's quarters," Dingles said, leading the way down the narrow corridor.

Dingles triggered the door to his quarters, and Liam was greeted by a beautifully laid out dinner table. Yasmin and several empaths stood by, ready to serve.

"Commandant," Jessie said, striding forward to shake Liam's hand.

"I'll leave you to it," Dingles whispered to Harbour. She smiled at him, laid a hand on his elbow, and sent him her thanks. "Always a pleasure," Dingles said softly, before he exited the cabin.

Harbour, Jessie, and Liam waited until the drinks and first courses were served. Liam murmured his delight about the freshness of the ingredients and the exotic mixture of his fruit drink, and Harbour and Jessie let him enjoy his meal.

As the main course dishes were cleared away and desserts served, Harbour signed to Yasmin to end their service. Yasmin nodded, ushered the other empaths out ahead of her, and closed the cabin door behind her.

Harbour waited until Liam was partway through his dessert before she said, "I must congratulate you, Liam, on some of your actions, which have been taken so soon after taking office. In particular, the shoring up of your officers by promoting Devon and your sergeants."

Liam had no expectation of that being kept from Harbour until after his announcement, and Jessie's passive expression said that Harbour had spoken to him in advance of this dinner.

"It turns out that I've got Devon for a limited time and must make the best of him," Liam replied good-naturedly. He regarded Harbour to confirm that Devon would leave when the *Belle* completed its next haul of slush.

It was Jessie, who laughed, and said, "Devon's definitely gone." He tapped his chest over his heart to indicate why.

"A lot must have happened during your journey," Liam offered. He had finished his dessert, and was tempted to lick his plate.

Without a word, Harbour passed the last half of her dessert to him.

When Liam glanced up in surprise at the proffered plate, Jessie said lightly, "If you don't want a response in the presence of an empath, don't broadcast what you're feeling."

"And how do you do that?" Liam inquired, ruefully twisting his lips, as he accepted the dessert plate and dug into it.

"With great difficulty," Jessie replied, laughing.

"To answer your remark about our journey, Liam," said Harbour, her expression serious. "Nothing personal happened between Devon and Aurelia. However, the experience bonded the explorers in ways that can't be explained. For instance, Tracy Shaver wants a berth on the *Belle*."

"I offered her a crew position," Jessie interjected, "but she said it had to be the colony ship. She said she wanted to be near the empaths."

"Did you give her a berth?" Liam asked Harbour. The stare he received had him adding, "Of course, you did. My apology, Harbour."

The tip of Harbour's head to Liam appeared to say that he was forgiven. *Watch your mouth, Liam,* he thought.

"The first mate, Nelson Barber, hoped to get his old position back but Flannigan has promoted crew in his absence. The captain did offer Nelson a severance bonus," Harbour said. "In turn, Jessie found him a spot as second mate on a different mining ship. The first mate has indicated he'll retire in another two or three years."

"My bet is Nelson won't last," Jessie offered.

"Because of what he experienced in the domes?" Liam hazarded.

"Exactly," Harbour replied. "And now that you're commandant, Olivia, Pete, and Bryan want to support the construction of the intravertors and platform. Captain Bassiter has already hired Pete's and Bryan's replacements."

"Which brings me to the subject I wish to discuss," Liam said. "But first, what about Jessie and you?"

"We'll be on station when the *Belle* sails with Jessie's ships," Harbour announced. She could see and sense the relief that Liam felt, and she sympathized with him. The commandant's position was a challenge, in and of itself. Add the nightmarish history of Liam's predecessor and the alien gifts, and it was enough to emotionally founder anyone.

"Let's retire," Jessie offered. He stood and led Liam into the study.

Harbour poured small drinks from a bottle that had lived in the captain's larder for centuries. Liam sipped at his glass and exclaimed, "What is this?"

Harbour silently handed Liam the bottle. After examining the label, Liam didn't seem any more enlightened.

"We don't know either," Jessie chuckled, hoisting his glass to Liam.

Harbour and Jessie settled together on the couch, and Liam chose to sit across from them in a comfortable oversized chair.

"Thank you, Liam, for matching my contributions to the eight explorers," Harbour said.

"It was the least the station could do for them," Liam allowed. "Has the council contributed?"

"No," Harbour replied, "and I don't expect to see anything from them."

Liam sipped at the ancient liquor, incredulous that such a thing existed. "I'm not sure how to proceed with the projects that support the rehabilitation of the planet's surface. The cost estimates for the present load of intravertor parts and the platform will empty the Pyrean Green fund and that includes the station's contributions."

"What about the downsiders?" Jessie asked.

Liam explained his efforts to pressure the council to match the topsiders' transfers into the Pyrean Green fund. "I'm hoping that adding the station's construction funds will galvanize topside investors, but I don't know what the council and downsiders will do."

"I realize you're frustrated, Liam," Jessie said, "but you don't need to fix this mess overnight. Take it slowly; think it through."

"What can we expect from the Jatouche and the Tsargit, Harbour?" Liam asked. "You've said in your broadcast that there are rewards. Too bad it can't be a shipload of coin."

"Real coin," Jessie teased.

"You know what I mean," Liam groused. "We need help funding our existing projects. But even if we manage to get the platform built and deploy a few intravertors, what do we do when the next shipment of intravertor parts arrive?"

"We documented the Colony's insidious expansion efforts," Harbour explained, "and, according to Mangoth, the Tsargit delegate, we'll be rewarded for our efforts. In addition, we did discover new races and one of the mysteries of the consoles. The former should cause the Jatouche to increase their reward, and the latter should serve both the Jatouche and the Tsargit."

"In what manner do you expect these rewards?" Liam asked.

"I've no idea," Harbour replied, shrugging. "The Tsargit is the alliance's governing body. According to Mangoth, their rewards are in whatever manner we want, within reason."

"So what and when do you intend to ask these groups to deliver?" Liam asked.

"I'm thinking on that, Liam," Harbour replied. "We need so much, and I'm afraid to ask for all of it and appear to be the envoy of a whining, upstart race."

"Or we could ask for too little and insult them," Jessie posited.

"That too," Harbour agreed.

Liam had hoped that his visit with Harbour and Jessie would provide an outline of a way forward and offer some insight into how to finance the ongoing projects. He drained his glass and sat back heavily into his chair. There was no hiding his disappointment.

"Maybe you're right," Liam said, staring at Jessie. "Maybe it should be done slowly, but I suspect that the topsiders' will to complete these projects over several decades isn't there."

-42-
Sika

Sika arrived on station and began her investigation. What was interesting to her was that none of the usual contacts, those paid by Dorelyn and other family heads, knew anything about who hired Roby. The more she dug, the more convinced she was that a stationer hired the assassin. It fit with what Sika had suspected, when she researched the means to reach Roby in medical.

Instead of pursuing the families' station contacts, Sika focused her efforts on locating Roby's connections. Spending time in poorer cantinas and visiting with coin-kitties, she identified a few of Roby's friends and many more of his accomplices.

Using various disguises and background stories, Sika met casually with each individual. She uncovered their weaknesses and spun tales about the type of work she could do for them. Frequently, she produced proof of her supposed skills and assets — coin, drugs, or false documents.

Sika was never disappointed in her failure to elicit the information she sought. The unsuccessful ending of a contact was a nonevent to her. She simply crossed the name off her list and moved to the next one, secure in the knowledge that persistence would eventually pay off. It always had.

One evening in a cantina located deep in the station, where gravity was near eighty percent, Sika approached one of Roby's associates. Her downside demure posture was not in evidence. She'd donned a worn pair of skins and some slightly ostentatious makeup. Sitting on a stool next to her target, she ordered a cheap drink.

Sandy eyed the woman sitting next to him. Everything about her suited him. He refused to pay for coin-kitties, but the opportunity to pick up a spacer on downtime was exactly his style.

"Evening," Sandy said to the woman. "In from a ship?"

"Yeah," Sika replied. "Two more days of downtime, and then it's back to the belt."

"I'm Sandy," Sika's target said, extending his hand.

"Portia," Dorelyn's assassin replied, giving Sandy a friendly smile and shaking his hand.

The pair shared their stories. Sandy worked in station maintenance, and Sika, as Portia, was a backup pilot. Slowly Sika worked her way around to her complaint. She didn't make enough coin to save for retirement, but she didn't intend to do the same old thing year in and year out.

"I had a deal set up with this stationer, but I make the JOS and find out he's dead," Sika said.

"That stinks," Sandy commiserated.

"We had this opportunity, you know," Sika lamented. "A good one. The kind where you have a good partner. Both of you know some of the same pieces of the operation, and each of you knows only some parts."

"Right, you had balance," Sandy said, trying to sound appreciative of the arrangement. "What was the deal?" he asked. He smelled opportunity, and his focus shifted from a night with a ship's downtimer to the possibility of picking up some extra coin.

Sika's eyes narrowed, as she regarded Sandy.

"I get it," Sandy said. "You have something on the side, and you don't want to share or you don't want to trust a stranger." He leaned conspiratorially toward Sika, and said, "I can help you now that you've lost your contact. My work in maintenance allows me to do a lot of things off the logs."

"What kind of things?" Sika asked.

"What kind do you need?" Sandy parried.

Sika finished her drink, and Sandy immediately ordered her another. He didn't need her leaving because of something as minor as a lack of coin.

"Thanks," Sika said, taking a sip of her drink. She pretended to be thoughtful before she said, "On my last downtime, I met this stationer, and we hooked up. Turns out he had a downsider connection, but he wasn't sure how to make use of it. The downsider had these customers, who'd pay him for the product, but he needed the people for all the steps in between."

"What was your part?" Sandy asked, more intrigued than ever.

"I came up with the idea of using spacers," Sika said.

"Spacers? Why?" Sandy asked.

"The shipment would be distributed over a considerable length of time, and it had to be kept hidden from the prying eyes of security," Sika explained. "Spacers would hide the stuff on their ships. I have six spacers on six different ships, besides mine. We'd spend a total of about fourteen months per year on downtime between the bunch of us."

"Yes, but it might turn out that no one was docked at any one time," Sandy pointed out.

"True. That's why we worked out a quiet storage place to leave the stuff for the next ship to dock," Sika temporized. "There might be a week or two without distribution, but the downsider said he was okay with that."

"That's actually kind of clever, Portia," Sandy said. "Security would suspect stationers and would be chasing their tails looking for them."

Sika murmured her agreement in her drink, as she took another swallow.

"How much was your contact offering for your services?" Sandy asked.

"My partner and I would get paid quarterly based on sales," Sika said, setting her trap. "That's why I liked this deal. The downsider was incentivizing us. We expected to split about eighty thousand a quarter, and we had to pay everyone else, customs, crew, storage, runners ... the lot."

"So, without your partner, can you still make this deal happen?" Sandy inquired.

"I've got most of the critical pieces," Sika replied, "but I don't have the customs connection, and I don't have runners, who'll be available, at a moment's notice, to pick up the product and deliver it anywhere on station, no questions asked."

"Well, you're in luck," Sandy said. Leaning close to Sika's ear, he whispered, "I've got a customs contact, and I've got many friends who'd be happy to run your product for a cut of that kind of payment."

Sika leaned away from Sandy. "I think I've said too much," she said, setting her unfinished glass on the bar. As she leaned forward and braced herself on the bar to stand, she felt Sandy's meaty hand grab her arm.

"What kind of proof do you need that my offer's not kinked?" Sandy hissed. "It's not like I can produce some kind of summary of my extracurricular activities."

"Who do you know?" Sika challenged in return.

Sandy leaned away from Sika and laughed. "Looks like we're at an impasse," he said. "It would be a shame if we can't resolve this. Then nobody's going to make any coin."

Sika stared at Sandy until she saw him fidget. She guessed that he was probably thinking he'd lost the opportunity. "I'll tell you one thing," Sika said, and saw Sandy focus on her. "My partner was a man named Roby. Apparently, he did something stupid and got killed for it."

"You bet he did. The idiot tried to kill Major Finian. He got taken down, and someone slipped into medical and dosed him," Sandy explained. "But, here's what you don't know, Portia. I told you that you're in luck. Roby was a close associate of mine. We've done jobs together for years."

"That would be nice to believe," Sika said. "But you were the one who pointed out you don't have proof of what you've done. You could be telling me what I want to hear."

"I could be," Sandy allowed, "but what if I could prove I knew Roby and knew him well? What would it be worth?"

"I'd split the profits seventy-thirty," Sika offered.

"If I've got to pay the runners out of my share, I need more. Fifty-fifty," Sandy replied.

"You can have forty. That's my final offer," Sika replied.

"Done," said Sandy, tapping his glass against Sika's. He polished off his drink, and said, "Come on. The proof is in my cabin."

Sika followed Sandy nearly a third of the way around the station's circumference. His cabin wasn't much better off than that of the cantina, where they had met.

"It isn't much," Sandy agreed, taking in Sika's scowl, as they entered the cabin, "but then again, you don't want to attract security's attention."

Sandy sat at his kitchenette table, where his monitor was set up. He laid his comm unit aside, and picked up another device.

"Whose is that?" Sika asked.

"Supposedly it belonged to a friend of my grandfather," Sandy replied. He hooked it to the monitor and searched out an account.

"That device looks new," Sika accused.

"It is," Sandy replied. "You don't expect us to keep a fifty-year-old comm unit around and assume it will work. It's been upgraded several times."

"You can't upgrade a comm unit without the owner," Sika argued.

"If you have the right contact in security, you can transfer the comm ID to a new unit. It costs you some coin, but it can be done," Sandy replied with a wicked smile. "Here ... here is what I wanted to show you."

"A financial account?" Sika inquired.

"Not any account. This is our stash. It's an account that's attached to a dead man," Sandy said. "This way none of us have huge deposits in our personal accounts that we can't explain."

"Okay, how does this answer my question?" Sika asked.

"Look at this line," Sandy directed. "Do you see the comm ID of that deposit?"

"I see an enormous amount of coin," Sika replied instead.

"It is," Sandy agreed. "Just the kind of amount you'd expect someone to pay to hire someone to kill Major Finian."

"I'm still waiting for my answer," Sika said, allowing the slightest display of impatience to leak out.

"Keep your skins on," Sandy growled. "When these deposits arrive, we meet and embed our comm IDs into the deposits for dispersal. You'll notice that this deposit is tagged with only one individual. Now, compare that ID to this device."

Sika took the offered comm unit. She was surprised to find it locked open. The IDs matched. She scrolled to the system settings and searched for the unit's owner. It was Roby's.

"Why do you have this?" Sika asked.

"I told you. Roby and I were close," Sandy replied. "Roby told me what he'd been hired to do. I argued with him that it was too dangerous, especially with Finian being shadowed by a security officer and an empath. But he insisted. He said he had a foolproof plan, and the payday was worth it."

"Not so foolproof," Sika commented.

"Yeah, but his loss is my gain," Sandy said, with a self-satisfied smile.

"You get to keep his coin?" Sika asked.

"No, rules of the crew. That coin has to be dispersed to everyone. I was referring to the fact that Roby's demise has led you to me," Sandy replied.

"I'm curious. Who was the person who hired Roby?" Sika inquired.

"Don't know," Sandy replied.

"Didn't you ask your friend in security?" Sika pursued.

"Look. I didn't ask for a good reason," Sandy shot back. "Someone has a great deal of coin and was willing to kill a security officer. That's someone I don't want to know."

"That's true," Sika agreed.

"So do we have a deal, Portia?" Sandy asked.

"We do, Sandy," Sika said, offering her hand.

"Great. When do we get started?" asked Sandy eagerly.

"I'll make contact with the downsider and tell him I've got the distribution details arranged," Sika replied. "When I'm on the return leg from the belt, I'll notify him and you of my arrival date, and you can organize your people. Two days after my ship has docked, we'll be in business. You and I will pick up the package at El customs. I'll secure it, and then we'll coordinate the runners and the delivery."

"Sounds good to me. You'll have to give me a heads-up when you dock. I'll need to check on my customs contact's working schedule," Sandy replied. "And now that our business arrangement is concluded, would you like to spend the night here?" Sandy offered, with a sly smile.

Sika's eyes narrowed, and she said, "You can have me or the coin, but you can't have both. My rules. You decide."

"I think you and I would have had a good time, but I'd prefer the coin," Sandy replied.

"Me too," Sika replied. She collected Sandy's comm ID and quickly left.

Sika waited until she'd traversed several corridors outward before she stopped and checked her comm unit. Surreptitiously, she'd taken an image of Sandy's account page. She wanted to ensure the depositor's ID for Roby's payment was clear. It was. It saved her having to go back and force it out of Sandy, which meant she'd have to manage a cleanup job. That wasn't her preferred manner of doing business.

* * * *

It was late evening, when Emerson received a visitor. He checked his comm unit, which held an image from his security cam mounted outside his cabin door. He didn't recognize the attractive, middle-aged woman.

"Yes?" Emerson asked, his voice issuing from his door panel in the corridor.

"I've a compensation gift from Dorelyn," the woman said softly into the comm pickup.

"Emerson retrieved his shock stick, which he'd yet to surrender to security, and held it to his side, while he triggered the cabin door. When the woman entered, Emerson swiftly closed the door behind her.

"Nervous?" the woman asked.

"Being careful," Emerson replied. "I've a good many secrets up here," he added, tapping his temple with his free hand. "Who are you?"

"I'm Joyce," Sika replied. "I execute delicate contract work for family heads."

"What's the gift, Joyce?" Emerson asked. He didn't like the woman. He hadn't invited her to sit down, but she'd already made herself comfortable on the couch.

"I possess a final transfer," Sika said, holding up her comm unit. "Consider it your last payment."

"Dorelyn could have made the transfer from her office. She didn't have to send you," Emerson challenged. He was getting suspicious of the woman.

"It doesn't work that way," Sika replied. "Your patron wants a guarantee that the secrets you possess will remain private."

"What kind of guarantee?" Emerson asked. For the first time, he was intrigued. What he knew was leverage, and he intended Dorelyn to pay dearly for his silence.

"You record your role as an accomplice in Governors Andropov and Panoy's machinations. You admit to taking their bribes," Sika explained.

"That's a lot to ask," Emerson replied. "Dorelyn could release the recording at any time."

"She's provided a recording of her own," Sika replied.

"And how much is the gift, Joyce, for this exchange of mutual recordings?" Emerson asked.

"One million in coin," Sika replied. She watched Emerson lick his lower lip. It was one of the ex-commandant's nervous habits that Dorelyn had carefully described to her.

"I want to hear Dorelyn's version first," Emerson stated firmly. His mind was racing, trying to anticipate every trap.

Sika promptly tapped her comm unit and played Dorelyn's recording. She paid attention to Emerson, while Dorelyn spoke. The family head had recorded a sincere-sounding and damaging admission of complicity in station affairs. Emerson had his lower lip pinned in his teeth. He was hungering for the coin.

"What's your method of exchange, Joyce?" Emerson asked.

"You make your recording on your comm unit," Sika replied, "then I transfer half the funds to you. After you verify the transfer of coin, you send me your recording. Then I send you your patron's recording and the other half of the coin. Is that acceptable?"

"Yes," Emerson replied cautiously. "Do you have a written statement for me?"

"As a matter of fact, I do," Sika replied. She tapped on her comm unit's screen and handed the device to Emerson.

Emerson accepted the comm unit and sat down at his dining table to scroll through the statement. The thought of recording it scared him, but the enormous payment drove him forward. He mollified his fear with the idea that he would possess Dorelyn's statement.

Emerson picked up his device to record the message and took a moment to wipe his lips. He held Joyce's unit in one hand, while he read the statement into his unit, which rested in his other hand.

After completing the recording, Emerson set Joyce's unit down and wiped his lips again. They'd begun to tingle, and he wiped them harder. The tingling turned into itching, and Emerson chose to lick his lips. "Excuse me," he said, "I need to get a drink of water."

The ex-commandant struggled to make it to the kitchenette sink. His legs felt weak, and he braced himself on the counter for support. Slowly, his legs and arms failed him, and he slid to the floor. Unable to speak, Emerson stared silently in horror at the woman.

Sika calmly stood, pulled a sealed bag from a pouch, and approached the dining table. She extracted a small bottle from the bag and placed it on the table next to Emerson's comm unit. Then she picked up her contaminated device and slipped it into the bag. She examined Emerson's comm unit to satisfy herself that the confession recording was displayed. The device would remain open and would provide a piece of evidence as to why the ex-commandant took his own life.

A look into Emerson's face revealed eyes that were watering and had difficulty tracking her. Sika waited for the final choke and gasp that were Emerson's last signs of life. Satisfied, Sika stripped off her ultrathin medical gloves and dropped them in the bag. She used a kitchenette towel to squeeze the bag's self-sealing activator. When it was closed and handling the bag by the towel, she dropped the bag and the towel into the pouch.

A last glance around convinced Sika that the job was complete. Per Dorelyn's request, the stationer who had hired Roby had paid the ultimate price.

At the cabin's door, Sika examined the security screen. No one was in the corridor at the moment. She used her elbow to trigger the door actuator and slipped out. As she walked down the corridor, she heard the whoosh of Emerson's door as it automatically closed after five seconds.

In a public facility, Sika disposed of her pouch, retrieved her change bag, and adopted the persona she used to ride the El. Adorned in the attire of a young wealthy downsider, she emerged from the facilities with glowing trans-sticks in her hair, a colorful costume, and an exuberant stride to match.

-43-
Rewards

Harbour and Jessie reviewed their personnel arrangements: who was going to Emperion, who would stay on the JOS, and who would work on the YIPS. Their ships would sail the next day for Emperion. It was time for another slush run, and they had decided to spend their final day aboard the *Belle*. Most of Jessie's crews, including the captains, were aboard the colony ship too, enjoying its amenities.

Birdie had the comm, and she was sipping on a fruit drink, when her comm monitor lit up, displaying the image of Jaktook and Drigtik.

"Welcome back," Birdie exclaimed, after accepting the call. "Is it just the two of you?"

The console's view widened, and Birdie enthusiastically greeted Kractik, who flashed her teeth in response to a warm reception.

"Wow, are you shipping the entire planet of Na-Tikkook here?" Birdie asked. She had a view of the platform, and teams of Jatouche were unloading crates, which joined growing piles on the deck. While Birdie chatted with the Jatouche, she messaged Harbour, Jessie, and Dingles. It said, "Jatouche are at Triton."

Harbour and Jessie came at a run onto the bridge, while Dingles worked to climb decks and cross half the length of the ship.

Harbour expressed her joy at the return of the Jatouche, and each one of them was wishing they were in her presence to receive some of that emotion via her empathetic power. Nonetheless, the console view, which Kractik had switched to encompassing the threesome, was a display of furry faces highlighted by rows of sharp, white teeth.

"Did Her Highness come with you?" Harbour asked anxiously. Immediately, the smiles were wiped from the faces of the Jatouche, and Harbour's heart lurched.

"It is with regret that I inform you, Envoy, that His Excellency's health, which hasn't been robust lately, has taken a turn for the worse," Jaktook lamented.

"What of your medical staff?" Harbour asked.

"That is the heart of the matter, Envoy," Jaktook replied. "The staff wishes to ease his suffering with techniques that would allow His Excellency to rest peacefully, but he will have none of their ministrations."

"Why not?" Jessie asked.

"Much has transpired since you left for Triton," Jaktook explained. "His Excellency insists on keeping his mental faculties alert so that he might advise Her Highness."

"Please send His Excellency my hopes for a speedy recovery," Harbour said.

"I'll convey your message, Envoy Harbour," Jaktook replied.

The manner in which Jaktook spoke told Harbour that there was little expectation among the Jatouche that their ruler would recover. Rictook's time among his citizens would soon come to an end.

Birdie signed to Jessie to ask about the crates.

"Jaktook, are you bringing three more sets of intravertor parts?" Jessie asked. "If so, it's not time yet."

Kractik shifted the console's view, and Harbour and Jessie had their first look at the mound of crates stacked across the deck. While they watched, the gate flashed, and more crates appeared.

"Are you bringing the next three years' worth of parts?" Jessie asked in awe.

Jaktook's sense of humor returned. None of the Jatouche wanted to dwell on their ruler's health. What was happening was inevitable and expected, although that didn't make it any more acceptable.

"His Excellency Rictook sends his regards, Advisor. The crates you see around us are the beginnings of twenty-seven intravertors," Jaktook explained. "These are part of the rewards that were promised for the services of the Envoy's exploratory team."

"I'm sorry to report, Jaktook, we've only managed to build two of the last six sets that you sent. Our financial systems are strained," Harbour said, with regret.

The threesome of Jatouche exposed their teeth, indicating knowledge of a surprise, and Harbour held her in breath in anticipation.

"Then it's good that His Excellency's generosity for your efforts, Envoy, are arriving now," Jaktook announced. He waved his hand at the nearly full deck of crates, and said, "These aren't intravertor parts."

A quick aside from Drigtik interrupted Jaktook, who continued. "Our engineer reminds me that in delivering my triumphant message I misspoke. These aren't similar to sets of parts we've previously sent. They contain everything necessary to construct complete intravertors."

"Twenty-seven of them," Drigtik interjected. "Based on your earlier statement, Envoy, I gather you could use another four shells."

"If you could," Harbour replied. She was embarrassed to be requesting more help than that which was being offered.

Drigtik touched his ear wig and spoke quietly, which made a note of the request.

"Envoy," Drigtik said, "I look forward to seeing my three engineer friends. Will they be available to work on the intravertor assembly with us?"

"With you?" Harbour inquired.

"Yes, Envoy, we don't expect you to provide the number of individuals necessary to assemble this many intravertors. It's recognized that Pyreans must work daily to earn their coin," Drigtik said. He appeared pleased that he'd adopted a human expression.

"When the equipment transfers are complete and your ship is near, we'll transfer through the gate a number of engineers and techs, who are most eager to assist in the assembly," Drigtik continued. "It's hoped that they can stay aboard the *Belle*. I'm afraid stories of the cantina, fruit juices, and empaths have circulated far and wide across Jatouche space."

Harbour had to chuckle at that one. Empaths had been isolated for more than the past century and the *Belle* for much longer. Then Aurelia Garmenti's troubles had opened the hearts and minds of spacers to their plight. Now it seemed that the spacers and empaths were the preferred company of aliens.

"As to your engineer friends, Drigtik, they'll be delighted to see you," Harbour replied, "although, I must warn you that they're deeply involved in another project, at this time."

"What would that be?" Drigtik asked, his eyes lighting with curiosity.

"They're designing a launch platform," Harbour replied. "Delivering the first intravertor by shuttle proved to be much too dangerous."

"We thought as much, at the time," Jaktook interjected. "But it was not our place to advise you differently."

"We would like to offer our help with this project," Drigtik said. "Please tell us in which aspects of its production you'd like us to participate."

Jessie reflected on the enormous cost of the platform and the shortage of Pyrean Green funds. In jest, he replied, "It would be wonderful if the Jatouche could design it, fabricate the parts, ship them through the gate, and help us assemble it." His grin was exaggerated to imitate the Jatouche display of humor.

"Done," Jaktook said. "If Olivia could bring us her concept, we could send it to Gatnack. He would love to work on this."

"My apologies, Jaktook, I was teasing," Jessie said. "That was an unfair request."

"Then you don't want our help?" Jaktook replied. He appeared crestfallen.

"We do," Harbour interceded, "but to us, it sounded unreasonable to ask for so much."

Jaktook's lips curled away to reveal his teeth down to the gums, and the three Jatouche chittered loudly.

"We were employing a human manner of communicating, Advisor," Jaktook replied, enjoying his joke. "We'd be honored to build your launch platform. It is His Excellency's wish that you be rewarded in whatever manner you need to regain your planet's surface."

Harbour was stunned. She couldn't believe their good fortune. Her concept of reward and the Jatouche concept were worlds apart. As that thought crossed her mind, she chuckled. *Worlds apart*, she repeated in her mind.

"Jaktook, you said that much has transpired. Can you share some of that with us?" Jessie asked.

Jaktook stood proudly erect and said, "Through the efforts of the exploration team and the evidence collected in the alpha and beta domes, the Tsargit has elevated the Jatouche. We're to have a representative in the assembly."

"Congratulations," Harbour and Jessie called out together.

"Have you chosen your representative?" Harbour asked.

"His Excellency has recommended Tiknock, our master scientist, and Her Highness has approved."

That Rictook had recommended and waited for his daughter's acceptance indicated to Harbour and Jessie how critical the ruler's health had turned. At a youthful age, Tacticnok was about to assume the Jatouche throne.

"What else has happened?" Jessie asked.

"We've received word of Mangoth's elevation in the Logar clan," Jaktook said.

"That's well deserved," Jessie replied.

Jaktook and Kractik flashed their teeth, which seemed an odd response to Jessie. "What?" he asked.

"Mangoth accepted the elevation and the accompanying rewards, except for one," Jaktook replied. "He was offered his choice of mates, and he refused."

"Refused?" Harbour queried. "I thought that was Mangoth's prime reason for joining our team."

"It was in the beginning," Jaktook acknowledged.

"And I'm sure that there were many Crocian females who were disappointed by Mangoth's decision," Kractik added, chittering her amusement.

"According to the messages we received," Jaktook continued, "Mangoth told the Logar clan leader that he had no intention of settling down on Crocia and raising a brood. He was reserving his life to be available to explore the galaxy's domes with the most magnificent Advisor Cinders and his future mate."

While Jessie laughed outright at Mangoth's characterization of him, Birdie, several crew members, and Dingles, who'd just arrived, stared in surprise at Harbour, who signed to them, "Alien speak. Ignore it."

Jessie caught his breath. He'd been observing the lighting of the platform. The significant team of techs had cleared two loads of crates from the platform, while they had been in conversation.

"Drigtik, exactly how many crates are required to construct twenty-seven intravertors?" Jessie asked. In his mind, he was visualizing the first enormous device attached to the underside of the Belle's shuttle.

"The equipment for the first eighteen intravertors will fill the second level corridor and the deck, Advisor," Drigtik responded. "We'll need your assistance in moving this material before we can bring the rest of the crates through the gate."

Jessie and Harbour regarded each other. The Jatouche intended to introduce a tremendous mound of equipment and numerous personnel to the YIPS, and the station wasn't prepared to store that much material and host the engineers and techs for free.

"The Belle," Jessie signed, and Harbour signaled in the affirmative.

"We'll send our ships your way," Harbour announced.

"How many cycles are they out from Triton?" Jaktook asked.

"They're at the JOS," Harbour explained, "but we can have them underway within a day."

"There's no hurry, Envoy," Jaktook replied. "Drigtik and Kractik calculate that it will take seven to eight days to fill the second level corridor and deck."

"Understood, Jaktook, we'll send you the appropriate workforce and vehicles to move your equipment," Harbour said. "Home for your engineers and techs will be the Belle," she added, with a smile.

"Fruit juices," the Jatouche threesome crowed, and Harbour and Jessie laughed.

"We'll be in touch," Harbour said, and Kractik ended the comm.

* * * *

Harbour turned to Jessie. Her face was a study in surprise, hope, and realization. "Twenty-seven complete intravertors," she whispered, as if saying it too loudly would dispel reality.

"And shells for another four," Jessie said in amazement.

Then Harbour let loose a quiet yip of pleasure and threw her arms around Jessie's neck. The bridge crew broke out in celebration, slapping one another on the back or hugging. Harbour let loose of Jessie and grabbed Dingles.

After a few moments, the joyous moment eased.

"Navigation," Dingles ordered. "Plot Pyre, Emperion, and Triton, and estimate the movement of the moons for the travel time of the *Belle* to Triton and back."

When the navigation officer was ready, his central monitor displayed the celestial bodies and the orbits of the moons during the time it would take the colony ship to make a roundtrip.

"Timing's everything," Jessie muttered, regarding the display, "and it's not with us today."

"Captain Bassiter, would you be so kind as to locate my captains, and could we borrow you and your quarters?" Jessie requested.

"Certainly, Advisor," Dingles replied. He pulled out his comm unit and made calls to Ituau Tulafono, Yohlin Erring, and Leonard Hastings, who were all aboard the ship.

"Coming?" asked Jessie, when he made for the bridge hatch, but Harbour didn't follow.

"You go ahead," Harbour replied. She turned to Birdie and said, "I need Olivia Harden. She's aboard the YIPS."

"Aye, aye, Envoy," Birdie remarked. She called the YIPS and got a comm operator. "This is the *Belle*. I've a priority request from Envoy Harbour to speak to Olivia Harden."

"Wait one," the comm operator replied.

It was a wait of several minutes before a voice said over the bridge speakers, "This is Olivia."

In reply to Birdie's questioning glance, which wanted to know if Harbour needed privacy, she signed, "all good."

"Olivia, I need you to locate Bryan and Pete, pack your personal things, and make for the *Belle*," Harbour said.

Dingles glanced away from his comm unit. The tone in Harbour's voice reminded him of a captain operating under emergency conditions. She sounded cool, calm, and authoritative, and he was grinning with pride.

"Problems, Envoy?" Olivia asked.

"Negative, Olivia, opportunity. The Jatouche have returned to Triton, and they're bearing gifts," Harbour replied.

"Wonderful," Olivia cried out excitedly. "I'll gather the men, and check the shuttle schedule."

"Negative on that last item, Olivia," Harbour interrupted. "Captain Bassiter, I need one of Advisor Cinders' shuttles to make a run to the YIPS to pick up our engineers."

"Aye, aye, Envoy," Dingles replied.

Harbour could detect Dingles' emotional elevation, and now that she had, she realized the entire bridge crew was broadcasting like starlight. It occurred to her that they were proud to have played a large part in resurrecting the colony ship, which had played a critical role in the encounter with the Jatouche. And it was the alien contact, which would help them regain the planet's surface.

"One more thing, Olivia, Drigtik wants whatever information you have on the launch platform," Harbour stated.

"But we've only begun to outline the requirements and sketch some concepts," Olivia objected.

"Then you'll have some time to perfect your ideas before you make Triton," Harbour replied. "If, however, you feel that you need to continue consultation, you can sit with Gatnack, while he completes the design."

"Gatnack came too?" Olivia asked. She was shocked the elderly Jatouche would make the journey.

"No, Gatnack is still on Na-Tikkook, Olivia, where you'll be going, if necessary. Now get your rear ends in gear. You're holding up the launch of our ship," Harbour shot back.

"Yes, Envoy," Olivia replied crisply.

Harbour made a slashing motion, and Birdie ended the connection. "Are you ready, Captain?" she asked Dingles.

"Yes," Dingles replied, adding, "Advisor Cinders' captains are on the way to my quarters, Envoy."

Walking the short distance to their meeting but in the corridor's privacy, Dingles asked, "Does this change your plans?"

"I wouldn't think so, Dingles," Harbour replied. "This operation is best left in the hands of capable captains and experienced engineers. There are conditions aboard the JOS that require my touch." She smiled at Dingles, and he touched two fingers to his brow in acknowledgment.

Harbour and Jessie sat at opposite ends of Dingles' salon table, while the captains arranged themselves in between.

"The Jatouche have returned with the parts for twenty-seven complete intravertors," Harbour began without preamble. "In addition, they intend to bring through the gate a multitude of engineers and techs to help with the assembly."

"Complete intravertors, not the bits and pieces like the first ones?" Yohlin asked.

"Complete," Jessie affirmed.

"What does this do to our sailing orders?" Ituau asked.

"Before someone responds to that question," Leonard Hastings, Jessie's most senior captain, said, "allow me to congratulate the two of you." He glanced toward Harbour and then Jessie. "Obviously, these are the rewards that you indicated you earned for your exploration. I hope our Pyrean citizens give you proper credit for your efforts."

"Thank you, Leonard," Harbour replied. "But whether we ever receive credit or not, I'm thankful that the possibility of reclaiming the planet's surface is becoming a reality instead of a distant wish."

"Harbour, I've dispatched a shuttle to the YIPS, as Dingles requested," Yohlin interjected.

"Thank you," Harbour replied. "Is everyone ready to sail now?"

The answers were negative, but they could launch within five to six hours after issuing crew recalls.

"Let's discuss the strategy here," Jessie said, bringing a focus to the discussion. "The Jatouche are filling the exit corridor and the deck with piles of crates, and that's only two-thirds of the intravertors." His statements generated surprise from his captains.

"And Harbour and I are in agreement that it will be necessary to host the Jatouche on the *Belle*," Jessie continued,

"There goes the coin for our slush hauls," Yohlin lamented.

Jessie stared sternly at Yohlin, as he said, "Everyone here has earned a huge amount of coin over the past several years, and it has been largely due to the *Belle*, which, mind you, was put into action through no effort of my people. If the colony ship needs to sit out a rotation or three of the *Pearl's* hauls, then so be it."

"The purpose of dedicating the *Belle* to the Jatouche is by necessity, Captains," Harbour added. "The YIPS can't accommodate the number of Jatouche engineers and techs that we anticipate, and we don't want them to host the Jatouche, even if they could. In addition, the YIPS will charge to store the crates until the assemblies are completed."

"And don't forget, the YIPS would end up storing thirty-three intravertors until we can complete a launch platform," Jessie explained. "Those would be additional fees."

"I wonder what we can charge the JOS to rent the *Belle* for hosting the Jatouche, storing the crates, and then the intravertors," Harbour mused.

A grin spread across Jessie's face, which surprised Harbour. She meant her statement in jest, but obviously he had a different idea.

"Let's focus on sailing orders," Jessie gently urged. He glanced at Harbour, who nodded her assent.

"The *Belle* will be the host for the Jatouche who arrive. However, we don't want to use the *Belle's* shuttle for the workloads. That will be reserved for our mining shuttles," Jessie proposed.

"What about to transfer the Jatouche engineers and techs from the surface?" Dingles asked, and Jessie indicated Harbour with a tip of his head.

"That decision is yours, Dingles, in concert with your pilots," Harbour said. "I'm sure the Jatouche would appreciate a ride in our new shuttle, but that moon landing should only be allowed if you and the pilots feel it's safe to do so."

"Now, as for orders for my captains," Jessie said, "Leonard, you'll sail for Emperion. Ituau and Yohlin, take the *Spryte* and *Annie* to Triton. You'll load as many of the crates as you can to facilitate transfer to the YIPS. What you can't take on, store onboard the colony ship."

"Thank you," Ituau said earnestly.

Jessie frowned and replied, "You're welcome."

"What?" Harbour asked Ituau.

"Yohlin told me that if I was tapped to make the next run to Triton that I should recommend her," Ituau explained. "Said if I didn't, she wouldn't speak to me for a month."

The table eyed Yohlin, who shrugged and said, "It was our ship and personnel who discovered the dome, and I've never had a chance to set foot on it."

The group chuckled, and Jessie ended his assignments. "The *Spryte* and the *Annie* return to the YIPS, drop their loads, and head to Emperion to help Leonard's crew load slush."

"It's going to be like the old days, Captains," Leonard announced. "Tight quarters, reheated meals, and no cantina." His remarks generated groans from Ituau and Yohlin, and Leonard grinned.

-44-
Favors

"I have an important favor to ask of you three," Harbour began. In front of her sat Lindsey Jabrook, Sasha Garmenti, and Tracy Shaver. "The Jatouche ruler, Rictook is dying, and I want to help him."

"How can we do that?" Tracy asked.

"Let me explain," Harbour replied. "Some important alliance decisions have been handed out after we left. They've been extremely positive for the Jatouche, due to our exploration. Rictook is resisting medical services that would dull his mind, while he's able to speak to his daughter, Tacticnok. I can think of only one thing that might be of value to him, at the present time."

"Us," Sasha declared, pointing to Lindsey and herself.

"Yes, empaths," Harbour replied.

"I can do this myself," Sasha offered.

"And we'll depend on your stamina and mental strength, Sasha," Harbour allowed, "but you'll need to be spelled, and Lindsey and you work well together."

Lindsey translated Harbour's words to be that her primary purpose would be to supervise Sasha.

"Why do you need me to go?" Tracy asked.

This was the tricky part of Harbour's request, and she was saddened that she wouldn't be telling Tracy the truth. However, her years of empath training from the likes of Lindsey and other senior empaths was that sometimes the manner in which you helped clients wasn't always by giving them what they thought they needed.

"You've been to Rissness, Tracy. You know what to expect, and Lindsey and Sasha could use your guidance," Harbour said.

"And if I don't wish to go?" Tracy asked.

This was what Harbour feared — that Tracy's experience in the domes and the loss of her brother had soured her on any further contact with aliens.

"Then I'd be reticent to send Lindsey and Sasha by themselves," Harbour replied. She felt a little stab in her heart at her duplicity. With or without Tracy, she would send empaths to help Rictook. She would have to choose another guide.

"I want to go," Sasha said defiantly. Deliberately the teenager didn't look at Tracy. Lindsey had taught her that her stare intimidated people.

Tracy looked at Lindsey, who wore a sympathetic expression. The thought crossed Tracy's mind that a berth aboard the *Belle* would mean sharing the ship with Sasha, and upsetting one of the most powerful and willful empaths wasn't a good start. She examined her reasons for not wanting to journey to Na-Tikkook. It wasn't the Jatouche. She liked them. Then it struck her. It was the gates. Their journey through the domes had been fraught with fear. The team never knew what they might find on the other end of a Q-gate. However, Tracy also realized that the other end of the Triton gate pair was Rissness. It was a known and, more important, a safe destination.

"I'll go on one condition," Tracy said, after her lengthy pause to think. "We journey between the Triton and Rissness domes and nowhere else. If these two journey anywhere else, I'm staying behind."

"That won't be a problem," Harbour said, staring straight at Sasha, "because if they even so much as climb on another platform at Rissness, I'll hear about it, and they won't have a cabin on the *Belle* any longer."

"I think that's a pretty clear message, don't you, Sasha?" Lindsey asked.

The women could see Sasha chafe at any restrictions being placed on her first opportunity to leave Pyrean space.

Sasha was tempted to argue, but her glance around was greeted with implacable faces. "I accept this condition," she said, controlling her ire.

"Not good enough," Harbour riposted. "Looks like everyone's staying aboard the *Belle*."

"Why? What did I do?" Sasha exclaimed.

Harbour could feel Sasha's power coiling, and she prepared to meet it. But Lindsey laid a hand on Sasha's arm, and the girl clamped her gates shut.

"You do recognize that you're speaking to the Pyrean Envoy, don't you, Sasha?" Lindsey asked. "She's responsible for our society's relationship with the aliens. If she feels she can't trust us in Jatouche space, then she can't risk us going."

"I said I was okay with Harbour's condition," Sasha objected.

Tracy realized the difficulty that Harbour and Lindsey faced with Sasha and possibly the reason she was being tasked to guide the empaths. She chose to step in and respond for Harbour. "Sasha, your power is great, but you haven't got much experience outside this ship, much less on an alien world. You tried to evade future conditions that might be placed on you by accepting one condition, at this time. It was a clumsy attempt to fool us."

Sasha forgot Lindsey's admonitions and glared at Tracy, who laughed in her face. "You were right, Envoy. While Sasha might be one of the most powerful empaths, we'd be better off replacing her with one or two other more mature empaths."

"I can be mature," Sasha said hotly. It galled her that in a short space of time, she'd dismissed most of Lindsey's training on how to cooperate with individuals.

And Harbour, for her part, couldn't believe the shift in Tracy's attitude. Then she recalled that it was Tracy who had been frequently called on to keep her brother, Dillon, in line. Perhaps the young woman had found a substitute for her brother. Harbour hoped Tracy was up to the challenge.

"Prove it," Tracy said.

"How?" Sasha replied.

"Think about your reply to the Envoy and try again," Tracy demanded.

Sasha wanted to ask which response Tracy referred to, but she knew that was being petulant. She felt hemmed in by two keepers, and it occurred to her that she'd just been strapped with an Aurelia substitute. Tracy reminded her of her sister.

"I promise to accept any conditions placed on me," Sasha said unhappily.

"Excellent," Tracy replied. "I have only one. You won't go anywhere, do anything, or say anything without the express permission of one of us."

"That's not fair," Sasha declared.

"That's my condition for going," Tracy said, who eyed Harbour and waited for a reply. In turn, Harbour gazed at Sasha.

"Well?" Lindsey prompted.

"Accepted," Sasha grumped.

"Excellent," Harbour said, clapping her hands once. "One critical word about Rictook's treatment. You know the Jatouche are highly susceptible to our powers. Lindsey, you'll determine the level of ministration with the ruler, and you'll teach Sasha to maintain that amount of power and no more."

"Understood, Envoy," Lindsey said, and then the women excused themselves.

Harbour strode to the bridge to send Jaktook a message. She found Jessie there reviewing the courses his ships would take to join the *Pearl*.

"Birdie, can we make a call to the Triton dome?" Harbour asked.

"Begging your pardon, Envoy, but I think you've spent too much time among the advanced aliens. We don't have an ID for our dome," Birdie replied.

"Contact Aurelia, Birdie. She's on the JOS," Harbour requested.

Jessie tapped the navigation officer on the shoulder and signaled him to wait. He was keenly interested in this conversation.

"Afternoon, Envoy. How can I help you?" Aurelia replied congenially to Birdie's request.

Harbour smiled at the maturity that Aurelia's voice projected. It was light-years away from the frightened and unsure young empath who Jessie rescued.

"Aurelia, can the *Belle* communicate directly with the Triton dome?" Harbour asked.

"Negative, Envoy, you don't have the tech with which to key the console," Aurelia replied. "According to Kractik, she's not aware of any alliance race that has that capability. However, you can get Kractik's attention."

"How?" Harbour asked.

"Can you hear me, Birdie?" Aurelia asked.

"Standing by, Aurelia," Birdie replied, poising her fingers over her comm board.

"Point a comm antenna, the strongest one you have, at Triton," Aurelia said. "Oh, is the dome side facing us?"

Navigation checked on Triton's position and nodded to Jessie. "It is, Aurelia," Jessie affirmed.

"Antenna's ready," Birdie sang out.

"Send a repetitive signal, Birdie, as if you were tapping out a music beat," Aurelia said. When there was no answer forthcoming from Birdie, Aurelia started snapping her fingers to some unknown tune, and Birdie copied the cadence on her comm panel.

Within a few minutes, Kractik's face appeared on a separate monitor, "Are you requesting contact, Envoy?" Kractik asked, when Birdie accepted the call and activated the bridge's vid pickup.

"I am, Kractik. I need to speak with Jaktook," Harbour requested.

"Please be patient, Envoy. Jaktook is below deck," Kractik replied. She touched her ear wig and mouthed something.

Harbour signed to Birdie to mute the bridge side of the Triton connection. When Birdie signaled that was done, Harbour said, "Aurelia, well done. That was clever of you."

"Good to know it worked, Envoy," Aurelia replied. "We can use this technique in the future to initiate communication from the stations or ships to the dome, as long as someone is standing by to recognize the console's reaction. Anything else, Envoy?" Aurelia asked.

"Thank you, Aurelia, you've been quite helpful," Harbour replied, and Birdie closed the connection.

While Harbour waited for Jaktook, Jessie sidled close and whispered, "I was dubious about what Aurelia could achieve trying to decrypt the dome's glyphs, but it's evident that she has a sense of the way the domes and the consoles work."

"I would characterize it as a form of intuition that perceives the minds of the Messinants," Harbour whispered in reply.

"That's a creepy thought," Jessie admitted.

"Empaths can be a creepy lot," Harbour riposted. She accompanied her remark with a wry grin, and Jessie bobbed his head in a combination of admittance and apology.

"Here, Envoy," Jaktook said, which drew Harbour's attention, and Birdie opened the ship's audio pick up.

"Jaktook, His Excellency has been extremely generous," Harbour said, "and I wish to reciprocate with a small gift."

"I'm sure His Excellency will appreciate whatever you choose to send, Envoy," Jaktook replied. "Will it be aboard your ships?"

"They will be," Harbour replied.

"They?" Jaktook inquired.

"This is a special gift from me to Rictook, Jaktook," Harbour replied. "Two empaths are prepared to attend His Excellency and alleviate the pain of his final days."

Jaktook's slender jaw fell open. When it closed, he said, "Truly a magnificent gift, Envoy. His Excellency, the members of the royal family, and Jatouche citizens will be forever grateful. Who's coming?"

"I'm sending Lindsey and Sasha," Harbour replied. When she saw Jaktook's eyes narrow, she quickly added, "Lindsey will determine the dosage that your ruler can accommodate, and she will teach that to Sasha. I expect His Excellency's treatment to last for many days. Only Sasha can keep up that length of continuous service."

"We trust your judgment in this, Envoy," Jaktook said, although to Harbour he didn't seem convinced.

"In addition, I'm sending Tracy Shaver to act as their guide," Harbour continued.

"How is she faring?" Jaktook asked with concern.

"I think minding Sasha will give her a new focus. That was her role with her sibling," Harbour replied.

"Tracy will enjoy her welcome among our citizenry, Envoy," Jaktook replied. "She has no concept of the gratitude that awaits a Pyrean explorer on Na-Tikkook. I would wish you to experience it."

"Perhaps, someday, Jaktook, but there are pressing issues here," Harbour replied. A small part of her was jealous. The thought of experiencing the gratitude of an entire race for what she had accomplished was enticing. This was as opposed to the decades of fear and other negative emotions her presence had engendered among Pyreans.

"So it is for all of us who've accepted titles and responsibilities, Envoy," Jaktook said. "As for myself, I would wish to be by Tacticnok's side in these final days of her father's life."

"We help our citizens where and how we can, Jaktook," Harbour replied. "Our ships are ready and will launch within hours," Harbour said, ending the comm.

Soon after the comm to Triton, Harbour and Jessie exited the ship. Before Danny undocked from the JOS terminal arm, Harbour had a final word for the two pilots. "You two be safe at Triton. Hear me?"

"He won't be," Claudia said, hooking a thumb at Danny, who frowned. "But that'll be my job. You can count on it, Envoy."

"I do," Harbour said, sending an affirmation of her affection for the couple before she exited the shuttle.

Jessie noted Harbour was exceptionally quiet, as they made their way down the terminal arm. "Thoughts?" Jessie asked.

"Hmm ..." Harbour murmured.

"I was wondering why you're so quiet," Jessie inquired.

"I suddenly feel a great emptiness," Harbour said.

"And rightly so," Jessie replied. "Why do you think spacers have such a bad reputation for the way they spend their downtime?" he asked.

"I hadn't given it any thought," Harbour replied.

"A crew is crammed into a ship. The captain and officers keep them constantly busy to prevent boredom and sloppiness. Then they battle the dangers of space, searching for metal on chunks of rocks. They'll race the days. Whether they're successful or not, the ship's dwindling resources will force them to return to the JOS. On station, they'll have a week, maybe two or three if they've made a good haul, to decompress. And you know what they'll be feeling?"

"A great emptiness?" Harbour guessed.

Jessie winked at her, as they joined the queue for the transition to the station. They hadn't been in line for long, when they heard the whoosh of the cap doors opening and heard, "Envoy, your cap is waiting."

Harbour looked up and saw spacers at the front of the line. They were waving her forward.

"That's your due, Envoy," Jessie said. "You're giving those spacers something else to live for besides the rigors of mining."

Harbour walked to the front of the line, with Jessie following. As she passed the spacers, she sent a wave of appreciation their way. Jessie and she joined the others already strapped into the cap, and Harbour had a moment to witness the smiles on the faces of the spacers she'd passed.

"Feel better?" Jessie asked, leaning close to Harbour, as the cap began to move.

"Much better," Harbour acknowledged, with a smile.

Left Out

In the morning, after a quick meal in her cabin, Harbour commed Liam and asked for a meeting. Two hours later, Harbour and Jessie walked into the commandant's office.

"I used to hate coming here," Harbour remarked, when Liam stood from behind his new desk to exchange greetings.

"And now?" Liam inquired.

"It's worse," Jessie shot back, and the threesome shared a laugh.

"I was curious if you could share the status of your investigation into Emerson's death," Harbour requested.

"I don't see why not," Liam replied. "The investigation is closed. It's been ruled a suicide by the medical director."

"Suicide?" Jessie questioned.

"All indications point to that," Liam said. "According to the medical director, Theo Formass, Emerson selected a plant distillate, which is commonly used as a tincture, but it requires a solution of fifty parts water to one part oil. Moreover, it's for topical applications. I've been told that spacers and stationers often have their skin rubbed raw by vac suits and maintenance gear. The tincture prevents infection of the exposed skin."

"Dreeson oil," Jessie exclaimed. "I've used it myself."

"According to Theo, who handled the autopsy, Emerson rubbed a quantity of the pure oil directly on his lips and ran his tongue over it," Liam explained.

Harbour shuddered at the image of a human being choosing to end his life that way. "Emerson must have been totally devastated by his election loss."

"Upset, pissed off, distraught," Liam enumerated, "I can believe any of those, but suicidal ... no. Emerson wasn't the type to take his life. After he had some time and regained his balance, he'd have found a way to regain a position of power ... topside or downside. That was the type of man he was, and if anybody should know that, I would."

"But you have no reason to suspect it wasn't suicide," Jessie pursued.

"Unfortunately, none," Liam replied. "That's why the case is closed."

"Let's talk about another subject," Harbour said, and she brought Liam up-to-date on the communication with the Jatouche and the effort of their ships, which had sailed yesterday evening.

"Twenty-seven complete intravertors, four more shells, and they're willing to build our platform," Liam said in wonderment. He sat back in his chair, and tears formed in his eyes.

"It's hard to take in," Jessie commiserated.

Liam regarded Harbour. "You did this," he said.

"We all did this," Harbour replied. "It started when empaths began sparing spacers from security incarceration. It accelerated when we rescued Jessie's sorry butt off Triton. One thing has led to another. It's always involved Pyreans fighting for a better life for us all. Some have helped; some have been obstacles."

"I've been racking my brain for a way to stretch the Pyrean Green fund to cover the costs of these projects," Liam said. "Now, I might be able to use the coin for other things."

"I wouldn't be too sure about that, Liam," Jessie said. "People donated their coin for a specific reason. I think you'd need permission to apply those funds to other projects."

"Besides, Liam, you might be paying it to us, or more specifically, to the *Belle*," Harbour added.

"Why's that?" Liam asked.

Harbour lifted an eyebrow at Jessie, who took that as a sign to initiate negotiations.

"Liam, you might want to calculate the following," Jessie began. "Storage of intravertor crates, storage of thirty-three intravertors until the platform is ready, and YIPS cabins for thirty to forty Jatouche engineers and techs."

"You don't really want to have the Jatouche hosted by the YIPS, do you?" Liam asked Harbour.

"No," Harbour replied, "but is it fair for the *Belle* to be offline while these projects go forward? They benefit all of Pyre, and that was the purpose of the fund."

"You also need to consider that the *Belle* and my ships have been providing transport from Triton to Pyre and back for the Jatouche and their equipment," Jessie pointed out.

"I propose this, Harbour and Jessie," Liam said, leaning back in his chair. "Detail the cargo space the equipment occupies, the work details, and the shuttle time to lift the Jatouche and materials from Triton, your transport charges, and your daily cost for hosting and storage, and I'll request the comparable items from the YIPS."

"Another thing to add to the mix is the energy delivered by the intravertors to the YIPS," Jessie added. "Launching thirty-three intravertors should power one-and-a-half lines of the YIPS. What's that worth to the stations?"

"I'll have to form a board of some sort who can advise me on the value of these things," Liam suggested.

"I can volunteer one person to be on your advisory board," Harbour said. "Speak to Dottie Franks. She might have been a little shaky, in the beginning, as a delegate. But she's become an ardent supporter of our alien relationships and the future of the planet."

"I appreciate the suggestion, Harbour," Liam said. "The advisory board can give me recommendations, and I'll apportion some of the Pyrean Green funds to reimburse you," Liam replied.

Liam was feeling fairly good about his negotiating position. That was until he heard Jessie say, "That's not good enough."

Momentarily, Liam was at a loss for a response.

Harbour heard Jessie's dismissal. She intuited that Jessie considered that their negotiating position was untenable, and he wished to abandon this discussion. An alternative occurred to her, and she voiced it. "I think there's another option for us, Jessie," Harbour said. "We should take our case to the Review Board."

"Why the Review Board?" Liam asked in surprise.

"We're in new territory, Liam," Jessie replied, liking Harbour's idea. "We've aliens, intravertors, the Pyrean Green fund, and an effort to resurrect the surface. These things might be more fairly decided by adjudication."

"Think of it as removing a weight from your shoulders, Liam," Harbour added, with a kindly smile. "You're new to this position. You shouldn't have to mark your command with this monumental decision."

Harbour stood, and said, "Good day, Liam." Then Jessie and she exited the office before Liam could summon a reply.

As the pair passed through the lobby, Jessie asked, "Are we going to give Liam an opportunity to compare costs?"

"No, I don't think so," Harbour replied. "I'd like you to prepare a summary of the costs, as you perceive them. Treat the *Belle* as a large mining ship for the purposes of transport, storage, and hosting. However, I want you to prepare an argument for the Review Board that compares the expenses that we're requesting to the losses you and I will suffer for keeping the *Belle* offline."

"I won't be able to complete this until our ships leave Triton, and we've detailed our efforts there," Jessie replied. "Then, I'll need Drigtik to give me an idea of the time to construct the intravertors and the platform."

As Harbour and Jessie walked through the corridor, they were hardly aware of the pedestrians' reactions to them. They were lost in their thoughts.

"We'll also need to take in the daily transport of Jatouche to and from the YIPS and any crates the *Belle* had to take on," Jessie mused. He stopped dead in the corridor and stared at Harbour. Then his face morphed into an enormous grin. He looked around, seeking a quiet place. Then he hooked Harbour's arm and strode off, adding, "Miner's Pit."

Harbour smiled to herself, as Jessie nearly pulled her along. Years ago, he had difficulty finding himself in close proximity to her.

At the Miner's Pit, Jessie smacked the door actuator multiple times. When the hatch slid aside, Maggie demanded, "Is the JOS going down? Should I pack and catch a shuttle for the *Belle*?"

Harbour grinned at Maggie, as Jessie pushed past the Pit manager and ordered a fruit drink for him and a green for Harbour. To Harbour's surprise, Jessie took a seat at the bar and patted the stool next to him.

"We're going about this all wrong," Jessie said urgently, when Harbour sat and swung her stool to face Jessie. "What do we need the YIPS to do?" he asked.

Harbour started to reply, thinking of the steps that were taken to produce the first intravertor. Then she reviewed the conversation with Jaktook and Drigtik, and suddenly those processes seemed obsolete. "I can't think of anything," Harbour said. "The YIPS has six intravertors in various stages of completion, but the Jatouche are promising to finish them."

"Exactly," Jessie said. "Why can't we assemble the intravertors on the *Belle*?" Jessie asked.

"Is it physically possible?" Harbour asked. "I mean, I know we have the bays, but can a single bay accommodate the construction?"

"Absolutely," Jessie replied. "An intravertor is shorter than your ship's new shuttle, which can land in any one of your bays."

"If that's the case, Jessie, does the *Belle* need to return to Pyre?" Harbour asked.

"That's an excellent question," Jessie replied. Maggie set their drinks before them, and Jessie pulled deeply on his fruit drink, while he mulled over his reply. "I don't think so. Not for the foreseeable future, but let me consider that question for a day or two."

The pair clinked their glasses together, celebrating their idea.

* * * *

Liam sat in silence, pondering the discussion that took place in his office. On the one hand, he felt he'd been outmaneuvered by Harbour and Jessie. On the other hand, if they were assuming part of the responsibilities for building and deploying the intravertors, they should be compensated.

The more he thought about it, the more grateful he became for Harbour's remark that she would take the matter to the Review Board.

Better you stay out of politics and stick to security matters, Liam thought.

The arrival of the Jatouche and their rewards for the explorers did simplify one matter for Liam. He was no longer desperate for the families' contributions. His grin was predatory, as he picked up his comm unit. This was one call he anticipated enjoying.

"Dorelyn, looks like your ship has sailed without you and the family heads," Liam began his conversation.

Dorelyn was meeting with Rufus and Idrian, and she placed a finger to her lips to silence them, as she placed her comm unit on speaker.

"What do you mean, Commandant?" Dorelyn asked.

"You've dithered making a decision to support the Pyrean Green fund, and now it's a moot point," Liam replied. "Oh, and greetings to whoever else is listening, as it appears I'm on speaker."

Dorelyn clenched her jaw. Her comm specialist was supposed to have perfected an app that eliminated the ambient sounds of a room so that a listener wouldn't know when their conversation was being shared. *Obviously, it's not perfect,* Dorelyn thought angrily.

"Why are our donations not welcome, Commandant?" Dorelyn asked.

"I didn't say they weren't welcome, Dorelyn," Liam replied cheerfully. "Fact of the matter is that the Jatouche have arrived bearing gifts. Apparently, Envoy Harbour underestimated the term reward for her team's exploration. The Jatouche are prepared to build out twenty-seven new intravertors, drives, shells, and all, and complete our other intravertors."

Liam could hear subtle whispering in the background. His grin got wider, and he fairly wiggled in his chair. The thought occurred to him that he was being petty. Then again, he'd been fighting the influence of the dome families his entire time in security. It was a delicious feeling to have the upper hand on them, at this critical time.

"Is this a promise of the Jatouche?" Dorelyn asked.

"Well, Jaktook told the envoy and her advisor that the dome's deck and second level could only accommodate the first eighteen sets of crates. The Jatouche said they'd have to wait for help before they could move the remaining units through the gate. According to Envoy Harbour, the piles were really high. So, I guess you could say that the promise has yet to be completely fulfilled."

Liam couldn't help the chuckle that escaped.

In Dorelyn's office, the threesome was thinking of any remaining points of leverage. Dorelyn held up a finger to cease the whispering.

"That's generous of the little aliens," Dorelyn replied. "But there's the launch platform that must be constructed. The expense of that will be far greater than a number of intravertors. You'll need the council's contributions for that, and we're awaiting the cost estimates."

Dorelyn sat back in her chair, relieved to have reversed the circumstances on Liam.

"Oh, my apologies, Dorelyn. I forgot to tell you," Liam said in an overly sweet tone. "The Jatouche heard about the engineers' choice of a launch platform, and they want to build that too. It seems they plan to design it, fabricate it, and ship it in crates through the gate. Isn't that amazing?"

"Amazing," Dorelyn replied. She was too dumbfounded to say anything else.

"Well, it was enjoyable chatting, Dorelyn. I must prepare for my Pyre-wide broadcast announcing the good news. I think topsiders will be overjoyed with what Envoy Harbour and Advisor Cinders have accomplished. It looks like I might be alive and well when the planet's surface opens up."

When the call ended, Dorelyn continued to regard her comm unit. Rufus started to speak, but she held up a hand to forestall him.

"The fools," Dorelyn whispered, and Rufus and Idrian knew who she meant. The council had debated too long. The families had missed their opportunity to show support for the Pyrean Green projects.

In Dorelyn's mind, she saw the council dissolve, and the families enter a period of economic war. In the meantime, the topsiders would have the help of the Jatouche to open Pyre for settlement.

"Is there an opportunity we might have missed?" Idrian asked.

"Thirty-three intravertors will be deployed after the Jatouche build the platform. I give them a year to complete those projects. After that, how many more intravertors are expected and at what rate?" Dorelyn replied.

"The scrubbing of the atmosphere and the cooling of the surface will take place in years instead of decades," Rufus marveled.

"We're forgetting one more thing," Idrian reminded his companions. "In Envoy Harbour's original broadcast, she mentioned the rewards of the Tsargit, the alliance council. If what we're seeing is the thanks of one alien race, what will be the rewards from the alliance?"

Dorelyn considered Idrian's words. A thought went through her mind: *There might come a day when downsiders will stare through the walls of their domes to regard the blooming fruit trees of topsider settlers.*

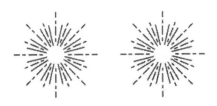

— The Pyreans will return in *Veklocks.* —

Glossary

Colony Ship (*Honora Belle*)
Beatrice "Birdie" Andrews – Comm operator on the *Belle*
Bryan Forshaw – Propulsion engineer on the *Belle*
Danny Thompson – Pilot of the *Belle*, copilot of its shuttle
Dingles – Nickname for Mitch Bassiter, first mate on the *Belle*, later captain
Harbour – Protector of the empaths, captain of the *Belle*, later envoy to Jatouche
Helena Garmenti – Mother of Aurelia and Sasha
Lindsey Jabrook – Previous Harbour
Makana – Artisan who decorated Aurelia's skins
Mitch "Dingles" Bassiter – First mate on the *Belle*, later captain
Nadine – Older empath
Pete Jennings – Engineer and ex-spacer
Sasha Garmenti – Younger daughter of Helena, Aurelia's sister
Yasmin – Harbour's closest friend, empath

Crocian (crow-she-un)
Mangoth of the Logar – Explorer
Norloth – Supreme Crocian body

Downsiders (Domes)
Dimitri Belosov – Former governor's dead nephew
Dorelyn Gaylan – Matriarch of Gaylan clan
Giorgio Sestos – Former governor's head of security, in jail
Idrian Tuttle – Dome family head
Jordie MacKiernan – Chief of security for Lise Panoy
Joyce – Alias of Sika
Lise Panoy – Governor of Pyre's domes
Markos Andropov – Former governor of Pyre's domes, in jail
Nevis – Emissary for Dorelyn
Portia – Alias of Sika
Rufus Stewart – Dome family head
Sika – Dorelyn's administrative assistant/assassin; aka Joyce and Portia

Jatouche (jaw-toosh)
Drigtik (drig-tick) – Fabrication engineer, grandson of Gatnack
Gatnack (gat-knack) – Elderly engineer at Pyre, metallurgist
Gitnock (git-knock) – Elderly scientist
Jakkock (jack-cock) – Linguist
Jaktook (jack-took) – Dome administrator, later advisor to Tacticnok, later master advisor
Jatouche (jaw-toosh) – Alien race
Jittak (jit-tack) – Military leader
Kractik (crack-tick) – Tech and relief console operator
Pickcit (pick-sit) – Master economist
Rictook (rick-took) – Jatouche ruler, His Excellency
Ristick (riss-tick) – Emergency medical director
Roknick (rock-nick) – Master strategist
Tacticnok (tack-tick-nock) – Daughter in the royal family, Her Highness
Tiknock – Master scientist

Mistrals (miss-trawls)
Zystal (zis-tall) – Mistrallian research director at Rissness Station

Other Aliens
Gasnarians – Original race on Pyre, extinct
Messinants – Ancient race that genetically tinkered with species and built the Q-gate domes
Norsitch – Alien race with dome connecting to the Colony, Norsitchians
Shevena (sha-vena) – Alien dome administrator
Tsargit (tzar-git) – Alien alliance council
Veklock – Alien race with dome connecting to the Colony, Veklocks

Spacers
Aurelia Garmenti – Eldest daughter of Helena, also known as Rules
Belinda Kilmer – Second mate on the *Marianne*
Claudia Manning – Copilot of the *Belle*'s shuttle
Dillon Shaver – Brother to Tracy, explorer
Ituau Tulafono – First mate aboard the *Spryte,* later captain
Jacob Deering – Senior mining tech

Jeremy Kinsman – Navigator aboard the *Spryte*
Jessie Cinders – Owner of a mining company, captain of the *Spryte,* later advisor to Harbour
Kasey – Tech aboard the *Spryte*
Leonard Hastings – Captain of the *Pearl*
Nate Mikado – Second mate aboard the *Spryte,* later first mate
Nelson Barber – First mate on the *Splendid Metal,* explorer
Rules – Nickname for Aurelia Garmenti
Tanner Flannigan – Captain of the *Splendid Metal*
Tracy Shaver – Sister to Dillon, explorer
Yohlin Erring – Captain of the *Marianne*

Stationers or Topsiders (the JOS and the YIPS)
Benny – Retired spacer
Cecilia Lindstrom – Sergeant in station security
Devon Higgins – Lieutenant in station security
Dottie Franks – Starlight cantina patron and investor
Emerson Strattleford – Commandant of the JOS
Evan Pendleton – YIPS manager
Gabriel – Latched On store owner
Hans Riesling – Starlight cantina patron and investor
Henry Stamerson – Head of the Review Board, retired mining captain
Jameson – Med tech
Liam Finian – Major in station security
Maggie May – Hostess and manager of the Miner's Pit, ex-spacer
Miguel Rodriguez – Sergeant in station security
Olivia Harden – YIPS engineer
Oster Simian – Starlight cantina patron and investor
Roby – Liam's attacker
Rod Fortis – Candidate for commandant
Sandy – Maintenance worker, associate of Roby
Terrell "Terror" McKenzie – Ex-corporal in security
Theo Formass – Medical director
Trent Pederson – Starlight cantina patron and investor

Objects, Terms, and Cantinas
Agri-dome – Dome dedicated exclusively to agriculture

Alliance – Group of races to which the Jatouche belong

BRC – Bone replacement copy, pronounced "brick"

Cap – Transportation capsule

Captain's Articles – Agreement a captain signs with the JOS

Coin – Reference to electronic currency

Coin-kat or coin-kitty – Male or female sex service provider

Colony – Entities entering by gate five in the Jatouche dome

Cube – Messinants communications device

Deck shoes – Shoes with patterned bottoms, which allow people's feet to adhere to decks

Downside – Refers to the domes on Pyre

Dreeson oil – Therapeutic medicine or poison depending on concentration and use

El – Elevator car linked between the orbital station and Pyre's domes

Empath – Person capable of sensing and manipulating the emotional states of others

E-trans – Electric passenger transport

Gik-kick – Jatouche short measure of time

Green – Replenishing drink of herbs and vegetables for empaths

Hook on – Expression that means pay attention now, response is "Aye, latched on."

Intravertor – Jatouche device used to cool Pyre's surface and clean the air

Latched On – Spacer supply house

Miner's Pit – Cantina owned by Jessie Cinders

Mist mask – Makeup mask

Mister – Dome bathing cabinet

Normals – Individuals who have no empath capability

Ped-path – Domes path for electric vehicles and pedestrians

Plumerase tree – Sweet fruit and an addictive narcotic, from the nut

Pyrean Green fund – Pyrean financial efforts to fund intravertor projects

Q-gate – Jatouche term for transportation gate

Review Board – Judicial body aboard the JOS

Rik-tik – Jatouche predator

Shock stick – Pyrean security's weapon

Skins – Preferred clothing of stationers and spacers

Sleepholds – Places for people to temporarily bunk

Slush – Generic term for frozen gases

Starlight – Expensive JOS cantina
Stationers – People who live on the Jenkels Orbital Station, called the JOS
Trans-sticks – Hair accessories of dome young people
Vac suit – Spacer's vacuum work suit

Stars, Planets, and Moons
Crimsa – Star of the planet Pyre
Crocia – Crocian home world
Emperion – Pyre's second moon
Na-Tikkook – Jatouche home world
Pyre – New home world of human colonists
Rissness – Jatouche moon, Messinants dome located here
Triton – Pyre's third, outermost moon

Ships and Stations
Honora Belle – Pyrean colony ship, also known as the *Belle*
Jenkels Orbital Station – Station above Pyre. Anchors the El car to
    downside, called the JOS, pronounced "joss."
Marianne – Captain Jessie Cinders' first ship, referred to as the *Annie*
Rissness Medical Station – Jatouche hospital, aka Rissness Station
Splendid Metal – Pyrean mining ship
Spryte – Captain Jessie Cinders' third ship
Unruly Pearl – Captain Jessie Cinders' second ship, referred to as the *Pearl*
Yellen-Inglehart Processing Station – Pyrean mineral and gas-processing
    platform, called the YIPS, pronounced "yips."

My Books

Jatouche, the third novel in the Pyrean series, is available in e-book, softcover, and audiobook versions. Please visit my website, http://scottjucha.com, for publication locations and dates. You may register at my website to receive email notifications of soon-to-be-released novels.

Pyreans Series
Empaths
Messinants
Jatouche
Veklocks (forthcoming)

The Silver Ships Series
The Silver Ships
Libre
Méridien
Haraken
Sol
Espero
Allora
Celus-5
Omnia
Vinium
Nua'll
Artifice (forthcoming)

The Author

From my early years to the present, books have been a refuge. They've fueled my imagination. I've traveled to faraway places and met aliens with Asimov, Heinlein, Clarke, Herbert, and Le Guin. I've explored historical events with Michener and Clavell, and I played spy with Ludlum and Fleming.

There's no doubt that the early sci-fi masters influenced the writing of my first two series, <u>The Silver Ships and Pyreans</u>. I crafted my stories to give readers intimate views of my characters, who wrestle with the challenges of living in space and inhabiting alien worlds.

Life is rarely easy for these characters, who encounter aliens and calamities, but they persist and flourish. I revel in examining humankind's will to survive. Not everyone plays fair or exhibits concern for other beings, but that's another aspect of humans and aliens that I investigate.

My stories offer hope for humans today about what they might accomplish tomorrow far from our home world. Throughout my books, humans exhibit a will to persevere, without detriment to the vast majority of others.

Readers have been generous with their comments, which they've left on Amazon and Goodreads for others to review. I truly enjoy what I do, and I'm pleased to read how my stories have positively affected many readers' lives.

If you've read my books, please consider posting a review on Amazon and Goodreads for every book, even a short one. Reviews attract other readers and are a great help to indie authors, such as me.

The Silver Ships novels have reached Amazon's coveted #1 and #2 Best-Selling Sci-Fi book, multiple times, in the science fiction categories of first contact, space opera, and alien invasion.

Made in the USA
Coppell, TX
17 September 2020

38206135R00263